CABIN FEVER

Mark Butler took a lurching step forward on his bare white feet and collapsed heavily to his hands and knees in front of Ricky. His voice, when he spoke, was the high, whiningly petulant voice of someone else, the voice of a shrew.

"On the fifteenth day without food, much as it pained us, we ate our brave dog," he said. He began to crawl shakily across the floor. His blue lips were stretched in a crazy, off-kilter grin. He crawled to where the cleaver lay, and picked it up. Slowly he got to his feet, clutching the table for support. He turned and lurched stiff-leggedly toward Ricky . . .

"On the fifteenth day without food, much as it pained us, we at our brave dog," Mark recited in his old woman's voice, advancing on Ricky. He raised the cleaver and swooped it down. It made an unpleasant whooshing sound as it cut the air. "Much as it pained us, we ate our brave dog." He raised the cleaver.

"Daddy!" Ricky screamed . . .

AFTER SUNDOWN

AFTER SUNDOWN

RANDALL BOYLL

CHARTER BOOKS, NEW YORK

AFTER SUNDOWN

A Charter Book/published by arrangement with the author

PRINTING HISTORY
Charter edition/February 1989

ISBN: 1-55773-190-X

Charter Books are published by The Berkley Publishing Group,
200 Madison Avenue, New York, New York 10016.
The name "CHARTER" and the "C" logo are trademarks belonging
to Charter Communications, Inc.

PRINTED IN THE UNITED STATES OF AMERICA

10 9 8 7 6 5 4 3 2 1

PART ONE

The Funeral

CHAPTER ONE

The night before Robin's funeral was a hard and sleepless one, but one that had to be faced if Mark Butler were to be a sane and presentable pallbearer in the morning. On the dark ceiling of his bedroom his mind played out endless scenarios of the little girl's accident, the upcoming funeral, and his own undeniable complicity in her death. He had, after all, given her the murder weapon for Christmas.

"Mark, for Christ's sake," his wife, Linda, said. Lying beside him on the bed, a rumpled shadow, she was offering her own brand of solace. "There's no way you can blame yourself. Blame the dog. Hell, blame the sidewalk. Anything but *yourself*. It's three o'clock in the morning."

Robin had been the daughter of Mark and Linda's friends the Pruetts, Glenn and Jill, local chiropractor and wife. They were a fine and happy couple whose daughter went skateboarding three days ago and was run down by the family dog, Beast. In the fall she broke her neck and died. Beast was apologetically licking her dead face when Jill Pruett came out of their neat suburban house and began to scream.

"I could have bought her that big stuffed giraffe," Mark said to the ceiling. "Anything but a skateboard."

"You gave the giraffe to Ricky. Would you rather have *him* dead?"

"I'd rather have nobody dead." Mark swung his legs out of bed and fumbled a cigarette from the pack on the nightstand. His own son Ricky dead, or the Pruetts' daughter? What did it matter? A child he knew and loved was dead. For crying out loud, a little kid was dead. The world sucked, yes it did.

"Put that out. You'll catch the bed on fire." Linda sat up and Mark felt her draw the covers up around her shoulders. A fine night, you bet. And tomorrow little Robin would be buried in dirt forever. It was beyond comprehension. You ride a skateboard, which your daddy's best buddy bought for you, and the family dog charges across your path, and you fall down and twist your neck in a neat three-sixty. Bam, you're dead. A child of six is dead.

"At least it wasn't our dog," Mark said.

"We don't have a dog."

"Thank God."

"Are you getting religious on me, Mark Butler?" Linda giggled then, a sound so harsh and out of place Mark winced internally. A child is dead, he thought with savage displeasure, and my wife giggles in the night.

"Cut it out," he snapped.

"Sorry."

Mark smoked and thought. Linda was just too damn carefree, had always been. She cared for religion, any religion, the way most people care for voodoo. Okay for other folks, but not for her. But at this moment Mark, never one for religion himself, began to wonder what sense the world made, and if it did, who was responsible for its atrocities.

Down the hallway he heard Ricky's bedroom door swing open and shut. Little feet came across the carpet and stopped at the doorway.

"What is it, hon?" Linda said.

"Cold." Ricky's voice was full of sleep. "Wet."

"He wet his bed, Mark. Will you look?"

Mark shook his head. "I've seen wet beds."

"Grouch."

Mark stood and stabbed his cigarette at the ashtray, catching the edge and sending it thudding to the floor with a shower of sparks. "What the hell do you expect?" he barked at no one, perhaps himself, and went to Ricky. Ricky's pajamas shone dull gray in the weak light from the window above the bed, making him a short headless ghost. Mark found his shoulders and guided him across the hall to the bathroom, found the light, and stood squinting while Ricky did his business.

"Finished, Ricko?"

"Finished, Daddy."

"To bed, then."

"It's wet."

"We'll change it." This was better, having something to do.

Anything to take his mind off Robin and the skateboard, a freak accident that couldn't have happened. And what must it be like for Glenn and Jill, spending this night at home while Robin reposed at the funeral home, never to wet the bed again, never to get up and complain about being cold again? The sun would burn to a cinder, the galaxies turn to dust, and after such billions of years Robin would still be six years old and still be dead.

"Ah, God," Mark moaned. He shook his head to clear it, and steered Ricky by the shoulders toward his bedroom door.

"Snowing out there," Ricky muttered.

Snow in April? Mark wondered. It was nicely cool here in Salt Lake City, but the only snow was in the surrounding mountains. They came to the door and Mark pushed it open with his foot.

"Should have seen that one," Ricky said. "Wish I had my knife."

"You're asleep, champ. Let's try dreaming in bed."

"Thirty-one days in a row," Ricky said, and gave out a miserable, childish chuckle. "Should have seen that one."

Mark hoisted Ricky into his arms, overcome for a moment by the innocent lightness of the child, and the sweet shampoo scent of his hair. Such big talk from a kid, this sweet kid. Robin, however, dead Robin, how would she . . . smell?

"Gah," he grunted, and shivered. The middle of the night was no time to be possessed by such thoughts.

"I wish we could eat," Ricky moaned.

"In the morning. Now to bed." Mark lowered him down, feeling with one hand to make sure the bed was dry, which it was. Good boy, well potty-trained. He spread the covers over him and tucked the crisp white sheet under his chin, then paused to take in the sight of this living child so safe in his bed. In the vague light that filtered down the hallway from the bathroom, the bed appeared as a white rectangle, Ricky's head as a pale circle capped with tousles of black hair. His eyes were peacefully shut.

Rest in Peace. Another thought, obtrusive and unwanted. Mark shook his head to clear it. These had been rough nights, these last three. Glenn was probably up this early, too, had probably not slept at all. His wife, Jill, might be up, too, perhaps sobbing on the living room couch, or looking through photo albums, or wringing her tear-soaked pillow out over the toilet—who could predict which—and what sense did this world make anyway when you began to imagine such goofy things?

"Sleep tight," he whispered, and went back to his own bedroom and Linda.

"Did you change the sheets, or just put a towel down?" she asked.

"Neither one." Mark sat on the edge of the bed and bent to pick up the ashtray. "He was just dreaming again. The bed wasn't wet at all."

"Same thing, huh?" She reached over and encircled his waist with her warm arms. "Cold in the middle of April."

"He's a weird kid." He set the ashtray right and lit another cigarette. "Hungry, too," he said after a puff. "Didn't you feed him?"

"Meat loaf, which he ate like a hog." She squeezed him once and let go. "Are you feeling better about Robin? You sound like it."

"No." Mark stood abruptly, overcome once again with thoughts of Robin. He hooked the cigarette in his mouth, and picked yesterday's clothes up off the floor. "I'd better go see Glenn and Jill," he said as he dressed. His shirt was wrinkled but it didn't matter. Nothing mattered, really, except making sure his two best friends weren't sitting home hating him for having bought a skateboard.

Linda sighed loudly. "Do you have to do this again? You spent all evening over there. What about work tomorrow?"

He turned, fastening his belt. "I'm taking the day off. The deadbeats can wait."

Linda crossed her arms over her knees and studied him. In this light her eyes shone cat-green, like weak emeralds. "I thought the proper terminology was problem cases."

"Problem cases, deadbeats, what's the difference?" He fished his shoes out from under the bed. That was one thing Glenn was always kidding him about—this messy house, this messy Butler family of finance company fame. But with a kid around, and both adults working full-time . . . well, it was just hard to keep things in order. Mark sat again to tie his shoes. "Christ, babe, I'm just the manager of two-bit loan outfit. The two-bit problem cases can hang on to their money this month. I've got two good friends next door who've lost their only daughter. The company can go to hell."

"For a while."

"Forever, for all I give a shit."

"I thought you loved your job."

The plaintive voice, that hard head of reason in a woman so unused to reason. Mark turned on her, full of sudden bitterness. "Are you that cold, Linda? Are you so used to dealing with death that it doesn't bother you at all? Jesus, Robin broke her neck three days ago. Worry more about her than about my stupid job."

"Life goes on," Linda said, sounding defensive.

"And death reigns supreme." Mark stood and went to the door, pausing a moment to turn. It was just perfect, so very perfect, to have to spend this night before the funeral arguing jobs and philosophy in the dark with his wife. And all because of a stupid skateboard, a stupid dog. "Just let me do what I have to do," he said.

"Torture yourself," she replied. "See how much it helps."

He went through the kitchen, out across the patio, and across the back lawn to the Pruetts' house. Things were not often tense with Linda and it felt cold and unusual to be arguing, especially considering the occasion. Under ideal conditions they might awaken this late, still groggy with sleep, and make love like a couple of teenagers sleeping out for the first time. And maybe, he thought as he swung the gate that opened on the Pruetts' lawn, maybe this is the first time we've had to face something this serious together. So much for love and lovemaking when a child has died.

Light was shining in the living room windows. Mark tossed his cigarette into the dark and stepped up to the patio door. He knocked briefly, then slid the door open and stepped inside. The smells in here were the Pruetts in a nutshell: super-clean, furniture waxed, carpets deodorized. The opposite of the Butler house, which smelled like home, just that, but doubtless like a junkyard to others. In the seven years they had lived at 1201 Westfire, Mark had watched his dream house deteriorate under the demands of a kid and a job while the Pruett Palace, 1199 Westfire, remained the same as ever, brand spanking new no matter how old it got. But that didn't matter now, nothing mattered. The smell in here was clean but full of emptiness. Robin was gone forever.

"Glenn?"

"In here, Mark."

Mark went through the kitchen into the living room. Jill, an

ashen face under tangles of dark hair, regarded him with a poorly
attempted smile from her perch on the couch. She did have a
pillow on her lap, he noticed, and it looked wet. She was wearing a pink nightgown with an open neck he might have found
alluring on any night but this. Her nose looked sharp and somehow pinched, like a talon. He had never noticed that before and
chided himself for looking at her so closely, so obviously. I'm
watching for signs of utter breakdown, he realized, and wondered suddenly how *he* would look under scrutiny. Guilty, probably. Guilty as he felt. The fatal skateboard.

"Are you up late," Glenn asked, "or awake early?"

"Both," Mark replied. Glenn was standing in front of the
fireplace, where the beginning of a fire lazily crackled under
thick logs. Glenn saw Mark glance at it quizzically, and
shrugged.

"Thought it might cheer us up. Chase the darkness, you
know."

"Sure." Mark moved beside Glenn and spread his hands toward the faint heat. "Should burn good pretty soon."

"It should, yeah."

"Nothing like a good fire."

"Right."

Mark turned and laced his fingers behind his back. Pictures
of Robin, blond-haired and cherubic, stared at him from the
opposite wall. In one she was perched at a fence before a fake
country scene. About four years old then, Mark guessed. The
picture had not hung there before tonight.

"What did you have for supper?" Glenn asked.

"Huh?"

"Supper. You know." Glenn made eating motions. "The in-
take of food."

"Oh. Uh, nothing, really. Some milk."

"I was thinking about food," Glenn went on, rocking slightly
on his heels as he talked. To Mark he seemed quite at peace
with himself, which was reassuring. To Jill, Glenn said, "Honey,
why don't you go make us some cocoa? I've got a chill I just
can't get rid of."

Jill looked at him vacantly, then slowly nodded and got up.
She walked to the kitchen trailing covers. Like walking death,
Mark thought. She looks like walking death.

"Tomorrow this house will be full of people," Glenn said.
"They'll bring lots of food, an ancient and honorable tradition.

There will be talk, some laughter, some tears, lots of condolences. And when it's all over with, Jill and I will be left with a house full of food and no one to eat it. See, Mark, I don't think I can ever eat again. My stomach's in a permanent knot. Jill hasn't had a bite since . . . since the accident. We're just wasting away.''

"I know," Mark said. "I haven't been able to eat much, either. And work—well, I just sit there like a lump. I'm supposed to close at least fifteen loans a week and—" It occurred to him that his own troubles would be of no interest to Glenn, so he shut up.

"Ham," Glenn went on in monotone. "Lord, how I hate ham. And everyone will be bringing ham." His hand moved up and he pinched the bridge of his nose. "I feel like throwing up."

Mark saw that he was staring at Robin's picture with a dazed and weary look, like someone who had just been beaten in a fight. Glenn had always been a solid, jovial man, big and robust. In his T-shirt his arms looked skinny now, the flesh sagging from the bones, his hands like big, useless clubs. Only three days, and look what grief has done to him, Mark thought. How can he survive this?

"I can't find my shoes," Glenn said. He turned his head and gave Mark a grim, defeated smile. "I've been walking around in my socks all night. Whenever I go to look for them I forget what I'm doing, and the funeral's tomorrow, and I'll have to go without shoes." He put both hands to his face and covered his eyes. "My daughter's only funeral and her daddy will have to go barefoot like some bum, like some fucking bum." He began to sob into his hands, and Mark hung his head, not sure what to do. This was not the first time he had been around Glenn when he started crying, but this time, this late in the night or early in the morning, depending on which side of the clock you approached it from, it was unbearable, the final blow. *I did this to him, ruined him like this. But no, no, it wasn't my fault.* Or was it?

By the time Jill came back with three cups of cocoa on a silver serving tray Glenn had regained some composure, but when Jill saw him she burst into tears herself. Mark took the tray from her and set it on the coffee table. A strong hand was needed here, he knew, someone to assert some authority over these two devastated people and instill some order in their lives. He had a short, crazy mental image of himself bellowing *Cheer up!* at the top of his lungs, but the image quickly dissolved and he was left with his own pain and the nagging worry that all of this was his fault.

"I'll look for your shoes," he said weakly, and wandered away to do it.

Something was wrong with Ricky's bed.

It was something his father had not noticed, what with his mind being occupied by other things, but something which Ricky, even in his state of half-sleep, noticed easily. It had started the night after Robin died.

Things were coming out of the mattress.

Not big things, or fuzzy tufts of padding, or even the coil springs that lay so neat and compressed under the mattress cover.

Wet things were coming out. Sharp things.

In his dream Ricky was cold, the mattress wet, the sharp things sticking into his back and buttocks and legs. Not hard enough to wake him up, but real enough to keep him from sleeping fully. In his half-dream, Ricky was no longer Ricky Butler, no longer a little boy.

He ground his teeth as he slept.

Wish we could eat.

Ice began to form on the posts of the bed. A thin mat of ice grew on the sheets, a shimmering, dreamlike coat, like diamond dust.

No rest, a voice in his head whispered as he lay there shivering. It was, perhaps, the voice of dead Robin; hard to tell under these freezing conditions. Robin and Ricky had always been special friends, living next door to each other like they had, being the same age like they were. It was Robin and Ricky who had brought the two families together under the bond of mutual parenthood; for as Linda Butler was fond of saying, with Jill around she didn't feel so much like the Lone Ranger. Swamped with diapers and feedings and teething in those early years, Jill and Linda would swap tales of mothering over a cup of coffee. Glenn and Mark would take turns watching the kids when the women were gone together. The two families grew together, sharing a friendship that would only stretch thin when the kids got to fighting, as kids will do. That time Ricky walloped Robin over the head with the baseball bat—that had been bad, accident or not. Or the time Robin shot Ricky in the eye with that gun that shot

Ping-Pong balls—things were tense there for a while. But by and large the kids got along well, and so did the moms and dads.

Ricky had seen Robin die. Ricky had been hiding in the bushes as she skated by and might, just might, have had something to do with Beast charging after her that way. Perhaps he had pulled the dog's tail, or given it a swat on the rear. In any case, Beast bounded out of the bushes and Robin fell down and when she fell she landed funny and she died staring up at the serene blue sky with her pretty blue dead eyes.

No rest.

The bedsprings creaked under their load of boy and ice. Slush dripped and ran from the bedposts, soaking into the carpet. Through the bedroom window a big white moon peered in, fat and cold. Ricky exhaled steam as he lay in tortured sleep, and sharp things stuck him through the mattress.

"Wish we could eat," he muttered, dreaming.

Sometime after sundown, Robin promised.

"They were under your bed," Mark said. He hoisted Glenn's shoes for him to see. "Right there all along."

A few minutes had elapsed since Mark left the living room, and in that time the Pruetts had managed to get their act together. Jill was back on the sofa, curled like a cat, sipping cocoa. The fire behind Glenn was a bit bigger now.

"Thanks, Mark," Glenn said, and smiled at him warmly. "Sorry about that."

Mark smiled back. "No problem."

"It's good to have you around," Jill said. "Too bad we're such rotten company."

"Consider yourselves forgiven." Mark winked at her, put the shoes on the floor, and picked up the cup left for him. "Besides, I have to earn my cocoa, don't I?"

Under other circumstances this might have earned him a chuckle, but tonight he considered himself lucky to get a smile, which Jill gave him. "How's Linda been?" she asked.

"Working." Mark took a big swallow and shrugged. "She would come over more often, but one of the other girls quit, so she's working extra hours." He hoped this excuse would set well, but doubted it. It was in fact true that one of the other girls at Johnson's Pharmacy had quit, leaving Linda to run the cash register and practically the store herself—old Ivan Johnson, the proprietor and pharmacist, tended to spend all his time in the back room reading magazines, because the store did more business in nickel and dime stuff than in drugs—but still, Linda could make an appearance here more often. Truth was, Mark guessed, that now with Robin gone she and Jill would have nothing more to talk about. And besides, carefree Linda just couldn't be bothered with other people's troubles. For a quick, intense moment he hated her for not being here to share the burden of these two ruined friends with him.

"I understand," Jill said, and by her looks, she understood quite well.

"Nice fire now," Mark said.

Glenn turned to regard it. "Yes, isn't it?"

They stood in silence. Mark thought of skateboards, and of the mysteries of a cruel universe.

"Did you ask him while I was gone?" Jill asked suddenly.

Glenn made a face. "Jill, really . . ."

"No," she said, and frowned. "No, I want it done. Tonight, if possible."

"Christ, woman," Glenn said. "Not tonight."

"What's up?" Mark asked casually.

"The dog." Glenn shook his head. "Jill wants me to kill it."

Of course, Mark thought. The shock is wearing thin, and now revenge enters the picture. How long before the revenge turns toward me? "I see," he said.

"I think it's silly," Glenn said with a dark glance at his wife. "A dog is just a dog. You can't blame the stupid dog."

"Can't I? We had Robin for six years. You bought that dumb dog three years ago. It owes us."

"That's absurd."

Jill's face became even more pinched. "It owes us," she said shrilly. "It owes us three years of my little girl's life. It owes us!" She set her cocoa down (didn't spill a drop, Mark noticed with dazed wonder), then picked up the pillow and crushed it onto her face. Her shoulders heaved with great, racking sobs. Robin stared, unconcerned, from her position by the fence post, still a cherubic four-year-old and still dead.

"Oh, hell," Glenn said. "Oh, hell." He put his cup on the mantel and stuck his hands in his pockets. "Mark, do you know where my rifle is?"

"Sure." Mark was filled with sudden dread. Another death, this one so quick on the heels of the last one? Did Beast have to die, too? "It's in your closet."

"Get it, will you?"

"Sure." He found his way into the bedroom, slid the closet doors apart, and found it there, a small Marlin .22 with its butt resting on Glenn's slippers. He hoisted it out and took it into the living room.

"Careful," Glenn said. "I keep it loaded. Burglars, you know."

"I know," Mark said.

"I'm doing this against my will," Glenn said to Jill.

She replied with a loud, muffled sob. If this kept up, Mark knew, she would indeed be wringing that pillow out over the toilet. And when she got done crying she might start to think about the other factors in this not-so-complicated equation of her daughter's death.

"Let's do it, then," Glenn said.

Mark followed him outside, where the air was cool and nice, no fit air in which to kill a dog or anything else. Glenn slid the patio door shut and whistled for Beast, a high, keening sound that made the hairs on the back of Mark's neck rise. *Come 'ere, doggy-boy. I've got a bullet for you.*

"Look, Glenn, you can't shoot a gun out here," he said.

"Why not?" Glenn's shoulders were hunched, and under the moonlight his eyes were moving circles of reflected light as he looked around for Beast. "We're not in the city limits, you know. A man's got a right to do what he has to do. A man's got a right to protect his own."

"What?" Mark followed him as he went to the toolshed that bordered on the alley, where two trash cans sat silver and serene in the moonlight. Trash day had been yesterday and bereavement or not, the Pruetts hadn't forgotten; both cans were empty. The Butler cans down the alley a bit were fly-blown horrors, split-open trash bags and banana peels from Ricky's breakfast six days before. "What are you talking about, man?"

"Beast," Glenn whispered loudly. "Beastie old boy, come here."

"Glenn, listen," Mark began, but Glenn was busy fumbling with the lock on the toolshed and didn't seem to hear. Just then Beast came bounding up and began to run in mad circles. Mark bent to ruffle his fur, this Beast, who looked for all the world like Fred MacMurray's dog Tramp on the old TV show *My Three Sons,* all hair and mournful eyes. How could anyone shoot this dog? And Glenn of all people, Glenn the healer.

"Just take him to the pound, okay?" Mark said to Glenn's back. "Let's don't shoot him like this."

"Shhh." Glenn got the door open and stepped inside. Beast followed him in, his tail thumping against the tin walls in a fast drumbeat. Something clattered and Glenn let out a stifled curse. "Where in the hell did I put that, anyway? Oh, in here." He came back out and Mark felt sure he had procured a trash bag to put the unfortunate Beast in. Instead, though, he was holding a bottle, which he held high for Mark to inspect.

"You know how much Jill thinks of booze," he said. "I keep this a secret." He unscrewed the cap and took a remarkably long drink. The smell of good whiskey floated with the cool night breeze, bright and pungent. He handed the bottle over and Mark had to think about it for only a second. It had been a long three days.

"Old Grand-dad," Glenn said. "One full fifth of forgetfulness, which is just what I need."

"Oof," Mark said, and grimaced as the whiskey made his esophagus catch fire and burn in a remarkably pleasant way. "Smooth."

Glenn took the bottle back when it was offered and swirled it in front of his face. Moonlight caught the foam, winking in mosaic patterns. Under this light he looked young again, not like the old man who had cried in front of the fireplace. It felt good to get out of that house, Mark realized. Death lingered in there like some thick, hanging fog. Out here it was better.

"I never used to let Robin play in the shed, you know. Afraid she'd get cut on my tools."

"Glenn, don't," Mark said.

"Not to worry." He took another drink. "I'm just stating a fact: out here is one place I wouldn't let Robin play. You try to protect your kids as much as possible. I realize, you see, I realize how utterly absurd her accident was. I am a doctor, though some might argue that, and I can be clinical to the bone. My daughter died for absolutely no reason, no reason whatsoever. Jill, though, she needs reasons." He handed the bottle back and went into a squat, beckoning to the dog. Beast dropped whatever he was doing at the base of the trash cans and jumped him, licking furiously at his face. "Good dog," Glenn said. "Good, good dog." He looked up at Mark. "Go ahead and shoot the rifle off. Just try not to kill anybody."

This was Glenn, all right, in command of himself and his

surroundings once again. Last year in August the two families had gone camping, really roughing it in the foothills of the mountains, and Mark had found to his chagrin that he was helpless on his own in the outdoors, utterly incapable of doing something as simple as starting a good fire, while Glenn could do anything, it seemed. The result of my having lived a sheltered life, Mark had decided, and let it go at that. But there was something about Glenn's demeanor, something that made you know here was a man who could handle himself. It was nice to be around that man again. Mark held the muzzle of the rifle a few inches off the ground, clicked the safety off, and pulled the trigger. The noise boomed like a good-size firecracker and rolled away across the hills behind the house.

"I'll drink to that," Glenn said, took the bottle, stood, and did just that.

"What about Beast?" Mark asked. "What do we do with him?"

"We spare his life, but part company forever. Jill might change her mind about the dog in a few days, or a few months, maybe never. Right now I have to do what she wants, so we'll drive the dog out to the mountains and let him go. By the time he finds his way back, if he ever does, she'll see things a little different, maybe. But for now I have to do what she wants." He handed the bottle over and sighed. "Maybe it's what I want, too. This is a tough time for rational decisions, you know. I think I hate that dog a little bit myself."

"I could keep him in my basement," Mark said. "Until things cool off."

"Mark old buddy, the way I see things now they'll never cool off. I've got a heat in my head you wouldn't believe." He took the bottle back and took three gigantic swallows. Behind his head the mountain's foothills stretched into the distance like lumps of cold silver bordered in black. In the mountains themselves snowcaps gleamed with weak reflected moonlight. Mark shivered a bit in spite of himself, looking up at them.

"Oh, he'll survive," Glenn said. "There's tons of wild game up there. Rabbits like you wouldn't believe. Rrrrabbits. Hah."

Glenn was getting decidedly drunk. On an empty stomach, with no sleep, it was no wonder. Mark himself felt the heady beginnings of a good buzz coming on. "Wascally wabbits," he said, and laughed, then wondered immediately if that wasn't the

wrong thing to do. You do not laugh when someone close to you
has died.

"Wascally, yeah." Glenn took a breath, looked at Mark, and
almost . . . *almost* . . . chuckled. That was a good sign.

"Gimme that goddamn bottle," Mark joked, and swiped it
from him. Anything to keep this new mood going. The old mood
was just too sick.

"Take it, take it." Glenn grinned with perfect white teeth.
You should have been a dentist, Mark had once joked. But a
fucking *chiropractor*??? With teeth like *those*??? That had been
a scream, a good buddy-to-buddy joke, once upon a time, once
upon a time before Robin died.

"Too much of this and we won't make it to the mountains."

Glenn shrugged. "A man can take more than you think,
Mark." His tone was suddenly subdued. Shit, shit, Mark
thought. The moment has fled.

"I need to talk," Glenn said. "To talk to you for once without
crying. I need to talk to you about Robin. It'll make me feel
better."

"If that's what you need," Mark said, "then that's what I'm
here for."

Jill came out on the patio, still a mess. "Did you do it?" she
hissed.

"Damn," Glenn whispered, and forced the dog to the ground
with his hands. Beast lay still, expecting a good petting. "We
did it," he called back.

"Oh," Jill said. "Oh, oh, oh." She began to cry, and stumbled back into the house.

"Go figure 'em," Glenn said, and winked.

"Never will." Mark took one more drink from the bottle and
decided he would love Old Grand-dad forever. All of it was
lifting, this pain, it was lifting like a load being craned off his
shoulders. The miracle of booze. Trouble was, booze extracted
its price. In the morning—just a few hours away now—he would
feel like shit.

"About Robin," Glenn said, standing. Beast bounded away.
"It's a funny thing, her being dead. Not funny funny, of course,
but *funny*. I miss her so bad it's tearing me up. She's been gone almost seventy-two hours now, and I feel like she's been gone
forever. But you know what kills me most?"

Everything, Mark thought. Probably everything.

"What kills me most is that if she were away at camp, or

taying the week at her grandma's, I might miss her a little bit.
ust the normal type of missing you do when your kid's away for
while. But here she is gone just about three days, a short three
ays, and I hurt so bad I'll never stop hurting. Is it just the
nowledge she's gone forever that hurts me so bad? Do I feel
orry for her for the life she's lost, or sorry for myself because
'll never see her again?''

"I don't know," Mark said. "I honestly don't know." Who
ould figure out grief? A chemical imbalance in the brain, one
night say. Self-pity, another might say. In either case it boiled
lown to one thing: misery. A big stinking shitpile of misery.

Glenn took a breath, hitched once, and let it out smoothly.
'Almost got going there again," he said. "Almost."

"Steady, old pal." Mark took another drink, very warm inside now.

"I've thought about killing myself," Glenn said. "But that's
a chickenshit attitude. Anyway, Robin wouldn't want me to. I've
got to remember what it is she'd want me to do."

"Of course," Mark said. "Of course."

"She'd want me to come home on time, and bring her candy,
and not be too grouchy when I've had a bad day cracking people's bones. That's what she thinks I do all day, crack people's
bones. She thinks her daddy's a choir-practor who breaks bones
for a living. Aren't kids just the cutest? Wasn't she?"

"She was."

"Goddamn right she was. My baby." He scrubbed an arm
across his eyes and sniffed. "And now she's fucking gone. God,
give me that bottle. I'm coming apart again."

Mark handed the bottle over. It was almost empty. "It's this
house, this miserable house," Glenn said, and waved the bottle
toward the patio. "Every one of my memories of Robin is tied
up with this place. I'm going to sell it. No, fuck that. I'm going
to burn it, right to the ground. Except Robin's bedroom. That
I'll turn into a shrine." He was weeping openly now. "Ah,
God, what am I saying? This booze has got me all screwed up."
He spread his arms and laughed. "I'm just a carefree bone
breaker whose daughter is dead. *Dead!* Can you fucking believe
it?"

"No," Mark said. This wasn't getting anybody anywhere.
Glenn's eyes were wild circles, his chin shiny with whiskey.
"Let's go back in the house."

"No!" Glenn staggered backward into the shed's wall, righted

himself, and grinned. "I intend to stay out here and get shitface
for the funeral. I refuse to attend my daughter's funeral sober
She wouldn't want it that way."

"Okay," Mark said. "Okay, Glenn."

Glenn made a self-righteous noise and worked on the bottl
some more. In the hills behind him a night bird chirped mourn
fully. "That fucking dog," he growled after a pause. "Kille
my baby."

"Glenn . . ."

"Fucking ran her down like a truck. And why? Running fo
a fire hydrant? Chasing fucking parked cars? The dog is stupid
Mark old buddy. The mutt is stupid."

"Just a dog."

"Beast," Glenn muttered, then loudened it to a cry. "Beast
Oh, Beastie! Come here, boy! Do come here, old chap." He
began to roam around, waving his arms and the bottle. At thi
rate the Iversons down the block would wake up and start phon
ing the sheriff.

"Goddamn dog," Glenn shouted. "Where in the fuck are
you?"

"Keep it quiet," Mark hissed at him.

"Why the fuck?" Glenn shouted. "Why the fuck?"

The man was not used to the bottle, Mark knew. In the space
of fifteen minutes he had become a lunatic. Jill appeared at the
back door and stuck her head out. "What's going on?" she demanded.

"Our baby's dead," Glenn screamed gleefully, spreading his
arms. "God has fucked us in the ass!"

"Glenn, stop that!" Jill stepped out. The night breeze pulled
her nightgown out like a pink Japanese fan. "Stop screaming
like that!"

At the Iversons' house a light went on. Beast came out of
nowhere and chased after Jill, snapping playfully at the hem of
her gown. She saw him and screamed.

The plot thickens, Mark thought dazedly.

"Fucking dog," Glenn shouted. "I'll kill you!" He began to
chase after Beast, who went nuts with joy. They played a short,
mad game of tag. Glenn fell to his knees on the grass, still
clutching the bottle, and began to sob. Beast relented and came
up to lick his face. "Gotcha," Glenn shrieked, hugging the dog.
The bottle clinked against his collar. "Shoot him, Mark! Shoot
the bastard!"

Mark came forward and raised the rifle. This was insane, utterly insane. Jill threw her hands over her eyes and stumbled backward, tripping over her own feet and landing on her butt with a soft *thud* that seemed to shake the ground. There was an earthquake of grief here, a tornado of misery. Mark raised the rifle, sighted it on Beast's hindquarters, and made up his mind.

"In the mountains," he said. "I'll kill him in the mountains."

"Then take him," Glenn said. "Take him and do it." He pushed the dog away and wobbled to his feet. "Do it before I strangle the bastard with my bare hands."

He went to Jill; man and wife, they stumbled into the emptiness of their house and slid the door shut.

"Come on, Beast," Mark said, and took him by the collar. A warm tongue licked his wrist. In the mountains behind them birds were starting to chirp their morning songs in earnest.

"Certainly glad I came," he said to no one, not even to the dog, not even to himself. "Certainly glad I did."

He put the rifle and Beast in his car and started it up.

CHAPTER TWO

Eddie Chambers, brother to Jill Pruett, Confederate soldier killed at Appomattox, German officer killed in the trenches of France, was smoking grass in the privacy of his motel room on Interstate 80 on the outskirts of Salt Lake City, where he had journeyed, courtesy of his thumb, from Ontario, Oregon, his hometown. If Eddie could be considered to have a hometown, that is. Truth was, Eddie had no hometown at all; if pressed he would have trouble identifying which century he had been born in.

"Through the heart," he muttered, and poked a finger at his skinny chest. "Right *here*."

In the year 1864 Eddie Chambers had suffered a blast of grape-shot through the heart, which had killed him. Of course, that was a different lifetime, and Eddie had had plenty of lifetimes, died plenty of deaths.

"Cleopatra, baby," he said, smoking grass. "Stroke me."

He was lying on the covers of a Super 8 cut-rate bed, watching an old Abbott and Costello movie in black and white on a Super 8 color TV, just smoking and watching, which was the only thing to do right now. He was wearing battered army fatigues with officer's insignia on the collar. He had been an officer in the Great War and had died during a mustard gas attack.

He coughed. He put a skinny hand to his mouth and retched. He coughed a lot, which he understood to be the aftereffects of gas. The fact that he smoked four packs of Marlboros and eight reefers a day did not bother him at all.

"Fuck it," he said, and sat up, wiping his hands on the bed-spread. Fucking Super 8, anyway, they could use a little phlegm on their furnishings. If Jill had not wired him four hundred dollars he would still be sleeping on a park bench in Ontario, and what did it matter, anyway? If Robin hadn't died he would still be there.

No, that was a depressing thought. It was one thing to be forced by past lives to live like a vagrant, tortured by previous deaths, another thing to have your only living niece get killed on a skateboard, a fucking for Christ's sake skateboard. This was a death that hit mighty close to home.

Eddie puffed on his joint and regarded his knobby knees. In the ashtray on the bedside stand a Marlboro burned merrily away, awaiting its turn. For Eddie smoke of both kinds was a way to chase the pain, this pain of knowledge. He was able to vaguely recall his past lives. Mostly this information came to him in dreams, especially now that he was eternally stoned. At other times he would flash to a previous lifetime, smell the cordite, feel the pain of dying. It was always that, the dying, that came to him the strongest.

"Und was ist los?" he said to the Super 8 carpet. It was the only German phrase he knew, one from his past life, the life where he died in the trenches. He had been a German officer for the Kaiser. There had been a spike on his helmet.

"Hoodenbagen," Eddie said to the rug. "Cardensagen." These were secret phrases from some unknown lifetime, phrases that had come to him just the other night when he was stoned to the gills on some respectably magnificent Colombian. It was eerie, really, the way foreign languages came to him while stoned. At times he shivered under the weight of his lives.

"Goddammit, Robin," he said. "You poor little kid."

He pinched one nostril shut and blew his nose into the air. He hoisted a leg and scratched his ass. On any other night he would be feeling quite pleasant. Tonight Robin was dead. Dead for the last three days. He wondered where her soul was, which level of being it had attained. Eddie himself was on the eighth level, which was just one below Nirvana, the ultimate. One more lifetime, this one, and he would be perfected.

It was three-thirty in the morning. He scratched his ass and thought. The funeral was tomorrow. It had been a miracle that Jill called him at all, what with him being the family's black sheep and all. Funerals are funny things. People got considerate all of a sudden. Jill hadn't so much as dropped a note over the past three years or so, but come to think of it, neither had he. And that fuckhead Glenn, the dude she married—had he con-sented to this? To having the family weirdo drop by to pay respects to the dead little girl? And how had Jill found him, anyway? The family had semiofficially disowned him back in '76 when they dumped his belongings on the front lawn of the family house in Ontario after that affair with the psychic. Eddie had found a cut-rate psychic through the want ads and invited her in for a reading. She had read his palm, felt the bumps on his head, pronounced him a mystic of the eighth level, and screwed him in the closet. A fine affair, really, until Mom came in with her feather duster and screamed. That had just about done it, that affair.

But Eddie couldn't help it. He really *had* had past lives. He was sure of it, and it tortured him.

He picked up the phone, dug a scrap of paper out of one fatigue jacket pocket, and dialed. After a few boops and beeps someone answered.

"Jill?" Eddie asked.

"Yes? What?" She sounded sleepy, or like maybe she had a cold.

"Did I wake you up?"

"No," Jill said. "No, you didn't wake me up."

"I'm in town," Eddie said. "Just thought I'd let you know."

She said a few more things. It all sounded tense. For a second Eddie thought he heard a man—probably that fuckhead Glenn—crying in the background. That was sad, too sad, really. No dude should have to cry. Not even a fuckhead like Glenn.

"What time tomorrow, and where?" Eddie asked.

She told him; she hung up. Tense, all of that, tense shit going down there. Eddie felt grief for them both. Pretty fucked up, this situation. Pretty sad. If only they would realize that Robin would be back someday, back as a better person, then they wouldn't cry. They would be happy.

He sat back in bed and smoked his joint from one hand, the Marlboro from the other. On the floor a beer sat, waiting to be finished. In his pocket was a Baggie containing enough pills to keep the whole German Army from sleeping.

"They should be happy," Eddie Chambers, black-sheep brother to Jill, said. "They ought to be happy for her."

He watched TV and scratched his ass. At thirty, he already had a king-size batch of hemorrhoids and a head of hair falling out. In a few days he would be out of money and on the streets again.

"They ought to be happy," he said again, and wondered why

he, who had died so many times, should be so saddened by this death.

Three years before Robin's death the Pruetts and the Butlers had gotten a wild hair and decided to spend a weekend at John Phillips' cabin up on Spike Mountain, one of the highest mountains of the Wasatch Range that borders Salt Lake to the east. That had been in July, when most of the snow had retreated from the surrounding foothills, leaving Spike Mountain sticking up like a well-enameled tooth. The drive up in the Pruetts' Chevy Blazer had been exciting enough, what with the melt-slicked, winding little road that led up the mountain being as dangerous as it was; the walk through the crusted, dying snow had been a real bitch. The air had been cool and fresh, the scent of pines exhilarating. Both of these wore thin during the two-mile march.

"Who in the hell would build a cabin this far off the road?" Mark had asked after the first mile or so. He was carrying a bag of groceries and Ricky, who had tired quickly of slogging through snow up to his little knees. The path was marked by stripes of faded red spray paint on the trunks of the massive pines that capped the mountain. To Mark the whole area looked too wild, too far from civilization.

"John Phillips would," Glenn shouted back. He was fifty yards in front with Robin on his shoulders, and pulling ahead. Her shining blond hair bounced with his big strides. Her giggles floated on the thin air like bubbles. She had been a remarkably happy child.

"May he rot in hell," Mark called back. "Let's take a breather."

"Breather my ass." Glenn took a few more steps and stopped. To Mark's satisfaction the steam clouds of his breath were almost as closely spaced as his own. Above them, between the branches of the pines, the sky was a deep and unending blue.

They sprawled in the snow, Linda and Mark and Ricky, Glenn and Jill and little Robin, who had three years left to live. Ricky attempted to make snow angels but was impeded by the crusty, half-melted condition of the snow. He got up and stomped the half-formed angel into mush.

"Does it ever get green here?" Linda asked.

Glenn cocked his head up. "The trees are green, evergreen. What more could you want?"

"Grass," Linda shouted. "Or at least some dirt."

"By August," Glenn promised. "The ground pokes through by August, and then October brings the snow again. Nature's eternal cycle. Ever heard of it?"

"Doctors," Linda said, and hurled a hastily made, wet snowball at him. "Always the know-it-alls."

It had been inevitable, perhaps, that such good friendship would spring up between these two families. Mark and Linda had bought the house on Westfire Road the summer before Ricky was born, while Mark was still in college. There had been a matter of a little financial help on the down payment by Linda's parents, but that would eventually be repaid. There was the matter of a loan that was a little too big for the Butlers to handle at the time, but the payments were eventually caught up when Mark landed the job at Capitol Finance, a strange job for someone behind on his mortgage to land, but land it he did. Once in place on Westfire, it had been Jill who broke the ice. At the time she was exuberant about her pregnancy, had come over to welcome Mark and Linda to the neighborhood, and discovered to her everlasting delight that Linda was pregnant, too. The bond was set right then; the two kids growing up together had cemented it tight.

"Come on," Jill said, and got up. Snow was pasted to her back like wet cement. "Come on, killjoys. The cabin's only another mile up the hill."

"Hill!" Mark and Linda exclaimed together.

"Baby hill," Glenn said, sprang up, and charged forward, kicking snow. Robin trailed behind, wailing for Daddy.

So they had come to Dr. John Phillips' cabin, which was nice indeed. The logs it was made out of were well hewn and well fitted. The chimney, a massive structure of stone and cement that took up fully a third of the south wall, had been remade just months before, after the old one had threatened, for years, to collapse. Inside, the cabin was sparsely furnished with handmade pine furniture, but it was nice, oh indeed. A Rockefeller would feel at peace here, Mark thought when he first stood inside. A president could hold Cabinet meetings here.

The women busied themselves with unpacking the few things that had been brought. It was only to be a weekend, a Saturday afternoon and Sunday morning, really, not a week. The provisions were sparse, but enough: some picnic food, and a case of beer. Jill had frowned on that, and loudly, but Mark had insisted. *Thou shalt not booze it up* was a commandment that

seemed to govern her otherwise carefree life. Someday, Mark
decided, he would find out why. An alcoholic father, no doubt.

The weekend went superbly. The kids, worn out by the ad-
venture, went promptly to sleep at seven on the hideaway bed.
The adults played pinochle on the coffee table, sitting cross-
legged on the floor, till everyone was stiff. Mark drank his beer,
respectably slowly, having to step outside only twice to urinate.
That, as far as Mark Butler, beer, and his bladder went, was a
record.

The girls got to talking. Mark became restless, wanting to
slug down more beer, wanting to get drunk and really enjoy, but
afraid to because of Jill.

"Hell, let's go outside," Glenn said after hearing enough
after-cards talk about the kids and the way they were so sweet.
"Grab your coat."

"Let me grab a beer first," Mark said, and scooted off to the
kitchen to grab two.

"Thanks," Glenn said when they were outside. He popped
the Budweiser open and watched the foam crawl across the top.
"Jill's funny," he said after a moment.

"Ah, jeez," Mark said. "Nah."

"Yeah, she is. Funny." Glenn shook his head and grinned.
"So are you, weirdo. You play pinochle like my grandma, and
she's dead."

"Prick."

They laughed together. Here in the dark, in the cold, there
was a wonderfully indefinable sense of mystery, something grand
about being under towering pines and starlit sky. Mark shivered
under his coat. It didn't get much better than this.

"I want to show you something," Glenn said.

"Not those filthy pictures again. You have a sick mind, you
know."

"Jerk. I'm talking serious here. There's a cabin a ways away
from here, or what's left of one. Want to see it?"

"What for?"

"For the hell of it, goddammit. Would you rather play pinochle all night?"

"I'd rather drink beer all night."

"So would I." Glenn took a long drink, incredibly long, then
pitched his can to the sky. Mark heard it fall in the snow a short
distance away, empty.

"Ahhh," Glenn said. "Mmmm."

Mark snorted. "You drunken bastard."

"You're just jealous." Glenn started forward. "Come on, I
want to show you this place. It's a bit of history."

"I hate history," Mark said, and followed, nursing his beer.

They walked until the lights from the cabin became hidden by
the thick, bellowslike branches of the pines. The dark was perfect, the scent of pine thick, like a wonderfully expensive in-
cense. Glenn stopped walking and turned. "Breathe it for a
minute," he whispered, and inhaled loudly. "The great outdoors. Can you imagine city people, New Yorkers or something,
who live all their lives without this? Christ, you can eat the snow
here, you can live on the pine smell alone. Can you imagine it,
being without this?"

I can, Mark thought. Call me a fool, but I can. "It's nice,"
he said, crushed his beer can, and dropped it in the snow.

"Nice?" Glenn tilted his face to the sky and laughed. In the
folds of the mountains, an echo laughed back, distantly. "It's
life, man. *Life*. Out here nothing dies."

"I dig it," Mark said. "Yes, I dig it."

"Bah." Glenn studied him, a whitely starlit face with black
shadows for eyes. "You couldn't dig it with a shovel."

They walked on. Glenn's boots crunched through the snow.
After an interminably long time his footfalls slowed, and he
turned. "Here they are," he said, his breath steaming out in
white, beer-scented clouds. "The Great Ruins of Spike Mountain."

Pitiful, Mark thought immediately, and then: We came all this
way for this?

"There's what's left of the framework," Glenn said, and extended an arm, pointing in squares. "Main cabin, stable . . ."

"Stable?"

"The old mountain men kept horses, y'know. What do you
think pulled logs as thick as these here to build the cabin?"

"Some cabin," Mark muttered. It was cold and his feet were
getting wet. He could find no beauty in these starlit shambles.
It was just a collection of rotting logs, and the jutting, bonelike
remains of the chimney.

"Let's walk through it," Glenn said.

They walked. A high step over the lowest remaining wall, and
they were inside, dark figures inside a large white rectangle, a
sketch on the snow as seen from above. The moon floated high
and cold in the blackness of the sky.

"Sort of gives you a feel for history, doesn't it?" Glenn said.

"Sort of gives me the creeps."

Glenn ignored the remark. "This was the hearth." He scraped at the snow with one foot. "Four feet by six. I've measured it."

"Whoopee."

"Jerk. The hearth was an important feature in old American homes. The only place where you could really get warm, I'd guess. This is where they did their cooking, too. Can you imagine a big pot hanging here? Rabbits cooking, deer meat, lots of times. When winter really hit they probably cooked a horse or two right here to save themselves from starvation."

"Professor," Mark said. "Professor of history Glenn Pruett. How nice to meet you."

Glenn scowled, then grinned. "You're a hopeless one, you asshole. You stand amidst history and crack jokes."

"I stand," Mark said, standing stoop-shouldered with his hands deep in his coat pockets, "amidst junk and freeze my bones off. Let's get out of here."

"Okay, okay. Just thought you'd appreciate the tour."

"Appreciate it I did. Let's make like sheepherders."

"And get the flock out of here?"

"Precisely. Just don't get the flock lost."

They went back. The women had grown tired of talking, and cards seemed useless. Mark and Glenn had another beer, this one less hurried, and around nine o'clock everyone went to bed. The weekend would later be considered a success, even though Mark would never figure out how nine o'clock could seem like an appropriate bedtime, being used, as he was, to sacking out at eleven.

And as the months and years went by, Mark no longer thought about that weekend at all. Until the weekend Robin died.

Mark did battle with himself as he drove out of town. Beast sat calmly on the passenger seat of Mark's Delta 88, watching the street flow by, occasionally sniffing at the glass. The rifle was in the back seat wrapped in a towel Linda had left there for reasons known only to her. Probably there since last summer, when they had gone wading at Salt Lake.

It would be really ridiculous to kill the dog, Mark told himself. Insane, really; when Jill and Glenn got done blaming Beast they would go looking for other scapegoats, and Mark was next in line. If he went ahead and killed Beast, the other child in the family, he would be doubly guilty. It was a silly thought, maybe, but a thought that had to be considered in this terrible situation. The Beast must not die.

But the Beast must indeed die; he had killed a child. It was a law of man: when an animal kills a human, it must be killed. Look what had happened last summer up in Yellowstone: that black bear that had gone nosing through some camper's tent. The man of the tent, taking umbrage, had beaned the bear with a skillet, and the bear, instinctively and reflexively, bit the man. Not a killing bite, really, but unfortunately for the man an artery was nicked, and the man's wife was not skilled in first aid. The man died, and so the park rangers went out with their rifles and shot the bear. Old Slouch, that had been the bear's name. It was in all the papers. Old Slouch, world's friendliest (if a bit testy) black bear, dead at the age of six.

Six. Like Robin. Yuck.

Mark drove east and thought. Beast sniffed.

There had to be some way out of this. If I don't kill the dog, Mark thought, and the dog does find his way home, they'll know I lied to them. In the week or so it takes Beast to find his way back, Glenn and Jill will be on the road toward healing. Beast will rip open the wound, simply by reappearing. Thus, Beast has to be kept away permanently. In other words, he has to die.

But on the other hand, if I do shoot the Beast, and it is later decided that the poor dumb dog was indeed poor and dumb and nothing more, then I will be regarded as the Man Who Shot the Pruetts' Dog, a hero in reverse, the well-meaning friend who blundered. This might bring attention to the blundering friend who not only shot the family dog but bought the fatal skateboard as well. Thus, Beast must not die.

"Ah, shit," Mark said, and rubbed his forehead. Westfire became country road, winding through the foothills of the Wasatch. His headlights threw sharp shadows behind the skeletal branches of the sagebrush; sunrise was still an hour away. To the east, behind the mountain, the sky glowed a pale, predawn orange, obliterating the stars in that part of the sky. It would be a fine spring day soon.

Beast stuck his muzzle against Mark's leg, looking up at him with his big, mournful eyes. *What's up?* he seemed to be asking. *Is it something I did?*

"Damn right it is," Mark replied. "Something both of us did."

He drove and thought; an hour rolled by. The stars disappeared, replaced by orange and blue sky. Beast wandered into the back and found something to gnaw on—probably a bone from some long-ago visit to Kentucky Fried. Hadn't Glenn once called this car the Meatwagon? Or was it the Trashmobile?

This was getting ridiculous—every minute he drove east called for an equal minute heading back. Mark put his foot on the brake and pulled over to the side of the road. Some morning traffic might be headed by soon and the time to do this was now or never.

"Come on, Beastie," he said, and got out. Beast shot out, ran around madly, sniffed at everything, and urinated on both front tires. "Ought to kill you for that," Mark muttered, and got the rifle off the back seat. He shut the door and leaned against it, waiting for something, anything, a decision, maybe. To kill or not to kill. That is the question.

Beast ran around. Mark played with the safety on the gun. There were no cars at all on this lonely, windblown stretch of road out near Kamas at the foot of Strawberry Peak, where nobody ever went. There was nothing at all to stop him from simply shooting the dog and going home. Besides, this ought to be gotten over with pretty quick; the funeral was to be at ten o'clock on this beautiful Tuesday morning.

"Come here, Beast," Mark shouted. Beast was far enough away now to be a roving speck, moving slow and purposefully between the sagebrush. His head popped up; he came loping, his ears flopping. Mark raised the rifle, sighted in, and pulled the trigger.

Beast didn't even notice the spurt of dirt in front of him. Mark had hoped he would shy away, maybe get it through his thick doggy skull that something dangerous was happening here. He fired again, making dirt jump, and then Beast was at his feet, questioning.

"Git," Mark shouted. It took effort to raise his voice, more effort than he wanted to expend. He was tired to the bone and the whiskey buzz had been replaced by a thumping headache. "Go on, scram!" he shouted.

Beast jumped up and licked his face. Mark pushed him away, spluttering, spitting out the dog germs, almost ready to get angry. "Go on, pooch," he said, and got back in the car. Beast looked on with open curiosity.

"Go chase jackrabbits," Mark said wearily, and threw the

rifle on the back seat. He put the car in drive and swung it in a tight U-turn, then sped away. A glance in the rearview mirror showed a lonely Beast in the middle of the road, watching. After a while he began to run after the car.

"Sorry, Beast," Mark said, and gunned it. It was the last he would see of Beast for a while.

That morning a mountain man, the last of a dead breed, stubbornest mule in the world, was taking a shit in the snow. His name was Allison Parker, Allie to his friends, of which he had just one, Jackson Pierce, who was back in the cabin making what he liked to call breakfast. Breakfast to Jackson was flapjacks, one good stack of which could support ceiling joists. Allie was out shitting because he had, for the last eight months, eaten nothing but flapjacks and venison, and was damned tired of it.

"Yahh, shit!" Allie screeched, shitting in the snow. There was an outhouse just to the rear of the cabin, an outhouse which had blown down in January during a storm and was no longer in service, so Allie was forced to do this ridiculous thing, hang his ass out under the morning sunshine and shit his king-size flapjack-and-venison loaf like some goddamn bear, and it was all Jackson's fault, him with his let's buy two thousand pounds of pancake flour for the winter.

Behind him the cabin in which he and Jackson lived sat in an irreparable state of decay, a leaning tin and tar-paper horror that Allie had built in 1946 with funds from the G.I. Bill, which wasn't very particular at that time who they loaned to. Outside the front door lay a ruined baby blue spruce, which Jackson had tossed out and burned during a particularly bad spell of cabin fever last Christmas Eve. Bits of wrinkled tinsel still clung to the unburnt branches, which had gone a sour and decidedly dead brown. On the broad shelf of Spike Mountain to which the cabin clung, the white snow was dotted with uncountable flapjack loaves, and wads of toilet paper that fluttered in the breeze like multicolored confetti. Smoke from Jackson's breakfast fire drifted out of a bent and broken stovepipe on the roof.

"Yahh, shit," Allie screeched again. He had begun screeching that a lot this endless winter, but then, over the years he had been losing his mind anyway so didn't really care much how much he screeched. In 1938 Allie had shot a man in Reno, served four years in the Nevada State Penitentiary for attempted murder, and was released to join the navy in 1942. The man he had attempted to murder was Jackson Pierce, whom he was still trying to kill, if only Jackson would hold still long enough. That was probably why Jackson stayed here in the first place: so he could keep an eye on Allie.

"God, my asshole," Allie screeched, and wiped it with a wad of toilet paper. He held the wad close to his eyes and inspected it. His mother had died of bowel cancer in 1930 and his father had died of bowel cancer in 1940. It was the one thing Allie feared. He had killed a bear once with a bowie knife and had not been as afraid of it as he was of bowel cancer. Someday, he knew, he would find blood on his toilet paper and then it would be all over. But for now he was clean.

"Nyah, nyah," his partner Jackson shouted, stepping outside. "Yer sniffing yer asswipes again."

"Fuck you," Allie roared, and hitched up his britches. "Peeping fucking tom!"

"Breakfast is ready, dipshit," Jackson sneered. His face was a soot-smudged circle, and his grandma-style glasses reflected sky. That was one thing Allie hated about Jackson—you could never see the bastard's eyes because of those damned specs. He even slept with them on. Someday he would die with them on. What Allie would never admit to anyone, though, was that on those long winter nights when the wind howled and screeched and the snow piled up on the roof like a giant flapjack, he was damned glad to have Jackson around. More than once they had gotten drunk on their homemade hooch and wound up doing the cancan or a dreamy waltz together, arm and arm like a couple of lovers. Allie preferred to believe he would like to kill Jackson, if only Jackson would allow it.

"What are we having this morning, buttfuck?" Allie asked, going inside. He stomped the snow off his boots and sat at the ruins of a table.

"Jacks du flap, you dildo," Jackson replied, and shoveled a stack out of a skillet onto a plate. "You were expecting something else?"

"Maybe some goddamn eggs and bacon. Maybe some fucking French toast. Maybe anything but this."

Jackson sat down. "Eat 'em and shut yer yap, fuckhead. We got another thousand pounds to go through."

Allie eyed his plate with cold hatred. "White flour causes bowel cancer," he stated flatly.

"Think I don't know it? Go on, eat. Eat till yer shit turns barn fucking red."

"You'd like that, wouldn't you?"

"Fuckin'-A right I would. Go on, eat before I stuff 'em down your throat myself."

Allie jumped up; the table leaned hard on its three good legs and fell on the fourth, snapping it entirely. The two engaged in a tussle. Flapjacks flew. Furniture, if you could call it that, broke. It was over in thirty seconds.

"Fucking yahoo," Allie shouted.

"Cuntface," Jackson cried. "Pussylicker!"

They set the table right and propped the leg underneath. More flapjacks were served. They ate, *sans* syrup or forks. In better times they had indeed eaten eggs and bacon, the bacon purchased at the Kroger store down in Heber, the eggs laid by the dozen or so hens they'd had before the coyotes got to them. Now both their Social Security checks had gotten cut and hard times were here. It was a tough life, roughing it here on the side of Spike Mountain, but one neither man would trade for the city. Jackson had shown up shortly after Allie built the cabin, ostensibly to kill him for attempting to murder him in 1938. After the gunsmoke had cleared and neither man was dead, an uneasy truce settled in. A big blow forced Jackson to stay awhile, and he just never left. When the right time came, both men assumed the grudge would be settled, one way or another.

"Done, dickhead?" Jackson asked after a while.

"Do I look done, fartface?"

"Want some more?"

"Not on your life."

They cleared away the dishes, washing them with handfuls of snow fetched from outside.

"Looks like spring's here at last," Jackson said when they were relaxing with a smoke.

"Shows you what you know, asshole. We're due for one more big blow."

"Says who?"

"Says me, you ignorant cocksucker."

Jackson snorted. "You been reading tea leaves again, cunt-breath? The sky's bluer'n hell, the snow's melting off, and the birds are back. It's fucking April, you know. Fucking April."

"April can kiss my ass. Look up at the peak, farthead. See the cloud cover up there?"

They looked out the window. The craggy spire of Spike Mountain was wreathed in a dirty white fog. The topmost trees appeared cut off about waist-high, just stumps.

"So?"

"So, you syphilitic fuckwad, it means we're in for one more good blow. Probably soon, too."

"Zat so? Ten bucks says you suck eggs."

"As if we had any fucking eggs!" Allie roared.

"A thousand more pounds of flapjacks," Jackson said. "I can't wait to see you screech when your shit turns red."

"That's the day I'll kill you, my friend."

"That's the day you'll try, you faggot."

They got up. They tussled. Furniture flew. On Spike Mountain, the clouds hung low and menacing.

CHAPTER THREE

Mark got home at quarter to seven, exhausted. The funeral was to be at ten o'clock and it was the last thing in the world he felt like attending. A loan convention, a Lions Club meeting, even one of those boring Chamber of Commerce meetings his area supervisor forced him to go to once a month, anything but a funeral. He went to the bathroom and took a long, hot shower, trying to scrub away the awful night and the thought of Beast in the rearview mirror, poor lost dog, poor lost Robin, poor lost family.

Linda was still asleep when he got out. Damn that woman, he thought, how can she sleep so well when the world's gone to hell like this? "Wake up," he said, and nudged her foot.

"Mmm," she said, and stretched. "I'm awake."

"How can you do it?" he asked, almost angrily. "Don't you know what's going on next door?"

"Sad stuff, I'd expect," she replied, and sat up in bed.

"Sad stuff?" Mark pulled his underwear on, then scouted through his drawer for a fresh T-shirt. "Is that the way you look at this, like something sad that's going to go away soon? Christ, Linda, you could show some sympathy."

"I do feel sorry for them," she said. "I do."

"Then go over and help them out, for God's sake!"

She drew her knees up to her chin. "God, indeed. Don't go getting religious on me, Mark Butler."

"Don't go getting religious on me, Mark Butler," he mimicked in a high, angry voice. "Do you know how tired I get of hearing that? And where the hell's a clean T-shirt?"

"In the dryer, probably."

"Can't you ever do something all the way done? Why don't you fold clothes once in a while?"

"Why don't you? I work, too, you know!"

"But not half the hours I do, I'll bet."

"Oh, yeah? So what? Think we could live on your income alone?"

They were fighting, all of a sudden. It had happened in the space of five seconds, the same old tired fight, the same old basic dilemma: What do you do when you live in a house you can't pay for? You put your wife to work, that's what you do. And as a result no one has time to do things like folding clothes, or picking up, or vacuuming once a month or so. Hence the Butler dump.

"Shitcan it," he snapped. "We've been through it before."

She ran her fingers through the short locks of her hair. "All right," she said sprightly.

Carefree. Instantly. Mark shook his head. A child has died, I'm standing here in my shorts with no T-shirt, and she doesn't give the slightest shit. "You amaze me," he said.

"Why, thank you."

He could have taken the bait, but decided not to. Ricky woke up and began to holler. Mark let out an exasperated sigh and said, "What's wrong with him now?"

"How should I know?" She got out of bed and stalked away.

Mark slammed his drawer shut, pinching half a dozen mismatched socks that hung out of the drawer like tongues. Most of them had holes in the toes. "Damned dump," he muttered.

"Mark!" Linda shrieked from the other room.

"What? *What*?" He went running, socks, holes, and drawer forgotten, and made it to Ricky's room in two seconds. "What the hell is it?"

"This mess, that's what it is." Linda had taken Ricky out of bed and was stripping his pajamas off. They were wringing wet. So was the bed, and the carpet under Mark's feet.

"Jesus H. Christ," Mark said. "He must have pissed a gallon."

"You let him drink Coke before he went to bed, didn't you?" She was furious, jerking poor Ricky around like a puppet. "You always let him do that. I told you he'd start wetting the bed if you kept it up."

"I didn't," Mark protested. God, but the floor was *soaked*. How could a little kid piss that much?

"Cold," Ricky murmured.

"Of course you're cold, honey." Linda got him naked and

urged him toward the bathroom. ''We need to put you in the tub.''

Mark got towels out of the linen closet—miracle they're not all in the dryer, an inner voice snickered—and spread them on the floor around Ricky's bed. The kid must've stood up and hosed it all over the place, by the way the towels were darkening in a circle around the bed. And the covers were soaked, too. That was disturbing. A wet bed is one thing, but to sit or stand there and spray it? These dreams Ricky had been having about being wet all the time were starting to affect him. And he had picked a particularly bad time to start acting strange; but then again, perhaps the time had picked him. In his concern about Glenn and Jill, Mark had been ignoring the problems Ricky might be having with Robin's death. After all, they had been close pals, those two, inseparable at times. These nightmares had started just after Robin died, if memory served him right, and memory was a faulty thing lately. Before, Ricky had been as normal as you please, if there was a before. Robin's death seemed to have placed a curtain over the past, as if everything that had gone before had occurred in some dimly remembered happy time, when the only concerns were what kind of TV dinner ought to be made tonight, and which bills ought to be paid this week. Now everything was a blur, a tired jumble of events. Ricky's troubles would have to wait until the Pruetts' troubles had been settled.

Mark got dressed, black suit and black tie, and went into the kitchen to find something to eat. His hangover was abating, replaced by a bit of hunger and a sour, dead-tasting mouth. He located the toaster behind a stack of newspapers and folded-up grocery bags, and set about making toast.

Linda came in. She looked like she would on any normal morning. He knew he looked as bad as he felt, which was like shit. She had no right to look that good.

''Are you making breakfast?'' She sat down at the kitchen table and propped her chin on her hands. Last night's meat-loaf leftovers lay on greasy plates by her elbows.

''I am not.''

''How about some toast, then? I'd like some.''

''Would you? Would you really?''

''What's with you?''

Mark snorted. What was with him? Linda was taking Robin's death a thousand times better than he; she wasn't going through his agony. Maybe that was it. Of course that was it. "I just don't feel like cooking," he said.

"Making toast isn't cooking."

"And making believe nothing's happened isn't normal."

"That's not what I'm doing. I'm simply carrying on with life."

"Business as usual, huh? I suppose that's why you've only been over to see Jill once since Robin's accident."

"She was hysterical. I don't like hysterical people."

"What do you expect? Their daughter's dead."

"I don't know what I expect." Linda stood up and got the bread off the top of the refrigerator, studied it for a moment, then put it back. "If we're examining anybody's actions here, I think we ought to be examining yours, Mark. You've spent almost every minute of your time over at Glenn and Jill's. That's not normal. You toss and turn all night and blame yourself that she died. That's not normal." She looked in the toaster; in the bathroom, Ricky splashed and giggled.

"I'm just concerned about them," Mark said defensively.

"And it's driving you nuts. Have you looked at yourself in the mirror lately? You've aged five years. You haven't shaved for three days and you're starting to look like a bum, fancy suit or not."

Shave? Mark ran a hand over his chin. By God, he hadn't shaved for a long time. This was no way to attend a funeral. "I'll take care of that right now," he said.

"The toast is almost up."

"I'll eat it later." He ignored her look and went into the bathroom."

"Hi, Daddy," Ricky said.

"Hi, champ." Mark went through the jumble in the medicine cabinet and found a somewhat rusty-looking Bic. A little more scouting found the shaving cream.

"Cold," Ricky said.

Mark lathered his face. "I'll bet you were. You and me are going to have a little talk about wetting the bed, Ricko, 'cause you're going to catch pneumonia at this rate." He began to shave, wincing. This blade hadn't seen an edge in months, but the new ones, if any were to be had, would be in some long-forgotten grocery bag someplace and he didn't feel like hunting.

"I'm getting cold," Ricky said, and in the mirror, Mark saw him stand up.

"Sit back down, Rick," he said.

"The water's cold, Daddy."

Mark moved to the tub and twisted the handle on the hot water spigot. "Now, sit down," he said.

"It's too cold." Ricky had his arms clasped to his skinny chest and was hopping from foot to foot. "Get me out, Daddy."

Mark bent down and stuck a hand in the water. The water was indeed cold—no, it was *icy*. Mark was reminded of the time Glenn had dragged him over to Duchesne on the Strawberry River for some fishing. The Strawberry was snow-fed, crystal-clear water that rushed its way down the Uinta mountainside, cold enough to numb your hand in five seconds. Glenn had gone wading in it, calling Mark chicken. Ricky's bathwater was that cold. He pulled his hand out and shouted angrily for Linda.

It was her turn to come running. "What's the matter?" she asked breathlessly.

"It's this freezing water, that's what's the matter. Are you trying to give Ricky pneumonia for sure?"

She bent and put her hand in the water, frowning. "But it was hot," she said. "Steaming hot."

"Right. And the Brooklyn Bridge is for sale." The words came out loaded with sarcasm, perhaps more than he had intended. Well, Christ, he hadn't slept all night, so what did she want? Ricky stood in the water, his teeth chattering. His lips had gone a pale shade of blue. "So get him out of there, will you?" Mark snapped, and turned off the water. "I have to finish shaving."

Linda got a bath towel and wrapped Ricky in it, then pulled him out. His teeth clicked like castanets. "Fuh-fuh-freezing," he said, grinning apologetically. "Sorry, Daddy."

Mark ruffled his cold, wet hair. "Not your fault, champ." He cast Linda a cool, weary glance. "Looks like your mom's not holding up as well as she thinks she is. Now, you better go get dry."

Linda shot him a look and they went out. Mark went back to his shaving, shaking his head. Poor Ricko. It had been a bad night for him.

Behind him in the tub a skein of ice formed on the water, so thin a waterbug might have gone crashing through it, if there could be waterbugs in a bathtub. Had Mark looked back he would have seen it and perhaps given the whole episode a lot more thought, but as it was he had other things on his mind. After a minute the ice was gone and everything was forgotten.

Until later.

• • •

"I'm not going," Linda said afterward when they were eating toast.

"You're not going where?"

"You know. The funeral. Count me out."

Mark bit into his toast, chewed awhile, and swallowed. Amazing, truly, just how tasteless plain toast could be. He got himself a glass of water.

"Well?" Linda said when he sat back down.

"Well, what?"

"Aren't you going to argue?"

"I am not."

"Fine, then." She fidgeted; she finished her toast and scraped the crumbs off the table onto her hand. "I just don't like them," she said at last.

"Nobody does."

"Well, count me out."

Mark shook his head. "Jill will never forget this, you know. You're her best friend. You'd really be letting her down."

Linda waved her arms angrily, one hand open, the other a fist. "Don't put pressure like that on me, Mark Butler. For God's sake, try to be understanding about this."

"Getting religious on me, Linda Butler?"

"No, I'm just asking you to understand. I don't want to go."

"Then don't."

"I won't."

"Fine."

"Fine."

Here it is folks, Mark thought. The world's strangest fight. We both agree on everything.

"I'm not going," she said again.

And that was that.

Later, after Mark and Ricky had gone, Linda sat at the table, alone. The sunshine through the dirty kitchen window was glorious; on TV in the family room a good game of Password was being played. She didn't have to be at work until five, and that left a lot of time to kill. It was nine-thirty.

This fucking dump, Linda Butler thought savagely. She swept her arm across the kitchen table, and ten things, a dozen things, plates, pans, plastic cups, clattered to the floor. It was a never-ending battle, trying to keep this dump clean. There was no space for anything. Mark didn't have time, she didn't have time. They simply didn't have time. They both had to work in order to send the bank their dump payments on time.

The TV blared: laundry detergent commercial. Sunshine lay in big squares on the linoleum at her feet. Linda began to cry. "Dammit," she said. She tilted her head back and tears rolled down her cheeks. *"Dammit!"*

There, that felt better. Get it out, get out all the bad feelings. There was a funeral starting in a half hour, and it was best that Linda not attend, for if she went, Linda Butler might tilt her head back during the middle of the ceremony, and scream. She might get up and run around like a lunatic. She might, just might, totally lose her mind.

She had watched the Pruetts' little girl Robin die. That wasn't the worst part, but it was a part. Chubby was the worst part.

Chubby was a cousin she had had, back when she was a little girl. Chubby's real name was Ferdinand and he had died a lot like Robin had, not on a skateboard, but while playing. Chubby was on a rope swing, his foot in the noose at the bottom of the rope that hung from the branch of a tree, swinging merrily. He let go of the rope to jump off but his foot hung up. He swung out, upside down, and when he swung back, his head hit the ground like a big hard volleyball. His head bounced. Chubby died. Linda saw it all.

Ah, God.

Remembering Chubby.

Remembering how much Chubby liked monsters. Remembering how Chubby liked to pretend he was the werewolf, sometimes, and how he would hide in the bushes behind Linda's Uncle Richard's house and jump out to scare her, when she was visiting, which was often, because Linda lived two houses down on Maple Avenue. Chubby would pretend to be the Mummy, one hand hooked into a claw, one foot dragging as he stalked her. And Chubby pretended to be a vampire, lunging out of nowhere to bite her neck playfully. Quite a kid, that Chubby. He was a year older than Linda but was okay, for a fat kid, anyway. He even played dolls with her once in a while, when none of his pals were around and monsters weren't on his mind.

The sun had been shining. It was a nice October afternoon. Chubby swung on the rope upside down, his foot in the noose, swung until his dragging head stopped him. The sun from where

Linda watched was big and autumnally cheerful, winking on, winking out as Chubby swung in front of it. Chubby swung, grinning with his bloody dead face in the dust. Chubby was still playing monsters, even though he was quite dead.

At the funeral, Linda was taken to the coffin by her mother. Linda did not want to see Chubby again; she had seen enough. But there was Chubby, all fixed up by the undertaker, looking peaceful and happy in his satin-lined casket, with just a few pink scratches under the layer of undertaker's makeup.

Kiss him, Linda's mother said. *Kiss him goodbye.*

No. No way. I will not kiss Chubby until he quits playing games.

Go on, people are looking, people are watching. Kiss your cousin Chubby goodbye, for heaven's sake.

And so she had bent down to kiss him, and in her mind, and maybe not, but maybe so, Chubby had lunged up to take a bite out of her neck, his yellowed teeth bared, his dry lips spreading, his hot dead-boy's breath whoofing out with a smell like old meat. Chubby was playing the vampire. Chubby was, as Chubby liked to say, *THE UNDEAD.* But . . . they buried him, anyway, and Linda Atterson, later to become Linda Butler, became hysterical at the funeral, and remained terrified of the dead, and now could not bring herself to attend the funeral of her best friend's daughter.

That was one part; the worst part, maybe. The other part had happened three days ago, on a sunny Saturday morning. Linda had been sitting on the porch watching Ricky and Robin play, and she had seen Robin go skateboarding past, and she had seen Robin take her fall. And after a second, when Robin didn't scream or get up and cry or even let out a moan, Linda knew she was dead. She knew it, the way she had known Chubby was dead when Chubby grinned at her with blood running up his upside-down face.

And Linda, seeing Robin, had simply gone back into the house.

"I'm sorry," she shouted, sitting in her messy house with its cluttered table and no space for anything. She balled her hands into fists, helpless fists. "Dear God, I am so *sorry.*"

The funeral started promptly at ten o'clock.

Mark, the self-appointed guardian of the Pruetts, chauffeured Glenn and Jill in their car to the funeral home. They sat in the

back seat, stiff and stony, couched in a net of grief and shock
that made them seem, to Mark's eyes, definably smaller. They
had shrunk, both of them. Jill was wearing a black grandma's
hat that sprouted heavy black mesh out the front, shielding her
face. Glenn was wearing a dark blue suit with a blue tie that was
badly knotted. He couldn't manage it, that tie seemed to say. In
his grief he couldn't even tie me right. That, and his shoes
needed polish. Mark chided himself for not having done it.

Ricky sat on the seat beside him, wordless.

He found their reserved parking space and they got out. The
sun was bright and incongruously cheerful overhead. In front of
the building sat the hearse, waiting for its load of child.

"I hate this," Glenn muttered.

"We'll get through it," Mark replied. Now, for no particular
reason, he felt strong enough to be the crutch they needed. They
would never need a friend this much again; he was determined
to do it right. With Jill between them, they made their way
inside. The director met them at the door and guided them to
the family section, where rows of pews already held a number
of people, some of whom Mark knew. There was Jill's Aunt
Polly, looking as fat as ever, and Glenn's brother Jack, the saw-
mill owner. Jill's mother and father, all the way from Ontario.
Glenn's mother, weeping. A slew of cousins and uncles and
aunts, all of whom looked up at Jill as she came in, all of whom
had the same questioning look on their faces. *Is she holding up
well? Is there anything I should do?*

Somewhere, organ music was playing. It reminded Mark of
church. He had not been to church since he was fifteen, when
his parents, solid Baptists, decided that his childhood Sunday
school attendance should have had sufficient impact on him, and
gave him the option of going to church or not. Big mistake; he
soon found other things to occupy his Sunday mornings.

People stood up and surrounded Glenn and Jill; Mark and
Ricky hung back. By rights they should be in the friends' and
visitors' section, which lay off to the right of this big, L-shaped
chamber. He looked around, unsure of what to do, and saw the
coffin sitting on its flower-draped bier at the head of the room
beside a speaker's podium. For one excruciating moment he felt
his stomach tighten, felt his sinuses sting, and thought he might
cry. Here was Robin. He had not seen her for so long.

There was a crush of relatives and friends around Glenn and
Jill now. The smell of flowers, thick as honey, hung on the air.

Mark took Ricky's hand and led him up to the coffin. "We're going to see Robin for the last time," he said. "Think you can handle it, Ricko?"

Ricky looked up at him. "I want to see her, Daddy."

So big, this kid, so big for his age sometimes. They made their way through the people and stood at the bier. Mark gazed down at Robin and his heart caught in his throat. She was beautiful. There were tiny flowers on a thread woven through her hair, a beautiful wreath. Her cherubic face was set in a half-smile, Mona Lisa style. She looked breathtakingly alive.

"Is she dead, Daddy?" Ricky asked. A fat lady beside them looked down at him, smiling grandmotherly.

"She's just sleeping, dear," she said, and waddled importantly off.

Big help, Mark thought.

"Is she, Daddy? Is she really dead?"

"Yes, son."

"Oh." Ricky went up on tiptoe and looked at her closely. "Hey, nerd," he said, and poked her shoulder. "Are you really dead?"

"Ricky," Mark warned, and looked around guiltily. "You can touch her hand, if you want to, but for Christ's sake don't poke her like that. You won't wake her up."

"Sorry." Ricky brushed a hand through his short hair and went up on tiptoe again. "Sorry, Robin."

Mark's heart caught again; with effort he pushed his emotions back.

"Goodbye, Robin," Ricky said, and touched her hand.

That was when her eyes moved.

Mark jerked, overtaken with sudden shock, a jolt of electricity through his veins. He passed a hand over his eyes and blinked. No, no. He hadn't seen that. He hadn't seen her eyes move under the eyelids. This was silly.

Ricky let go of her hand. Her eyes moved again, the lids raising slightly as the irises passed underneath. It was very cold all of a sudden, too cold to breathe, too cold to survive. Mark felt gooseflesh jump out on his body, a thousand hard needles pricking his skin. He stumbled backward from the coffin and thudded into someone.

"Hey!"

Conversation stopped; people looked. A woman went sprawling on the floor, her handbag spilling with a jingle of keys and coins. Mark ducked his head and grabbed for Ricky's hand, white-faced, ignoring the woman. "Sit here," he said, and put Ricky in a chair. "Stay there."

He forced his way through the knot of people and found Glenn. The organ music stopped; people began to sit down. He knew he was making a spectacle of himself. He took Glenn by the sleeve and pulled him aside. "Glenn, listen," he said, and stopped himself. What was he about to say? That Robin wasn't dead? Fine thing, insane thing, to say to the bereaved father. He passed a hand over his face. Had he really seen that?

"No more condolences," Glenn said heavily. He was the old man again, the old man who had stood in front of the fireplace and cried into his hands. He looked crumpled inside his suit, a well-dressed doll going flat. "I've heard all the condolences I can take, Mark. Just tell me that you loved her as much as I did, and I'll be . . ."

"No, it's not that. It's . . ." He hunted for words, found none, and shrugged. "It's nothing." Glenn was in too much of a fog to realize that a woman had just been slammed to the floor here, that his best friend had sprung away from his little girl's coffin as if on fire. Glenn was seeing nothing. "We'd better sit down," Mark said.

"Yes. Yes, we should." Glenn pulled away from him and sat beside Jill. Someone strode slowly up to the podium carrying a Bible with a big purple tassel hanging out of it. Mark looked across the room and saw that Ricky was looking around, ready to get up. The kid was just too little to be left alone for long. Guiltily, practically on tiptoe, Mark found his way back to him and sat.

"Words are difficult to find on an occasion like this," the minister said, opening his Bible. People were sniffing; the minister himself sniffed. "But words we must find. A child lies here before us, her soul already in the hands of her loving creator, and we are left with questions."

Yes, we are, Mark thought. Already he was pushing the incident from his mind. He hadn't really seen it, after all. There had been too many nights without sleep; there had been too much grief. He hadn't seen anything at all.

"Only God in his loving mercy knows all the answers," the minister said. He was an older man with a head of white hair. How many senseless deaths has he seen in his life? Mark wondered. How many times has he had to stand before the grieving and give solace where no solace can be given?

"We find our solace in the words of God," the minister said, as if reading his thoughts. "For only by listening to the Almighty can we know of his plan for the lives of each and every one of us."

Ricky slipped his hand into Mark's. Mark squeezed it, thinking. What would this day be like if it were Ricky lying up there instead of Robin? How could man fear hell, when so much hell is available right here on earth? The living live, and then they die. The dead stay dead forever.

But her eyes moved.

They did not. Preposterous.

They moved.

No. The dead are dead, the dead stay dead. Unless, of course, the dead aren't quite . . . dead.

Mark blotted out the minister's words, filled with a cold and dreadful certainty. Robin's eyes had moved, yes they had. That meant she wasn't dead. In the fall, see, she had been knocked unconscious, been put into a coma, and now she was waking up. Of course. Little Robin had been in a coma all along.

No.

Couldn't be. Medical science knows the living from the dead. Besides, when a person comes to a funeral home they fix them up, embalm them, take out their blood and replace it with something, antifreeze or formaldehyde, something. Something like that.

"Ow," Ricky whispered. "Daddy, *ouch!*"

Mark started; he had been gripping Ricky's hand too hard. The minister droned on. People sniffed and cried. His collar was too tight, his tie a vise around his neck. Dammit, he had seen it. Her eyes had moved. She wasn't dead.

"Stay here," he whispered to Ricky, and put his hand back in his lap. "Don't move till I get back."

"Where you going, Daddy?"

"Just over here. Stay put." Mark got up, aware that no one gets up in the middle of a funeral without a damn good reason. He put a hand over his mouth, hoping the people looking up at him would assume he was overcome with grief, and found his way to the back. In the hallway that led from the front door he saw a portly young man standing with his fingers interlaced in solemn repose on his belly, a man who was watching the proceedings with a professionally sympathetic eye. An usher, then, or someone in charge. Mark went up to him and cleared his throat softly.

"Yes?" the man inquired. He raised his heavy eyelids with mild but sympathetic interest. "How can I help you?"

"Uh," Mark said. That's nice, his mind sang out. You approach this fat man with an unaskable question and you say "uh." Good going.

"Down the hall to your right," the man said, and gestured. "It's marked."

"No, no," Mark said. "I don't need a rest room. I was, ah, wondering if I might speak to someone in charge. The director, or someone who knows something about, ah . . ."

Embalming? Is that what you were going to say?

"About what? Perhaps I can help." The man adjusted his hands on his belly. He wore large rings, Mark noticed. This had to be the funeral director's son. Hadn't he heard once that these people get rich doing this kind of thing?

"Yes," Mark said. "Yes, I suppose. I was wondering, see, wondering about these funerals, yes. I was wondering if in every case the deceased gets, I mean is, if the deceased is, um, prepared. Prepared for burial, I'm trying to say."

"Prepared?" The fat man blinked. "I don't understand."

"You know." Mark made useless motions. "You know."

The man stared at him. In the other room, the minister droned on. People coughed in the stillness, and someone was sobbing. Jill, probably. This was all just too much.

"I mean," Mark said, drawing closer, "was the little girl in there embalmed? Was she embalmed before the funeral?"

The fat man blinked, and blinked again. Then his eyes grew larger. "What a question, sir," he said at last. "There are strict laws governing this kind of thing. I assure you that the Monaghan Funeral Home operates to the strictest letter of that law. So of course the little girl was embalmed, if you must know. Of course she was."

Of course she was. "Thank you," Mark said. "Thank you so much."

He turned away, relieved. It had been silly, this little encounter, pretty silly. Of course Robin had been embalmed. Of course.

He went back to his chair to watch the rest of the funeral.

• • •

Eddie Chambers, brother to Jill, was stoned out of his mind when he entered the Monaghan Funeral Home ten minutes after the proceedings had started. For breakfast he had devoured two Quaaludes, a handful of peyote buttons washed down with five beers, inhaled the smoke from two joints (good Colombian, of course), and smoked an additional five Marlboros. This was, even for him, unusual fare. He generally had Hostess twinkies for breakfast, but today his stomach was knotted, just too tight to hold down food. He detested this funeral business.

Eddie breezed past the fat man in the hallway, Eddie a skinny, gaunt-faced figure in an oversize army fatigue jacket, trailing behind him the odor of burnt leaves and beer for the man to enjoy. Beneath his uncombed brown hair his eyes were wide and wild, shot through with scarlet veins. To the casual observer, and in the Monaghan Funeral Home there were plenty of these, Eddie appeared to be on his last legs. Even the minister, droning on at the head of the room, paused in his speechmaking long enough to cast Eddie a suspicious glance. Eddie resisted the urge to show everyone in the room the finger and just stomp out. If he hadn't spotted Jill off to the left he might have done just that; instead he sidled into a pew beside some old woman with blue hair, nudged her to get her to move over, and sat heavily on the slickly varnished wood.

"Did I miss anything?" he asked her. When she didn't reply he began to look around suspiciously. "They don't pass the plate here, do they?" he asked, breathing hard on her.

She made a disgusted face and ignored him. He settled back, already forgetting that he had asked her anything, and proceeded to let the peyote work on him. Peyote didn't give him a buzz, per se, but it did relax him a little with the marvelous way it changed the color of everything. The minister, for instance, had flaming-red hair and a purple face. Jill's fuckhead husband was orange, sitting over there beside her, orange enough to have Sunkist stamped on his fuckhead's face. And this lady with the blue hair had violet bags under her old lady's eyes. She smelled like a flower factory.

"Umm," he moaned, inhaling her fragrance. "Dig *that*."

She scooted as far away as possible from him, holding a hanky over her nose now. Eddie chuckled to himself. It was the prettiest hanky he had ever seen. And come to think of it, everything here was pretty. Even the coffin was pretty, sitting up there all burnished brown and white satin.

"Hi there, Robin," he whispered, able to see just the tip of her nose and the knuckles of her little hands. "Batman's here."

For a short time there a few years ago Robin and Eddie had really hit it off, back that summer when Eddie had stopped by the Pruetts' long enough to say hi and grab a free meal. That had been when Eddie was on his tour-the-country trip, riding an old Indian motorcycle he had bought with the money he'd earned pumping gas in Ontario. He'd swung down this way to see the Pruetts' kid before the kid got too old to appreciate weird relatives, and he and Robin had played Batman. That was all, really. They'd played Batman, but every time Jill got ahold of Eddie she mentioned that Robin still remembered him, still remembered playing Batman with him, and when would he be back by to see them all? Someday, he would promise, and someday had come at last. He was here.

"So, how do you dig being dead?" Eddie whispered. Having been dead so many times himself, it was puzzling to Eddie that he could not recall what it was like. He could recall being born a few times, dying a lot of times, but nothing in between. Was there a heaven up there where an angelized Robin now flew around like a large cherubic housefly? Or was it a dead zone where you simply existed in blackness while awaiting the next lifetime?

"Tune in on me, babe," he whispered, mentally tuning his antenna to the dead. "Tell me what it's like."

"*Really,*" the old woman said. "Please be quiet."

"I can dig it," Eddie mumbled, and folded his arms across his skinny chest. It was tough, being a hippie when all the hippies were gone. Old folks like this lady just couldn't dig it anymore. What had happened to the days when some of the old ladies wore beads and flowers and grooved on the young generation? Now everyone was dignified and crass.

The funeral dragged on and Eddie grooved on the colors, turning his antenna this way and that, trying to pick up on Robin. It was an exasperating task, one not helped by the minister's endless yakking. Eddie decided it was easier to tune in while asleep, so he closed his eyes. Besides, better to sleep through this ordeal than take it awake. Colors danced on his closed eyelids, beautiful violets and reds. He strived to achieve form out of them, to make coherent the images that were trying to form, but nothing happened. This was, he decided, a lousy place to make contact.

When the service had ended and the people were filing out, Eddie opened his eyes. An unhappy procession was going past dressed in their Sunday finery, most of them people Eddie had never seen before, some of them painfully known to him—the relatives, especially Mom and Dad. He stayed put, letting them leave, knowing none would want to talk to him and grateful for it. After the coffin had been shut and carted out by the pallbearers Jill and Glenn came past, both of them exuding misery. Eddie looked up at Jill and smiled.

"Hi, sis," he said.

She smiled back, weakly. "Hi, Eddie. Nice of you to come."

Glenn regarded him with amiable disdain. "How you been, Eddie?"

"Staying cool," Eddie replied, biting his tongue to keep the word *fuckhead* from rolling out. Glenn was just too straight, this fraud doctor with his fancy house and cars. Eddie realized that he actively hated the man, yet could not put his finger on the reason why. Glenn had always treated him kindly, the way one might treat the family dog, allowing it table scraps and an occasional pat on the head, but in no way granting it equal rights. That was the galling thing, really; Glenn was the type of man Eddie's parents had always hoped Eddie would become: staid and stable.

"Need a ride to the cemetery?" Glenn asked.

Eddie shook his head. "Thanks, man, but no."

"Aren't you coming?" Jill asked. She looked away and waved at someone who was leaving, then turned her attention back to Eddie. "We don't mind driving you. Really."

"I know, I know. It's just that I've had enough of this, if you understand me." He groped for words. How could they know that he was close to solving the old riddle, where do you go when you die? "I just have to be moving."

"Okay." Something passed in Jill's eyes, a quick twinge of extra sadness, maybe. "It was nice of you to come, anyway."

"Yes," Glenn said. That was something else Eddie couldn't stand: the way Glenn said *yes*. He couldn't be like other people and say *yeah* sometimes. It always had to be yes with a couple of extra hard *s*'s on the end. Fuckhead.

Eddie stood up. He yawned and stretched, looking around. The lady with blue hair had taken a quick powder out the door. "So," he said, "I'll be seeing you two sometime."

"Don't make it too long, Eddie," Jill said, and Glenn nodded.

"Yes, stay in touch this time. For Jill's sake."

"Sure," Eddie said. "Sure enough."

They left. Eddie stayed awhile, watching the fat man who had been in the hallway go up front and begin collecting the flower vases together. If there were vibes around, vibes that could put him in touch with Robin, they would not be found here. Too much interference. Also, he needed a beer.

He went outside and started the long trek back to his motel.

CHAPTER FOUR

The graveside service was short, held under a piercing blue sky while sun shined down with eye-smarting, hopeless cheerfulness. It was fully seventy degrees, unseasonably warm for Salt Lake City this time of year, a perfect day to water a winter-dry lawn, a perfect day for children to play outside. Robin was lowered into her grave at eleven thirty-five.

Mark glanced away from his watch, mentally noting the moment, searing it into his memory. It occurred to him that someday, some misty future day, he would be put into the ground himself. People would be there to mourn, Linda would be there all gray and old, and the sunlight would be shut out on him forever. It was a suitably depressing thought.

He was standing beside Jill, a crutch for the weight of her arm. Glenn was on her other side, composed, almost placid. His face was a dreadful thing to see, all full of mustered strength and unnatural lines, the face of a man whose need to collapse weighed on him like lead. He kept rubbing a finger under his nose, kept glancing at the sky as he did so. The sun burned down, and Mark watched everything as if in a dream.

The service ended and people filtered away to their cars. Mark and Jill and Glenn and Ricky turned away after a moment, a sad, silent chorus line, and went to Glenn's car. Jill faltered twice on the way, overcome with crying. Her knees bobbed under her black dress, out of rhythm with her steps.

"A few more, honey," Glenn said. "Just a few more."

"My baby," she sobbed. "Oh, my baby, my baby."

They made it to the car and got in. "I'm hungry," Ricky said after they got under way.

"Quiet," Mark said, and drove out of the cemetery, gratefully leaving behind its tombstones and its endless expanse of lawn.

"Oh, Jesus," Glenn said in the back seat, and exhaled loudly. "That's over. That's finally over." He was quiet for a moment. "Except for the rest. The wake, and the accompanying condolences, the accompanying hams. God, how I hate ham."

"I know," Mark said, and found Thirty-ninth Street, which led homeward. Tuesday morning traffic was down to a few cars on this side of town.

"I wonder how many people will be coming?" Glenn said. "It'd be best, you know, if just a few would show up. Wouldn't it, hon?"

Mark heard Jill's veil rustle as she nodded. Glenn leaned forward and put his arms across the back of the seat, resting his chin on his hands, watching traffic out the windshield. He was still remarkably composed. "If Doc Burris would show up, that would be all right. The Gleasons, too, they'd be all right. But I'll bet my bottom dollar every human being I've ever known or treated will be waiting at the house, all loaded down with condolences and ham." He chuckled miserably. "Condolences and ham. Sounds like a Dr. Seuss book."

Ricky looked up at him. "You mean green eggs and ham. I read that book."

"Sure you did, son," Glenn said, and tousled his hair. "The big boy can read now. Kids grow up so fast, you know? Robin was a whiz at reading."

"I'm hungry," Ricky said, and Mark remembered that he'd had no breakfast. Things go topsy-turvy, and the little items get forgotten. Little things like feeding your kid.

"You can eat for both of us, champ," Glenn said, and tousled his hair again. "You can eat my ham for me."

Ricky grinned up at him. "Okay."

Glenn leaned back and put an arm around Jill's shoulders. Everyone was silent for a long time then. Glenn's Mercedes purred over the road, a marvel of German engineering. Mark set the cruise control at fifty-five when Thirty-ninth became highway, and settled back for the long drive to the suburbs. For an instant he felt a warm, inexplicable sense of camaraderie with these three, sojourners on life's rocky road, all of them. Death had entered their lives but they were still intact, battered and worn but still intact. Death always lurked out there, beyond the safe confines of this car, a gruesome monster with an endless hunger, but for now death had sated its appetite. Robin had died, but life went on. They were safe, alive and safe.

Ricky nodded off, swaying in the seat beside Mark as sleep stole up on him. Mark pulled his head down into his lap and positioned the boy's legs out across the seat. These were fine velour seats but Glenn surely wouldn't mind having Ricky's shoes up on them; Glenn was too busy with himself right now. Jill had become a pallid statue behind her veil, Mark could see in the rearview mirror; she was staring ahead without expression, lost in her world of grief. The time would come, and probably shortly, when she would snap out of it long enough to wonder why she had ever demanded that her dog be shot, and wonder why her well-meaning neighbor had done it. So far neither had asked just what really became of Beast, but Mark knew what the assumption was, that he had shot the dog. It occurred to him that he still had Glenn's rifle in his car.

"Hungry," Ricky murmured in his sleep. His face felt cold against Mark's thigh. *"Huuuuungry . . ."*

Damn that Linda. So busy eating toast and making arguments she had forgotten to feed the boy. Mark could have done it himself, but dammit, he was busy with Jill and Glenn's troubles. And this business about not coming to the funeral . . . what a disaster. Glenn had asked about her, Jill hadn't. Maybe Jill already knew something Mark didn't—like what a cold, uncaring fish his wife was, for instance. What a cool and carefree woman she was, deep in her heart of hearts, for instance. Or how quickly she could end a friendship when the common bond of kids no longer existed.

"Endless days," Ricky whispered in his sleep, and Mark glanced down at him. The side of his face was twisted and white. He was drooling from the corner of his mouth, darkening Mark's trousers in a small circle. "Should have seen *that* one," he whispered, and bit into Mark's leg.

"Jesus!" Mark yelped quietly. Ricky's little teeth, biting almost playfully at first, were now clamping down with real force. He had a sizable chunk of Mark's skin and pants in his mouth and was working his head from side to side, moaning. Pain that had been a tickle at first expanded into real torture. The kid would simply not let go.

"Ricky," Mark snapped, and pulled at his hair. *"Ricky!"*

His jaws clamped harder. Mark tugged his hair. It was comical, really, being bitten by your own kid like this, like he was some kind of dog or something, but the situation was losing its humor fast. Christ, but it *hurt*. "Ow," Mark said involuntarily.

Glenn perked up. "What say?"

Mark threw him a quick, worried smile. "It's Ricky." He
shook Ricky's head with his hand. "He's biting the hell out of
my leg."

"Huh?" Glenn leaned forward and looked down. "He's
asleep."

"I know that." Mark squirmed, trying to pull away. This was
turning into real agony. "He's trying to take a chunk out of
me."

Glenn reached down and patted Ricky's bottom. "Wake up,
champ. You're dreaming."

Ricky turned and twisted. Mark had a quick vision of himself
arriving at Glenn's house for the wake with a big piece of meat
missing from his thigh, and Ricky standing there all woozy and
sleepy with a blood-dripping hunk of flesh hanging from his
jaws. "Christ," he blurted, "dammit, Ricky, *stop*!"

Ricky woke up then, and the pain was gone. He sat up and
looked around groggily. "Thirty-one days," he said, seeming
forlorn. His lower lip, wet with saliva, puckered out and he
began to cry. "So cold," he wailed.

"What's the matter with you?" Mark snapped.

"He was having a nightmare," Jill said. "Robin used to have
them."

"In the daytime, for Christ's sake?" Mark wiped a hand across
his pants, trying to control his anger. There was a bit of fear
there, too, he had to admit. These things Ricky had been doing
in his sleep lately were getting spooky. What if the kid had a
mental problem?

Jill took Ricky's shoulders and shook him gently. His eyes
began to lose their dull sheen and he stopped crying. "We
home?" he asked after a few seconds.

"Just about, honey," Jill said. Mark and Glenn exchanged
glances.

"He'll be all right," Glenn said. "It's the stress, you know,
with Robin and all."

He was right, of course. Deep inside Ricky's mind unhappy
things were happening. As a child, though, he had yet to find
suitable ways to express his grief. Hence the dreams. Hence
everything. Mark sighed, too tired right now to analyze this
thing any further. Ricky was having sleep problems, and that
was that. They would pass, like everything else in this world.

They came to Glenn's house, where cars were parked everywhere but on the lawn, found the spot that had been left for them in the big circular drive, and got out. People were milling around carrying covered dishes, waiting for them. The smell of baked ham hung in the warm morning air like the exhaust from a restaurant, making Mark's stomach jump with expectation. It had been a long time since he'd tasted real food.

Jill went inside, followed by Ricky, but Glenn hung back, receiving more condolences, still taking them with a smile and a decently heartfelt thank-you. This group, at least, was mercifully smaller than the crowd of people who had descended upon the funeral home. Mark stayed with Glenn, there to receive his sideways glances that spoke so much. It suddenly felt good to be this big man's best friend, and be able to read his eyes so well. When they had first met some seven-odd years ago Mark's first impression of Glenn had not been a good one. Back then Mark had just bought the house next door and was wildly scrambling to make the payments, working full-time as the collection specialist for Capitol Finance, working evenings at the Jiffy Car Wash down on Grant Street, and Linda was baby-sitting for extra cash. Glenn's cool demeanor, his neat house, and his fleet of Mercedes (two at the time, actually) had made Mark feel like some kind of upstart, the poor kid from the wrong side of the tracks who would never be quite as cool or as rich as Glenn Pruett. That feeling had passed as they got to know each other, though. Down past Glenn's foggy demeanor was a good heart and a quirky sense of humor.

"Shall we?" Glenn said now, indicating the door. "Or shall we have a picnic on the lawn?"

They went inside. The hum of conversation and clink of cups on saucers were a welcome change from the usual ghostly silence that had hung here these long days. Mark spotted Jill off in the kitchen, slicing a huge ham that sat on a bed of crinkled aluminum foil. Sandwiches were being made, potato salad was being dished out. The dining room table had become a smorgasbord. Mark wandered over to it, dodging between knots of people, and helped himself to a green olive. It was salty enough to make his jaws ache for more. He found a napkin and made himself a ham sandwich, heaping it high. The last act in Robin's tragedy was almost over; it was time to start eating again. He found his way back to Glenn, who was engaged in conversation with a man Mark recognized as John Phillips, one of Glenn's friends from the other side of town. He was a fellow chiropractor, Mark knew that much.

"Mark, you remember Dr. Phillips," Glenn said as he approached.

"Sure do," Mark said, and shook his hand. John Phillips wore huge tortoiseshell glasses that magnified his eyes enormously. His bald head was the perfect capper for those eyes; he looked like a character in a far-out Larson cartoon. "How have you been?"

"Been fine, Mark. I was telling Glenn here that if he wants to get away, my cabin is the perfect place to do it."

"Get away?" Mark eyed Glenn questioningly. "Are you going to get away somewhere?"

"Thinking about it, and thinking hard," Glenn replied. "It's this house, see. Everywhere I turn, I'm reminded of Robin. Not that that's bad, but it hurts. It's like opening the wound a thousand times a day. And Jill, look at her. She spends half her day in Robin's room, sitting on her bed, crying over her teddy bears. I just thought that maybe a few days away from here would help us."

"It certainly would," Phillips said. "And there's no better place than my cabin." He pulled a key chain out of a pocket and worked a key free from it. "It's yours for as long as you need it," he said, and handed the key to Glenn. "Now, the place may be a bit of a mess, what with winter and all, but if none of the windows have been broken or the roof hasn't caved in, you'll be all right." He laughed a little. Mark had the definite impression that here was a man who wanted someone to go and clean his mountain cabin for him so he could use it this summer without all the bother.

"I'll think about it," Glenn said, and slipped the key into his pocket.

"Do that," Phillips said. "In the meantime I'll be making myself a plate."

Glenn waved a hand. "Eat, eat," he said, and Phillips walked away toward the table. Glenn looked at Mark wearily. "And a good time was had by all," he muttered.

"Chin up. They'll be gone soon." Mark bit guiltily into his sandwich.

"And then I've got the emptiness to face. I don't know which is worse, Mark. All the hubbub, or no hubbub at all. Christ, but this is hard for me." He looked dangerously near tears again.

Dammit, I'm tired, tired of everything. I really do think I ought
to take Jill up to Phillips' cabin for a few days. I'll have my
secretary cancel all my appointments and just go. It's not as if
I'm an M.D., you know. Nobody's going to die if I just up and
leave.''

"That's true," Mark agreed. "Maybe you ought to go."

"Then it's settled." Glenn looked relieved, and put a hand
on Mark's shoulder. "Want to go with us, Mark? We'd love to
have your company up there. Linda and Ricky would enjoy it."

Mark shook his head. "Sorry, but I couldn't. I'm not an M.D.,
either, but the office would fall apart if I left. I've already missed
two days, and my regional manager is a calendar watcher."

"Don't you have any vacation time earned up? I'll bet you
haven't taken a week or two off in years."

Mark thought about it. What Glenn said was true—he hadn't
taken a week off in several years. But it was one of those deals
a manager tended to fall into: you begin to think, after a while,
that things just can't run right unless you're there. It was probably an illusion, but still . . .

"No, better not. Maybe this summer sometime. I've been
wanting to take Ricky down to Disneyland, so I'd better hold off
till then."

"Suit yourself. But the invitation stands, if you change your
mind."

"Not much chance of that," Mark said.

Mark and Ricky went home at three, after everyone else had
left. The closest of Glenn and Jill's friends stayed the longest,
thinking, perhaps, that they had some sort of territorial rights
on the Pruetts and their grief. Mark stuck it out the longest,
feeling that he *should* stay the longest; he had, after all, been
with them through this thing from the start. Finally the Millers
left, followed by the Pearsons, and eventually even Doc Phillips
got tired of sitting around and made good his departure. Jill and
Glenn both looked beat; it had been a long morning, a long
afternoon. He knew they dreaded the coming of night, and
promised to come back later. First, though, there was business
to take care of with Linda.

He had begun to feel the first throbbings of a decent headache
around two, and by the time he trudged across the yard with
Ricky it had become a real thumper. There were aspirins in the
medicine cabinet, which he intended to get, but not before he

was finished letting Linda know what he thought of her behavior
these last few days. It had been a burden, a real burden, acting
as Glenn and Jill's major consoler, and now that the position
was almost ended it was time to settle accounts with the woman
who had left him in the lurch to do this job alone.

"We're home," he announced as they came in. He hoped
momentarily that Linda was out; that would give him time to
lose this headache, time to cool off. What he had to say now
might be harsher than was intended.

"In the kitchen," Linda sang out.

"You go change your clothes," he said to Ricky, and Ricky
scooted off to his bedroom. Mark went into the kitchen, loos-
ening his tie. "Have a nice day, did you?" he said acidly.

"Quite nice," Linda said. She was standing at the sink, washing dishes. The built-in dishwasher that had come with the house
had gone on the fritz months ago, and there never seemed to be
time for Mark to delve underneath and see just what the problem
was. A valve, or something. The last time it had gone out the
repair bill was almost two hundred dollars, and that was two
hundred dollars the Butlers didn't have to spare.

Mark leaned casually against the countertop. "Nice funeral
you missed," he said.

"Did I?" Her tone was spright—Mark read it as her usual
don't-give-a-shit attitude. Damn her for this, he thought. Damn
her for being this way.

"You know," he said, "somehow I hope Jill never speaks to
you again."

"Oh?" Linda turned back to her dishes. "Why shouldn't
she?"

"Because you missed her daughter's funeral, that's why." It
was starting to spill out now, all the anger and exasperation.
"You hang around here like nothing at all has happened. Robin's
dead, and you stand here washing dishes."

"Somebody's got to once in a while, Mark. This house is a
cesspool as it is. You want it to get worse?" Anger was starting
to flare deep in Linda's green eyes. She shook soap from her
hands and put more dishes in the water. "You've been so busy
playing the good neighbor that you've forgotten we have problems of our own. The light bill is a week past due. The house
payment is due today. Those are *our* problems. We spend every
cent of every paycheck we make, and we never get ahead." She

plunged her hands back into the dishwater and hoisted out a plate, which she scrubbed furiously, flinging water.

"Those are the problems we've always had to live with," Mark said. "If we want to keep up with the Joneses we've got to spend like the Joneses."

"But where does it get us? For eight years we've been working like slaves and we're still nowhere."

What does this have to do with Robin? Mark wondered, and following that: Why does every argument turn into an argument about money? "You've lost the subject," he said. "We were discussing your pitiful behavior toward Glenn and Jill."

Linda rinsed the dish and went for another. "My pitiful behavior! Mine? You should see you, Mark Butler. You've become Glenn's favorite dog, following him around all the time, trying to be like him. Why don't you go to chiropractor's school, if you want to be like him so much?"

"I don't want to be like him so much. That's silly."

"And what about Jill? What are you after with her? Don't think I didn't see you last night, standing in their backyard with her floating around wearing a nightgown. Did you get a good look at her, Mark? See anything you liked?" She was furious now, her scrubbing hand a blur, her hair falling across her eyes.

"That's preposterous," Mark said evenly. "And you've got a sick mind, thinking something like that. Christ, their daughter just died."

"And life goes on, like I keep trying to tell you. It's time you stopped trying to be one of their family and started worrying about being one of ours. You've got a job you're ignoring."

"So I took two days off. I've earned it."

"And what if you lose it? What happens then? What happens to the house?"

"You don't lose a job for missing two days. Besides, I've got an assistant manager. Leon can run the place as well as I can."

"Leon the Loan Man? You told me he was a jerk."

Mark frowned. What did this have to do with anything? "So what if he's a jerk? He's filling in for me, that's all. The place won't go down the tubes in two days."

"Well, maybe you should call him. Just to make sure everything's all right."

"What the hell for? And why are you so concerned, all of a sudden?" What had happened to the original argument? Linda had a remarkable talent for twisting things around to her advantage. What she was aiming at, Mark knew well enough, was the career he had chosen in this life. As the manager of Capitol Finance he brought home a slim fifteen thousand a year. You do not bring home fifteen thousand a year and live on Westfire Road in the heart of the Westwind Subdivision; you bring home something upwards of thirty. Maybe someday if he were promoted to regional manager his income would climb that high, but such a promotion was still years away. Until then, there would be fights, and the fights, no matter what started them, would wind up being about money. Yet Mark knew that Linda didn't hate his job, or even the slim paycheck he brought home from it. It was this house. It was like a big sponge, sucking them dry. It had been a young and starry-eyed couple who decided to buy it.

Linda turned away from the sink and began to snatch cups off the table. "I'm concerned about everything," she said. "I'm concerned about stretching every dollar we make. I'm concerned about our marriage falling apart because we never see each other. I'm concerned that we'll never have another baby because we just can't afford it. You do want another baby, don't you?"

"Sure," Mark said uneasily. This was an idea they'd been kicking around since Ricky was two, but it had been kicked and kicked and never made it to the goal line. It would be swell to have a baby brother or sister for Ricky, but that would mean Linda couldn't work, and if Linda couldn't work, they couldn't afford to live. Unless they sold the house, that is. Mark had a secret fear that if they ever lost the house, they would wind up living in a trailer somewhere. When he was a junior in high school his father had lost a particularly good junior college teaching position and been forced to take work as a substitute high school teacher for the better part of a year. That had involved moving, and for three miserable months Mark and his two brothers occupied the same bedroom in a dilapidated, rusting Streamline mobile home. Those three months had been a miserable experience. Perhaps that was why he had dreamed for so long of owning a nice house like this one on Westfire. But now that they had it, what would life be like if they lost it?

"It's this house," Linda said. "It takes everything we've got. How did we ever think we could keep up eight-hundred-dollar house payments for twenty years?" She took in a breath, hitched once, and spoke again. Her face was set and determined. "I think we ought to move, Mark. Put the house on the market and look for something else. We just can't afford it anymore."

"No," Mark said immediately. "We've got to hang on to it."

"But we can't, Mark. It's draining us dry."

"We've made it this far, and we can make it some more. It's not that bad."

"Isn't it?" She shook her head sadly and dropped cups into the dishwater. "I have to go to work at five. You normally come home at five. Ricky's in school all day, so I only see him mornings and weekends. You I only see at night and on weekends. It's not normal, Mark. A family should be together. If we had a cheaper house we could live on your income. And it would be nice." She brushed her hair away from her eyes with the back of one hand. "Besides," she said, "with Robin gone it just isn't the same anymore. Glenn and Jill were the only ones in the neighborhood with a kid Ricky's age. The Normans only have teenagers. I want to move."

"No way," Mark said. "We've invested too much."

"With the equity we could make a down payment on another house, a smaller one. Besides, we don't need four bedrooms. They're just repositories for junk. We could get by with two, like most people."

"No." Mark rubbed his forehead, massaging his headache. Linda just didn't understand. You do not move down the ladder of material wealth; you constantly move up. It was a law of modern man, or something. "There's no way we're moving."

There was a weary, determined look in her eyes now. "We can't keep up this pace, Mark. We're so busy working we don't have time to enjoy life. And you know how short *that* can be."

"Tell me about it."

She stopped washing dishes and leaned tiredly on the counter. "And there's one other thing I want to tell you. I can't live in this house after what's happened."

"You mean Robin? What's that got to do with the house?"

"She died on our front sidewalk, that's what. That little girl died on our property."

"So?"

"So everything. Call me irrational, but I just can't live here after what's happened. We're going to move."

"We are absolutely not going to move."

"I'll quit work."

"Then we'll go bankrupt. Is that what you want?"

"What I want is to live a normal life."

"We do. Lots of people live like us."

"Name two."

Mark sighed. This wasn't getting anybody anywhere. "Look," he said, "everything's just too topsy-turvy right now to think clearly. Let's give it a day or two, and then start this all over."

"I won't change my mind," Linda said, and reached for a glass that was perched atop a pile of plates. It toppled off and shattered on the linoleum like a small bomb, spraying shards.

"Another one bites the dust," Mark said with a lopsided grin, and bent to pick up the largest pieces. Linda went into a squat to help him. They eyed each other for a moment, their noses almost touching, speaking with their eyes.

"We move out of this dump," she whispered after a bit.

"We clean it up and stay," he whispered back. "We stay forever."

"Please?" She kissed him lightly on the cheek. The smell of her was suddenly enticing, the smell of long giggly nights in bed, the smell of soft breasts and secrets kept in the dark.

"We think about it," Mark said, relenting. "At least we can do that."

They picked up broken glass, gingerly. "Thinking hard?" Linda asked, smiling.

"Thinking about lots of things," Mark replied. He carried his share of the glass to the wastebasket. "Glenn and Jill are going up to John Phillips' cabin for a few days. He invited us along, and I said no, but if you think it would help you out if we got away for a few days, then what the heck?"

She looked at him with shocked dismay. "Oh, Mark, no. You've got to get back to work. And who would fill in for me?"

"I've got Leon the Loan Man. Don't you have a Leona the Pharmacy Girl or something?"

"Well, there's Peggy Williams. She's just part-time, so she could probably—oh, what am I saying? There's no way."

"There's always a way. I think it would do us good."

She got a broom and dustpan and went to work sweeping the remaining bits up. "It'd take a lot of thinking," she said finally. "And Ricky's got school."

"The dear lad could stand to miss a few days. Besides, he's already a genius, that boy of ours. And after what's happened, I think he could stand a break, too. Fresh mountain air, and all that. It would clear our heads."

Linda carried the dustpan to the wastebasket and tipped it inside. "When are they leaving?"

"I don't know. Nothing's been finalized, as far as I know."

"Well, let's just think about it."

"That we can do."

"I mean it, Mark. Let's think about everything real hard. I still want to move."

"And I still don't want to. But up on Spike Mountain we can think about it all."

"We'll see," she said.

"Yes, we'll see," Mark said, and went off to find out what Ricky thought about the idea, feeling strangely victorious, as if he had used Linda's own tactic of twisting things around to gain the upper hand. He had, after all, successfully postponed the decision of whether to move away or not. Too many years had been spent here, too much money sunk, to just chuck it all and move into some two-bedroom cheapo shack someplace. Up on Spike Mountain, away from all this, Linda would have time to see things more clearly.

He found Ricky sprawled on the bedroom floor, still in his suit, poring over a Mickey Mouse book. "Hey, Ricko, how would you like to go up to that mountain cabin again?"

Ricky looked up. "You mean with all the snow and stuff? That place?"

"That's the place."

"Yuck," Ricky said. "I hate snow."

"Well, you big party pooper." Mark picked him up and swung him around. "Come on, go along with us. We'd hate to have to leave you behind."

Ricky giggled. "Okay, Daddy, but I don't think I'll like it."

"Sure you will, champ. Sure you will."

It was almost settled.

CHAPTER FIVE

By morning Eddie was at the Tremonton exit on Interstate 84, still a good ways from Ontario, still trying to get the hell out of Utah. Hitchhiking was becoming a dying art, he had decided around midnight, tired already of the cars and trucks that rushed past him and his outstretched thumb without stopping. There was just too much bad news about hitchhikers being broadcast these days, too many lurid stories about Murder on the Road, for a decent person to hitch a decent ride. To the American motorist, the word "hitchhiker" now denoted *killer*. It looked like he would have to walk the four hundred miles back home.

By comparison, the trip down to Salt Lake and Robin's funeral had been a breeze. Eddie had caught a ride with a big Allied Van Lines eighteen-wheeler shooting east out of Portland via Ontario, and the trucker, a skinny, bearded dude named Buford Robeson, had shared both his ride and some of the Falls City beer he kept in a big blue Coleman cooler on the passenger-side floor. That had been a fun trip, really; nothing at all like this endless walk. There had been only one ride so far during the night, the short hop from Salt Lake to Tremonton, in a big red Cadillac driven by a cocky, overweight insurance salesman in a plaid suit who tried to sell Eddie an accident and health policy as he drove. Got business in Tremonton, he had said at the exit when Eddie refused to buy any insurance, pulled over, and gotten Eddie out. He had then proceeded straight on 84, ignoring the Tremonton exit. That was at six o'clock this morning, about the time Eddie decided he hated hitchhiking. You never know what kind of weirdos you'd run into.

He stuck out his thumb at a car. The car, a red Escort, swooshed past. He dropped his hand and continued to walk, holding his thumb lackadaisically out by his waist, dispirited and ired. The air smelled of morning cold and diesel exhaust, the smells of the lonely road. It occurred to him that he had not eaten for days, and he dug a cigarette out of his field jacket pocket, a crumpled Marlboro, and lit it to assuage his hunger. It tasted like a dry turd, but at least it was something to take into his body, something besides dope. His senses were dull, his head a thundering jackhammer, his eyes dry husks in their sockets; too much beer and too many pills. This junkie's way of life was a rotten way to live, but one he knew well.

There had been a time in the life of Eddie Chambers when he was as normal as you please, a gawky high school freshman with a mild case of acne and a severe case of high school jitters, but then he had been introduced to dope, descended into the world of it, and it made, for a while, his life a lot easier. The crowd he hung out with in school had generally been a freaky lot, longhairs all of them, dope eaters and pot smokers, flea-ridden ass-scratching bums by nature, who now, in their thirties, made their livings off welfare or crime, you can take your pick. Eddie, on the other hand, had come from a decent and respectable family and had to work hard at fucking up his life. There had even been a time, not all that long ago, when Eddie tried to go straight, get a job, eat three squares a day. The job had been as a motorcycle mechanic at the Ontario Honda & Suzuki, an occupation for which Eddie had only mild talent and less interest. That job business hadn't worked out, not for long. The pressure of the straight life was just too much for Eddie to bear, because Eddie needed his dope, it turned out, like your average mammal needs air. Best of all, at this late stage of his life, was the fact that he didn't give the slightest shit that he was going down the tubes. His only concern was for the pain in his head.

"Oh, fuck," Eddie breathed, walking down Interstate 84. He held his head in his hands and groaned. This was a king-sized dope hangover, this one. His guts burned like fire. His breath wheezed in and out of his ruined lungs. His head spun. "Oh, fuck," he repeated.

Cars roared past, drowning him with their blasts of wind. His clothes flapped against his bones. If there can be living death, he thought miserably, quaking with self-pity, then I am currently it.

After about an hour someone swung over to pick him up. Eddie jogged to where the pickup truck had stopped, a green Dodge that had seen better days, then slowed when he saw that

the driver and his passenger were wearing cowboy hats. Could
be trouble, he knew. Cowboys and out-of-date hippies do not a
good mixture make. And the truck bore Idaho plates: Idaho,
home of potatoes and rednecks.

"Where you headed, partner?" the passenger asked when
Eddie cautiously approached. "We're going toward Boise." He
was wearing a faded blue shirt and bright orange suspenders.
Might be a good sign, Eddie thought.

"Oregon," he said. "Ontario."

"What the fuck we got here?" the driver said. He cocked his
hat back and took a swig of Coors from a can he fished out from
between his meaty legs. Looked to be about fifty, to Eddie's
bleary eyes. A mean old cuss, without doubt.

"Just me," Eddie replied. "Eddie Chambers."

"I smell dogshit," the passenger said, leering at Eddie. "You
got dogshit on you, boy? Dogshit in that woman hair of yours,
maybe?"

"Thanks, anyway," Eddie said. He had hitched with these
types before. Either they ribbed you for a while and then got
friendly, or they ribbed you for a while and then got mean.

"Thanks for what? We haven't done you any favors, boy. Not
yet, anyway." He grinned at the driver. "Not yet, anyway."

"Yeah." The driver grinned back, his eyes full of secret mirth.
He had a jagged scar running the length of his nose, Eddie saw.
Doubtless picked up that trophy in a bar, courtesy of someone's
ring on someone's fist.

Eddie backed away from the truck, shuffling through the gravel
beside the road and holding his hands out apologetically. "Sorry
I bothered you guys. Guess I can just walk."

"Naw, naw." The man wearing the orange suspenders
grinned. "We can't leave a woman walk all by herself out here
in the middle of nowhere, now can we, Dave?"

"Guess not," Dave said. Dave smiled. The man named Dave
smiled like a man might smile when he sees that he has successfully picked a fight in a bar and the man he has picked it
with is too scared to fight back. "She might drop her Kotex and
bleed to death. Nope." He shook his head decisively. "We can't
have that. Get in, boy."

Eddie found that it was getting hard to scoop breath into his
mouth. "No thanks," he wheezed. "Gotta walk."

"I said get in, dammit!"

That shout, as loud and as commanding as any he had ever

heard, did it for Eddie. He spun in the gravel, his jungle boots seeming slow and incredibly heavy, and lifted his feet to run. The man wearing the orange suspenders came out of the pickup in one lithe motion, grabbed him by the shoulders, and hurled him against the side of the truck, which rocked on its springs, creaking. "Don't you dare fucking run, longhair," he said, leaning Eddie backward over the bed of the truck. Eddie heard his spine crackle under his coat. "You and your fag pals are already running the fucking country, so don't *dare* run from me. Dave!"

Dave got out. He came importantly around the truck. "Looks like we got us a situation here," he said. He wiped his nose. Eddie saw everything upside down: blue sky, white clouds, Dave hovering over him like an undertaker. His nostrils looked huge from this position, big enough to disappear into. This had to be a hallucination, all of this; for one intense moment Eddie flashed back to a trip he had taken on LSD a few years back, in which the world became a black hole and he was a star, shining brightly. He was the center of the universe, and these two angry planets were in his orbit now. It was time for the Big Bang.

They hauled him up and dumped him into the back of the truck. There were tools back here, and a spare tire. Eddie tried to grab for what looked like a wrench, a tire iron whose chrome had gone to rust, but Dave reached down and shook it easily from his hand. "Fucking puss," he muttered, and cracked Eddie across the head with it. There was a bright moment of pain, and Eddie found himself fighting tears. Dammit, dammit, why did this have to happen now? Why did it ever have to happen? The world of the hippies was gone forever. There was no peace and there was no love.

"By george, I think the lady's going to cry," Dave said, seeming stupefied. "I think we hurt her feelings."

The other man giggled. "Hit her again, Dave. Knock her ass all the way out."

"No, Christ, there's cars going by." Dave dropped the tire iron and took a handful of Eddie's coat. "You can ride with us, scumbag, but you ride in the back." Eddie could smell his breath, sour with beer. On any other day these two might be normal folks, decent and proper; hell, on Sunday they probably went to church, Eddie thought dazedly. And at church, the congregation all wears orange suspenders.

Dave and his friend got back in the truck; Eddie raised up

weakly and considered jumping out. But then the truck started
up with twin spurts of rock from under the tires, and it was too
late. The truck rattled and thumped, picking up speed, and Eddie
lay back down with the spare under his head for a pillow, his
eyes closed to the smarting overhead sun. The bump on his head
hurt, but not as bad as the dope hangover that was threatening
to extinguish his life. This was one hell of a way to hitch a ride,
he had to admit, but it beat the hell out of walking. He cleansed
his thoughts and let fate take him where it wanted to. And after
a while he fell into a light and troubled sleep.

What woke him up was the road. Something had changed.
The truck's snow tires had put out a high, steady whine on the
highway, but now that was gone. And things were getting bumpy.
Eddie sat up with the wind whipping his hair out in front of his
face and watched the road receding.

Dust. Dirt and dust. The cowboys were taking him off on
some side road.

Fear welled up now, hot and glassy. What had happened before was just a little roughhousing, a couple of good old boys
too drunk to know the difference between offering a ride and
demanding one. Eddie had been through stuff like that before;
his frazzled appearance seemed to incite ordinary people to ex-
traordinary rage. On the open road it wasn't a problem, but out
here was nothing but sagebrush and sand. The freeway was a
bright ribbon perhaps a mile away already.

One of them lives out here, a hopeful, lying voice in his head
said. *They're taking you there for a little late-morning breakfast.
For brunch, you see. They're taking you home for brunch.*

He knew what the main course would be: old hippie. He went
up on his haunches, clinging to the side of the truck for balance,
his knobby knees tucked under his chin, ready to jump out if
old Dave would just slow down a little. The truck rocked and
bucked under him, threatening to spill him out before he could
jump, if he decided to, a matter that was still up in the air. Dave
was doing at least forty on this bumpy back road, which was
not a speed at which a man would want to hit the dirt, no sir.
Brain fried by dope or not, Eddie was no fool. He held on, his
heart thumping wildly in the hollows of his chest, waiting for
the truck to slow.

It did, finally, as it followed a sharp curve in the road. Dave
applied the brakes and Eddie jumped, his arms flailing like the

arms of a man determined to fly. The blur of the earth rushed up to stop him, tall sagebrush and sand, and he tumbled five or six times, spraying dust. At last he stopped, flat on his back, limbs splayed out but unbroken. He probed his mouth with his tongue, tasting strange salty things, and discovered he had bitten the inside of both cheeks. Not bad, all things considered. Not bad at all.

He looked over and saw the truck disappearing, a green dot trailed by a spume of dust. Good old Dave and his buddy were going to have to eat their brunch all by themselves, by God. Eddie let out a whoop, screeching at the sky. On this tortuous road of life he had finally won a victory. When the truck was out of sight he stood up, shaking with exultation and the last remnants of his fear, and began to walk back to the freeway, keeping a watch behind himself. His dope hangover was gone for now, chased out of his body by the more powerful dope of adrenaline, the brunch of champions. He grinned as he walked, aware for the first time in a long time just how good it could feel to be alive. The air was warm and clear, the sky a dazzling blue, the smell of sage light and muskily sweet. A bird was calling out a cheerful greeting somewhere, and up ahead lay the road and Ontario. Perhaps, when he got back, he would let his body clean itself out and then go look for a job, try the straight life one more time. There was, after all, only one more lifetime left ahead of Eddie before he reached the ninth level of existence; no sense, perhaps, wasting this one bombed out of his mind all the time.

He was thinking these delusory thoughts when the truck made its reappearance behind him, prowling slowly. Eddie ducked down behind a tall sagebrush, glad for his green coat and the camouflage it offered. What, he wondered, did these dudes want, anyway? They had had their fun; if they hadn't been lying about heading for Boise they were sure as hell wasting a lot of road time.

"Where in the fuck'd he go?" he heard one of them shout, distantly. The truck rattled and groaned, creeping toward him. Eddie wished he had had sense enough to get a few hundred yards off the road; too late now, though. He would just have to trust this big bush to keep him hidden. The truck came closer, weaving drunkenly on this narrow bit of road. The man wearing the orange suspenders was sitting out the window, holding on to the roof with one hand and a Coors can with the other.

"Fucking peehole," he heard Dave say. "Chickenshit bastard."

They went past, close enough for Eddie to get a faceful of exhaust. He remained frozen for a second, then turned his head to follow their progress. The man in the window looked directly at him, swept on with his gaze, then snapped his head back around. For a moment the two men stared at each other, Eddie feeling the strength drain from his body, the other starting to grin. "Spotted him!" the man cried, and pounded on the roof. "We got the fucker!"

Gears clashed; the pickup roared backward. Eddie stood up, his stomach knotting, his head beginning to thump. What did these dudes want from him, besides a little fun? Things were just getting too bizarre. The truck stopped and both jumped out.

"Now, look here," Eddie said. It was in his mind to run again, but they had a truck, and besides, he was a being on the eighth level of existence, the next to the highest; surely he could reason with these fools. "What is it you want?"

"A piece of your ass," Dave said, grinning.

"But why? What did I do?"

"Ain't what you did, son. It's how you smell."

Eddie stood his ground as they advanced. "There are lessons to be learned here, men," he said with as much authority as he could manage. "In the grand scheme of things we are all co-inhabitants of the same heavenly sphere, albeit on different levels." Eddie had learned this from reading book after book on reincarnation. They all said pretty much the same thing, but he had read a ton of them. What it boiled down to was this: You start out low and work your way up. A couple hundred lifetimes down the road, you become perfected and assume a permanent spirit existence, no longer burdened with anything but happiness. It was divine law, and Eddie believed it with all his heart. "I am able to teach you," he said, trying to keep the panic out of his voice. "I have the understanding of uncountable lifetimes, the knowledge to help you advance. Please."

Dave and his friend stopped. They scratched their heads.

"Nuts?" Dave asked.

"Bonkers," the other agreed.

They took him by the elbows and threw him out onto the road. Eddie grunted, landing hard on his stomach. He sat up, tasting sour things. "Guys, please," he said. Terror was a living thing inside him now, crawling and hissing. "If you'll just listen to reason."

"Reason with this," Dave said, and kicked him in the face. Everything became crystal clear for Eddie in that second—there could be no reasoning, and these two meant business. But why? Why did he incur so much hate, no matter where he went?

The man with the orange suspenders hauled him up by the jacket, and cocked his fist back. No rings on that hand, Eddie noticed. Here we have a simple man.

Pow. Eddie saw stars, comets, the gates of heaven opening for him. Pain crawled over his face and nestled in his eyes.

"That one did him good," Dave said, breathing hard. "Let me try one."

Eddie was hauled up again. He flopped in his clothes, hung there from a pair of fists like bones in a sack. *Pow.* He went down again, getting a mouthful of dirt. The mud and the blood and the beer, Johnny Cash sang in his left ear. Harps played in his right. It was the music of the spheres.

"Kick him in the nuts," one of them said. It was getting hard to tell who. "Kick his balls clean off."

"Hippies ain't got no balls, dipshit. They got ovaries." He kicked Eddie in the side. These are decent men, Eddie thought dimly. They will not violate my nuts. With that thought came the terrible hissing word *castration* to his mind. In the movies, at about this time, one of the heavies would produce a knife and proceed to deflower the hapless hippie. But this was not the movies, and these were decent men.

Rough hands hauled him up again. He opened his eyes and saw Dave's broad, smiling face. "You dropped something out of your pockets," Dave said, and handed Eddie to the other, bending down to retrieve something off the ground. He straightened, snorting. "Damn, Fred, lookit here. The hippie sumbitch has a medical condition." He held up a Baggie full of red and white pills. "You suppose he's got a heart murmur, or something?"

"Could be, Dave. Why?"

" 'Cause he looks like he's about to have a heart attack, that's why. What say we give him his pills?"

"Yeah." They both grinned. Eddie watched them, filled with fascination and dread. The Baggie hung from Dave's outstretched hand like a small pendulum, swinging, swinging. There was two weeks' worth of 'Ludes and reds in there. Even a few tabs of acid, top-of-the-line Windowpane. Perhaps forty pills in all.

"Eat 'em, hippie," Dave said. "Eat 'em all."

Eddie shook his head. Blood was running from somewhere between his eyes, a slow trickle of it. He had an overpowering urge to scratch his nose.

"Oh, you'll eat 'em, all right. Fred!"

"Yo."

"Hold the weasel's mouth open. Weasel, you bite this man and you die. Understand?"

Eddie struggled as he was pressed to the ground. Fists rained down on him. He felt fingers fumble with his lips, felt fingernails scrape across his teeth. He was pushed into the ground and held there by Dave's cowboy boot on his chest. Fingers scrabbled at his mouth, and he clamped his jaws to keep them out.

"Looks like we'll have to pry him open," the other said. "I'll get the tire iron."

"Do that," Dave said. "Do that."

The tire iron was produced. Eddie watched the man named Fred, Mr. Orange Suspenders, lower it toward his face. He pressed his lips tightly together, knowing it was useless, that they would break all his teeth out if they had to. It was at that moment that he realized why he was eternally the victim, why people hated him for no reason that he had yet been able to fathom: he was different. Not so much externally, but internally. He was on the eighth level, a level perhaps only a hundred others had yet reached (Jesus Christ and Buddha topping the list) and it was for this reason they hated him. Somehow people sensed his uniqueness, and despised him for being so far superior.

"Brothers," he said, and then the tire iron was in his mouth tasting like old dental fillings. It was cold and rough on his tongue. "Pwease," he said past it. "Pwease lishen."

Dave emptied most of the Baggie into his open mouth. "Take your medicine, fleabag," he said. "Swallow it down."

Eddie swallowed. A pill or two slid down the parched constriction of his throat. He coughed and gagged.

"Hell, get that thing out of his mouth before he pukes," Dave said, and the tire iron was pulled out and stuck against his Adam's apple. A bit of his own saliva dribbled down his neck. "Now, swallow," Dave growled. "Swallow them all down."

Eddie swallowed. He was crying again without realizing it. His lifetimes had given him a love for humanity that was too deep for ordinary men to understand. It would be centuries before these two souls would reach his level; for this crime they might well be reborn bugs. It was for them that he cried, and for the hot uncaring sun that burned in his eyes without reaching down to help him. Somehow, in the space of the last hour, the synchronization of the universe had gone out of whack. Eddie

Chambers was eating enough dope to kill him. A lifetime such as this should not have to end this way. In the trenches of France and at Appomattox he had died a hero's death. There was nothing heroic about this one. When the pills had all been swallowed (some of them chewed up, tasting bitter, bitter) Eddie was forced to finish the rest of the bag, and then for good measure he was forced to eat the bag. Dave and Fred, for whom he cried, beat him up a little more and then left him, a crumpled figure on a dusty back road, and when they arrived in Boise six hours later they would tell this tale in a bar, to much laughter and much agreement that they had done the right and proper thing.

"It's a rotten system," Glenn said. "You set yourself up for a fall with every step you take."

He was sitting on a stool in Mark's kitchen, his heels hooked over the rungs, drinking a Coke from a tumbler—the same kind of tumbler Linda had broken the day before, the last of the set that had been a wedding present eight years ago. Mark was emptying groceries from three large bags into a huge picnic basket, listening to Glenn talk. Linda was in the bedroom, packing clothes. The trip to Spike Mountain was scheduled for the morning, and he was getting things ready. Glenn had dropped by to deliver the picnic basket, which was one of his extras. That was the kind of guy Glenn was—he seemed to have two of everything. "Every step of this life sets you up," he said. "Your job, your kids, your wife. From the day you're born, you start setting it up, and when it comes crashing down, that's when you realize what you've done."

"I don't follow you," Mark said, placing the hot dogs in the basket beside the buns. "What fall?"

"The fall of your dreams. Look here, Mark. Listen to a wise man. When you're born you have nothing but the skin on your bones. No house, no mortgage, no wife, no kids. It's best to stay that way. Impossible, I know, but the best way nevertheless."

"Are you guys bringing relish?"

"I don't think we have any, so you better pack it just in case. But when you're born, see, you don't have these mental obligations. You haven't set up the system that can destroy you."

"Mustard? Ketchup?"

"Pack them, too. Should I get the feeling you're not listening to me?"

"What? Who?" Mark grinned. "No, go on and ramble. I'll shut up."

Glenn took a drink, looking thoughtful. The ice cubes in his glass clinked softly. "Do you remember what it was like before Ricky was born? How you felt about him? Of course you don't—there was no him to think about. Maybe you thought that some-day you'd have a kid, and that you'd love that kid, but to you that kid was just a bit of your imagination, something hard to picture in your mind's eye. By having that child you dreamed of, you set yourself for a fall. A possible fall, I should say. You created something that can hurt you terribly."

"Meaning? And dare I ask if you and Jill packed salt and pepper?"

"We did, and you daren't, and what I mean is this: if Ricky dies, you will go through unimaginable hell. Don't look so shocked, Mark. I'm not trying to scare you, just stating a fact. If Ricky dies, you will go through hell. Believe me."

"I do," Mark said. For a while there things had seemed like the old days, the days before tragedy blotted out happiness. Glenn was drinking Coke and rambling on, philosophizing, as he called it. Now the subject was back to the new Hot Topic: death. Mark began to wish Glenn could shake it, but knew it was too soon for that. He would have to talk this thing out until his mind was free from it. He would have to talk it to death.

"If Linda dies, you will go through hell. If you lose your parents, you will go through hell. Hell, even if you lose your job, you'll probably go through some hell. Hell hell hell. Ho ho ho." He chuckled miserably and took another drink. "Where was I? God, Mark, I think this Coke is getting me drunk. Did you spike it?"

"Did not," Mark said. "Maybe the caffeine's giving you a rush."

"Maybe it is. Anyway, here's my point. By acquiring a wife and children, by doing the normal things a person does as he grows up, you set yourself up for disaster. Imagine these people who have ten children—the odds are good that one of those children will die somehow before reaching, say, twenty-one—imagine the heartbreak they've set up for themselves by having so many kids. It's best to be a hermit, I believe. No wife to die on you, no kids to go out and play one morning and . . . and."

Don't do it, Mark thought helplessly. *Don't start crying.* He picked up the picnic basket and set it down on the countertop with a bang. "This will be hard to carry up that mountain," he said. "Imagine the fun *that'll* be."

Glenn sniffed, looking foggy. The awareness came back into

his eyes and he smiled. "You can make it, old man. You can make it up that mountain."

"Tomorrow morning, eight o'clock sharp. I assume we'll be taking my car."

"The trashbucket? Please, no. We'll take the Blazer. With four-wheel drive we'll probably be able to drive right to the front door, way the weather's been. I'd hate to have to leave your car stuck up there. It might rust, and Lord knows it can't take any more of that."

"Ah, you rich people. Always making fun of the downtrodden and oppressed."

"It's a hobby." Glenn winked. "Seriously, though, I think we ought to take the Blazer. I don't feel much like walking all that way again, like we did last time. I really think we could make it all the way to the cabin, avoid the blisters."

"Whatever you say." Mark closed the lid. Enough food in there for three carefree days for the three of them. And if he knew Glenn, he'd bring enough to feed an army. Perhaps even a little jar of that rotten caviar, like the last time. "Who's bringing the beer?"

"Ugh, don't say beer. My head's still thumping from that whiskey the other morning."

"Cancel the beer, then."

"No, bring some if you want. Hell, bring a dozen cases. After I get some of that mountain air in my lungs I might be well enough to get plastered again. Just don't let Jill see it. She's really down on drinking, after what happened." He paused and cleared his throat. "Uh, about Beast, Mark. Did he, uh, suffer much? When you shot him, I mean."

"Suffer?" Mark thought about it. To lie, or not to lie? Hell of a question. "I guarantee that the Beast did not suffer," he said, feeling guilty and evasive. Perhaps the truth should come out, but not now. The wounds were still too fresh.

"We shouldn't have made you do it. That was a hell of a thing to ask you to do. But I'm glad you did."

Great, great, Mark thought. *What if Beast finds his way home today?*

"How did they take it at the finance company?" Glenn asked, mercifully changing the subject. "Was there moaning and groaning and gnashing of teeth?"

"Hardly," Mark said. "Leon has been itching for a chance like this. He wants to prove he can run a branch office all by himself, so I told him to go for it."

"How about your boss? That MacKenzie fellow?"

"Bill? Bill's cool, for a change. I called him at that great corporate headquarters in the sky and told him I'd like to have a week off. He agreed that I had a lot of vacation time built up, asked me if the office could run smooth without me, and wished me a happy vacation. It couldn't have gone better."

"That's good." Glenn finished his Coke and set the glass on the counter. "I'm hoping this outing will get Jill and Linda back together. I think Linda's been afraid of Jill, afraid of what she's going through. I think maybe this hit a little too close to home for her. It could have been Ricky just as easily as Robin. She knows about the setups and the falls, I think. Have you talked to her about it?"

"I have, but without your eloquence. Your philosophizing, I think you call it."

"A philosopher I am," Glenn agreed.

Mark found himself a stool and perched on it. "I'm sorry she wouldn't go to the funeral. I think she feels bad, too."

"She really shouldn't. I would have missed it if I could have. I hate the things, and I swear I'll never go to another one." He smiled. "Not even yours."

"I won't have a funeral," Mark said, grinning. "I want you to take me out back and stuff me in a trash can."

"Agreed," Glenn said. "By the looks of this house, I'd say it'd be a fitting burial."

They laughed. It felt good to laugh again. Mark wished it could always be this way. *But what about the setups and the falls? Who will be next?*

"Guess we're set for tomorrow morning," Glenn said. "Eight o'clock, and all will be well. We'll load up and get the hell out of Westwind for a while. It'll do us good."

"It sure will," Mark agreed.

For Linda, packing clothes in their big red suitcase while the men droned on in the kitchen, there was one other matter besides packing that had to be settled before she would be ready for the trip. There was the small matter of her mental state, which was not good. Not that she didn't want to go, not that at all. She felt the experience would be good for all of them. The dark cloud of death hung over this house, over these two houses on Westfire Road, and it would be a relief to leave them behind, if only for three or four days. Yes, it would be good to get away. A cleansing time for all their souls. There would remain, however, the small matter of her mental state, and her relationship with Jill. The two were intertwined, interchangeable. Linda was afraid, and what she was afraid of was Jill.

It was silly and she knew it, but her feelings couldn't be denied. She folded a pair of Mark's jeans and stuffed them into the suitcase harder than she needed to, growing angry at herself. This whole business was as tragic as it was silly. She knew she had failed miserably as a friend to Jill, was probably failing miserably now and would continue to fail miserably until the end of time. The fear that had blossomed in her mind when she saw Robin fall and not get up had not abated, but had grown, grown eyes, grown heads like the Hydra of mythology. That fear was the fear of death, and the fear had transferred itself to Jill. Jill was tainted. Her child had died.

When Linda was six years old and her cousin Chubby died, it had been Chubby's mother who had instilled the fear of death in Linda. Chubby dead had been a mere curiosity, a staring Chubby-face with bloody lips and dirt in his hair, an upside-down kid playing a new and interesting game. Chubby's mother, Linda's Aunt Martha, however, had taken the whole matter quite seriously—the whole family had taken it quite seriously, come to think of it—and it was around that time that Linda began to understand what DEATH was. DEATH was something that got you when you made a boo-boo and hung yourself by the foot. DEATH meant you could get dirt in your eyes and not even blink. DEATH kept you from giggling while you were lying in a big polished wooden box with your family moaning and crying all around you. And DEATH meant you were playing monster for good.

That business with Chubby in his coffin—Linda knew with every bit of her rational being that Chubby had not tried to bite her. Forced by her mother, she had bent down to kiss Chubby's dead cheek, and in all probability she had brushed his lips as she bent down, perhaps had skinned his lips back on his dead dry teeth and felt them there, cold and bare, and imagined with the imagination of a terrified six-year-old that Chubby was trying to bite her. That had to be it. That was bad enough, but what had happened to Aunt Martha later on had been just as bad. Aunt Martha became weird from then on, became reclusive and morbid and no fun at all. Before Chubby died she had been the type to serve up cookies and milk when you were visiting and came in from a hard afternoon of play, but afterward she was just mopey. Eventually she lost a good bit of weight, her hair got frizzy and tangled, her eyes grew big purple bags. There was talk that she was losing her mind, and when Linda was seven Aunt Martha was sent away by Uncle Bill to a place called a nuthouse, the place where people who had a close encounter with DEATH went. When Aunt Martha got back (and this was many years later) she had grown gray-headed and vague. Pumped her full of dope, Linda had heard Uncle Bill say one time. Fried her goddamn brain, she had heard him say.

So this was death, and its aftermath. First you died, then the people around you cried, then your brain got fried. It was a lyric simple enough for a child to understand. Died cried fried. Welcome to the world of the dead.

Linda pushed the lid of the suitcase down now, biting her lower lip thoughtfully. Her rational side knew that her fear was silly, based upon childhood recollections as it was. Robin had died and people had cried, no doubt about it, but Jill was a strong woman and would pull out of her grief with time. There would be no brain-frying going on around here. Tainted as she was, Jill would pull out of it.

Maybe. With the help of her friends, maybe. Who had helped Aunt Martha?

Linda picked the suitcase up by the handle and hefted its weight off the bed. No picnic, carrying this thing up the side of that windblown, forlorn mountain. Mark would have a heart attack. Oh, well, it was his trip, his idea to go. The worst part would not be carrying this thing up the mountain, oh no. Heavy as it was, it would be a picnic compared to the drive in the car, because Jill would be in the car, probably still smelling of funeral flowers and grief, and Jill was tainted (silly thought, silly thought, she told herself angrily) and would be there, too.

"Stop thinking like a child," she said aloud. "You'll get along just fine."

Somehow, though, she knew they wouldn't. Jill had been tainted by DEATH.

CHAPTER SIX

Around sundown on April 18, the evening before the Butlers and Pruetts' scheduled trip to Spike Mountain, Allie Parker came out of the squalid cabin he shared with his archenemy, Jackson Pierce, to cut a chunk of supper venison out of the skinned carcass of a deer that hung from a post jutting from the gable of the cabin. He tromped through the circular path in the snow around the cabin, his breath steaming out of his nostrils (it had been growing noticeably colder in the evenings lately), his bowie knife in his hand, came to the deer, and hitched in his breath with surprise.

"Yaahhh, *shit*!" he screeched at the top of his lungs. "Jackson!"

Muffled, from inside the cabin, came Jackson's reply: "Fuck you!"

"Lookit here," Allie roared. "The goddamn coyotes been at this thing again!"

A coyote, or coyotes, or a dog, something had indeed been dining on venison. The hanging rear legs of the deer were chewed down to the bone; the hindquarter looked as if someone had raked it with barbed wire. The deer twirled slowly on its rope against the backdrop of the sunset, hanging from the neck, a five-day-old kill. Even a bit of its forelegs had been gnawed on. Big critter, then, or a high-jumping coyote. Maybe even a bear, though a bear more than likely would have pulled the deer down and snapped the frayed old rope. That fool Jackson had forgotten to buy rope last trip down the mountain. Instead he had bought two thousand pounds of flapjack mix, the murderous bastard. It took a good week's worth of hunting to bag a decent mule deer, and now half of the eating part of it was gone. That meant another long hunt, or the rest of the spring eating Jackson's murder weapons.

Allie stormed back into the cabin and fetched his rifle, a rust-eaten Winchester lever-action .30–30, off the pegs on the wall. "Gonna bag the fucking critter," he swore, and sheathed his knife in his boot.

"Getting kind of late for hunting," Jackson said. Already he was whipping up another batch of bowel cancer, beating it in a bowl with a long spoon. "It'll get dark on you, dipshit."

"Eat my bag," Allie snapped.

"As if you had one, you puss."

Allie swung the gun around and pointed it at Jackson. "Don't cross me, anus-breath. I'm in no mood for it."

"You best be pointing that gun elsewheres, unless you want it sideways up yer ass!"

Allie considered shooting Jackson on the spot and ending this forty-year stalemate, but decided it could wait. He would need help skinning the coyote when he bagged it tonight; maybe in the process his trusty bowie knife could slip and accidentally cut Jackson's miserable throat, by God. It was a good thought, anyway.

"I'll be back in an hour or so," he said, and went for the door.

"I'll save yer supper for you," Jackson replied sweetly.

"Save it up yer ass," Allie said, put on his coat, and went out.

The sun was already fading off the horizon; there might be a good hour's worth of seeing-light left. He examined the ground around the deer, made positive identification of a single coyote, and headed east, following the tracks up the slope. There were bits of meat in the snow the first few yards; the coyote was carrying a raggedy piece in his jaws, then. Doubtless he'd stop after he thought it was safe and eat it. A couple miles, maybe, and Allie would spot him. Then there would be a coyote-hide blanket on his bed to warm his feet.

The trail led into the trees; no place else it *could* go. Allie's cabin sat in a clearing, one he had made himself with an ax and a lot of time. Surrounding it was dense evergreen forest, stately pines and low, sweeping spruce trees. Some of the low branches, hidden from the day's sunlight, still bore traces of the dusting of snow they had received a week ago, the last time it had snowed. Unseasonably warm, it had been lately, but now what had been

elted on the trees was turning back to ice, glistening in the
ding light like gems. The air was heavy with cold and the scent
f pine, and a deeper, almost indefinable smell Allie knew well
nough. It's gonna snow soon, he thought. It's gonna snow to
eat the devil.

The trail veered north, then west, then south and east again.
he paw prints were easy enough to spot in the three inches of
rusty remaining snow; old Wiley was trying to throw him off
1e trail by zigging this way and zagging that. Old Wiley E.
Coyote was a smart old cuss, no doubt about it; he couldn't
now he was being trailed but he did have sense enough to take
recautions. Allie charged up the mountainside as fast as his old
owlegs would carry him, blowing out clouds of steam that the
ght evening breeze let drift a few yards ahead of him before
issipating. He was a human locomotive following an easy track.
And it felt good to be out on the hunt again, away from Jackson
nd his flapjacks and his bullshit.

The minutes ticked by, marked by Allie's rapid footsteps as
e chugged his way up. His boots crunched over the snow, a
ound that was swallowed up by the trees and the stillness. When
he branches became too thick to penetrate he was forced to
ircle around, his head low to the ground, his shoulders hunched
s he hunted for the trail again, which he found easily every
ime. At last the trees began to thin a bit, and up ahead Allie
eard the coyote howl.

He stopped, breathing hard, and listened. Off to the right a
it, and a hell of a good distance away. Wiley was calling to
im, mocking him. You'll never catch me, Wiley seemed to be
aying. But you can sure as hell try.

"Shit if I won't," Allie said, and grinned, exposing missing
eeth. He knew the face of this mountain like most folks knew
he face of their wristwatch. The coyote was up near the area
where that fancy-pants doctor had built his cabin some ten years
ack, that big sprawling log job with the big plate-glass win-
lows. Allie had been up there several times, and more than once
ad cupped his hands around his face to look through the win-
lows of that miniature mansion. More than once it had occurred
to him to kill Jackson, burn the shack to the ground, and just
take squatter's rights on that fancy place. Hell, no one was ever
up there, anyway, save for five or ten days out of the year, and
during that time Allie could live in the woods. Besides, the people were never there in the wintertime at all. But a certain sense

of decency had kept him from doing it, a remnant of his civilize
years before he became a mountain man, the old days when h
had had to comb his hair and wash his clothes like normal folk
Killing Jackson presented no great moral dilemma; squatting o
somebody else's property did.

The coyote's yapping cry rolled across the hilly landscape i
quick sharp tones, high and excited. Allie homed in on it an
set out again, kicking snow and fallen twigs out in front of hi
pounding feet. Branches slapped at his face, filling his scruff
beard with pine needles. He was grinning now, knowing exactl
where he was going. Old Wiley sounded like he was on the high
falutin doctor's damned front step. The trees gave way at las
and Allie went into a crouch, eyeing the place, breathing slo
and measured.

No coyote. So much for his hearing, which had been goin
bad of late, anyhow. The wooden steps that led up to the fanc
carved front door were warped and split now, he noted wit
smug satisfaction. Fancy-ass doctor or not, his cabin was begin
ning to show its age and its neglect. God alone knew why h
had built it so high up, where no road would ever be.

Allie struck out across the lawn, if you could call it that; i
was a bare expanse of snow dotted with tufts of weeds and
few wooden shakes that had blown off the roof during the las
few big storms. One of the big plate-glass windows on the hous
was cracked, he noted with further satisfaction. Through it h
could see the ghostly humps and outlines of furniture that ha
been covered with sheets. If that roof was leaking there woul
be one hell of a mess inside, fancy place or not. Allie decide
he would take his shack over this place anytime. It was just to
big and modern to ever keep up. Skirting the house to the left
he worked his way down the gentle slope of the side yard, stil
following paw prints. The snow here on the knoll where the
cabin sat had melted off pretty bad, but there were still track
in the mushy ground, and a narrow path through the weeds where
a small body had recently passed. Smiling, flushed from the mac
pace he had been maintaining, Allie moved as silently as he
could, feeling that he was drawing near at last.

"Gonna getcha, you thieving turd," he whispered.

As if in reply, the coyote howled again off to his left. And
damned far away again, the slick little bastard. Allie broke into
a dead run and dived through the trees with his breath roaring
in and out of his lungs. Cold branches pawed at his face and

ied to tug his rifle out of his hands. Cursing, he shut his eyes
nd pressed forward, knowing the trees would be thinner inside
here the sunlight never penetrated. Pretty soon they did thin
ut, and he was able to make his way without too much imped-
nent. The trees were tall here, shutting the weak light of the
vening sky almost entirely out. There was little chance of track-
ig the coyote in here, but Allie was too stubborn to give up just
ecause it was getting dark. He plunged gamely on, a little slower
ow, feeling his age. He was one year shy of seventy and no
pring chicken anymore.

The coyote howled again. Closer this time. Allie grinned and
lowed to a shuffle, raising his rifle, ready to aim if anything
loved. Coyotes were a funny lot, jumpy as a bride and just
enerally skittish, but when mealtime came they just *had* to stop
nd eat. Allie had seen times when he practically had to take a
aseball bat to them to get them off a hanging deer. Stubborn,
ley were. And sometimes mean. And this loner was a rarity.
hey usually ran in packs.

The forest broke off and became clearing again. Not properly
 clearing, Allie noted, but a place where the trees were a hell
f a lot shorter. Up ahead he saw the bulk of something big and
lark, and for a moment had the crazy idea that someone had
larked a bus in here. That thought fled quickly as he saw that
he windows of the bus were gaping holes in the ruined, falling-
lown walls of some ancient cabin. He took one hand from the
un and scratched his head. Why the hell hadn't he ever run
cross this before? He thought he had traversed every inch of
his mountain. He circled the cabin, his nostrils full of the damp
mell of rotting wood, inspecting the gutted shell of what had
nce been a pretty respectable log house. In the gloom he could
ee the remains of a chimney jutting up from the earth like a
aceless totem. The wind whispered secretively through the sur-
ounding pines. A chill spread through his veins. Why hadn't he
nown this place was here before? Who had built it?

"Fat lot of shit it matters," he muttered, and turned away
rom it.

The coyote was facing him, perhaps twenty yards off. A big
piece of deer meat was still clamped in its jaws. The two eyed
:ach other, both startled, and then the coyote broke into a loping
un. Allie raised his rifle and popped off a shot. The mountain-
op echoed with it, rolling thunder. He worked the lever and

fired again, cursing the light. The coyote dropped the meat, tucking its tail between its legs as it ran.

"That won't save you," Allie said, and fired again. A branch snapped off a tree a foot above the coyote's head.

"Goddammit!" Allie levered the gun again. The coyote was doing his zigzag routine again, and doing a pretty good job of it. His path brought him around to the far wall of the cabin where he disappeared.

"Yaahhh, *shit*!" Allie ran around to the other side, tripping over roots and one time falling down. The forest erupted with another *Yaahhh, shit*! as he got up again with dead pine needles stuck to his face. He swiped a hand at them and continued the chase. Now the coyote had gone into the shell of the cabin and was halfway to the other side and the blackness beyond. As he skirted the cabin Allie fired again, and this time the coyote tumbled to a stop on the hearth with the fireplace and chimney sticking up behind him like a tall tombstone.

"Rest in peace, cocksucker," Allie said, and went over to it.

Dead. Deader'n shit, as Allie was fond of saying when he thought of the day he would kill Jackson. The thieving bastard was dead. And what a chase it had been.

He hoisted the coyote onto his shoulders and found that it was bleeding all over his coat. Disgusted, he dropped it to the stones with a decidedly dead *thump*. "Fuck," he growled, and pulled his bowie knife out of his boot. Better to carry the bastard's thieving skin back instead of the whole useless carcass, anyway. He knelt down and slit the coyote's throat. Blood washed out dark and steaming, filling the air with a smell like stagnant swamp water, and soaked into the spaces between the stones. Nice hearth, Allie noted mentally. Someone went to a lot of trouble to make this big thing, back in the days of yore.

When the flow of blood had slowed he began to gut the coyote, pulling out handfuls of steaming entrails. These smelled like farts, Jackson's greasy farts. Allie smiled, thinking of the day when he would gut Jackson like this, pull out the rotten bastard's heart while it was still beating, if possible, and stuff it down his throat. That was a nice thought, and he savored it as he worked. Deftly, he opened the coyote from throat to sternum and began to work the skin off. At which point he sliced off the end of his thumb.

"Yaahhh!" he screamed. "Shit!" He examined it—a small slice, really—but it was hard to tell which blood was his and which was the coyote's. He could be bleeding to death without knowing it. He dug a tattered snot rag out of a pocket, wiped his thumb off, and held it close to his eyes. From the severed tip, fresh blood welled, a miniature volcano overflowing. He let out a whimper. Mountain man or not, he hated pain, and this was worse than the hemorrhoids Jackson's flapjacks had given him. He flapped his hand and droplets flew into the dark mouth of the fireplace. Fine time to cut off his thumb, really fine. A man could bleed to death on the long walk back, a man could die of pain. He knotted the handkerchief around his thumb and pulled it tight with his teeth. Fucking coyote, anyway. It was all his fault. And Jackson's, just for good measure.

A faint hissing sound made him stop with one end of the cloth still in his teeth. He frowned, the net of wrinkles around his eyes deepening, his heavy brows coming together. *What the hell* was *that?* It sounded like air hissing out of a tire, and the tire sounded like it was stuck in the fireplace somewhere. He turned his head, cocking it to catch the sound. In the deep, black maw of the old dead fireplace the noise grew louder. Allie went on his hands and knees and crawled toward it, his thumb forgotten. By God, by the smell of it, something was *burning* in there.

Flame sprang to life in the scatter of old wet sticks and pine needles that had, with time, accumulated in the fireplace. In the sudden bright glare Allie saw drops of his own blood on the sticks, drops that were bubbling merrily as the flame consumed them. And then the fire went out. Foul-smelling smoke drifted on the air, thick and cloying. "Well, what the fuck?" Allie murmured. The skin on his back and forearms was prickling up, and more than a touch of fear was warming his old heart. Just what in the hell was going on?

A new sound made him turn. The coyote was trying to get up. Allie stared at this, numb with disbelief and a growing, primitive sort of terror. The coyote wriggled, sluggish and seeming dazed, and staggered to its feet. A thick rope of intestine hung down from its open belly. The fur on the side where it had lain was matted with blood. For a moment it stood, wobbling, then took a drunken, lurching step toward him, then another. Its open eyes gleamed in the dying light. Then its back paws became tangled in its own entrails and it tripped, falling forward. Its jaws snapped shut with a click. One more movement, a spastic jerk of one paw, and it was still.

"Damn," Allie breathed, open-mouthed and staring, still on his hands and knees. Saliva dribbled from his lower lip. "Jesus and Mary, what's going on?" He shuffled forward and poked an exploratory finger at the coyote. Nothing. The critter was indeed quite dead. In his life Allie Parker had seen a few of the strange things animals could do. There had been times when he had come up to a freshly shot deer stretched out in the woods and nearly been gored when the animal sprang suddenly to life. In one instance the deer had been shot clean through the heart and pulled that stunt. How did they do it? How did they come back to life for one or two seconds? And how had this coyote pulled it off with no blood and no guts left in its body?

He used his knife on the coyote. He stabbed it again and again. He was ruining the hide, but so what? He stabbed it in a frenzy, angry now, angry that some weasely critter could have scared him so. He would make sure the son of a bitch stayed dead this time. After a while he stopped, breathing in ragged gasps. Damn this bastard for scaring him like that. No true man of the mountains should ever have to be that scared by one lousy coyote. Jackson had wrestled him to the floor and held a knife at his throat more than once, and even then he hadn't been as scared as this. How had the critter done it?

Spastic reaction. Nerves, that was all. Just nerves that still had a bit of life left in them.

He got to his feet, satisfied. Nerves. Yeah.

So explain the fire, asswipe. Explain that away.

He went to the fireplace and stuck his foot inside. Old wet sticks, nothing else. Natural combustion, natch. What was it they called it? Spontaneous combustion? Sure, that was it. Old wet sticks that caught themselves on fire. All quite natural, Allie old boy. All quite natural.

He picked up his rifle and walked away, jumped the low ruined wall of the cabin, and sauntered on his way. The smell of smoke was still in the air. He glanced back and the coyote was still dead. Nothing unnatural had happened here. Nothing at all.

He made his way through the forest, his pace quickening as he went. There was a sour taste in his mouth, the aftermath of fear, and he was getting skittish. Night birds squawked at him. For the first time in his life, Allie was afraid of the woods after dark.

There was a noise behind him, a sound like something small shuffling to its feet and stumbling off through the trees. A deer, a fawn. He swore to himself that it was only a fawn. That did not stop him from stepping up the pace, though, so that by the time he broke out of the forest into the clearing where the high-falutin doctor's place lay, he was going at a dead run.

Eddie Chambers was taking a trip. Lying on a back road outside Tremonton, Utah, a discarded scarecrow under a rising slice of moon, he was tripping out. Out of his head. Eddie Chambers was taking the ultimate trip to Overdose City.

He moaned, thrashing his head this way and that. Colorful things were going on inside it. Earthshaking things. His hands and arms moved in sudden spasm. His legs buckled upward, his knees knocking at his chin. His eyes were open, seeing nothing. Twenty 'Ludes and twenty reds, four tabs of LSD mixed in for good measure. It was a devil's brew. Eddie was flying higher than he had ever flown before. And dreaming very disturbing dreams. Seeing very disturbing things. Feeling things that seemed very, very real.

There was blackness and thunder around him. Horses were galloping past, their hooves clopping the cold damp earth like drums. Flashes of light. Bright things in the sky, falling stars.

"Sie kommen," someone said to him. It was German but he understood it perfectly well. *"Die Engländer kommen."*

There was a rifle in his hands. There was a bayonet at the end of it, fully eighteen inches long. He was lying against the sloping wall of a trench while bombs burst all around, lighting the darkness with brilliant flashes. Clods of earth rained down on him. Shrapnel whistled over his helmeted head. Flares on parachutes lit the sky dull orange. He was terrified, terrified beyond description. Death was all around him. Wounded men and horses screamed. *Sie kommen.*

"Vorwärts!" someone shouted, and Eddie was aware of men getting up, men clawing their way out of the trench, silhouetted against the bright bursts of bombs like frantic dancers under a strobe light. Noise was all around him. Noise filled the world.

He got up. His feet gave way under him and he fell. Someone came up behind him and kicked him in the butt. *"Vorwärts!"* He got up again. A soldier beside him, a shadowy shape, screamed and fell to the ground. Eddie ran, knowing that he was not Eddie, knowing that he was not here. He was . . . he was . . .

Werner Guttman. He was Werner Guttman, born in Berlin,

educated there, destined to die here. Bombs rained down and he
ran. He was Werner Guttman and he ran because someone had
kicked his butt and told him to, not because he wanted to, but
because he had to. He was not an officer, as he had always
imagined, but a simple foot soldier about to die in the fields
of . . .

Flanders . . .

Yes, on the fields of Flanders. Biggest operation of the war so
far. 1917. The Germans were on the offensive, on Flanders field
where poppies grow. A million men would die here. Werner
Guttman would be one of them.

Bombs rained down, making dull thudding noises this time
instead of explosions. White haze crawled over the ground. Eddie
saw a shell hole and dived into it, too full of fear to do anything
else. He fumbled for his gas mask, opened the canister that
contained it, tried to put it on his face. White haze snaked into
the shell hole. Eddie held his breath, fought the straps of the gas
mask, tried to pull it on. He was working in a world of white.
His lungs burned and throbbed. He needed to breathe. He needed
for all the world to breathe, but the gas mask wasn't on yet, so
he breathed anyway because his body commanded it. He began
to cough and retch. His lungs were on fire, his throat constrict-
ing, his eyes watering. He coughed, and breathed, and coughed,
and breathed. And grew light-headed. His gas mask fell from
his hands unused. His head fell back onto the ground. He
twitched a couple of times. He died.

Lying on a road outside Trementon, Utah, trapped in a nightmare, Eddie began to scream at the uncaring night sky.

By ten o'clock that night, Ricky was tucked in his bed. Linda
had dutifully taken him to the bathroom, dutifully seen to it that
he had nothing to drink after six. She did not want to go through
another bed-wetting episode.

He lay in bed, fully awake, not wanting to sleep because sleep
brought nightmares. A big square of moonlight lay on the carpeted floor beside the bed. Toys were heaped in that square
because Ricky's room, like the rest of the house, was a mess all
the time. There were times when his mother told him to *clean
up your room*! but he usually just played around until she had
forgotten about it, and she always did because she was just too
busy with other things to worry too much about how his room
looked, anyway. Ricky did not mind the room being a mess. At

least when it was a mess, he could wake up in the night with
terror welling up in his throat and know with one glance that he
was home and safe. Clutter denoted home to Ricky. A cluttered
house is a house full of love.

He lay in bed with his eyes wide open, afraid to shut them
because of what went on whenever he did. Whenever he shut
them drowsiness stole over him and he began to dream. About
wet things. About sharp things coming up through the sheets. It
had happened every night since Robin died. And every morning
he was in trouble for wetting the bed.

A breeze rustled outside and the shadows cast by the branches
of the big elm in the front yard danced in the square of moonlight, a thousand pointing fingers. The big Mickey Mouse clock
on the wall ticked reassuringly. Mickey's big white-gloved hands
pointed at numbers Ricky could barely understand, seeming to
glow in the moonlight. Ricky could not tell time yet but he liked
the way Mickey's arms were in different positions all the time.
You could stare at that clock and not see a hint of movement,
but slowly, secretly, Mickey was moving. And time was ticking.

Sundown, a voice whispered.

Ricky drew the covers up tighter under his chin. His eyes were
wide and white. That voice, that was a scary thing. It was the
same voice every night, calling to him from far away, calling to
him from everywhere. It was a secretive, whispering voice, a
voice all dim and full of weariness.

"Leave me alone," Ricky said with as much courage as he
could muster.

Sometime . . .

It was very cold in the room. Ricky could see his breath all
of a sudden. Ice was forming on the windowpanes, turning the
moonlight into rainbows. Fear crawled up Ricky's spine like a
hissing snake, and he drew in his breath to scream.

Hungry . . .

Ricky let his breath out in a whimper, overcome with a new
sensation that replaced fear. There was a knot in his stomach, a
cramp in his stomach that nearly doubled him up. He was suddenly, desperately hungry. Hungry enough to eat a million Hostess cupcakes, hungry enough even to eat some of the cold yucky
meat loaf that was in the refrigerator in the kitchen. Hungry
enough to eat a horse.

So cold, the voice wailed. It was no longer a whisper, no
longer so very far away. The voice was in his head, quite clear

now. It was a hard, grating voice, the voice of a man that Ricky could almost recognize. Not his father, or his grandfather, or even Glenn Pruett, the only men Ricky really knew. It was the voice of a man and it was as familiar as his own.

Sometime after sundown, the voice cried, and the covers on the bed began to glisten with a dusting of ice crystals. Sharp things sprouted through the sheets, sticking into his skin like needles. Ricky turned his head on the pillow and watched things grow from the mattress, things like shoots of yellow grass. He pulled one hand from under the covers and ran his palm over the stubble on the sheet beside the pillow. Whatever was growing there was a quarter inch long now. It was, it was . . .

Straw. Straw was growing from his mattress. Straw and ice.

"Mommy," Ricky said evenly. His tongue felt like a cold dead lump in his mouth. His heart pounded in his throat. "Mommy!"

Footsteps approached. The ice became water. Water dripped onto the floor, ran down the windowpanes. The straw disappeared, sucked back into the mattress.

Brigham, the voice said.

"Mommy!"

Brigham!

"Leave me alone!" Ricky cried.

No forgiveness, and no rest.

"Mommy!"

The door swung open. The light snapped on. Linda stood there, her eyes narrowing, anger spreading across her face. "Well, buster," she said, frowning at him, "looks like you did it again."

This time he got a spanking.

PART TWO

The Cabin

CHAPTER SEVEN

They arrived at ten o'clock Thursday morning. In Glenn's four-wheel-drive Blazer they had no trouble driving all the way up to the cabin through the thin crust of snow; dodging the trees had been the worst part. In retrospect, it would be the glimpse he got of Beast that would trouble Mark most about that rainy, miserable drive with the Pruetts up to Spike Mountain. The glimpse he got of Beast, and the fight Glenn and Jill had.

The morning had started out lousy. Mark had rolled over in bed and lifted the curtains, expecting to see another glorious, sunshiny day like the last four had been, and was disheartened to see rain trickling down the window. It was seven o'clock in the morning and looked like it would be a shitty day all day.

He got out of bed and dressed. Linda stirred in her sleep, mumbling. Ricky was in bed, too, curled up between her arms. Mark shook his head, looking at him. That boy had mental problems. His room was going to have to be fumigated pretty soon if he kept pissing all over the rug and walls like that. A miracle that it didn't stink like a hamper full of wet diapers already.

He tickled Linda's foot to get her going, got his hand kicked for his trouble, and went into the kitchen to make coffee. By eight o'clock he had everyone up, had breakfast in them, and they were ready to go. Sort of. Ricky seemed troubled and cranky, and Linda wasn't in a much better mood. Now that everything was set and they were ready to walk out the door, she was having second thoughts.

"I could lose my job for this," she growled at him as he handed her the picnic basket. "It's silly."

He picked up the suitcase and headed for the door. "Too late to back out now," he said. "We've already made promises."

"What if burglars break in while we're gone?" she asked, following him grumpily.

"When did you become such a worrywart?" He held the door open and shooed them out. There was a pretty good drizzle falling; the gray sky seemed low enough to reach up and touch. Next door he could see Glenn leaning into the Blazer, packing things inside. Swell day for an outing. Mark locked the front door and shut it, tested the knob once, and headed across the yard.

"The Butler clan cometh," Glenn said when they had splashed their way up to him. He was wearing a bright orange hunting vest and boots that came up almost to his knees. "Go ahead and get in out of the rain, guys," he said, and opened the Blazer doors for Linda and Ricky.

"You look like you're going to an English fox hunt," Mark joked.

Glenn smiled. "I just might hunt me some fox. You still got my twenty-two?"

Mark had to think for a moment. "In my car, I think. Do you really want it?"

"Never go into the mountains unarmed," Glenn said. "Up there, there be bears."

"Against which a twenty-two is about as good as a BB gun."

"Between the eyes." He tapped his forehead. "You must shoot them between the eyes."

"The great white hunter, eh?" Mark got the rifle, not really concerned about bears at all, and put it on the floor in the back. Jill came out of the house looking glum and lost; she exchanged stilted pleasantries with Linda. In a few minutes they were under way, Mark and Glenn sitting up front, Linda and Jill and Ricky in the back. There was silence for a long time as they drove, punctuated by the slapping of the windshield wipers and an occasional yawn from Ricky. The silence between Linda and Jill seemed enormous. Mark feared there might be a rift between the two women that could never be healed, and still didn't fully understand it. Linda was just a little too cold, a little too . . . scared. Yes, that was it. She acted like she was scared of Jill. He made a mental note to ask her exactly what it was that was bugging her. But that would have to wait until later.

They were an hour into the drive when Mark saw Beast. He had been looking out the side window, drowsing a bit, dully watching the dead highway scenery flash past. Glenn hadn't had much to say, and Mark didn't feel like talking, either. It was too early in the morning, and the weather was just too depressing. We should have had sunshine for this, Mark thought, looking at the leaden sky and the soggy landscape. It would have made things more bearable. They were getting up into the high country now, where the first pine trees began to make their appearance. There were a few crusty-looking patches of snow on the ground, and Glenn was driving with both hands on the wheel as if afraid of ice. Fine day, Mark thought dismally. Bee-yootiful.

That was when he saw Beast. Of course it couldn't be Beast, not this far from where Mark had left him, but it did *look* like Beast, all soggy and dispirited, walking between the trees with his head down. Glenn was only doing thirty on the curves and Mark had ample time to look at the dog, hoping no one else was. As they drove past, the dog looked up, and its eyes seemed to catch Mark's, even from this distance. By God, if it wasn't Beast, it was Beast's twin.

Mark glanced over at Glenn. He was studying the road, frowning slightly. At least he hadn't seen the dog; that would have raised too many questions that Mark didn't feel like answering now. And from the back seat there hadn't come any cries of recognition, no horrified shriek from Jill. That would have been the real capper for this gloomy trip, having to explain why he hadn't killed Beast after all.

"Ah, jeez," Glenn said.

Mark's heart beat a little faster. "What's the matter?"

"All this gloom and doom," he said. "Why can't everybody cheer up? Last time we drove up here we were singing songs, having one hell of a time. Now it's like a morgue in here."

Jill snorted. "That's a terrible thing to say, Glenn. You know it wouldn't be right to be cheerful."

"How would Robin have wanted it? You think she'd want us to sit here all depressed? Hell, no, she wouldn't. She'd want us to be happy."

"That's the spirit," Mark said.

"Damn right it is. Ricky?"

Ricky poked his head up over the seat. "What?"

"I'll bet you've learned some great songs in school, haven't you? Why don't you sing us one?"

He frowned. " 'Cause I don't feel like it, that's why." With that, he sat back down.

"The kid's a grump," Glenn said softly to Mark.

"Tell me about it."

"How about 'Row, Row, Row Your Boat,' people? Anybody know *that* one?"

"I wish you'd be quiet," Jill said.

Glenn cast her a sharp glance in the rearview mirror. "We're on this trip to try and cheer up, Jill. It won't work unless we work at it." He smiled at Mark. "Come on, kiddo. 'Row, row, row your boat, gently down the stream'—sing along with Mitch here. 'Row, row, row—' "

"Stop it!" Jill snapped. "Just stop it."

"I will not stop it. If Robin was here she'd be singing at the top of her lungs, and I'd be singing along with her. So would everybody else. So we'll dedicate this one to the memory of our daughter, and sing like it's the last song we'll ever do. 'Row, row, row your boat—' "

" 'Gently down the stream,' " Mark sang halfheartedly, feeling sheepish and stupid.

" 'Merrily, merrily, merrily, life is but a—' "

"Stop it!" Jill shouted.

"I will not stop it." Mark could see that Glenn was gripping the steering wheel hard enough to bend it. His knuckles were white, the cords in his hands standing out. "I will sing this one for Robin, and sing it with great gusto. 'Row, row, row your boat, gently down the stream . . .' "

Jill burst into tears, but Glenn continued grimly on. He sang two or three refrains, then tapered off. Mark could see that his eyes had become shiny with tears.

It looked like it would be a long three days.

"I guess we're here," Glenn said now. They had been sitting silently in the truck, looking at the cabin. No one seemed anxious to get out. A light snow was falling out of the leaden sky; thin fog drifted mysteriously between the trees. Mark opened his door and was surprised at how much colder it was up here compared to the city, and how sharp the scent of pine was. Hopefully John Phillips had left a good stack of firewood the last time he was here, because if not, there would be a lot of cutting and chopping to do, something he didn't look forward to. As Glenn and everyone else knew, he was not much of an outdoorsman.

The rest got out and stood glumly in the snow. Even Ricky stood with his shoulders hunched, eyeing the scenery without enthusiasm. Glenn found the key and went up the steps to the door, worked on the knob for a moment, then swung it open.

"The magic castle," he announced. "Inside we shall forget our cares and worries. For three days, at least."

They went inside. Here the smell was damp and sour, the smell of emptiness and disuse. Mark had remembered the place as being smaller, cozier, but that was a trick of the mind. The living room alone was big enough to park five cars in, and there were two bedrooms off in the back. Mark had the feeling John Phillips had money to burn, erecting a place this size to be used once or twice a year. Too bad it was starting to fall apart.

"Broken window," Glenn remarked. "And look at the ceiling."

Water had been leaking through, discoloring the plaster in big concentric rings. The hand-hewn beams even appeared to be sagging, but that had to be an illusion caused by the gloom and the shadows. The place looked downright creepy.

"It'll be better when we get a fire going," Glenn assured everyone. "Why don't you girls get those sheets off the furniture? It's like a mausoleum in here."

They set about doing it, and Mark took the picnic baskets into the kitchen. It struck him as absurd to have a kitchen here at all—there was no running water for the big double sink, not even a hand pump. During their last outing here Glenn had mentioned a mountain stream not too far away, somewhere out near the old cabin, from which water could be hauled in buckets, but that was a bit too rustic for Mark's taste. Probably a bit too rustic for John Phillips' taste, too, which is why the good doctor didn't spend much time at his summer resort.

He went along the row of cabinets, opening the doors for a brief inspection, finding a lonesome pack of plastic forks in one of the upper cabinets and a forlorn-looking roll of Reynolds Wrap in one of the lower. Under the sink he discovered to his amusement that there was no plumbing, just a plastic bucket with some decidedly old-looking water in the bottom. You look beneath the veneer, he thought, and you find that we haven't improved ourselves much since the olden days.

"Anybody hungry?" he asked, going into the other room. He got a few head shakes and a mumbled no from Glenn, who was stacking logs in the fireplace from a pile beside the hearth. "Ricky?"

"Not hungry," Ricky said. He sighed. "I want to go home."

"Home?" Mark went to him and swept him up in his arms. "You want to go home already, champ?" He spun him around,

making Ricky giggle. "The fun's just beginning, kiddo. As soon
as we get a fire going we'll roast weenies and marshmallows.
And later tonight when it gets dark we'll sit around and tell ghost
stories. We'll scare you right out of your pants."

"Oh no we won't," Linda said.

"I guess we won't," Mark answered, realizing that Linda was
right. The ghost of Robin was already hanging over this group
like a dismal cloud, threatening to ruin everything before it
started. No need for ghost stories; what was needed here were
fun stories. "Then we'll tell each other fairy tales, nice ones
about princes and princesses."

"Sleeping Beauty, Daddy?"

"Sleeping Ugly, if you want." He put Ricky down and grinned
at him. "We'll all tell a tale, and see who's the best tale-teller."

"That'll be fun," Ricky said.

"Darn right it will."

"I think I've got it going now," Glenn said, and straightened.
"My Boy Scout days finally paid off. Look at that blaze."

It wasn't much of a fire, just a couple lackadaisical fingers of
flame, but it would grow. Soon the room would be light and
cheerful. "Let's hear it for the Boy Scout," Mark said. "He's
helping us chase the blues away."

"Darn right," Glenn said. "We're going to be cheerful, have
a good time, and leave here with a new attitude. I guarantee it."

Mark believed it. If they all tried hard enough, they could turn
this outing into something special. It would just take some work.
He rubbed his hands together, grinning. "Now that we've got a
fire going, what say we go outside and make a snowman?"

"Count me out," Linda said. Jill shook her head, looking at
him with her sorry, misty gaze, a bundle of folded sheets in her
arms. She looked sick, almost emaciated. It wrenched Mark's
heart to see her this way. In better times she could be fun in a
sassy, teasing kind of way.

"I doubt if you've got enough snow," Glenn said.

"Doubt never built a snowman, man. Come on, Ricko, let's
go make one and name him Frosty."

Ricky shrugged. "I guess so."

"Of course you guess so, you sourpuss." He opened the door
and breathed deeply. "Ah, smell those Christmas trees, smell
that fresh air! Come on!"

They went outside. In a few minutes they had a soggy ball of
snow rolled together, one full of grass and dead weeds. Things

looked pretty hopeless, Mark had to admit. It was no bigger than a basketball, and they had traversed most of the yard to make it. Snow was falling in sparse flakes. At this rate, it would be days before the ground was covered. The sky was full of promise, though. If Mark was any judge of weather, it would be snowing pretty hard soon.

"Maybe it'll be better tomorrow," he said, and stuck his wet hands in the pockets of his coat. He shrugged apologetically. "Sorry, Ricky."

Ricky scowled at the ground. In the blue snowsuit Linda had dressed him in he looked like a figure out of a Currier and Ives engraving, the little boy in blue trying to have some winter fun. His cheeks were bright pink, his hair a dark curl protruding from under his hood. Mark felt a wave of love and pity for him; it was obvious how badly he missed his playmate. All through this winter he and Robin had played together, built snowmen, gone sledding on pieces of cardboard in Glenn's sloping backyard. The sound of their giggles, shrieks, and fights had become a regular thing in the neighborhood. He went to Ricky and put his hands on his shoulders. "What's the matter, Ricky? Do you miss her pretty bad?"

He shook his head. "She was just a dumb girl."

"A dumb girl, but still pretty special, huh?"

"I guess so." Ricky looked up at him, squinting. "Dad?"

"Yes?"

"Do we have to stay here? I don't like it."

Mark picked him up and hugged him. "It's just for a little while. Besides, we'll have fun."

"I won't. I remember this place, and it's no fun."

"You do?" That was amazing. Ricky had barely been four when they came here last. "What do you remember?"

"I remember sleeping in that bed. The one with the straw."

"Straw bed?" Not in a cabin like this. John Phillips' beds were equipped with Beautyrests. Probably dank and moldy by now, but Beautyrests nonetheless. "There aren't any beds with straw here."

"By the fireplace," Ricky said, and began to cry. "Take me home, Daddy. Please."

Mark pulled his hood down and ruffled his hair. "Go home right after we get here? No way, baby. We're tough woodsmen, and we'll stick it out. Okay?"

"No!" Ricky pressed his face into Mark's neck, almost choking him with his arms. "Please take me home, Daddy. Please!"

Gently, Mark disentangled himself. This wasn't like Ricky at all to be so tearful, so morose. Ricky was a tough and resilient kid. "Hey, what's bothering you so bad? Tell Daddy about it."

Ricky looked at him levelly. His eyes were bright with tears. "Bad things happen here, Daddy. Bad things."

He was confused somehow, Mark knew. The bad things had happened down in Salt Lake. Up here there was nothing but hope, and good times yet to be had. "What bad things?"

Ricky held him tight again. "I don't know. Just bad things."

"Nonsense. Nothing can happen up here but good things. Take my word for it, kid. Nothing bad is going to happen."

"Promise?"

Mark set him back on his feet. "I promise, Ricky. And I want you to promise me something, too."

"Okay." He thought about it, frowning hard. "What?"

"I want you to promise me you won't wet the bed while we're up here. There probably aren't that many covers and sheets, not enough to spare, anyway. And besides, you'll be sleeping in bed with Mommy and me again. You wouldn't want to make us all wet, would you?"

"No, Daddy."

"So promise me you'll wake up if you have to go to the bathroom."

Ricky scowled. "I don't need to promise. I haven't been wetting the bed, anyway. It's been getting wet all by itself."

"Oh?" Mark smiled, trying to be understanding. "And just how does this miracle occur?"

"What's a miracle?"

"I mean, how does it happen? How does the bed get wet all by itself?"

"I dunno." He shrugged. "It just does. And straw grows out of it."

Interesting, Mark thought. But why is there never a child psychologist around when you need one? "Tell you what," he said. "I'm going to show you where the bathroom is, and tonight when you have to go I'll take you there myself."

They walked around to the back of the cabin. Twenty feet from the back door, facing east, was John Phillips' outhouse. A half-moon was cut in the wall above the door; on the door itself a woodburned sign proclaimed "Hold Thy Nose." There was no more memorable experience in the world than having to get up in the freezing night to use this place; doing it during the last trip here had made Mark wonder how man had survived before Sir Thomas Crapper invented the indoor toilet. Mark swung the door open and let Ricky peer inside.

"That's a toilet?" he asked incredulously.

"A one-holer," Mark replied with a chuckle. "The smell mercifully muted by the cold, but a seat guaranteed to give you instant frostbite."

"Huh?"

"Nothing. I just wanted to show you that this is where we go to the bathroom. If you have to go in the night we'll just let you do it outside somewhere close to the cabin, but during the day-time this is what we use. Okay?"

Ricky nodded gravely, "Okay, Daddy. Now can we go back in? I'm getting cold."

They went back around front and went inside to warm up at the growing fire.

That evening, with the fire burning cheerily and all the kero-sene lamps they could find blazing to chase the shadows, they roasted wieners on sticks Glenn had cut and whittled for the task, and ate some of Jill's bean salad, a dish Mark liked espe-cially but could never convince Linda to make at home. After everyone was done and the paper plates had been tossed into the fire Mark got a bag of marshmallows out of one of the picnic baskets and roasted a few for Ricky, the only one who seemed interested in burned marshmallows for dessert. Talk was inter-mittent but pleasant; it became easy to imagine that time had not passed at all since the last time they had been here, that Robin was just off in one of the back bedrooms and would re-appear shortly, her blond hair done up in pigtails, a teddy bear clutched under one arm. Mark told Ricky a made-up tale about three spiders who went for a walk on the moon, and halfway through it the boy fell asleep on the floor.

"That was a cute story," Glenn said. He was sitting in a wicker chair by the fire, regarding Ricky's prostrate form. "Bor-ing, but cute. Better than taking an overdose of Nytol, it looks like."

Mark smiled. "Wise ass. I never said I was a storyteller."

"Neither will anybody else." Glenn grinned back at him.

"Now that the kid's asleep, I've got a tale of my own to tell. Anybody care to hear it?"

"No ghost stories," Jill said.

"Nothing ghostly about it. This is a true story, told to me by John Phillips several years ago. I mentioned to him that I'd found that old falling-down cabin near here and he told me the story behind it. It's interesting as hell, and all true."

"More history?" Mark asked. "Are you playing the professor again?"

"Indeed I am. Allow me to adjust my mortarboard, get my notes in order, and I shall proceed."

"Poke me once in a while if I doze off."

Linda leaned over and poked him. "Shh!"

"Settle down, class," Glenn said. "There will be a pop quiz at the end of the lecture, so listen hard. In the year 1856, a date which may or may not be accurate, there lived in the hills of Pennsylvania a young lad by the name of Benjamin Hastings. Benjamin was a tall, skinny fellow, dark of hair and complexion, with a long, brooding face and deep-set, smoldering eyes. He—"

"Smoldering eyes?" Mark interrupted. "Have you been reading those cheap romance novels again, Glenn?"

"Shaddup, kid, or you'll get an F."

"Well, excuuuuse me!"

"Oh, quiet," Linda said. "Let him tell his story."

"Thank you, madame. In the year 1856 young Benjamin Hastings, this tall, smoldering-eyed lad, happened to become acquainted with a few members of a band of Mormons who were passing through Pennsylvania on their way to Utah from New York. There was at that time a wave of persecution going on in New York State, and most Mormons who valued their skins were making the long trek to Utah and freedom. Among this band of traveling Mormons was one Esmerelda Smith, no relation to Joseph Smith, who we all know was the—what?"

"I know," Linda said. "Joseph Smith was the founder of Mormonism."

"Give that gal an A plus. At the tender age of fifteen Joseph Smith encountered an angel, and the angel directed him to unearth a chest containing golden plates, upon which were inscribed the history of a people who had emigrated from Israel to the New World, way back in the days of yore. Joseph Smith translated the writings on those plates into what is now known as the Book of Mormon, and thus founded the religion known as the Church of Jesus Christ of Latter-day Saints. For this he was hounded, persecuted, and eventually shot. But like any persecuted people, the Mormons endeavored to persevere, and found that persevering was easier if they headed west, away from the zealots who would do them in. Thusly, a band of fleeing Mormons passed through Pennsylvania, where our hero, Benjamin Hastings, ran into them, we know not how, and got to know Esmerelda Smith.''

"I think I need a beer for this," Mark muttered.

"No drinking in class. Now, who knows what invariably happens when boy meets girl?"

"Girl gets pregnant," Linda said, and giggled. Mark saw a hint of a smile fleet across Jill's drawn features, and their eyes met for a fraction of a second. Quickly, he looked away, embarrassed for no discernible reason. Again he thought of the skateboard, and of Robin, and of the whole sorry mess.

"No," Glenn said, "in those days such things did not happen. What did happen, though, was that our gawky, backwoodsy Benjamin fell into instant love with Esmerelda, or Ezzie, as he liked to call her."

"How could you know that?" Linda asked.

"Simple. I am embellishing."

"Lying," Mark said.

"Through my teeth," Glenn agreed. "But the bare bones of the story are fact. Benjamin Hastings met and eventually married Esmerelda Smith. He left his home in Pennsylvania and went with her to Utah, which was known at that time as the State of Deseret. And he converted to Mormonism. Became quite a fanatic, as new converts often tend to be. Believed every inch of the Book of Mormon, and followed it faithfully. Which meant, in those olden days, that he began to take more wives. In 1868, after twelve years of happy marriage to Ezzie, a fair young lass named, ah, Dorothy Jones, entered his life. Ben, now in his thirties, had an itch that just had to be scratched, so, under the laws of the State of Deseret, he scratched that itch by marrying Dorothy. Perhaps he was unhappy because Ezzie had not borne him any children; perhaps he felt called by God to take on another partner."

"Perhaps he was a horny son of a bitch," Mark said.

"The world will never know. At any rate, he married Dorothy, and the three of them lived happily for many years. Then

in, let us say, 1888, Esmerelda, now in her fifties, up and died. By
now Benjamin was a crotchety old bastard, still childless, still
looking for a woman to bear him an heir. He was a farmer, and
a pretty good one, and had a nice big house, but the patter of
little feet was conspicuously absent. This bothered old Ben,
weighed heavily on his mind. Dorothy was getting too old to
have children, and it looked like the two of them were going to
die childless. And then along came Jennifer, a pert young lass
of twenty-one, who stole old Ben's heart. Pretty, she was, fair
of face, fine of figure, a good catch for any man. And for reasons
known only to her, when Ben professed his love, she recipro-
cated, even though he was thirty years her senior. Young Jennifer
fell in love with old Ben.''

"Maybe it was his smoldering eyes," Mark said.

"More likely it was his money. Ben was a good farmer, and
might even have had some business interests in Salt Lake. I
believe he owned a general store and a stable. He might even
have had part interest in a local bank. You've heard of the Hastings National Bank, I presume.''

"Never.''

"You really should get around more. Let's go ahead and assume old Ben was rich, rich enough to attract young Jennifer to
him. Rich enough, in fact, to convince her to marry him. They
were wed in the fall of 1888, and by spring, lo and behold, she
was heavy with child. What effect this had on Dorothy I don't
know; she was probably reduced to the role of housemaid. How
two women can live under the same roof and not kill each other,
I'll never understand. But they did, take my word for it. They
got along splendidly. Until 1890.''

"And then?''

"And then their idyllic life was shattered when the Mormon
church outlawed polygamy. Here was Ben, living a strict and
proper Mormon life, following the teachings of the Book of Mormon, believing in it with all his heart, and suddenly the church
was telling him that he could no longer have two wives. Telling
him it was, in fact, sinful. It was the church's acquiescence to
the laws of man, and pressure from Washington. It must have
made Ben's blood boil. It would be like the Catholic church
today telling the faithful that they can no longer take commu-
nion. Imagine the uproar that would cause.''

"Wine sales would plummet," Mark agreed gravely.

"Dipshit." Glenn paused to put another log on the fire, then dusted his hands. "Well, Ben decided he wasn't going to give up his way of life that easily. He was a tough old bird, that Ben. By then Dorothy was no spring chicken, but because he had married her long before he married Jennifer, it was Dorothy he would have to keep, and Jennifer he would have to give up. But she was pregnant with his only child, the child he had waited so many years to have, and you can bet your booties he didn't want to let her go. So what do you suppose he did?"

"Built the old cabin," Mark said. "Moved his family up here to the mountains."

"Precisely, but you don't get an A because you knew what this story was about. Yes, Ben cashed in all his chips and built a magnificent cabin right here on Spike Mountain, up away from the people whose change of rules in the middle of the game had so devastated his life. He sold everything he had and became a mountain man, a real hermit. You can bet that if he was crotchety before, he became a regular bear now. Probably shot a government man or two who ventured up here to try and take his Jennifer away, so after a while people just left him alone. Oh, I suppose he had to go to town once in a while for supplies, but by then he was so mean nobody bothered with him. Let the old coot stay up there on that godforsaken mountain if he wants to, they probably said. And so a few months went by, and Jennifer had her child, a boy they named Brig am, after Brigham Young, the man who brought the first Mormons out west. A few years passed, and then a few more, and then the history of Benjamin Hastings takes a bizarre turn.

"In the winter of 1896, six years after Ben and Dorothy and Jennifer moved up to Spike Mountain, old Ben came down out of the mountain and wandered into town looking like a man who had passed through the gates of hell itself. His eyes no longer smoldered; they were burned-out cinders, empty and glassy. He stumbled barefoot into Salt Lake City, lurching like a drunk. His hands and feet were black and rotting with frostbite and gangrene. Gangrene had already claimed his ears and nose; most of his hair was gone. He was little more than a skeleton. He was taken to a doctor, where his hands and feet were amputated in an effort to stop the spread of gangrene."

Jill stirred in her chair. "Oh, yuck," she said, and shivered.

"It gets yuckier."

"Then stop."

Mark sat bolt upright. "No, don't! I want to hear the rest."

"Well, I've had enough," Linda said. "Jill, shall we go make the beds?"

"A super idea," Jill said, and stood up. "Anybody remember where the linen closet is?"

"Over there," Glenn said, and pointed to the blackness of the hallway that led to the bedrooms. "Back there in the dark."

"Then I'll stay here," she said, and sat down again.

"Better plug your ears, then. Old Ben's gangrene got worse. It spread up to his knees, and from his hands, up to his elbows. The doctor sawed on him some more. The gangrene spread. The doctor sawed. Pretty soon there wasn't much left to cut; Ben had no arms or legs left. And he was screamingly insane by then, too. He made too much noise to be kept in a regular hospital, so they put him in an insane asylum. Armless, legless, utterly crazy, Ben spent the rest of his life like a slug, screaming his lungs out. They sent a rescue party that spring up to Spike Mountain to try and find Dorothy and Jennifer and the boy; by then the snow was melting off, but was still over five feet deep. It took them nine days to fight their way up to Ben's cabin, and by then, of course, it was too late.

"They'd run out of food, see. The merchants at Salt Lake would later recall that Ben hadn't come down that fall to purchase supplies—the weather had just been too bad, the storms too fierce. Something, probably bears, had gotten to the horses, so there wasn't any horsemeat. Ben Hastings' mountain retreat had become a pit of no escape. They found Dorothy dead in bed, nothing more than a skeleton with some skin on it. And Jennifer, pretty young Jennifer—she was dead, too. She'd hanged herself from the rafters rather than face starvation. It was freezing inside the cabin and so she was preserved just as she was, except that over the months her neck had stretched until it was over three feet long and her knees were bumping the floor."

"Glenn!" Jill cried, loud enough to make Ricky jump in his sleep. "Stop it!"

Glenn grinned at Mark. "They never found the boy, young Brigham. But they did find . . . bones . . . in the fireplace. And old Ben? Well, he just wasted away, armless, legless, no ears, no nose. He even went blind before he died."

"How long did he live?" Mark asked.

"After he wandered down out of the mountain? Another six years. He lived like that for six years."

"Jesus," Mark said. He put his hands together and shivered. "What a story."

"That's what I told John Phillips. I told him he was a cruel bastard for making up such a story."

"You mean it's made up?" Mark cried. "You got me going like this, got me all scared, and it's a made-up story?"

Glenn smiled wickedly. "Ah, but is it? John Phillips rarely comes up this mountain anymore, even though he spent over thirty thousand dollars to build this cabin. He says things happen up here, things he can't explain. Noises in the night. Screams in the distance. Rattlings and groanings, and things that move by themselves. He says that one time all the lamps blew out at once, leaving him scared to death in the dark, even though there was no wind. And once he found bloody human footprints in the snow outside. Bare footprints, made by bare feet. Old Ben's bare feet. His ghost still wanders this mountain, looking for a way out."

"Well, I've had enough," Jill said, and stood again. "Linda, if you'll carry a lamp, I'll find some sheets and blankets. Let's leave these two alone with their ghost story."

"True ghost story," Glenn said. "Embellished, but true. John Phillips spent two years tracing the history, reading old newspapers, talking to old geezers who heard the story from their grandfathers when they were children. It scared him, honey. Scared him bad. I wouldn't go back in those bedrooms alone."

"Oh, pooh," Linda said, got up, and picked up a lamp. "I'll be glad to help you, Jill."

They went down the hallway to the bedrooms, two figures moving cautiously in a circle of light. "I think they'll be friends again now," Glenn said, watching them go. "Nothing like a good fright to bring people together."

"Is that why you told that story, even though nobody wanted to hear it?"

"Could be," Glenn said. "Could be." He regarded the fire, smiling to himself. "What say we put on our coats and hike over to the old cabin again? Care to see it?"

Mark shook his head vehemently. "Care to drop dead, old buddy? A million bucks wouldn't get me over there at night."

"Maybe tomorrow, then."

"Yeah. Maybe tomorrow." Mark stood, stretched, then bent to pick up Ricky. "The kid's dry," he said, feeling his pants.

"He's probably over it by now. I suspect it was just a temporary reaction to what happened."

"Probably." Mark hoisted Ricky to his feet, shaking him lightly. "Wake up, Rick. Time to go to the bathroom." He looked at Glenn. "I hate doing this, waking him up when he's just gone to sleep. It takes forever."

"Has to be done," Glenn said.

Ricky groaned, swaying on his feet. "Cold," he muttered. His eyes were still closed.

"It's going to be colder outside," Mark told him. "Come on, open those baby blues and walk with me." He went into a squat and took Ricky by the shoulders. "Open them up and look at me, champ."

Ricky opened his eyes. In the light from the fire they looked yellow and glassy, the way, Mark thought, old Ben Hastings' eyes must have looked when he came down out of the mountain. Ricky looked drugged. He turned his head slowly to stare at the fire, and his mouth fell open. "Thirty-one days," he said quite clearly, then opened his mouth so wide Mark could see all of his back molars, and screamed.

"Jesus," Glenn barked. Ricky's scream was high and piercing, a scream of utter terror. Reflexively, Mark shook him to make him stop. The women came rushing out of the hallway, their faces pale in the bobbing light. Ricky tumbled into Mark's arms, sobbing. Linda came over and snatched him up, giving Mark a hateful glare.

"What in the world did you do to him?" she demanded, stroking his hair.

Mark spread his hands. "Nothing! I was just trying to wake him up. Honest." For no reason at all he felt guilty, as if he had given the boy a punch in the mouth instead of a gentle shake. "You know how he's been lately."

"Robin went through a spell like that," Jill said. "She'd wake up screaming in the night, scared us to death. It's just nightmares."

"Yeah," Glenn agreed. "Nothing to worry about." In his face, though, Mark could see that he was indeed worried. That scream had been so loud, so full of terror and . . . *sadness*. Though it seemed hard to explain, Mark had detected a note of sadness in Ricky's cry. And that had to be because of Robin.

"He'll get over it," Glenn said, as if reading Mark's thoughts.

"Sure," Mark said. "He just needs time." He took Ricky

back from Linda and went outside with him. They stood by the open back door and Ricky urinated in the snow, shivering. "Cold," he said.

"Getting that way," Mark said. "Are you done?"

Ricky zipped up. "All done."

"Ricky?"

"Yes, Daddy?"

"What did you mean when you said thirty-one days?"

Ricky looked up at him and shrugged. "I don't know. I didn't know I said it."

"You've been saying it an awful lot lately."

"Sorry, Daddy."

"Don't be sorry. Just try and think what it might mean."

Ricky frowned. "I think it means that it's an awful long time. A really, really long time."

"Thirty-one days is a real long time? For what?"

"For anything. For everything. Isn't that right?"

Mark laughed. Go figure kids. "I guess it is," he said, and they went back inside to get ready for bed.

CHAPTER EIGHT

A clock was ticking. The sound of it woke Mark out of a light and troubled sleep, a sleep in which vague unhappy dreams scurried like ghosts through his mind. He had a recollection of tossing in his sleep, of trying to pull enough covers up over his neck to keep it warm. It was freezing back here in the bedroom so far away from the fireplace, and there were not enough covers to keep the cold out. And there was no clock, come to think of it. A clock was ticking, and there was no clock.

He opened his eyes and saw shapes and shadows. The bedroom was small, the walls dark oak paneling. Two windows allowed gray light to filter in, reflected light from the snow outside. Linda was a shape under the covers beside him, Ricky nestled next to her with his head on her outstretched arm. Something was ticking—clicking—with a steady *slap slap slap*. Mark sat up in bed and realized that things were getting wet. Freezing, and getting wet. Thin bits of ice crackled as he threw the covers aside with dismay. He put his feet on the carpeted floor and found that it was wet, too.

"Cold," Ricky muttered.

Had he done it again? That ticking was water dripping somewhere, no clock at all. Water was dripping off the bed, plinking drop by drop into a puddle somewhere on the darkness of the floor. Mark put a hand under the covers and felt Ricky's legs, which were warm and dry. No, not this time.

Ricky moved in bed. He sat up, pulling the covers away from Linda. Sleepily, she turned on her side.

"What a mess," Mark said.

"Get out," Ricky whispered. He clambered out from under the covers and put his feet unsteadily on the floor. For a moment

110

he stood facing the doorway, swaying from side to side, mumbling to himself. Asleep, obviously.

"Ricky?" Mark said, then stopped himself. What was the rule for waking a sleepwalker? Don't do it abruptly? Or don't do it at all? Ricky went to the door, weaving a little, and disappeared in the hallway. Mark stood and followed him, frowning with concern. Maybe all this talk about bed-wetting was having some effect at last. But could he find his way to the door, open it, and do his thing while asleep? Mark doubted it. "Ricky?" he whispered behind him as they went past the other bedroom, cautious not to wake Glenn and Jill. "Ricko?"

The boy continued his steady, wavering progress, padding softly on his bare feet. Past the kitchen, where the picnic baskets sat ghostly and silent on the countertop, and out into the huge main room, where a dying fire still crackled in the fireplace. It was warmer here. Outside, the wind moaned gently through the eaves, and Mark imagined he could almost hear the patter of snowflakes as they fell onto the roof. This cabin did indeed seem like a magical place, nestled here under the pines so far away from man and his world, man and his troubles. Up here there might be bears, as Glenn had said, but there was also tranquility, a fair trade-off.

"Ricky?"

Ricky went to the front door and opened it. Cold air crawled across Mark's feet as he walked up behind him. Ricky hesitated a moment, then stepped out onto the wooden steps, then down into the snow, which by now had fallen to a respectable two inches. A light wind marched across the dark hilltop, kicking up spirals of snow like dust. Mark hesitated, expecting to hear Ricky cry out from the shock of suddenly finding himself standing here in the cold, to wake up and look around with alarm and bewilderment. Instead, he turned right and walked past the cabin's big plate-glass windows as if determined to make his way into the woods beyond. His head rolled on his shoulders at times, and he began to make crying noises.

Poor kid, Mark thought, grimaced, and tiptoed out into the snow himself. Ricky stopped a little ways past the corner of the cabin and stood as if sniffing the wind. Mark could hear his teeth chatter; it had to be under twenty degrees, and all he was wearing were his flannel pajamas, the ones with yellow Pac-men all over them. Ricky raised his arms to the sky, turned in a slow, awkward circle, tilted his head back, and began to weep openly.

Mark went to him with snow crunching up in freezing clots between his toes, already shivering himself. He took Ricky's hands and pushed them back down to his sides. "Wake up," he said sternly.

Ricky's eyes were already open. "Brigham," he cried, looking utterly forlorn, utterly lost. He suddenly pulled away from Mark and went down on his knees, where he scooped up handfuls of snow and began to eat them.

Brigham. That's what Glenn had said the boy's name in the story was, the boy who disappeared up here on Spike Mountain over a hundred years ago. Mark pursed his lips, watching Ricky, scowling. In his sleep, Ricky had heard Glenn's tale. Somehow, subconsciously, it had taken root in his mind and hung on. "Get up," he said, and put his hands around Ricky's waist.

"Tonight we eat," Ricky whispered fiercely. His face was wet with melted snow. Mark hoisted him up and hobbled back to the cabin, carrying him in the crook of one arm. The wind was beginning to gust now, spraying him with snow, cutting through his pajamas like an icy knife. In the forest the treetops swayed mysteriously, dark spires against the moon-whitened backdrop of clouds. Mark shivered, glancing around himself as he walked. If there be bears, he thought, then they be out here somewhere.

They made it inside without being eaten. Mark took Ricky to the fireplace and stood him on his feet. The wind was really whooping it up now, groaning across the top of the chimney, making the flames dance. Through the windows Mark could see snow billowing outside, coming down in an almost solid sheet. It looked like it would be one hell of a storm, this one. The snowflakes were as big as half-dollars. He felt a twinge of unease but dismissed it from his mind; that Blazer could crawl through anything nature dumped on them. And if they had to they could leave in the morning before things got too deep.

"Feeling better?" he asked, warming his hands.

Ricky nodded. "Why did we go outside, Daddy?"

Mark had to smile. "That's what I was going to ask you. Have you ever heard of sleepwalking?"

"Sure." Ricky stuck his arms out straight in front of him, all ten fingers pointing forward. "That's when you walk around like this."

"If that's the case you'll have to brush up on your technique, Rick. And next time, try to stay in the house." He brushed flakes of snow from Ricky's hair, thinking. Just what do you do with a kid who has as many troubles as Ricky seems to have? The bed-wetting, the sleepwalking, the odd words and moans and groans coming out of him—just what do you do with a kid like that? Send him to some eighty-dollar-an-hour child psychologist who'll wind up telling you what you already know, that the boy's best friend was killed recently and that his child's mind simply can't process that morbid bit of information yet? Or do you just let him be and hope he comes out of it with his mind intact?

It came back to him then what had happened right before Robin's funeral, the way he had seen Robin's dead eyes move when Ricky touched her hand. To imagine something like that— you talk about someone having trouble dealing with death. Maybe Ricky wasn't the only one here who needed a psychologist. But Mark felt he was well on the road now toward accepting Robin's death as unchangeable fact, so perhaps it was only a matter of time until Ricky started down that road himself. It would be the only way to deal with her loss. Mark flung the moisture from his hands into the fire, where the drops hissed and crackled. "Do you have to go to the bathroom now?"

"I guess," Ricky said, sighing. "But do we have to go outside to do it? I'm cold."

"It'll just take a second." He took Ricky by the hand and led him back to the door. "Just stand on the steps and let her fly. No one will mind. And try not to get blown away." He turned the knob and the door blew open as if a bear had been leaning against it, tearing the knob from his hand and banging into the wall. Mark had a quick, worried thought that maybe the knob would have punched a hole through the paneling, but a sudden horrified shriek from Ricky made him forget that. He recoiled, instinctively pulling Ricky back away from whatever danger was out there.

A coyote was standing at the base of the steps.

A very sick coyote, by the looks of it. Its fur stood up in dirty knots. Something dark was caked to its side like a mat. Its eyes gleamed dull yellow, sunken like the eyes of an animal dead and left to rot in the sun. It took a staggering step on its bony legs as if to come up the stairs and invite itself in.

Mark stepped back, found the edge of the door, and slammed it shut.

Rabies! What we have here, he thought, his heart hammering with sudden dread, is a rabid coyote. Oh, joy.

"What was that dog doing out there?" Ricky asked, hugging his knees.

"No dog." Mark's voice was husky and rasping. "A coyote. A rabid coyote."

Ricky looked up at him, apparently more curious now than afraid. "What's a rapid coyote?"

"Rabid. With a *b*. Rabies." Mark opened the door a tiny crack and pressed an eye to it. The coyote was still there, still watching. And something was wrong with its chest, he saw now. It had been cut there, and deeply. White breastbone gleamed in the dark meaty slit.

"Jesus," Mark breathed, shutting the door again. He and Ricky had been out there not three minutes ago. So much for bears. There were worse things up here.

Glenn came out, sleepy-eyed, knotting his bathrobe. "Who shot off a cannon?" he asked.

Mark turned. "That was the door banging. Hell of a storm brewing outside, and worse." He motioned him over. "Take a look at this." With a thumb, he pointed outside. "Just open it a crack. We've got a coyote with rabies on the front steps."

"Really?" Glenn opened the door and peered outside, then shut it quickly. "Ah, so," he said, turning back. "Ah, so."

"Now what? We do Charlie Chan imitations all night?" Mark giggled in spite of himself; the shock of seeing that bedraggled creature had made him giddy.

Glenn shrugged. "I don't know. I don't think we're in any danger. It'll probably just go away by itself. We'll be all right."

"What about the storm?"

"It'll taper off. It's springtime, you know. It never snows more than four or five inches at one time."

Jill rushed out then, followed by Linda. "What was it, Glenn?" Jill asked.

"Dorkface here let the front door blow open." Glenn bent and inspected the paneling, shaking his head. "Doc Phillips will have your hide for this."

"Only if he finds out," Mark said guiltily. "Besides, the place isn't in very great shape, anyway. And he should have doorstops."

"Agreed."

"What's Ricky doing up?" Linda demanded.

"Trying to use the bathroom, only there's a coyote outside. A rabid one."

"So? Shoot it."

There we have Linda in a nutshell, Mark thought. A problem
rises, no matter how complicated, no matter how complex, and
Linda has the answer: shoot it and move on. Don't let anything
tand in the way of your happiness. But perhaps it wasn't a bad
ttitude, and a lot more like the old Linda. The new Linda was
a hesitant, indecisive whiner; things were looking up.

"It *is* an idea," Glenn said.

"A beauty of an idea, except for one thing, O great white
headhunter. We left the rifle in the Blazer."

Glenn nodded, chagrined. "Ah, so."

"Here we go again with the ah-so's. Tell you what, Charlie—
you keep the coyote busy and I'll run for the truck."

"Swell. I'll show him my repertoire of card tricks. That should
do it."

"Guys!" Jill waved her hands. "Just forget about it till morn-
ng. The coyote will probably just go away by itself."

Glenn nodded. "True. I vote we sleep on it."

"But Ricky has to go to the bathroom," Linda said. "He can't
go outside."

"There's a bucket under the sink," Mark suggested.

"He can use it," Glenn said. "It's no big deal."

Linda took Ricky by the hand and went into the kitchen. Mark
heard cabinet doors open, and a moment later a muted tinkle.
"Problem solved," he said. "Put four of the world's greatest
minds together, and no hurdle is too great."

"Always the jokester," Jill said, and smiled at him warmly.

"Now let's put our minds together and solve this," Mark said.
"The roof leaks over my bed. Everything's soaking wet."

"Well, shit," Glenn said.

"Not in that bucket you don't. Now, what do we do about my
bed?"

"Fix the roof in the morning, I guess. There were some shakes
lying on the ground, I saw. Maybe if we hammer them back it'll
stop the leaks."

"You brought a hammer, I suppose?"

"No, but we've always got your head." Glenn laughed. "We'll
figure out something. Meantime we'll share our blankets and
you guys can sleep by the fire. Right now, I think I'll get me a
bite to eat." He picked up a lamp and took it to the fireplace,
where he lit it with a burning stick. Warm yellow light grew in

the room. "I am famished," he said, looking puzzled. He stood and looked at his watch. "It's only one o'clock. That's strange."

"Not strange for you," Jill said. She looked at Mark apologetically. "He eats like a pig. And always wears his watch to bed."

"I'm familiar with the swine," Mark replied. Come to think of it, and now that Glenn had mentioned it, he felt hungry, too. Fabulously hungry. He was with good friends, Jill was perking up, Ricky's problems had been solved—Good God, boys and girls, why not have a bite to eat? "I could use something, too," he said.

Glenn smiled. "To the kitchen, then."

Mark cracked the door open again and looked out before he went. Surely the coyote had wandered off by now, or dropped dead in its tracks. But no, it was still there, keeping some bizarre vigil over the front door. Its head hung so low now that its muzzle was in the snow. The eyes showed no hint of intelligence in the brain behind them. The last stages of rabies, no doubt about it. The thing would be dead by morning. And it was a good thing, because by the way the snow was piling up, they might have to be leaving about then, too.

He followed Glenn and Jill into the kitchen, feeling a bit puzzled. It had only been a few hours since he'd eaten—eaten like a hog—and here he was hungry again. His stomach was a dull knot, his mouth already watering at the thought of more bean salad and hot dogs. And potato chips, though he wasn't sure if any of those were left. And mustard, delicious yellow Kraft mustard on a bun. It was strange to be hungry this way.

"We've got tons," Glenn said, pulling items out of the baskets. He spread food in an array on the counter.

"I'll eat tons," Mark replied, eyeing it all hungrily.

"Save some for me," Linda said, putting the bucket back under the sink. She straightened and brushed a hand through her hair. "I can't believe I'm so starved." With a sheepish grin, she got a raw hot dog out of the package and bit the end off.

Mark's stomach gave another lurch, this one hard enough to make him wince. What the hell was going on? He felt as if he hadn't eaten in days. He got a hot dog and took half of it with one bite, savoring its cold, smoky taste. When it was gone he got another, then rifled through one of the baskets for a spoon. Jill had opened the bean salad, and the smell of it was making him woozy. When he had located the spoon, he dug in, eating straight from the big Tupperware container.

Glenn had a hot dog in one big hand and a bun in the other, alternating bites between them. "Good stuff," he said with his mouth full, and grinned. "Good thing we brought plenty."

"There's a jar with carrot and celery sticks in here someplace," Jill said, rummaging through a basket. She produced it triumphantly. "Enough for all of us."

They ate. The kitchen was full of crunching and smacking, of Saran Wrap being torn off containers and aluminum foil being unwrapped. Mark noticed Ricky off in the darkness of the corner, watching them. "Hey, Ricko," he said, indicating the food, "don't you want a bite?"

"Not hungry," Ricky said.

"Suit yourself." Mark found a jar of hot dog relish and ate a spoonful. It was marvelous in his mouth, so tangy and cool. He ate another spoonful, amazed at himself. He felt he could eat a horse, with or without the relish. When Linda came up with a fresh bag of Frito Lay barbecue potato chips he tore the bag open and dug in, feeding himself with both hands the way Ricky would eat popcorn, making a mess on the floor.

"Hog," Glenn said, and snatched them away. The bag crackled unhappily in the hands of its new owner. Mark felt a sudden moment of anger and almost said something, then stopped himself. There was plenty here for everybody., And besides, the chips belonged to the Pruetts, anyway. He got another hot dog, becoming dimly aware that something strange was happening here. Four grown people were eating as fast as they could eat. The floor was being littered with crumbs of hot dog buns and potato chips, splatters of mustard, beans from the bean salad. Linda had her head over the bowl and was shoveling it in like a thirsty man ladling water from a bucket. Jill's mouth was so full she looked like a chipmunk, and she was stuffing it even fuller. And Glenn—he was rummaging through a picnic basket with a treasure hunter's gleam in his eyes, clutching his Frito Lay prize to his chest with one arm as if afraid it would be taken from him.

Tonight we eat. Ricky had said that. And it was tonight, and they were eating.

But dammit, he was *hungry*.

"Save some for me," he said, laughing. Here was all the food in the world. Here was everything he could ever wish to eat.

And somewhere in the depths of one of these monster baskets was a Hormel canned ham. A whole ham—and Glenn hated ham. That was good, because if Glenn liked ham, well, there just might be a fight. Right now, hungry as he was, Mark felt he could fight someone for a taste of that ham. Punch someone out, if he had to.

Tonight we eat.

"Gangway," Mark cried, and pushed Jill aside, looking for the ham.

At about that time Allison Parker was getting hungry, too.

He awoke and sat up in the battered, rough-hewn bunk that served as his bed, bonking his forehead on the bed above him where Jackson Pierce lay sleeping. Consternation crossed his heavy features as he rubbed the bump on his head. There was a great rumbling emptiness in his belly, a growing ache spreading across his midsection like a stain. It had hit him from out of nowhere, pulling him out of a dream with terrible suddenness. He rubbed his head absently, thinking of steaks and potatoes and heaping bowls of vegetables, his mouth watering, his eyes widening as he envisioned these delights in the dark. Outside, the wind howled and groaned, flapping the tar paper on the roof.

Jackson awoke, too, and sat up, swung around, and dangled his smelly feet over the side of his bunk by Allie's head. "Damn," he murmured.

Allie elbowed his feet aside. "You awake, too, asswipe?"

"Fucking hungry," Jackson said. Allie heard him scratch his beard. "What the fuck's going on? We just ate supper a couple hours ago." Supper had been, of course, flapjacks and venison. "I'm feeling like a midnight snack."

"Bacon," Allie said dreamily. "Poached eggs in hollandaise sauce. Peanut butter on hog jowls."

Jackson snorted. "Yer making me sick, buttfuck. What I want is one of those Big Macs like we got down in Kamas last fall. Two all-beef patties, special sauce, lettuce, cheese, pickles— holy Hannah, I think I'm going to die."

"Feel free," Allie said, and got out of bed. He padded to the potbelly stove, his long johns drooping at the ass and flapping at his ankles, opened it, and tossed a log into the orangeness inside. "But before you die," he said, "run out and pick me up a pizza." Allie had eaten pizza once at the Pizza Hut in Kamas, first the toppings and then the crust, and had pronounced it good if a bit too messy for his taste. That memory roared at him now, snarling like a beast, clawing at his throat. He could very easily kill for a bite of pizza about now, and his preference was to kill Jackson for it.

Jackson hopped out of bed, grumbling to himself, pulled on his boots, and made for the door. "I'll cut the steaks, cocksucker," he said, locating his knife. "You whip up some flapjacks."

"*Yahh, shit!*" Allie screeched. "I've got a taste in my mouth for pizza pie, and you want flapjacks! Eat shit!"

"Yer the only shit I see around here, dogbreath. Shut up and start cooking." With that he went out, swearing at the wind and Allie and God. Allie caught a glimpse of a full-blown blizzard roaring outside before the door blew shut.

"Goddamn pissant," he grumbled, and lit the lantern that hung from the ceiling on a wire in the middle of the cabin. Scowling, raging mad, he shoveled handfuls of pancake flour out of the big one-hundred-pound bag in the corner and threw them into a bowl. There was also a bowl of melted-snow water standing on the table, and he dumped a bit of this into the flour. When he had located a spoon he began to whip the mess into something respectable, if you could call a sure case of bowel cancer respectable. Damn, but he was getting tired of flapjacks.

"Cock*sucker!*" Jackson shouted, coming back in. "The critters got our deer!"

"What? Again?"

"Plumb clean stole all of it."

Allie's lips spread in an ugly growl. "You dumb cocklicker, if you'd have tied the son of a bitch up higher they wouldn't have got it." He advanced on Jackson, waving his fists. "I'm starving to death and you go and fuck things up." He hauled back and let loose with a roundhouse punch, which Jackson easily dodged.

"Don't go blamin' me, asshole. If I'd have tied it any higher we couldn't have got to it ourselves."

This bit of logic did nothing for Allie's temperament. He swung at Jackson again, missed, and spun in a clumsy circle. He hauled back again, sighting in on the white orbs of Jackson's spectacles, when a gleam suddenly came to his sleep-bleary eyes. "Rabbit," he said, and dropped his fist. "I wonder if we got any rabbit in them traps."

"Them traps been dry for three months," Jackson said.

"Flapjacks ain't hardly no proper bait," Allie noted sadly. "Still, though, it might be worth checking."

"Suit yerself, duckshit."

Allie dressed as fast as he could. His hands were shaking with hunger and expectation. Imagine a rabbit, a real rabbit in a pot. Rabbit stew, yessir. If there was a God in heaven there would be a rabbit in one of the traps.

"Get a pot cleaned out," Allie said as he pulled on his coat. "I'll be back in half an hour." There were, in fact, twenty traps set in various locations in the forest, and these would take a good half a day to check. Allie had in mind to check two or three and then give in and eat flapjacks. It was either that or drop dead from hunger.

"So long, fuckface," he said, and opened the door.

"Don't get blowed away, blowjob."

He went out, slamming the door hard enough to rattle the shack. The night enveloped him in a swirling world of black and white, and he pulled his fur hat down lower on his ears. At least the snow wasn't too deep yet, he noted, though it was beginning to pile up pretty fast. A few more hours and it would be something to contend with. He set out toward the first trap, which was located just east of the cabin, out toward the doctor's place in a clearing that seemed a likely place for rabbits to hang out. There had been a lot of dispute between Allie and Jackson as to exactly where the traps ought to be located, since both men considered themselves expert woodsmen. In Allie's opinion, a trap could be put just about anywhere and eventually would snare something; Jackson believed you ought to find the rabbit holes first and place your trap right beside one. To this Allie said something to the effect that you couldn't spend your whole life looking for rabbit holes, to which Jackson had replied that Allie didn't know what the fuck he was talking about, about which time Allie tackled him and they rolled around in the snow for a while, scattering shiny new traps. This had been twenty years ago, and in the interval the traps had produced all of four rabbits and a few gray squirrels, and had meanwhile given in, by and large, to rust and broken springs. But a few of them still worked, and it was these few that Allie intended to check.

He pressed forward into the wind, squinting as snowflakes pelted his face. There was a regular blizzard going on out here, bending the trees and making the branches scrape together and talk to each other with secretive voices. The sky was pale gray, it in an almost unnatural way by the unseen moon above them. Allie held his coat closed at the throat as he fought his way up the mountain, cursing under his breath. Some fine spring, this was. The low-hanging clouds that had shrouded Spike Mountain for four days were finally putting on their show. This was a real banshee, this storm. With any luck the shack would blow away and take Jackson with it.

Allie forged ahead, guided more by memory than by sight. The traps he had in mind to visit lay roughly on the same route he had taken yesterday while chasing the coyote, that damned coyote with the two lives. Thinking about that now made Allie feel a little spooked, but he washed it from his mind and concentrated on rabbit stew. His hunger was a painful knot in his belly, his mouth a watering faucet. He spit between his feet as he walked, and the wind carried it a good five yards to the south. About forty knots, gusting to sixty, he reckoned. And it might get worse. Already his coat and pants had gone white. He glanced back toward the cabin, having second thoughts, but already it had been swallowed up. Too late for turning back, anyway. He had his mind set on rabbit.

He looked ahead, trying to pinpoint familiar trees. Hollows in the blowing snow made weird, swirling shapes out of the dark. He almost walked headlong into a tree and stopped, sensing the wind, locating himself on a mental map. X was the shack, and a purposeful dotted line indicated his path. Another X indicated the first trap, the one in the clearing. And here in the thickness of the forest, a stick figure indicated Allie, watching, getting his bearings. Allie the mountain man, who until yesterday thought he knew every inch of this mountain. He walked again, moving the stick figure and its trailing dotted line in his mind, going in what he knew to be the right direction. The wind moaned, cutting through the trees, making them dance. He saw animal shapes, people shapes. A peculiar feeling began to grow around the knot in his stomach, a feeling like the one he had gotten yesterday when the coyote got up on its dead legs and walked. He realized he was getting spooked, old Allie of Spike Mountain was getting spooked by the wind and the shapes the snow made out of the dark. He wished now that Jackson had decided to come along.

It was when he came to the clearing that he saw the woman standing in the snow. The ground here reflected enough light to see her clearly, a stick figure wearing a dress that rippled and

billowed with the wind. Allie came closer, squinting, puzzled.
Was the high-falutin doctor at his fancy cabin? Was this his wife
or some drunken party guest, lost in the storm?

"Help me," the woman said. Her voice was so mournful, so
plaintive and high. Allie went up to her, traps and rabbits forgotten. In this light he could see the outlines of her face, the
hollows of her eyes. She was wearing only a baggy dress that
rippled and flapped. Her hair was a brown flag whipping out
beside her head.

"You lost?" Allie asked.

"Help me," she said. She pointed east, up the hill. Her teeth
were chattering, and Allie hurried himself out of his coat. Mountain man or not, he had a high respect for womenfolk. He draped
it over her shoulders, aware of the cold that dumped itself on
him like a bucket of ice water without it. The doctor's place was
another five hundred or so yards up the mountain, and no man
would freeze himself to death in the short space of time it would
take to get there. He turned and struggled forward toward it,
facing the full fury of the wind head-on now. His beard split
itself into two halves and blew back around his neck, tickling
the lobes of his ears. He turned, motioning for the woman to
follow, but she was right there behind him, holding his coat tight
to herself, bent to the wind that shrieked through the trees like
tortured voices. Allie plunged on, a bit irritated at this distrac-
tion but beginning to see the brighter side of things. If that doctor was up there it would mean he'd brought food with him, and
any man's reward for saving someone from this storm ought to
at least be a solid meal. And doctors, Allie figured, weren't
likely to be eating flapjacks this time of night. Venison maybe,
because it was a delicacy for fools and city folk, but not flapjacks.

He came to the area where the trees thinned out and broke
out into the open, his arms clutched to his chest to keep the
wind out. He stopped, catching his breath, feeling his age and
the lack of good food. He unclasped himself long enough to
point to the doctor's cabin, where there were lights in the windows. The woman drew up beside him with the arms of his Davy
Crockett coat flipping out behind.

"Help me," she said in her high, mournful voice, and walked
past him without a glance in his direction.

You've been helped, Allie thought, and followed her, thinking
of his coat and the good meal to be had inside. It had been a

long time since he'd had to be civil to anyone and it would take some getting used to, but for a good steak or some pheasant under glass, which all doctors ate, it would be worth the effort. And, come to think of it, it would be nice to see some new faces for a change.

The woman walked across the snow-swept knoll and went past the cabin, bent to the wind. Allie stopped, befuddled, and watched her go across the big expanse of lawn toward the trees at the far side of the clearing. She was, he noticed now, barefoot beneath her long dress. Barefoot in the snow, and courting frostbite with every step. He hurried after her, mightily concerned, about to freeze to death himself. Was the woman daft, or just plain out of her mind from the cold? She was going back into the forest now, back into that blackness where the trees grew so thick, the blackness out of which Allie had come running only yesterday night after his encounter with the coyote. Allie passed the doctor's cabin, looking sideways at it, filled with disappointment. Hell, the doc had even brought his dog, which was waiting by the front steps. That dog would probably get a better meal in the morning than Allie himself had had in months. That dog probably ate better than most mountain men. And that dog seemed to have spotted him, because it was walking this way.

Allie broke into a trot, not wanting to lose sight of the woman and most certainly not wanting to lose a chunk of his ass to Fido. But the dog wasn't even growling, wasn't even barking, and Allie managed to outdistance him with no problem. He plunged into the thickness of the trees, able to see only the barest outline of the woman as she walked. He put his arms in front of his face to shield it, snapping branches and showering himself with fragrant pine needles. She was crazy from the cold, that had to be it. He reached her and caught at the hem of his coat, wanting to stop her, maybe turn her around and slap her to her senses. That would be something, having to slap a poor frozen woman. But better that than to have her wandering around like this.

His coat fell away from her, but still she walked. Allie fetched it up, making it into a ball and tucking it under one arm, then reached out with his free hand and grasped the woman's arm, turning her to face him.

"Help me," she pleaded, pulling away.

"Ma'am," Allie said desperately, "begging your pardon, but

your place is back thataways." He pointed, but it was useless in
this dark. "Here, let me carry you. You've got no shoes on."

He bent awkwardly, extending his arms and managing to drop
his coat, a genteel suitor in a suitable pose. Instead of hopping
into his arms, however, the woman turned and walked again.

"Goddamn dumbass high-falutin weirdo," Allie muttered, and
put on his coat, whose fur was now full of pine needles that
stuck his neck like pins. He considered just leaving her, just
turning and leaving her, but the civilized side of Allison Parker
would never allow that. Sighing, defeated and demoralized, he
went deeper into the woods, keeping track of the woman more
by sound than by sight. He counted fifty paces, a hundred paces,
then a hundred and fifty, a woman on bare feet in this weather,
and what kind of superwoman was she, anyway?

The trees thinned out and Allie knew with sinking sureness
where he was, and why. This weirdo city-slicker superwoman
had found a poor dead coyote back here and wanted to show
somebody. Help me, indeed. Only a psychiatrist could help a
case like her. Allie stopped, breathing hard, his nose and cheeks
tingling from the cold. What a wild-goose chase, yes indeedy,
and for what? To be lured back to this creepy old place, to see
that goddam walking carcass again? He wished suddenly that
Jackson were here, good old Jackson with his thick little spectacles and smelly feet. Then Allie could blame him for being the
dumbass, and punch his stupid lights out.

He was turning to go when a light popped on up ahead. Another light popped on, then another. Squares of light, three windows of yellow light, appearing out of the darkness. A slit of
light appeared, a door widening open. He saw the form of the
woman silhouetted for a moment, then heard the solid bang of
the door falling shut against its frame.

His internal homing system searched itself for answers. He
had been at point A, had traveled a zigzagging path, and should
be at point B. But point B was the falling-down old cabin with
a dead coyote on the ruins of a hearth. Up ahead were the lighted
windows of a cabin by no means falling down. In this wind,
chasing this madwoman—had his internal system shorted out?
Didn't he know this mountain by heart?

Yeah, you thought you did yesterday, too, a sneering inner
voice said. Buttfuck, you had found another cabin where no
cabin should be. The city slickers are closing in on you, building
their places faster than rabbits can dig holes. You are a dumbshit.

Cursing under his breath, Allie moved closer to the cabin, his mountain man's senses outraged at this newest trespass. There had, by God, better be a free meal inside, and an explanation from superwoman. Probably she had been wearing those funny see-through boots women wore, those clear-plastic jobs. And if she needed help, then by God it had better be help setting the table.

He went up to the door and pounded on it, all full of unease and indignation. His stomach twisted and growled. There was no answer.

"Invite me in, goddammit," he shouted. The wind spat snow at him in a blustery reply. He hammered the door with his fist, no longer civilized, no longer genteel. There was food inside and you bet your ass he deserved some. He hammered the door without mercy, picturing Jackson's face there on the wood. He would pound Jackson's face to a pulp, smash through the wood, and bust in if he had to. By all that was good and holy, he was *hungry.*

No answer. Allie felt for a knob and found a block of wood instead, the same type of knob that graced his own modest home. Fuming, stripped of the remains of his rusting courtesy, he pulled the door open and stared inside, squinting at the light.

The woman had gone to bed and covered herself up. There was a lantern on a stand by her bed. A fire crackled in a huge fireplace, sending out a blast of heat. Allie stepped inside, instinctively removing his hat. The woman looked pale and sick. He was about to mumble some sort of apology when something caught his eye that sucked the words back down his throat.

There was blood on the hearth. A big blot of it, as if someone had recently killed something there, a coyote perhaps, and slit its throat there. There were paw prints in the blood, paw prints arrowing across the floor to where Allie stood with his hat twisted in his hands.

Same place as last night. Only far different.

"Help me," the woman said. She had turned her head and was looking at Allie. Reflected flame danced in her fevered eyes. Her cheekbones were high, the skin pale and taut across them, her mouth a sunken rind. *"Help me,"* she whispered in her high, reedy voice.

"Dear Jesus," Allie whispered. There was a stink in the air, he noticed now, a stink that emanated from the bed. It was the thin high smell of disease and pestilence.

"Help," the woman said, and pulled one hand out from under the covers to beckon to him. The skin of her arm was yellow and waxy, the arm itself a bony, emaciated twig. Allie went to her, his heavy boots thumping unsteadily on the floorboards where no floorboards should be. He got to her bedside and looked down on her helplessly.

"I'll get you a doctor," he said, his voice husky with shame. To think he had let her walk through the snow, let her walk at all in her condition. It looked, to his unpracticed eye, like a bad case of jaundice and malnutrition. How long had she lived here alone?

Here? he asked himself. *Where is here? Last night there was nothing here but old rotted logs and a broken-down chimney. You are dreaming, Allie Parker. Last night you got into the home-made hooch and drank yourself insane.*

"Tonight," the woman said, staring up at him.

Allie nodded. "Yes, tonight."

"The boy?"

Allie looked around quickly. Some nice handmade furniture, a roaring fire, a metal tripod with a big pot hanging on a chain from it. Water was sitting in it, sending out a lazy waft of steam. No boy.

And no blood on the hearth. How had *that* happened?

"No rest!" the woman shrieked, loud enough to rattle the windows and send a shiver up Allie's spine. "No rest, and no forgiveness!"

Delirious. Allie wrung his hat in his hands, not sure what to do. Then he thought of the doctor, the high-falutin doctor and his cabin not far from here. He would take her there.

"*Brigham!*" she screamed. Her eyes rolled up in her head, yellow eyes threaded with red.

"Hold on!" Allie cried. With one swift motion he peeled the blanket off her and bent to take her up in his arms. It was the smell that made him pause, made his eyes glance nervously down her body to see if she had, in her sickness, soiled herself.

She was naked. Her legs were shrunken sticks, the thighs curved and hollow. Her triangle of pubic hair was a stark black contrast to the diseased yellow of her skin. Her stomach was swollen like the belly of a starved child, and as Allie watched in horror, the skin split open with an explosive burst of internal gas, spewing matter in clots. Her intestines lay exposed, gleaming wetly. Worms crawled in the dark, pus-filled crevasse.

"No rest!" she screamed, arching her back in spasm.

Allie stumbled backward, nearly tripping over his own feet. The smell was unbearable. Matter was seeping out of this woman and pooling on the sheets under her buttocks, dripping thickly on the floor. A large cockroach lumbered out of the opening in her belly, its feelers twitching, and fell into the liquid, where it struggled feebly, drowning. Allie clapped his hat over his mouth and retched into it, his eyes huge, his skin crawling as he backed away.

"The boy!" the woman screamed, convulsing on the bed, making it rattle.

Allie turned, white with terror, and made for the door. He opened it in one swift motion and burst outside, his hat still clutched to his mouth, all thoughts of food forgotten forever. He lifted a foot to run but the civilized part of him, the part that forty years of living with Jackson Pierce had not erased, made him hesitate. This diseased woman should not die alone.

He turned back and the cabin was gone. Snow swirled down on the jutting remains of a chimney. The wind carried the smell of rotting logs and the faint remains of a dying scream. Nothing more.

"Jesus," Allie whispered hoarsely. He was shaking all over, shaking so badly his hat fell from his hands and his knees knocked together. He turned again, determined to run this time.

The coyote was standing in front of his feet. Its mouth hung open as if panting. Slowly, leisurely, it licked its chops with a dead black tongue.

Screaming, Allie ran from it.

CHAPTER NINE

"Do you hear that?" Linda said, startled up into a sitting position on the floor.

Mark, lying beside her, had his hands under his head and was studying the beams that ran across the ceiling, and the glow of the fire that danced between them. It was impossible to sleep on the floor in front of the fireplace though it was definitely warmer than the bedroom had been, but out here it seemed you could hear things better. A moment ago the hooting wind had begun to carry a higher, more macabre tone. It was the distant sound of a man screaming.

"The wind," Mark said, not believing it too well. It was, of course, the ghost of Benjamin Hastings; a schoolboy could have figured that out.

"I don't like it here," Linda said, nestling down and hugging him. Her hair, full of the fragrance of yesterday morning's shampoo, tickled his face and he brushed it away.

"It's doing Glenn and Jill good. And I think it's doing us some good, too." He reached up and pressed one of her breasts with his hand. "I think my fire's getting stoked. Let's get naked."

"Mark!" She pushed his hand away. "Ricky's right beside us."

"He's asleep." Mark chuckled. "Wouldn't it be romantic, making love while a ghost howls outside? So utterly Victorian."

"So utterly perverted, you mean."

The screaming had stopped; now there was only the wind, gusting and moaning.

"A deer," Mark said. "Midnight mating call."

"Sure."

They lay in silence, listening. The fire popped and crackled reassuringly. After a time, when the wind no longer imitated

128

distant screams, Mark let his mind dwell on other things. Like food. He patted his stomach, and burped. What a feast that had been, what a strange midnight feast. He had eaten almost half the ham; Linda and Jill had polished off the rest. What was left in the picnic baskets now might feed them once more, and then it would be time to leave. A strange little vacation, this one.

"I hear footsteps," Linda whispered.

Mark listened. "Probably Glenn."

"No, I mean outside. Someone's running."

Mark got up and went to the window. Snow fell in the darkness outside, kicked up into odd shapes by the wind. For a second he thought he saw something that could have been a man charging past the cabin, but then the illusion—if it was an illusion—was gone. "Nothing out there," he said, and went to the door, opening it a crack. The coyote was gone, its paw prints already blown over with snow. He shut the door and went back to Linda, but since it seemed impossible to sleep on a floor that was a little too hard and cold for his taste he sat on the sofa, picked his cigarettes up off the end table, and lit one.

"That coyote's left us," he remarked.

"Thank God."

"Getting religious on me?"

"It was just an expression, you know that. Stop using my own tactics on me. When the day comes that I decide to go back to church you'll be the first to know."

"And the first to die of surprise."

"I wish you'd quit smoking," Linda said suddenly.

Mark looked down at her, surprised. "Where did that come from?"

She went up on her elbows. "I mean it, Mark. You're going to kill yourself with those things. And besides, they cost too much."

Mark frowned. "You sure have become a worrier lately."

"I do worry. I worry about a lot of things."

"You sure never used to."

"That was before."

Mark smoked and thought. That was before what? He voiced the question, though he already knew the answer.

Linda sat up and hugged her knees with her arms. "Before . . . things . . . happened. Before Robin got killed."

This was true, Mark admitted to himself. Before Robin died Linda had been easygoing, almost carefree. Bills went unpaid

and she shrugged them off. The house was an eternal mess and
she didn't complain—or do much about it. Mark worked his low-
paying job and she seemed satisfied. But now, now . . . she
worried about the house. She worried about Mark's job, and
what would happen to them if he lost it. She seemed older. Not
necessarily wiser, but older.

"I think you've had to face a lot of hard realities lately,
Linda," Mark said.

She sighed. "We all have."

"It gets easy to cruise along in life, never thinking about the
fact that death lurks out there for each of us. Robin proved to us
that we're not immortal, I guess.

"Now you sound like Glenn."

"The great guru philosopher? Maybe some of him has rubbed
off on me. At any rate, and the way I see it, we've all done a
lot of growing up lately. Maybe it *is* time to start taking things
more seriously." He stubbed his cigarette out and dusted his
hands. "Therefore," he said, grinning, "I shall endeavor to quit
smoking. Starting next year."

She grinned back. "And I was expecting miracles."

"You want a miracle?" Mark stood and went over to her. He
lowered his pajama bottoms, exposing himself. "Touch *this*, and
it shall arise."

Linda giggled. "Pervert. And in front of your own sleeping
son. Cover up."

Mark did, laughing. "That was a reverse mooning." He sat
down beside her and caressed her thigh. "It's kind of romantic,
isn't it? A good fire, a big old cabin, nothing out there but the
moon and the stars . . ."

"And the snow."

"And the snow, and the screams, and the ghost of the old
monster Benjamin Hastings."

"Brrr." She put her arms around him. "Don't scare me,
Mark."

Mark kissed her lightly on the cheek, nuzzling her ear with
his nose. "And when, my dear, have you ever been scared?
Except by *this* monster?" He took her hand and placed it firmly
on his crotch.

She jerked away, scowling. "Do you really want to know, or
is this a prelude to rape?"

"A good fright is always a prelude to rape. The guru says
so."

"I was scared," she said after taking a long, thoughtful breath, "by my cousin once. Scared bad."

"Old Sammy? Pimpleface?"

"Not Sammy. Chubby."

"Some family, yours. What in the world did this Chubby do to you?"

Linda looked at the floor. "He died," she said softly.

"Oh." Mark found her hand and squeezed it. "Sorry."

"I saw him die, see. We were playing and he got his foot hooked in this rope and smashed his head in. It was almost like Ricky and Robin, the way it happened so suddenly and with me watching. But the worst part was, they made me go to the funeral. They made me kiss Chubby before they closed the lid on him."

"Yuck."

"Yes, yuck, yuckier, yuckiest. It scared me to death, having to do that. I imagined he tried to bite me. Somehow, I imagined that."

Mark thought of Robin, and her eyes. The imagination was a wonderful and terrible thing, especially in kids and thirty-two-year-old finance company managers.

"That's why I couldn't go to the funeral with you. I can't stand them. I might have flipped out or something. I didn't want Ricky to go, either. No child should have to endure something like that."

Mark considered it. "I don't think it did him any harm," he said at last.

"Something's harmed him, Mark. You know how weird he's been lately."

"He'll be fine. See, he's sleeping like an angel now."

Linda leaned over and stroked Ricky's face. "I don't want anything bad to happen to him in his life," she said. Her eyes were misting over, becoming wet. "I love him too much to ever see him hurt. I never, ever want anything bad to happen to him."

"It won't," Mark assured her. "As long as he's got us, nothing bad will ever happen to him."

He hugged her; she hugged him back, almost fiercely. There was a moment when neither spoke, and then she pulled away, looking at him demurely with her wonderful cat-green eyes.

"Rape time?" Mark asked, his voice soft and urgent.

"Rape time," she said.

They made love quietly, careful not to wake Ricky. He was, it seemed, getting his first good night's sleep in a long time.

Eddie Chambers was dying. Again.

It was his second night lying alone on a lonely, windswept back road near Tremonton, Utah. He lay with his head in a muddy pool of vomit, with saliva dribbling from the corners of his mouth, with his eyes open, vacant, staring.

He had been having convulsions for three hours. His heart, which usually skittered along at a good eighty beats per minute, had slowed down to about forty. Tired, overdosed, his body was about ready to call it quits for this lifetime. Yet his brain still functioned, the electrical and chemical impulses overloaded, scattered, winking on and off with terrible intensity inside his head.

He was hearing screams, too.

The Black Death had swept across England like a low, crawling cloud, brought by the rats from the tall ships that sailed from France, where the plague had already claimed a million lives. A dead ship manned by a dying, flea-infested crew had docked at London the year before, in 1603, but before the ship could be set afire with its crew the rats had already tight-walked the mooring ropes and begun the dance of death for a nation.

Eddie heard garbled voices, saw garbled things. It was dark here, he was in a cellar, piles of corpses to his left and right, the dying picking their way between the bodies, crawling their way to a dry spot to die in. Coughing and moaning filled his ears. And the stench, the stench—the stench was coming from himself. His body festered with sores. The lymph glands in his neck had swollen and burst, trickling slow pus to the cobbled floor. He searched his fevered mind for a name, an identity, and came up with:

Jonathon Stone.

He was Jonathon Stone and he was dying of bubonic plague in a cellar in London in the year 1604, God dear God, would this ever end?

He coughed. His chest sparked with pain, dying pinpoints of pain. His skin had gone black in blotches all over his body. He was wearing nothing, his clothes had been burned, he was covered with a sheet that was pasted to his body with blood and pus from his sores. Someone crawled up beside him and hit the floor with a flat thump. Jonathon Stone turned his head and was looking at the gaping mouth and rotted teeth of a dead man.

He wrenched his mouth open and screamed. The cellar swallowed it, a bottomless echo. Death was everywhere, death capered and danced like a gleeful madman in this cellar, death was a grinning reaper with a madly swinging scythe.

Jonathon Stone hitched in his breath, hitched again, closed his eyes, and fell into the endless black hole of death.

Eddie Chambers, lying on a back road, jerked and flopped with new convulsions, vomited new things. For him, the dance of death was not over. Not yet.

"Food!" Glenn cried.

He came out of the bedroom dressed for a new day, blue jeans and an eye-smarting red shirt, cowboy boots with pointy toes. Mark, bleary-eyed and sleepless, saw him make a beeline for the kitchen.

"Save some for us poor folk," he shouted at him, not really meaning for it to come out as hard and crass as it did. But unbelievably, he was hungry again. He had been hungry since the last time he got up to throw another log on the fire, when his watch told him it was five thirty-five. Linda had been complaining, too. They had decided to hold off on the eats until everyone was up. Now it was seven o'clock, and as far as Mark was concerned, the time for holding off was gone.

"You're not even going to get dressed first?" Glenn asked as Mark and Linda came into the kitchen.

"Early bird gets the worm," Mark replied, and inspected the inside of their picnic basket. "Worms is about all we've got left, too." He dredged out another pack of hot dogs—getting sick of those—a can of Spam, and half a loaf of Wonder Bread.

Jill came in, already dressed. She was looking bright-eyed and decidedly chipper. In her blue jeans and red shirt and cowboy boots—too cute, this couple, Mark had long ago decided when he had seen the number of matching outfits they tended to wear— she appeared vivacious and alluring. It was nice to see her this way.

"Save some for Ricky," Linda said, opening the Spam.

"He can have all of that shit, for all I care," Glenn said, eyeing the Spam with disgust. "Me, I've got the pickles."

"A hearty breakfast," Mark agreed. "It looks like we're getting down to the last of everything."

"And the weather sucks." Glenn drew aside the thin curtain that draped the kitchen window. The window was rimed with snow and frost, making portholes of the panes. It was a dreary gray outside. He dropped the curtains and smiled grimly. "Whose nutty idea was it to come up here in the first place?"

"Yours," Jill said.

"Yours," Mark said.

"I was against it," Linda said. She had made a sandwich and was wolfing it down. "I was afraid the weather would turn bad on us."

"Oh, you were not." Mark squirted mustard on a piece of bread and made himself a sandwich. "You didn't want to come here because you don't know how to act around Jill anymore."

"Mark!" Linda turned on him, her eyes bright with amazement and shock. "That's not true!"

"Oops," Glenn muttered. "Honesty time."

Mark busied himself with the pickles, wondering what had prompted him to let *that* particular cat out of the bag. But it was high time that Linda faced this thing with Jill and cleared up whatever bad air remained between them.

Jill put her hand on Linda's arm. "It's okay, honey. I don't know how to act around myself most of the time."

Linda patted her hand. "It's just that . . . it's just that . . . I feel so *sorry* for you, Jill. I loved Robin so dearly, and I hurt so bad for her that I can't imagine what you're going through. There are times when I just don't know what to say. And I'm so afraid I'll say the wrong thing."

Mark took a bite of pickle, glancing at Jill. Her eyes were filling with tears. The cat, he decided, might have been better off left in the bag.

"I'm sorry I missed the funeral," Linda said. "And I'm sorry I've been such a lousy friend to you." Now she was becoming tearful, too. "I wouldn't be surprised if you hate me by now."

"Hate you?" Jill smiled as a tear spilled down her cheek. "I've been too busy being miserable to hate you, Linda. I've been so sunk in grief the world seems like a fog to me. The last few days since—" here she took a breath, glancing over at Glenn as if seeking support—"the last few days since Robin . . . died . . . have been the loneliest of my life. Nobody could have cut through that loneliness. I didn't miss you at all." She clapped her hands to her cheeks, her eyes widening. "Oh, I didn't mean it to sound that way. What I meant was—"

"I understand," Linda said gently.

"Friends at last," Glenn blurted a little too loudly, a little too cheerfully. "Now shake hands and make up."

The two women embraced, patting each other's backs, Linda still in her pajamas and Jill in her cutesy outfit. Mark felt a bit of a lump in his own throat and forced it back, elsewise he and Glenn would wind up hugging and the whole lot of them would look, to the casual observer, like a bunch of nuts.

"The food's as good as gone," Glenn said when things had gone back to normal and the emotion that seemed to fill the kitchen like crackling electricity had cooled to an acceptable level.

"And the weather does indeed suck," Mark added.

Glenn sighed and leaned against the countertop, crossing his exquisite boots atop each other. He glanced outside again. "Thus does the trip come to an end. We should have had the affair catered, and listened to the weather report for this area." He shrugged. "But what difference does it make? We've had about twenty-four hours of fun, we've crawled out of the doldrums, and we can sing songs on the way back."

Jill looked at him sharply, then softened. "Yes," she said, "we can sing."

"Hallelujah. Mark boy, get your ass dressed and we'll go see what kind of damage the weather's done to us."

Mark went into the bedroom, grimacing at the freezing water that squished up under his bare feet from the soaking carpet, located his suitcase and boots, and took them back into the living room. "No peeking," he said as he passed the kitchen, and got a few chuckles and a low whistle from Jill in reply. Ricky was awake, lying on his stomach with his chin propped on his hands, watching the fire. "You'd better go grab some food," Mark said, bending to give his bottom a swat.

"I'm not hungry, Daddy," Ricky replied.

"You're the only one," Mark said. "But just to humor me, go eat a sandwich or something."

Ricky left, and Mark shed his pajamas and proceeded to pull on some jeans and a shirt. When he had his boots and coat on he and Glenn went outside.

"I see our furry friend wandered off," Glenn said, glancing around.

"He was already gone when I checked a few hours ago," Mark said, and pulled the door shut behind them. He pushed his hands deep inside his coat pockets, hunching his shoulders and looking around miserably. It seemed abnormally dark for this time of morning. The storm was still blowing along at full force, hooting around the corners of the cabin, whipping his hair and making his ears tingle. Powdery snow billowed down, spatting against him like stinging sand. Already it had drifted all the way up to the doors on the windward side of the Blazer, which sat looking cold and forlorn and very stuck a few yards away.

"No problem," Glenn said as if reading his mind. "She'll plow right through this stuff. We'll make it down."

"We'd better." One Spam sandwich did not make much of a breakfast, apparently; already Mark was feeling hungry again. And if they got stuck, and had to dig all day? This boy just might starve to death.

"I'll warm up the truck," Glenn said. "You grab our gear."

Grateful to be out of the cold, Mark went back inside. Linda was dressing Ricky by the fire while he ate a sandwich. Jill came out of the hall with a suitcase and handed it to Mark. "Short vacation," she said with an apologetic shrug.

"One whole day," Mark agreed. "Maybe we'll try again in the summer, and keep the five P's in mind."

She looked at him quizzically. "The five P's?"

"Sure. Prior planning prevents poor performance. That way we won't have another fiasco like this one."

"It wasn't a fiasco," Linda chimed in. "I'd say it went pretty well."

"I'll have to side up with her," Jill said. "We got quite a bit accomplished." She went to Linda and hugged her. "We're pals again, see."

Mark rolled his eyes. "To think that my wife and my best friend's wife have turned into lesbians. What a shocker."

"Oh, you." Jill wagged a finger at him. "Just get out of here."

"Yeah, I'll leave you two lovebirds alone." Mark went outside, laughing. Thick white smoke churned from the Blazer's exhaust, and Glenn was brushing the snow from the windows with a scraper.

"Fucking freezing," he said. "Did you bring any gloves?"

"Never thought to." Mark put the suitcase inside and went back, got his own, and put it inside.

"Keep the picnic baskets up front," Glenn said. He was in the truck now, racing the motor. "We'll eat on the way home."

"I don't think there's anything left," Mark told him.

"There's pickles, for sure. I'm dying for a pickle."

Mark laughed again. "Our wives are a couple of queers, and you're pregnant. What kind of weirdos have I gotten linked up with?"

"Admit it," Glenn said, grinning. "You're a closet fag, too, queenie." He leaned over and squeezed Mark's knee. "Want to play horsie, big boy?"

Mark slammed the door on him and got the picnic baskets out of the kitchen. Jill and Linda were draping the furniture with sheets, putting the wet ones nearest the fire. Mark made a mental note to remind Glenn to tell Doc Phillips about his leaky ceilings before any real damage was done. If this kept up there would be collapsing plaster to contend with.

"All set?" he asked, fiddling with the doorknob. Now that it was time to go he was in a hurry to be off. "Ricky, you warm enough?"

Ricky looked like a little blue mummy in his snowsuit and wrapping of scarf. Why is it, Mark asked himself, that we dress our kids like they ought to be for the weather but don't bother to do it for ourselves half the time?

"I'm hot," Ricky complained.

"Then outside with you. Girls, do you need any help?"

Linda frowned. "Why do you always ask that when I'm just about done with something?"

"Because I plan it that way, that's why." Mark escorted Ricky out, grinning, and deposited him in the back seat. "All set, Glenn?"

"The motor's humming and she's in four-wheel drive, sir. Nothing can stop us now."

"Do I get to ride shotgun again?"

"Only if I get to feel your leg while I drive."

"Then I'll take the back."

"Suit yourself. I prefer the feel of my wife's leg, anyway. Yours seems to be hairy."

They laughed, and Ricky giggled. Jill and Linda came out, and Jill shouted to Glenn, asking if they shouldn't throw some snow on the fire to put it out.

"It'll be all right," Glenn shouted back. "Just leave it, and make sure to lock the door."

"That reminds me," Mark said. "Shouldn't we have replaced the firewood we burned?"

"That little bit? Phillips hauls it up here by the pickup truck full. He won't miss it. Besides, what are we going to chop wood with? Your cutting wit?"

"Surely he's got an ax here someplace."

Glenn turned in the seat and regarded him. "Do you really want to chop down a tree right now?"

"I most certainly do not."

"Then let's get the heck outta here."

The women got in and slammed the doors shut. The windows immediately fogged up, and Glenn turned on the defroster and wipers. "As soon as I can see," he said, "I'm going to show you just what this baby can do in the snow. You won't believe it."

"I won't believe anything until you can get me warmed up," Mark said. He clutched his knees and shivered. "God, what a miserable day."

"Onward, then," Glenn said. "Down into the sunny city." He put the truck in drive and gave it gas. "Here we go."

The motor revved. Mark tensed slightly, unconsciously leaning forward a bit in anticipation of movement, but nothing happened. The Blazer rocked slightly as Glenn gave it gas, let up, gave it gas again.

"That's strange," he murmured. Mark saw Linda and Jill exchange quick, worried glances. "Acts like the brakes are on." Glenn leaned down and jiggled the brake release. "Strange."

"Go, man, go," Mark said.

The truck began to creep forward while the motor roared. Mark thought it was like trying to pull a heavy trailer up a steep hill—which they decidedly were not doing.

"Frozen wheel bearings," Glenn said. "Has to be."

They lumbered forward, down the gentle slope of the hill, belching exhaust in a silver cloud. The motor howled and blatted. Mark could feel the way the big tires spun out at times, grinding through the snow and down to the earth below. The windshield wipers marked time to their slow progress.

"We'll make it," Glenn said through gritted teeth. "The old bitch has never let me down yet."

Mark knew little about auto mechanics but the idea of frozen grease in the wheel bearings slowing them down to five miles per hour when they should have been doing eighty by the sound of the engine seemed implausible. It was as if the wind were blowing hurricane force at them head-on, trying to push them backward. It was a weird illusion, a weird feeling. Mark found that he was gripping his knees hard, mentally urging the Blazer on. They came slowly toward the treeline and Glenn spun the wheel to the right, following it, seeking the opening where John Phillips had had the trees cut in preparation for a road that was never completed. Two miles of gravel was an expense that even Phillips couldn't handle, Glenn had said once.

"Where'd it go?" Glenn asked, craning his head around. He rubbed steam off his side window with a forearm and peered out. "Where the hell did it go?"

They were circling the cabin, driving in a ring perhaps two hundred yards in diameter with the cabin at its hub. The churning snow drove in blinding, nearly horizontal streamers across the mountainside. Looking over, Mark could see the way the smoke from the cabin's chimney was torn to tatters and whisked away in seconds, the way the snow had piled up in drifts almost to the windows on the southern side. The storm, it seemed, was growing worse, really raging now. He was glad to be in the truck, and not out there in that mess. An Eskimo would drop dead in such weather.

The truck roared, chugging uncertainly forward. For a moment, as the wind gusted hard against the truck, Mark had the unsettling feeling that they were tipping over, that the wind had reached such a velocity that it could blow this truck over like a toy in a hurricane. The trees bent and swayed outside, their boughs dancing wildly in the wind. "Some fine day," he remarked as casually as he could.

"You bet." Glenn was looking around intently. "And where in the hell is the lane?"

"It comes out facing the front of the cabin," Jill said, pointing. "You went past it."

"I did?" Glenn turned the truck in a slow, tight circle. Snow spatted against the windows, not melting, building up. He drove along the treeline, searching.

Ricky touched Mark's leg with one mittened hand. "I'm scared, Daddy," he said.

Mark squeezed his arm. "Nothing to worry about, babe. Pretty soon we'll be out on the highway and out of this storm. You'll see."

"Okay," Ricky said, and then muttered something that would have made Mark believe, if Linda were someone other than

Linda and he were someone other than himself, that Ricky had
been going to Sunday school lately.

"What did you say?" he asked, frowning.

Ricky looked at him and shrugged. "I said, no rest, and no
forgiveness. Is that bad?"

"No, it's not bad, Ricky, but where in the world did you ever
come up with such a thing?"

Ricky studied his mittened hands, twisting them in his lap.
"The voice said it," he said at last.

*Oh, swell. Just when you think the kid's problems are gradu-
ally being solved, he begins hearing voices.* "What voice?" Mark
asked gently.

"The voice in my sleep," Ricky said.

The big terrible burden that was trying to settle itself uncom-
fortably on Mark's shoulders lifted as suddenly as it had come.
Voices in his sleep. Nightmares, that was all. The boy was not
yet certifiable. He looked at Linda and saw the relief on her
face, too.

"This is impossible!" Glenn barked.

Mark leaned forward and prodded his shoulder. "Are you
lost, bwana?"

"Hell, the truck won't hardly run and the lane's disappeared.
The storm's about to blow us over and I can't see shit." There
was an inflection in his tone that cooled Mark's humor like a
dash of cold water in his face. He sounded angry and exasperated and . . . scared. And when the big guy started getting scared
it was time for the rest of the boys and girls to start getting
scared, too. Mark rubbed the steam off his window with his
hand and peered out. Their position was right, from what he
could tell, and the lane should be here somewhere. After all, for
Christ's sake, this was where they had come up yesterday. But
it was all just trees now, an endless thick wall of mammoth pines
that groaned and swayed in the bitter wind.

"Somebody tell me I'm losing my mind," Glenn said, and
let off the gas. The truck came to a quick halt, idling roughly,
rocking in the wind. Mark could hear the springs under him
creak, hear a loose tappet clacking in the engine. Glenn scratched
his head and sighed. "Maybe we just can't see it through all this
snow," he said, and opened his door. He stood half in and half
out of the truck, leaning on the door. Freezing air and snow
swirled in past him.

What happened next would serve, in Mark's mind, as the

starting point for the series of events that would lead up to the inexplicable death of Glenn Pruett and the tragedies that were to follow. For Mark this moment would forever be stamped in frozen recollection on his mind, the moment when the world of normalcy suddenly tilted out of kilter, when the rational series of events that had brought him to this mountaintop took on a more sinister aspect. For at this moment the truck began to tip as if lifted by an invisible giant's hand, began to tilt impossibly on its side while Jill and Linda shrieked in horror and Mark uttered a startled squawk that sounded, even to his own ears, remarkably like the squawk of a chicken.

Ricky screamed. Mark grabbed for him as the truck went over, hugging him protectively, reaching out with one hand for something, anything, to grab on to. The suitcases behind him slid across the carpeted cargo floor and thudded against each other. Out of the corner of his eye Mark saw the trees, then the tops of the trees, then sky. The Blazer seemed to wobble, tilting at the point of no return, and then fell heavily over on its side. The picnic baskets skittered across the seats and fell open, spilling their load of silverware and unused paper plates across the windows with a jingling crash. The motor roared wildly for a second, rattled down to a wheeze, and quit.

Mark was sprawled on top of Linda, not moving, not yet ready to believe this had happened. He could see the tangle of Jill's hair over the top of the seat. The gray and dreary sky shone in the passenger-side window above him, while the windows on this side had gone black. The familiar interior of the truck had become strangely new and crazy. And there was Glenn's arm sticking through the crack between the frame and the driver's side door, his hand opening and closing, clawing at the air and Jill's hair, Glenn's familiar arm that was now pinched down to nothing at the elbow. The truck had fallen over on him.

"Glenn!" Mark shouted. He scrambled away from Linda, pushing Ricky aside, clawing up the seat for the door handle above him. He was able to get the door open (it was remarkably heavy at this angle) and clambered out as if from the hatch of a submarine. Cold wind caught his face, choking off his breathing momentarily. Over the roof of the Blazer he could see Glenn sprawled in the snow on his back. He had tried to jump and almost made it. Almost.

"Glenn!" Mark slid down across the roof and landed badly.

There was brief pain in his ankles. "Glenn," he shouted into the whistling wind. "Are you all right?"

Stupid question, stupid question. Glenn's face was contorted, his mouth moving soundlessly. With his right hand he was clawing at the Blazer and his captured arm. Mark squatted, took hold of the edge of the roof, and tried senselessly and heroically to lift the truck.

Glenn groaned, writhing in the snow. Inside the truck, Jill began to scream. Mark reached up, caught the lip of the roof, and hauled himself back up. The truck rocked slightly under his weight and Glenn groaned again. Mark lifted the door open and leaned inside.

"Everybody out," he said. "Quick."

Linda handed Ricky up. Mark took him by the arms and swung him out, slid down the roof a ways and let go. Linda came out next, her face ashen, her eyes questioning. Mark could feel her trembling as he helped her down. "He's alive," he said.

"Thank God," she whispered, and this time there was no rebuttal to that simple statement.

Jill was huddled inside, her eyes wide and wild. "His arm," she said, looking up at Mark, pleading. She had Glenn's hand in her own hands and was kneading his fingers. Blood was spreading in a slow ugly stain along the arm of Glenn's coat. "He's getting cold, Mark."

"He'll be fine," Mark said, and reached down to her. "Come on out and help me lift the truck."

"Lift the truck." She nodded, white-faced. "We have to lift the truck." She climbed out quickly, bracing her feet on the steering wheel, raising her arms to Mark. He hoisted her out and let her slide down the roof, then jumped back down.

"Everybody *lift*," Mark said, and squatted again. His fingers found the thin strip of the rain gutter and closed around it. Jill and Linda went down, digging through the snow for a handhold. "Okay, on three," Mark said when they were ready. "One, two, *three*."

They lifted. Mark heard his shoulders pop, felt his freezing fingers slip. Jill and Linda grunted like weight lifters. The Blazer rocked slightly, only slightly.

"Okay, again," Mark said. This was no good, he could see that already. In order to free Glenn's arm they would have to raise the truck almost all the way back up to get the door open even slightly. Three strong men couldn't do it; one man, two women, and a boy had no chance at all. Still, though, they tried.

"One, two, *three*." The Blazer rocked. Glenn made noises, stifled screams. Mark saw Jill look down at him, saw her eyes fill with tears. Her feet slipped in the snow and she plopped down beside him.

"Oh, Glenn," she wailed, pressing her face to his chest. Snow was collecting on her face, in her hair. She cradled Glenn's face in her hands and kissed him. "Don't die, Glenn!"

He smiled at her. "I'm not dying, babe," he said. "Just a minor fracture." He looked up at Mark. "Buddy, get this tank off of me."

"We need leverage," Mark said, blowing on his wet and freezing hands. "Something big."

"There's a bumper jack in the back," Glenn said. His teeth were chattering and he looked white, far too white. Stuck out here, Mark knew, he would freeze in hours. He climbed back up the roof, got inside, and threw the suitcases aside. The jack was beside the spare tire under the cargo floor, a simple bumper jack with a big metal base. It was as good as useless but he hauled it out, anyway. He snatched the keys out of the steering column and climbed out, shivering himself now in spite of the exertion. The temperature was still plunging, the wind still roaring and blowing. Linda had her arms clasped to her chest and was walking around stamping her feet, with her hair scattering wildly around her face.

"Blankets," Mark said. He pointed with the steel arm of the jack toward the cabin. "You and Jill go get all the blankets you can find. Ricky, go with them. See if you can find a hatchet or an ax."

He handed Jill the keys, and the three of them ran off toward the cabin. Mark stared at the fallen truck, full of exasperated fury.

"Going to chop off my arm, old buddy?" Glenn asked.

"Going to chop down a branch or something to make a lever, old buddy. A whole tree if I have to."

Glenn pursed his lips. They were going blue on him, Mark saw. His eyes were taking on a waxy sheen. Old buddy was going into shock. "What knocked us over?" he asked almost dreamily.

"Must have been the wind." Mark worked the jack to its lowest position and tried to stick it under the edge of the roof.

No good. He set it aside and went on his knees beside Glenn.
"Hang in there, Glenn," he said. "The girls have gone to get
some blankets."

"Yeah, I know. You're hollering orders like a general." He
frowned. "What the hell knocked us over, Mark? It was like we
were—pushed. Like something just lifted us right up and over.
Did you feel it?"

Mark zipped Glenn's coat up all the way to his neck and dusted
the snow off him. "Yeah, I felt it."

"The wind couldn't have done that. It couldn't have."

"Well, something did."

"I tried to jump. Chickenshit that I am, I tried to jump. I
should have jumped back in." He closed his eyes and shivered.
"It's getting hard to think."

"Don't think, then." Mark took Glenn's free hand and stuck
it in one of his pockets. It was like handling a clump of ice.

"The lane's gone," Glenn said. "It's all grown over." He
opened his eyes again, fixing Mark with a dull, worried stare.
"You tell me how trees can grow overnight, Mark. You tell me
where the lane went."

"It's out there. We just missed it."

"Not two times, we didn't. It's gone. Like it was never there."

"Nonsense." He patted Glenn's shoulder consolingly. Snow
was collecting on his forehead and cheeks and nose, small flakes
that melted slowly and ran off his face in thin rivulets. Now his
skin was gray, almost bluish. Bright drops of blood marked the
snow where his arm ended and the door began; his elbow had
been crushed to the thickness of a finger. Mark felt a surge of
nausea like a smooth glassy fist in his stomach. That arm was
ruined, probably for life. Once they got the truck off of him
there would be a pell-mell race to a hospital, a race against time
and loss of blood. It occurred to him that a tourniquet was called
for here, so he took off his belt and wound it around Glenn's
upper arm, buckling it tight.

"Boy scout," Glenn murmured, shifting in the snow. "A real
trooper." His eyes fluttered shut. For a moment Mark felt a cold
rush of dread, a frightening certainty that the big man had just
died. Then he saw that Glenn's chest still moved, that his breath
was still visible as thin wisps of fog which the wind snatched
from his lips and nose. Mercifully, he had passed out.

Jill ran up with a load of blankets in her arms. She looked
about as bad as Glenn, pallid and shaking. "Is he . . . is he?"

Mark shook his head. "He'll be fine." They wrapped him in blankets. As far as Boy Scout work went, it was all Mark could think of to do. He had in mind now to get a big stout tree limb and lever the truck up a bit, get Glenn out, and then . . . and then what? Carry him down the mountain? Rig up a stretcher and do it that way? Fashion a sled out of nothing and go tobogganing down the mountainside? What?

"Don't worry," he told Jill. "We'll get him out of this. Somehow."

She looked at him; they exchanged a long, silent stare. "How?" she asked finally.

Mark didn't know how to answer that.

CHAPTER TEN

Mark ran back to the cabin, passing Linda on the way, who had come out bearing a load of blankets, a crazy-color quilt, a white flannel comforter, the blue blanket that had been on their bed and was probably still wet, and some sheets. The wind whipped at their corners, seeming about to tear them from her arms. It looked as if Glenn were to be mummified. She cast him a short, worried glance as they passed. "I didn't see any ax," she said, and was gone.

Mark burst into the cabin, banging the door open again. He felt cold and uncertain and frightened. This whole thing was beyond the scope of anything he had ever experienced before; he knew about as much about first aid as a Tenderfoot scout. He had never before been in a car wreck, had never really even seen one close up. This was too real, too real to grasp. And the blood seeping from Glenn's crushed elbow was real, too.

Frantically, he searched the cabin, looking for something that could be used as a pry, and an ax or hatchet as well. Ricky had been deposited by the fire and still stood there, his little face a round white O, his eyes wide and questioning, his arms hanging limply at his sides. "Daddy?" he said.

"What?" Mark got on his knees and looked under the sofa. Nothing.

"When are we going home?"

Mark lifted the sofa cushions. "As soon as we can. Now just keep quiet."

"But I wanna go home."

"*Quiet!*" It was rare for Mark to lose his temper with the boy but this was no time to have to be putting up with a whining kid. Mark left the cushions in disarray and rushed into the kitchen, muttering to himself. He opened cabinet doors and

146

slammed them shut just as quickly. This was ridiculous. If he were John Phillips, a man who could afford to have firewood hauled up here by the truckful, why would he bother to have a hatchet at all, and if he did, where would he keep it? Mark checked under the sink and saw only a bucket with a little pee in the bottom. He slammed that door, too.

Somewhere. Somewhere there had to be something. This was a dire emergency and a man with a cool head should be able to come up with something. He went into the hallway toward the bedrooms, pressing his open hands to his temples, grimacing. There was a small penknife in his pocket. Would that be of any use?

"Daddy?"

"What!"

"Is Glenn going to die?"

"No, Glenn is not going to die. Now shushup and let me think."

"What are you looking for, anyway?"

"An ax."

"What's an ax?"

Mark turned on him, furious. "A thing with a blade you cut trees down with! Now leave me alone!"

Ricky made a mournful face. "There's a saw out by the back door. Is that what you mean?"

A saw? Of course. A saw would be perfect. Mark took the time to give Ricky a grin. "Show me," he said.

They went to the back door, unlocked it, and swung it open to the blizzard outside. Snow ripped through, dusting the floor. "Where?" Mark said above the noise.

"Leaning against the house." Ricky stepped outside, and came back toting a rusting, decayed-looking hand saw. He offered it hopefully. "Will it work?"

"Damn right it will." Mark bent and gave him a light kiss on the cheek. Observant kid, this. He pushed the door shut and sprinted across the room. "Stay in here and don't come out, Rick. Mommy will be back pretty soon." And with that he went out, holding the saw in both hands, a grim smile of determination on his face. It would be a simple matter now to cut down a tree, stick it under the roof, and lever the truck back up on its wheels.

If it works. But how many things in life really work out the way they should?

Mark pushed that thought from his mind and ran to the tree-line, sizing up the trees, choosing one that looked strong and straight and not too thick, not too thin. He passed Jill and Linda, who were busily mummifying Glenn, waving the saw and offering them a thumbs-up. And Glenn was right, he saw now: there was no longer a lane here. That would take some figuring out, but it would have to wait until later. Much later. Mark doubted that he ever wanted to figure it out. A chill passed through him as he knelt by the tree he selected and began to cut it. Just how *do* you explain trees growing up overnight?

An illusion caused by the storm, that's how. When things settled down, a lane would be there, the one-car strip John Phillips had paid to have cut through the forest, deliciously winding, scenic, and pleasant as it always had been, the trees on either side marked with blotches of red spray paint to help show the way. There was just too much snow, too much blowing going on to see clearly.

He cut the tree. Two inches deep into the soggy wood the blade began to bind up, and he started a new cut above the old one, angling down. Pretty basic, he thought. First you notch the tree, fellow Boy Scouts, and then you make notches all the way around. Presto, it falls down. Light cold sweat sprang into existence on his forehead as he worked. Branches hung down around his head, swatting his face with needles and occasionally showering clots of snow down the back of his neck. The wind hissed along the ground, kicking up snow. The backs of his hands were white with it, and freezing. He allowed himself a moment to warm his hands under his coat. The smell of pine was thick enough to gag someone here, the wind blowing hard enough to bowl someone over. And at night? What would it be like out here at night in this blizzard?

He didn't allow himself to dwell on that. He would have Glenn out of this mess long before nightfall. He began a new notch, battling the saw, which warped and bent at almost every shove with a high, melodic twang. Not a good saw, this. More rust than metal. He finished the notch and knocked the wedge of wood out with his fingers. The tree swayed above him, not close to falling down yet. It was about eight inches in diameter, perhaps twenty feet tall, and he had barely begun to do damage to it. He shifted position, working his way around the base, sawing and pausing, sawing and pausing. His breath was beginning to whistle in his throat, and his arms ached. His little two-inch notches were taking more out of him than he would have believed.

At last he began to see real progress, and the tree started making promising little cracking sounds as it bent to the wind. He finished the last notch and waited, hoping for it to fall, anxious to see which way it would go. It hung on stubbornly, though, held in place by a sap-covered stalk no thicker than four inches. Mark attacked this one with fresh determination, cutting it about halfway through, and then the saw got stuck and he didn't have the energy to pull it free. He put his hands on his knees and rested, breathing hard, the shirt under his coat pasted to his body with sweat, the cold air rushing in and out of his lungs and burning in his throat. He scooped up a bit of snow and put it in his mouth, grimacing at its coldness and the way it made his teeth ache.

He saw something then that made him stop in mid-swallow, something that caused his eyes to widen and the hairs on the back of his neck to tingle. On the bark of a tree less than a yard away, at about shoulder height, was a red stripe of paint. And on another tree about two yards behind him was a stripe of paint. He snapped his head around, noticing this for the first time. Red paint was what Phillips used to mark the lane, whether as a traveler's aid or to tell the crew who had originally cut the lane and pulled the stumps just where to work, Mark couldn't know which. But on the tree in front of him, and the tree behind, were stripes of red paint.

He was kneeling in the lane. Cutting a tree where no trees had been yesterday.

And something else was different, too.

This tree was on the treeline—had been on the treeline. It was—had been—one of the last trees that formed the edge of the clearing.

Now there were more. Mark was inside the forest at a depth of maybe three, maybe five trees. The treeline had advanced toward the cabin. The clearing, John Phillips' big circular clearing, was shrinking.

Mark shook his head, grinning lamely, his dark hair falling down across his forehead, tickling his eyelids. Trees do not sprout up like this, he thought insistently. You simply made a mistake, boy. What with Glenn being in the fix he is, and with all this pressure, you simply made a mistake.

He went back to the saw and all the strength went out of his lungs. He uttered an involuntary wheezing gasp and fell backward on his haunches.

The saw had grown into the tree. The tree he had spent the last twenty minutes cutting was no longer full of notches like fat pie wedges around its circumference, no longer dripping sap onto the snow. It had healed. The saw stuck through the virgin bark, the handle on this side, the tip sticking through the other side, as if it had been driven there with a hammer.

Mark stood up. His mind insisted placidly that this could not be, that some terrible mistake had been made here and that soon all would be right with the world. He scrubbed the heels of his hands across his eyes and looked again.

The amazing saw-in-a-tree trick. The handle bobbed lazily up and down, pushed by the wind. Presto, Boy Scouts. Here is how you fell a tree.

He made his way past the trees that had not been there before and sauntered into the clearing with his hands shoved deep in his pockets. It occurred to him to whistle. His best friend in this world was lying not ten yards away with his arm smashed in the door of an overturned truck, possibly dying, and the saw that might have saved him was no longer available, was temporarily indisposed and embedded in a tree where it could not be. Mark's mind retreated from reality a bit, went gray for a moment. Linda trotted over to him, her hair a wild brown tangle, her cheeks as red as the stripes of paint on the trees. He noticed that she was very pretty.

"Mark?" She stared at him. "What did you *do*?"

"Do?" Mark shrugged. What was the point? What was the point of anything, when wacky things like instant trees and magic saws can exist in the normal world?

"Mark?"

It came to him that he would not tell her, should not tell her any of this. It would be his secret, as if he were a child who had found a shiny silver dollar on the street and would spend it at his secret leisure. He would lie awake nights and think about this secret, and eventually, when he had everything straight in his mind, he would tell. But not until then.

"The saw broke," he said simply. He looked back, half expecting to see trees sprout up in bursts of pink pixie dust, but there was only the implacable forest and the snow belting down upon it.

"Oh." She was near tears. "What will we do?"

"Get help, I suppose." His mind was still occupied, still gnawing on this pesky secret problem.

"Where?"

"The road, I suppose." Magic trees and conjurer's saws, and perhaps a grinning God who looked down upon it all and pronounced it good. Too much.

"There won't be anybody on the road, Mark. They'll have closed it off when the storm hit."

"Maybe not." The cold was cutting through his coat now, freezing his wet shirt against his skin and bringing with it a sense of normalcy. Glenn was trapped. That was all that could matter now. The secret things would have to wait for later. "The snow's not all that deep yet, where it hasn't drifted. There might still be traffic on the road, maybe a snowplow. I'll walk down and get some help." He zipped his coat up higher, shivering now. "How's Glenn?"

"Not good." Linda sniffed and wiped away the tears that had begun to track down her remarkably red cheeks. "The pain is really starting to hit him bad. It won't be long before he's out of his mind with it." She slipped her arms around Mark's waist and hugged him fiercely, like a child wanting protection. "How long will you be gone?"

Mark put his hands in her hair, cradling her head. Her scalp was amazingly warm, making his knuckles ache. From all that sawing, he thought. All that useless sawing. "It's two miles down to the road, so let's say I need half an hour per mile in this weather. That's an hour there, an hour to get help, an hour back. If I'm not back in three hours . . ."

She blinked at him. "What?"

"If I'm not back in three hours, call the cops." He smiled and kissed her forehead. "Take care of Ricky while I'm gone."

"He's fine," she said. "In the cabin."

"Regardless." He glanced back again at the enchanted forest. Perhaps somewhere in there lurked the rabid coyote, stumbling around in a daze of hydrophobia. All this snow should be driving him mad about now. And what do mad coyotes do? They bite, that's what. But the chances were that the thing had simply wandered mindlessly away and was miles from here by now. And the chances were also good that the coyote wasn't rabid at all, just wounded and dazed. From where Mark had stood he had seen the deep cut along its breastbone, and the dried blood on its side. One hell of a dogfight, that's what that coyote had gotten

into. He disengaged himself from Linda, went to the truck and
clambered inside, found Glenn's .22 rifle, and handed it down
to her. "In case the coyote comes back," he said simply, and
she took it from him with wide, knowing eyes.

He jumped down and went around to Glenn. "You okay?" he
asked.

Glenn squinted up at him from his multicolored cocoon of
blankets. His eyes were glassy and feverish-looking, his lips
skinned back from his teeth in a grimace of pain. Snow clung
to his eyelashes. "Doing fine," he said, not sounding fine at
all. The blot of blood on the snow where his arm ended was a
regular puddle now. So much for the effectiveness of the tourniquet.

"I'm going to walk down to the road and get us some help.
You hang in there."

"Will do," Glenn groaned weakly.

Mark was struck again with the seriousness of this situation,
something his mind was trying to refuse, as it had refused to
believe that the trees were advancing on the clearing or that the
saw was stuck in the tree. He wanted to close his eyes, open
them, and find himself sitting in the back seat of the Blazer
halfway back to Salt Lake City, with Glenn belting out ridiculous children's songs and Ricky happily clapping his hands. That
was the way this should have gone, the way things were supposed to be. He did not want this tremendous burden of responsibility, did not feel that it should be his. Nothing should have
happened the way it did. Nothing.

He turned and struck out across the clearing, bothered now
by a new problem on top of all the others. He passed the treeline
and entered the deeper gloom of the forest, keeping an eye out
for the paint stripes, frowning at the curious but familiar feeling
that was spreading through his midsection, the feeling that had
been dogging him and the others seemingly from the moment
they arrived on Spike Mountain.

He was hungry again.

It was just going on and on for Eddie Chambers, getting better
and better for the young-old Man of a Thousand Lives lying in
the dirt of a forgotten road near Tremonton. He was bathed in
sweat although the temperature was barely holding steady at
sixty-five degrees this fine spring morning, April the 20th, 1988.
The heels of his cracked and splitting combat boots had dug

deep ruts in the dirt. His flailing arms had created a dirt angel in the dust around his body. His hair, which had been in dire need of shampoo even before his ordeal started, was splayed out from his head in brown ropes. His skin had gone a wan and jaundiced yellow. He had pissed his pants, not once but five times, but that was minor compared to what he had done into the backside of his underdrawers, not once but three times.

This new life that he was seeing, this long-ago life that may or may not be the stuff of dope and dreams, was playing out with ghastly clarity, as all the others had. The name came first, seeming to coalesce out of the endless blackness into a single concrete idea, a name hurled out of the dark, loud as the slap of a hand across a face: *Otu.*

Other noises. A growl, deep and echoing. Behind him a soft wind hooting past the opening of the . . . *cave* . . . and crickets chirping madly outside.

Otu. Bear, in the language of man before language was understood and writing invented, when pictures carved in stone and painted on cave walls told the story of heroic deeds done in dank, deep caves like this one.

A growl. A roar, the roar of pain. The bear was wounded, cornered. Otu, leader of his tribe, advanced into the dark maw of the cave with his back to the wind and the others who had come with him, who had wounded the bear on the plain and followed it to this spot, the cave of no return. Otu alone against bear, bear versus bear.

Eddie chuckled in his sleep. His hands moved in spastic fashion. He thrust his spear here and there in the dark, his eyes wide and searching, loincloth flapping gently at his thighs. Bearskin loincloth, from the last kill. Bear versus bear wearing bear.

Eddie chuckled. The night was warm and good. Fresh blood would flow, fresh loincloths and blankets would be made from the skin, there would be fresh meat for the feast. Otu was confident. His spear was carved ash, light and strong, the stone blade of it lashed firm and secure with leather lacing. The tribal sorcerer had blessed it, made it invincible and true. Otu advanced into the cave, one hand lightly tracing along the stone wall, the other thrusting and withdrawing the spear, thrusting and withdrawing it. His tribemates howled and cheered and danced for him at the opening of the cave, prancing figures in the starlight.

The bear roared and the sound of it echoed, echoed. It snuffled in the dark. It made wet smacking sounds. The smell of it seemed to fill the world, dank fur and hot breath, the smell of death in the stifling dark. Otu smiled. Now he was upon it. He drew back his spear, holding it high over his shoulder, trusting the God of the Hunt to direct his aim. He threw it, uttering a solid *oof* from the force of his effort. The spear whistled through the air and clattered against stone. The bear roared and was upon him.

Otu screamed. Claws raked down his face, laying it open in hideous gashes. Hot blood splashed down his chest. The bear's cold questing nose pressed itself into his throat, the bear's jaws opened and for a moment Otu could smell its hot carrion breath, feel its saliva spray out in droplets across his neck.

The bear crushed his throat in the terrible vise of its jaws. It lifted him and shook him. His legs jiggled and flopped. His toenails scraped the dirt. With his fists he beat the bear on the eyes.

And he died, not too slowly, dimly aware of warmth flooding through his body like soothing sleep, aware of a bright light that seemed to glow and dance in front of his eyes, beckoning. In the days when man wore skins and feared a hundred angry gods, Otu, leader of his tribe, died.

Eddie breathed in gasps, still seeing that light, reaching out for it. Dying for it.

Mark was having a tough time of it.

It was impossible to travel a straight line so he found himself zigging here and zagging there, wriggling his way between stands of trees that had grown thickly together, making wide detours where pine branches hung too low to the ground to dodge under. It was the second-growth trees that gave him the most trouble, the scruffy, stunted pines and spruces that were no taller than a man but thick with dead, skeletal branches that blocked his path. The ground was covered with perhaps six inches of snow here, nude in circular patches under the trees, drifted to a depth of one or two feet in the open areas, of which there were few. The wind was barely a whisper in the dense growth but rumbled overhead with a noise like steady thunder. If not for the red paint stripes marking the way he could very easily get lost, he knew. Thank God for John Phillips' foresight.

Yeah, John Phillips' foresight. Somehow he knew his lane would disappear one night—happens all the time in these here mountains, don't you know—so he painted these markers with that in mind.

Once again Mark decided not to dwell on that, because dwelling on a fact that was patently impossible was simply a prelude to insanity, the funny farm, padded rooms and basket weaving. Once there had been a lane and now there wasn't. Period. Case closed.

He walked on, knocking branches out of the way and getting his face dusted with snow, keeping an eye on those tall trees to his right and left that had the paint on them, generally keeping his eyes off the ground because there were snowed-over remnants of tire tracks there, Blazer tracks from yesterday morning that did not wend between the trees but simply dead-ended into them. Looking at those was too puzzling, too mind-boggling. A branch sprang up and caught Mark full in the face, pushing him backward a bit, and he plunged on grimly, smashing it aside with his arm. He estimated he had traveled perhaps a mile, perhaps a mile and a half. A glance at his watch told him it was almost nine. They had locked the cabin and started out at seven-thirty, which meant Glenn had had his arm crushed in the door now for an hour and a half.

He would lose that arm for sure. An hour and a half with no blood to the hand, no circulation to the fingers, and with it being as cold as it was . . . well, he would lose that arm for sure. Another fact to be dealt with. Mark wondered what it would be like to have a one-armed neighbor. Mark wondered what it would be like to *be* a one-armed neighbor, and then what it would be like to be a one-armed chiropractor, and that thought struck him with such force he stopped momentarily before plunging on, his brow wrinkling, his eyes narrowing. There could be no such thing as a one-armed chiropractor. How can you crack people's bones, as Robin had said, with only one hand? Mark had never been to a chiropractor but had a pretty good idea what they did. Manipulate your spine. Pop your neck. Rotate your shoulders, and realign your pocketbook. All with good, strong, almost-doctor's hands. Glenn's career was ruined. That was a fact.

But maybe not. Neurosurgeons were doing wonders these days. Why, you could get your whole hand cut off and they'd sew it back on, make it work (after a fashion) again. Perhaps they could save Glenn's arm. After all, it wasn't as if it were amputated, just crushed. The nerves and all that would still be there, still be hooked up. Everything was just—flattened a bit. Mark had

seen the white gleam of elbow-bone for a second as he tried to
lift the truck. A simple broken arm, then. A simple fracture of
the medulla-petulla ulna-oblongata, or whatever the hell it was
you had in your elbow. Sure, they could fix it up.

If he didn't die first.

Mark hurried ahead, casting his eyes left and right for the
reassuring red paint stripes, blinking as branches sprang into his
face and scratched his cheeks and chin. His breath steamed out
in great silver clouds, drifting with the muted wind. Once he
spied a sparrow hunched in the safety of a thick net of branches,
eyeing him nervously from its perch on a nodding branch. Lonely
sojourner, looking for a spot out of the wind. Mark felt a great
and sudden affection for it, poor hungry creature alone in these
woods.

He wondered how it would taste. That thought fetched him up
short again, made him frown deeply. Who would dream of eating a sparrow? No good meat on a bird that size. What was
needed here was a big white flapping chicken, plucked and
shucked and ready to be . . .

Eaten.

Food.

Mark eyed the sparrow, breathing hard, his mouth watering.

Madness.

He walked on, shaken. The trees with paint stripes on their
bark were closer together here, as if old John Phillips had started
out from the road with a nice full can of paint and realized later
on that he ought to be sparing with it. The road had to be nearby,
had to be. The slope was gentler, and here was a shelf where
the way stretched out broad and flat. Somewhere down here was
a gravel road that wound down the mountainside like a snake
and broke out on Route 134, which led back to Salt Lake and
civilization.

Mark stopped. On the tree to his left was the last stripe of
paint, this one in the form of a big fat arrow that pointed up the
mountainside, the way he had come. Below it was a black-and-
white metal sign with a spray of bullet holes in it, a sign that
informed passersby that this was private property. This was the
marker that indicated the start of the lane. He turned in a slow
circle, looking. The wind chugged overhead. Snow drifted down
on his face like fine powder. He bent down and dusted the snow
away from the ground with his hands in a big swipe like a windshield wiper would make.

Gravel under the snow. He had found the road.

And so had the trees.

Spread out before him was a wide, virgin panorama, a big calender picture of white sky and snow-dusted trees, rolling away to the farther mountains of the Wasatch, which stood like green furry camel's humps so far, far away, obscured by the falling snow. There was no road snaking down to the valley below, no road and no cars, no road and no snowplow chugging its way up it. No thirty-mile winding stretch of gravel. No rescue for Glenn, in other words.

Just trees.

Mark went up to the nearest one and kicked it. There was a satisfying thump, a bit of rustle as the branches shook. Snow sifted down on his hair. It was a small tree, really not much more than a good-size Christmas tree. All of them here in the road were, as if the bed of gravel they grew in were not conducive to good tree-nourishment. But then again, maybe it was. They had, after all, grown to this size overnight.

Too much.

Mark snorted to himself. He tipped his head back to the sky and denied everything, closed his eyes and smiled. It was the satisfied smile of a man who refuses to believe what he sees because he knows that it simply is not there. He opened his eyes, opened his mouth. He looked around with his mouth hanging open, his eyes slightly narrowed, as if expecting to be hit in the face with some new and deniable reality.

"Bullshit," he said at last. A sparrow twittered briefly from some distance away, then was quiet. The wind seemed to have died down now, too. An eerie stillness hung over this beautiful panorama, a silence heavy with mystery, as if nature were proud of its abnormal handiwork and was presenting it, breathless, for Mark to see.

"I don't believe it," Mark said. He shook his head. "I don't fucking believe it."

The wind started up again, sighing. The new trees rustled. Mark would have been surprised, but not too surprised, to see them get up on their roots and walk. They were, after all, walking into the clearing two miles behind him.

What now? he thought desperately. *Try to walk the rest of the way? Thirty miles in a driving snowstorm with no gloves, no hat, no . . . food? And what if the highway's gone, too? What if the world is gone, turned overnight into one gigantic forest?*

Nonsense, his logical mind retorted savagely. *There is a rational explanation for everything that occurs on this earth. Everything.*

Something moved to his left, a dark blur in the corner of his eye. He whirled, his hackles rising involuntarily, his lips drawing back in a snarl. The wind gusted against his face, tossing his hair back to expose a somewhat receding hairline. Blown snow stung his eyes.

A coyote was sitting on its haunches under the tree marked with the private property sign and red arrow. Baleful yellow eyes glared at Mark. Between its front legs Mark could see its belly, which was a dark gaping slit in the brown of its fur. The coyote licked its chops. There was a flat smacking sound as it did so. Mark could see, to his horror, that its tongue was not pink but black. The blood caked to its side had gone black, too.

The coyote stood up and walked away. It lurched drunkenly, its bony ribs thudding against a tree as it passed. Its tail dragged the ground. It crashed into the underbrush and was gone.

Checking on me, Mark thought. It was an absurd idea but it clung to his mind just the same. *Checking on me.*

He waited awhile and then started the long walk back to the cabin. There was nothing else to do.

CHAPTER ELEVEN

He made it back in less than an hour—somehow it seemed easier, even though the going was uphill; the wind was at his back, urging him along, and even the trees, these miraculous trees, no longer seemed so thick and tangled—and broke out on the clearing shortly before ten. His legs ached and his lungs seemed to have turned to frosted glass. The temperature was surely below fifteen now. His face felt raw and chapped, his hands like cold clubs at the ends of his arms.

Jill was sitting in the snow beside Glenn, tears spilling down her cheeks. Glenn had become even paler, his cheekbones high and sharply outlined on his face, his eyelids sunken and gray. His skin seemed to be stretching taut over his skull, papery white and papery thin. The edges of the blankets that enfolded him flapped in the wind. Mark was reminded of pictures he had seen of the desolation of World War II battlefields, where overturned vehicles sat stark and cold in the snow, and bodies of Germans and Americans lay in various postures of frozen death. There was a battle going on here, too, he realized: the battle to save Glenn's life.

And what if the trees keep coming, Mark? Do they stop when they reach the Blazer, or do they just grow right up underneath it?

That was a disturbing and impossible thought. Up to now he had not seen any trees grow, had only seen seen them *there*. If they were indeed shooting up out of the ground they were doing it secretively, when no one was looking, the way a plant seems to turn its leaves to track the sun when no one is watching. Mark gauged the distance between the treeline and the truck to be no more than fifteen feet now. Before he left, it had been more.

"I'm back," he said simply as he walked up to Jill.

She looked up at him. Her eyes were red-rimmed and weary,
her cheeks the color of bright roses. She had Glenn's right hand
in her own and was kneading his fingers. Mark saw her look
over his shoulders, look past him. No, he thought dismally.
There's nobody here but me. The Boy Scout failed again.

"What will we do?" she asked. She nodded down toward
Glenn. "I think he's dying."

It had now been two and a half hours since the accident, and
the pool of blood where Glenn's arm ended was the size of a
dinner plate, a red hole in the snow. In spite of the blankets his
teeth were chattering. He opened his eyes and looked around
dazedly. "Who?"

"It's Mark, buddy."

His eyes found him. They were dull and dazed, the mindless
plastic eyes of a mannequin. He opened his mouth, grunted,
seemed to reconsider. "Watch out for the bitch," he said at last.

Mark and Jill exchanged glances.

"Getting dark," Glenn said. "Endless days and nights. Watch
out for the bitch."

Jill broke into fresh tears. "It's the pain," she said between
sobs. "He's been talking that way for an hour. Something about
a bitch, watch out for the bitch." She looked up at Mark with
such a mournful expression that his heart went out to her. He
wished he could hoist her upright and enfold her in his arms and
make all her pain, the pain of Robin's death and the pain of this
new tragedy, simply disappear. Looking at her, sitting helpless
and dejected in the snow, he was struck with such a wave of
pity and . . . love . . . for her that he felt his knees go momentarily weak. On the dark screen of his inner mind he saw a quick,
fleeting vision of himself holding her, hugging her, kissing her
. . . could feel her breasts pressing against his chest, feel her
breath hot and sweet on his lips . . .

He shook his head, frowning suddenly. What in the hell was
he thinking of? *Glenn's lying here all twisted and broken and
you're fantasizing about his wife, for Christ's sake. Are you nuts?*

"You'd better go in the cabin and get warmed up," he said,
taking her hands. They were cold but delicately soft. He felt
those oddball thoughts tug at his mind again and willed them
away. "Go on, Jill, or you'll freeze. Throw another log on the
fire and tell Linda to come out. I'll find some way to get Glenn
out of this, I promise. Somehow, we'll get him out."

She pulled herself up with his help and walked away with her

lustrous black hair whipping out beside her head, weaving a bit
from the force of the wind gusting against her body.

Her precious body, Mark thought, and brought his hand halfway up to his face, intending involuntarily to slap it. Only a jerk
and a cad and a crudball and a pervert would be thinking these
things now. He hated himself with sudden brief intensity, hated
himself for failing Glenn and for lusting after his wife for no
reason, no reason whatsoever. Everything was going wacko here.
He was, apparently, losing his mind.

"Too much," he muttered, and went down on his knees beside Glenn.

"The bitch," Glenn murmured.

"Hang in there, Glenn." Mark brushed snow from his face.
"I'm going to find some way to get you out of this." But wasn't
he lying? The snow was piling up and would soon bury Glenn,
bury the truck, bury the world. Out here in the clearing it was
really pelting down, big fat flakes the size of the Susan B. An-
thony dollars Ricky collected back home in a jar, piling up in
drifts that already covered one headlight and a bit of the front
grille of the truck. In a matter of hours, perhaps, it would be
deep enough to bury Glenn altogether, and then the problem of
how to save him would be solved, because you can't solve what
you can't see . . .

Out of sight, out of mind

. . . and Jill would need some powerful consoling, Jill with
her precious body and hot lips.

Mark hung his head, his eyes squeezed shut, his chin pressing
down against his chest. Is this the way insanity began? The new
trees and the saw-in-the-tree were real. His mind had accepted
that fact at last, and here he was, going quietly cuckoo because
the adult mind is not meant to accept the unbelievable, cannot
accept it, blows a fuse if asked to. He was going insane because
he believed.

"Watch out for the bitch," Glenn whispered.

Mark opened his eyes. "What bitch, Glenn?"

Glenn grinned a knowing, mysterious grin. His teeth looked
yellow against the whiteness of his face. There was a stubble of
whiskers on his cheeks which lay starkly black against his skin.
His tongue snaked out and licked his blue lips. "The bitch runs
the show now," he said. His free hand walked up Mark's sleeve
like a slow pale tarantula, pausing at his shoulder. "I've been

seeing her, Mark. In the sky. She rides a broom now, Mark. She's highly pissed.''

''There, there,'' Mark said.

''She's planting trees, Mark. I see her.''

Mark's heart beat faster in his chest. ''What?''

''She's towing the sun with her broom, Mark. Towing it backward.''

Mark took Glenn's hand in his own. It was cold, too cold. If there was life left in that hand, it had ebbed, gone backward like the sun he was talking about in his delirium. Mark looked up into the sky, almost ready to believe anything, and saw only clouds the color of ashes.

''Watch out for the bitch, Mark. She knows. She wants things. She's hungry.''

''So am I, Glenn. We all are, I suppose.'' And wasn't that just too odd? They had eaten like pigs last night.

''It's getting dark,'' Glenn said.

Mark looked at the sky again. It did seem darker. But that was just the clouds, these snow-showering, low-lying clouds. They were piled on each other, scudding across the sky in a dreary march to the tree-studded horizon.

''Watch out,'' Glenn said. His eyes fell shut. Blood dripped from his arm, slow and sticky-looking, onto the snow. The wind rocked the Blazer slightly, making it creak. Mark stood, feeling cold and forlorn and utterly helpless. Tears tried to spring, hot and unbidden, into his eyes, but he pushed them back. This was no time to get maudlin, no time to give in to fear and hopelessness. There had to be a way, some way, to get Glenn out of this. If the roles were reversed Glenn would be feverishly combing the cabin, looking for something to pry the truck up with. A big, steady man like Glenn would not stand around with tears just this side of his eyelids watching his best friend slowly die in the snow.

Mark trotted back to the cabin just as Linda came out. She stood on the steps with her hands deep in her coat pockets, her shoulders hunched, watching him. ''What happened?'' she asked as he came up.

''I couldn't find anybody,'' Mark said, evading the truth.

''So what now?''

''I don't know. I honestly don't know.''

She pressed herself close to him. ''It's getting dark,'' she said, looking over the top of his head to the sky. ''Darker than it already was. Doesn't it feel to you like evening? As if the day had already passed?''

Mark shrugged. "I'm beat from walking, I know that." As a chair-bound finance company manager the farthest he usually managed to walk in a day was from the front door of the office to his car, and from the car to the front door of his house. The four-mile hike felt like a hundred to him now.

"I'm starving," Linda said. She gave him an offhanded smile. "Isn't that funny? After all that's happened, I'm hungry."

"Funny," Mark said.

"As if I hadn't eaten all day, like that. It seems like the day's over, and it's time for supper."

"It's still morning." Mark pulled the cuff of his coat away from his watch and checked the time. Ten-fifteen. It did indeed feel like evening. The wind was abating a bit now and darkness seemed ready to descend. His stomach gave a low, purring growl.

"I must be a monster, thinking about eating while Glenn's lying out there . . .''

Go on, say it, Mark thought dispiritedly. *Go on and say he's dying. We might as well admit it.*

"Lying out there alone," she finished, and walked off toward the truck.

The light of day was fading. Mark watched Linda walk away, sure of it now. In a few minutes it would be night. Impossibly, it would be night.

"Madness," he muttered, and went inside the cabin to look for something, anything, that would free Glenn from his trap.

Jackson Pierce and Allison Parker were eating a meal in peace. The storm howled around their shack, blowing dry puffs of snow through the cracks in the walls, hooting across the stove-pipe on the roof and making the potbelly stove chug, but not as bad as before. The light of day was fading, and things were calming down a bit.

"Pretty fucking early to be getting dark," Jackson remarked.

Allie nodded. He had been white-faced and stony ever since last night. Something powerful unpleasant on his mind, Jackson reckoned. It occurred to him that Allie was plotting his murder. After all these years, perhaps it was about to happen. Jackson had watched an Alfred Hitchcock movie down in Hanna one time years ago, and in it the murderer got all quiet and thought-

ful just before he struck, and when he struck, he struck hard.
Knifed this guy, he did. Knifed him in the back.

"How's your flapjacks?" Jackson asked gently.

"Taste like dogturds, as usual," Allie said.

"Too bad there weren't no rabbits in them traps."

Allie eyed him levelly, picking crumbs out of his beard.
"Don't talk to me about them fucking traps, Jackson. I don't
never want to hear about them traps again. I don't never want
to see them traps ever, and I don't want to hear that word ever."

Jackson ruminated. "Traps traps traps," he said after a minute. Better to make the murderer make his move prematurely,
in the white heat of anger, than to have him coldly plotting the
deed over a pile of steaming flapjacks.

"Shut yer yap," Allie warned.

"Traps traps traps," Jackson said. "Here a trap, there a trap,
everywhere a trap trap."

The table got upended. Flapjacks flew. They tussled for a
while, but neither man really had his heart in it. After a bit
things got set to right and Jackson fried up more flapjacks.

"We been eating like pigs lately," he said, dishing them out
of a big iron skillet.

"That we have," Allie allowed.

Jackson eyed him. He didn't seem any more murderous than
usual, so he forgot about Alfred Hitchcock and his dumbass
movie. "What's put a spook into you?" he asked when they
were seated and eating again.

"Don't want to talk about it."

"You get yer dick caught in one of them traps, did you?"

"No."

"You know why them traps was empty, dontcha?"

"Shaddap."

"Because you've got to put them by the rabbit holes, dimwit.
I told you that all along."

Allie ate in silence.

"You stick em by the holes and when old Br'er Rabbit comes
out, whammo, you've got his ass. Get me?"

Allie showed him the finger. The wind hooted and screeched
outside, but not as bad as before.

"Damn strange day," Jackson offered. From the grimy window behind his head he lifted lace curtains that time had turned
a dim piss-yellow, and craned around to look outside. "Gonna
be plumb shit-black out there inside of ten minutes."

A white face rose up in the window. It moved its lips.

"Fuck," Jackson said. He jumped up and the table flew over on its side. Flapjacks rolled across the floor on their rims, hit the walls, and spun there like big brown tiddlywinks. Allie went over in his chair and landed on his back.

"What did you do that for?" he roared, getting up. A flapjack was pasted to the middle of his flannel shirt like a large button. He peeled it off and slung it against the wall.

"Thuh-thuh-thuh," Jackson spluttered. He pointed with a shaking finger to the window. The face was still out there, deathly white in the dark, speaking without sound.

"Holy Toledo," Allie breathed.

"It's a dame," Jackson said. He made for the door.

"Stop!" Allie jumped in front of Jackson. "Don't go out there. It ain't no dame. It ain't even really there."

"Bullshit."

"Believe me." Allie took the front of Jackson's shirt in his hands. "If you go out there you'll regret it."

"And if you don't let go of my wardrobe you're going to regret it, barfbreath."

Allie let him go. "Fuck you, then," he snarled.

Jackson opened the door. Snow and wind charged in. He leaned out, ready to shout out to the woman, but she was already waiting there. Her arms and shoulders were wrapped in a cro-cheted black shawl that whipped out beside her in the wind. She was wearing a simple pleated dress and black old lady's shoes. Her hair streamed long and dark.

"Help us," she said.

Jackson threw on his coat. "Trouble up at the doc's place?" he asked worriedly.

"Help us," she said, and wandered away.

"You coming?" he asked Allie.

"I been bitten by that bug before," Allie replied. He was by the bunk beds, cringing. His face was screwed up so terribly that Jackson thought he might be ready to cry. Jackson got his earmuffs out of his pocket and set them on his ears, flipped Allie the bird, and went out.

Night was settling over Spike Mountain. Looking down the mountainside to the valleys below, Jackson could see that it was lighter there. The clouds seemed to have formed a dark, brood-ing cap over the mountaintop as black as the woman's shawl. That would take some figuring out. Jackson scratched his head,

looking around. Probably some freaky weather phenomenon
like the inky black thunderheads that preceded a summer storm.
Stratocumulus clouds, or some of those altonimbus jobs. Jackson was a semieducated man, holding a diploma from the West
Side Elementary School in Payette, Idaho, where he had grown
up. It had been a casual trip to Reno in 1938 that ended up
with him being shot and wounded by Allison Parker in the
botched murder attempt that brought the two men together.
Like Allie, Jackson assumed that someday the score would be
settled and one of them would die. He knew which one it would
be.

He followed the woman up the slope. He could smell her
perfume on the wind and liked it far better than Allie's perpetual
B.O. She was kind of pretty, too, except for being so deathly
pale, he noticed now as he caught up to her and walked by her
side. And she was strong, clomping through the snowdrifts as if
they weren't there. It had been a woman who looked something
like this that had caused the murder attempt. But while Jackson
was in the hospital and Allie was in the Nevada State Pen, the
woman, whose name both men had now forgotten, had gone and
married some asshole architect from California and moved away.
That's women for you.

"What's your name, sweetie?" Jackson ventured as they
neared the doctor's place.

"Help us," she replied without so much as glancing his way.

"That I'll do, ma'am, but I think we ought to at least know
who we are so things won't get confused. My name's Jackson
Pierce, but you may call me Jack." He adjusted his earmuffs,
smoothed his hair. Perhaps, he decided, if things went right
there might be a kiss stolen here before long. Most likely this
was that fancy doctor's daughter, and everybody knew doctor's
daughters were spoilt and rich and sexually savvy. Jackson's heart
leaped with expectation. Doctor's daughters were always carrying on with older, more suave and mature men. He licked his
hand and mashed his cowlick down, combed his beard with his
fingers as he walked. His crotch tingled pleasurably. How long
had it been since he had bedded a young calf? 1938? That long?

She led him past the doctor's place, avoiding the clearing,
dodging nimbly between the trees. Jackson followed, love-
struck, barely noticing the distance they had walked or the
direction they had taken. Presently a cabin loomed out of the
darkness. The woman stopped at the front door.

"Help us," she said softly.

"You bet," Jackson panted.

She led him inside.

A hangman's noose dangled in the center of the room from one of the rafters. There was a wooden chair underneath it. In the fireplace, a nice little fire crackled pleasantly. Off in the corner there were a couple of beds.

"No rest, and no forgiveness," the woman said, and climbed onto the chair.

"Now, hold on here," Jackson said. "Honey, nothing can be so bad that you'd want to—"

She put the noose around her neck, kicked the chair away, and hung on the end of the rope, twirling slowly, her old-lady shoes twitching. Bones cracked as her neck broke.

"Honey!" Jackson screamed.

As he watched, thunderstruck with horror, her neck began to stretch. There was a ripping, gurgling sound. Blood trickled out of the corner of her mouth, dripped down her chin and the elongating whiteness of her neck, and stained her dress in dappled red blotches. Her feet descended neatly to the floor. She danced a wobbling tango, her shoes thumping the floorboards. Her neck was two feet long now. Her eyes bulged in her purpling face, blinking owlishly. Her feet skidded out behind her. She jerked and flopped like a fish on a hook. "No rest," she screeched in a wheezing, strangled falsetto. Jackson caught a whiff of her breath. It was damp and rotten, the smell of her perfume now as old and rancid as dead flowers.

Her knees touched the floor. Jackson backed away, terrified, his own eyes bulging, his heart jackhammering in his chest. The woman's shawl fell from her shoulders and flopped to the floor. Things squirmed in it.

When her neck was three feet long and her hands were almost touching the floor Jackson turned, hurled the door open, and fled outside.

There was a coyote waiting for him there. It looked up at him, seeming to grin.

Jackson jumped back from it and tripped over his own feet. He put his arms out, pinwheeling them for balance, and fell backward, expecting to crash against the wall of the cabin. Instead he fell heavily on his butt. He looked back, his eyes wide and terrified, and the cabin was gone but for a rotting shell and a tall, crumbling chimney.

Jackson covered his eyes with his hands and screamed. The mountains echoed with it.

Back in their shack, Allie nodded to himself, hearing it. He had been bitten by that particular bug before.

Linda heard it, too.

She was crouched beside Glenn, talking to him in low, soothing tones, holding his hand, when a high, grating scream rolled out of the forest off to her right and echoed down the mountainside. She felt the hair lift off the back of her neck, felt the skin on her thighs and back crawl. There must be an animal nearby, she thought, a wounded animal in the woods. A bear, perhaps, or an elk. Something big.

She stood up, debating whether or not to run back to the cabin. Glenn lay in a stupor, mumbling to himself occasionally. It was as dark as night now, just as dark as night. The clouds let barely a glimmer of light through, a flat dusky yellow that gave everything, the Blazer, the trees, the cabin, even the snow, a dirty and unreal look. Still the snow pelted down in huge flakes, piling up, piling up. Linda shivered, filled with desperation and a shrill kind of fear. Her feet were freezing and her face felt like a cold hard mask. If she ran for the cabin she would be slow and clumsy, and whatever was out there in the woods could overtake her easily.

She put her hands lightly in her pockets and waited, tense. The trees surrounding the cabin sighed and swayed, looking cold and utterly foreboding. Linda was a city girl, born and brought up in Salt Lake City, no stranger to the mountains but no friend to them, either. The mountains were wild and unknown, and this mountain, this Spike Mountain, was too high and far away to be a good place for anything. There was no electricity, no running water, no warm bathroom, no safety. John Phillips was a fool.

Yet three years ago she had come up here with Mark and Glenn and Jill and had a wonderful time, enjoyed the mountain air and the hard crust of snow that never seemed to leave. They had gone hiking and sledding and played cards till the cows came home, and she had enjoyed it. But now, this time—nothing seemed right. Even the mountain itself seemed different, wilder, less hospitable. Or maybe it was just her, grown older now, old enough to see that play is just a brief interruption from work, that duty and responsibility made demands on you that you couldn't ignore, that when you're thirty years old silly side trips to silly mountains no longer served any purpose at all.

She brushed her hair away from her face, looking warily around, turning in a slow circle. She was wearing ordinary shoes and the snow had already dug itself in around her ankles, wetting her socks, making her miserable. She had a pair of cowboy boots in the suitcase but things had been happening so fast around here she hadn't thought to put them on. They were, after all, supposed to be in the truck heading home. They should, in fact, have been there already.

Something touched her leg and she jerked away, a scream of her own building behind her lips, but it was only Glenn, reaching out, his hand making slow figure eights in the air. His eyes were closed and save for that wandering hand he looked dead in this queer yellow light, a blanket-wrapped corpse on a field of snow. Linda felt her fear grow instead of ebb, felt warm panic building inside her. If Glenn died out here alone with her it would be too much, her mind would jump back to Chubby the way it had jumped back to Chubby when Robin died, and she would go insane. Her brain would be fried like her Aunt Martha's had been.

Slowly, full of guilt, she began to walk back to the cabin. Something crashed through the trees up ahead and burst into the clearing, some wild thing with waving arms and pistoning legs. Linda fell back involuntarily, her hands clapping themselves over her mouth. Whatever it was—a *man?* a *bear?*—it was kicking up great clouds of snow with every frantic step as it sped across the western rim of the clearing, just at the treeline. Huge steam clouds of breath puffed out of it.

Then she heard it mumble: *oh damn oh shit oh hell oh God oh damn oh shit* . . .

A man, then. Linda raised her arms over her head, waved them there. "Hey!" she shouted.

The man turned, looking at her as he ran.

"Wait," she shouted.

The man stopped. He had a big beard, she could see now. He wore little round spectacles that reflected drab yellow sky. He held his hands in front of himself as if to ward off an attacker. Linda slogged through the snow toward him, another human being, a man with hands, someone to help them get the truck off Glenn. They were not alone here anymore.

"Help us," Linda said when she was close to him.

The man did a curious thing then. He let out a whoop and seemed to catapult six feet up into the air, as if a springboard had been hidden in the snow under his feet and had chosen this moment to let go, shooting him skyward. He was framed for a moment against the sick yellow backdrop of the sky. Then he landed spraddle-legged, stuck his arms out in front of himself like a sleepwalker, and ran. Snow flew in clouds behind him.

"Wait!" Linda screamed. "Help us!"

Whooping, the man ran. His legs were a blur. He smashed his way into the trees, moaning and gobbling, and crashed away. Within seconds he was gone, the needled green branches closing in on themselves again, and the only sounds left were the brutal roar of the wind and the short, staccato cry of a distant night bird, angry at being disturbed.

What the hell?

Linda turned and went back to the cabin, her fear overcome now by curiosity and an overpowering sense of unease. There was at least one other human here with them, an actual soul on this windswept, forlorn mountaintop, and he was scared, more scared than they were. Scared to death, by the way he acted. Scared out of his ever-loving mind.

But of what?

Mark was dismantling a bed. Angry, frustrated, simmering inside with helpless rage, he was taking the bed apart in the bedroom where he and Linda and Ricky had slept before the leaking ceiling drove them out. The long sideboards of the bed might make useful prying tools, he had decided after exhausting every other possibility in his mind, and so that made them the last best hope. A slim hope, but hope. He tossed the wet mattress and box springs off to one side and kicked the headboard free, then wrenched the footboard off. Each piece was seven feet long, roughly, and would have to do.

There was no other way.

He carried the boards out into the hallway, banging them against the walls but not caring. Ricky was dozing on the couch, Jill standing stoop-shouldered by the fire, lackadaisically using the poker to prod the logs. The stack beside the fireplace was noticeably smaller now; Mark estimated that in another few hours it would be time to start cutting some wood. Har-de-har on that one. The saw was occupied, the ax nonexistent. If John Phillips were to show up suddenly Mark just might wallop him upside the head with one of these big boards about now. Him and his stupid cabin, anyway.

"What are those for?" Jill asked as he passed her.

"Don't ask," he said.

Linda burst in, breathless. "There was a man out there," she blurted.

"Yeah?" Mark's eyebrows arched hopefully, crested, then fell. "What do you mean, there was?"

"Was. He ran away." She slammed the door. "I chased after him but he ran away."

Mark put the boards down. "Which way?"

"You'll never catch him," she said. "He was going like a jackrabbit."

"Why? What did you do?"

"I just asked him for help, that's all. Didn't you hear a scream a while ago? I think it was him."

"I was tearing a bed apart. Jill?"

She looked away from the fire. There were big bruised-looking pouches under her eyes, and her hair was a tangled wet mess. Falling apart, Mark thought. In her own way, she's falling apart. Like me. "I didn't hear anything but the wind," she said.

Linda moved by the fire and spread her hands toward it, shivering. She did a little dance, tromping snow off her shoes. "I almost froze to death out there," she said.

Jill burst into tears. Linda looked at Mark, giving a little helpless shrug. She put an arm awkwardly over Jill's shoulders. "Don't worry, honey. Glenn will be fine."

"He'd better be," Jill said. She sounded determined despite her tears, determined and almost angry. "If Glenn . . . dies . . . I'll kill myself." Her eyes sought out Mark's, fiercely shiny. "Do you hear me, Mark? If you let him die, I'll kill myself. I mean it."

"He won't die," Mark said, feeling inwardly unsure and . . . guilty. Guilty because the only things he had been able to come up with to save Glenn were these two miserable boards, which were going to be no use whatsoever. If the tables were turned Glenn would have already saved him by now. He was sure of it.

"Jill," Linda said, "don't say such things. Glenn will be fine."

"Liars!" Jill shrieked, making Ricky jump and mumble in his sleep on the sofa. "He's dying right now!"

"No, Jill, no. Mark will get him out of it."

"How?" She covered her face with her hands. "How?"

Linda caught Mark's gaze. *How?* she mouthed silently.

Mark could only shake his head. Once again he felt that strange and overpowering attraction to Jill, felt that he should go to her and hold her in his arms, pull her hands away from her face and cover it with soft, soothing kisses. The thought was so strong, the vision of it so clear, that he ground the palms of his hands into his eyes to make it disappear. Still it lingered, though, a bright, slowly fragmenting picture inside his mind.

He picked up the boards and went outside. The wind was a bare whisper suddenly, the silence clear and perfect. Mark would not have been surprised to see stars glimmer overhead, cold and distant, but there was only the low ceiling of clouds and that flat, milky yellow light. The snow seemed to be falling out of nowhere, falling out of everywhere. The upper side of the Blazer had collected nearly a foot of it.

"Glenn?" Mark called as he approached.

Nothing. A cocoon on the snow. Mark was seized with a superstitious fright, a certainty that Glenn was no more than a stiffening corpse now. His footsteps slowed and faltered.

"Glenn?"

A sudden gust of wind swirled around the Blazer, tossing spirals of snow around the bumpers. Something inside the truck rattled briefly like a harsh whisper in the dark.

"Glenn?"

"Who?" Glenn called out. It was the slurred voice of a drunk. Mark felt his heart resume its normal beat.

"The bitch," Glenn whispered as Mark crouched beside him. His eyes were closed. "Towing the sun."

"I'm going to try and pry you out of this, buddy. Hold on."

"Bitch," Glenn said. He spat the word.

Mark worked one end of one of the boards under the roof, inserting it perhaps six inches under the door pillar beside Glenn's extended arm. He set the other board on edge beneath it to form a short fulcrum. The end of the board that formed the lever was three feet off the ground, wobbling. Mark steadied it with a hand. With this contraption he guessed he might raise the truck five or six inches. With luck the door might fall open enough to free Glenn's arm. Then he could wriggle free and bleed to death in the heated comfort of the cabin.

"Jesus," Mark whispered, shaking his head.

The wind gusted again, making the blankets flap. Snow stung

Mark's eyes as he moved to the end of the board and pushed it tentatively. A trial run, and then the real thing. He would need Linda and Jill to pull Glenn free if this worked. The wind died down, and he went at it.

The board bent under his weight. The truck creaked and groaned. Mark noticed the smell of gasoline here. It had probably all leaked out by now. He pressed harder. The lower board flipped sideways and the lever collapsed.

"Ouch," Glenn said, clearly and distinctly. He opened his eyes.

"Minor setback," Mark said, setting the board right again. It occurred to him that this was going to cause Glenn excruciating pain. But wasn't the simple fact that his arm was crushed pain enough? How can you multiply the unbearable?

He went to the end of the board and pressed down decisively. It bowed in a long arc, but the truck creaked again and came off the ground an inch or so. Mark smiled. With a thicker fulcrum—a stack of firewood, maybe—he just might be able to raise it enough. The door only had to fall open two inches to make this work. He pressed the board down until the end of it touched the ground. It was bowed tremendously.

"Bingo," he said, grinning, and the board broke in the middle with a crack like a gunshot. The Blazer settled heavily on its side again. Mark went over on his face, saving himself by pistoning his arms out and catching the ground with his hands.

Glenn screamed. His free hand went up and clawed at the Blazer's roof. His fingernails screeched across its shiny red paint. Watching him helplessly, Mark felt those tears try to jump in his eyes again, felt his sinuses become hot and watery. This was stupid, this was preposterous. You cannot raise a fallen truck with two sideboards from a bed. You need help, lots of it. "I'm sorry," he said, crawling over to Glenn. Glenn's face was twisted into something drawn and haggard, his eyes screwed shut. Mark had never seen such an expression of utter pain in his life. Yet other than the long, growling cry, he had not screamed again. His hand fell from the Blazer's roof and thumped to his chest, opening and closing at nothing, like a dying crab. His knees were arched up in a spasm. The unbearable had been multiplied after all.

Mark stood up, wavering on his feet a bit, and swiped at his nose with the back of one hand. He bent again and adjusted the blankets back over Glenn's feet, full of unspoken apologies for having hurt him so. But now what was to be done, other than simply stand here and watch him die? Fresh blood was dripping from his arm, making dark runners in the snow. The end of Mark's belt trailed through it like a blacksnake, his useless belt that seemed to be doing no good at all. Glenn was bleeding to death, maybe dying of shock. And there was nothing, not one single thing, that Mark could do.

Except maybe amputate his arm.

He frowned, sick at the thought. Amputate it with what? A butter knife? Saw through the flesh where the bone was broken and separate Glenn from his arm forever? And what good would that do? He'd bleed to death for sure then. Unless Mark hauled him in to the cabin and cauterized the stump at the fire. Imagine the screaming that would be going on *then*. Jill would go insane. Hell, Mark would go insane.

It was a dumb idea and he let it drop. He could no more saw through Glenn's arm than he could saw through his own. There had to be another way. Linda said she saw a man, a man who ran away. There were other cabins on this mountain, most likely, and the people who lived in them would surely have an ax with which to cut down a tree. With some help and a fallen tree, they could pry the Blazer up.

But where were these cabins? Where did the running man live?

Mark struck off across the clearing, full of resolve that was practically devoid of hope. Spike Mountain was a big mountain, a huge rolling piece of real estate that climbed to the sky higher than any others in the Wasatch, a big knot on anybody's map, a lump on the globe. Somewhere here were other cabins, summer cabins where rich people came to relax from the grind of their opulent lives. And in one of them, at least one of them, someone was home. That someone would have an ax. That ax would save Glenn's life.

He went east across the clearing, determined to find some help, plunged into the forest, and practically bumped into the two women who were waiting for him there.

CHAPTER TWELVE

"We need help," Mark said fervently. The shock of running into these two at the edge of the woods had caused him to recoil stiff-leggedly backward as if he had come face-to-face with a bear, and now he stood before them with his heart racing in his chest and confusion whirling in his mind. The women were standing together beneath the dark umbrella of a gigantic pine, two dark and faceless shapes. The woman on the right had some dark thing draped over her shoulders which the wind also fluttered. She clutched it tightly to herself with her fists pressed to her chest. The other took a step toward Mark.

"Bring him home," she said.

Mark frowned. Bring who home? "There was an accident," he said, turning to point through the trees to the Blazer. It lay like a dead beetle on the yellow-white field of the clearing. "A friend of mine is trapped underneath. If I could get some people to help lift the truck we can get him out. Did you come up here with other people? Where are you staying? Is your cabin nearby, and . . ." It came to him then that he was jabbering like a madman. He pressed the back of his hand to his lips, organized his thoughts for a moment, and spoke again. "I need help," he said simply.

"Home," she said again, and turned. Together, the two women walked away from him, back into the woods.

Home? What, to their home . . . is that what they meant? What were these, foreigners? Mark gnawed nervously at a fingernail, watching them go deeper into the dark and shadowy forest. After a moment he followed, pushing aside branches with his hands, frowning so deeply his forehead started to hurt after a while. What kind of weirdos had he run into here? The Weird Sisters up ahead were walking practically arm in arm, wending silently through the trees, not stooping under overhanging branches or pushing them aside but just plowing right through them, leaving jostling barriers for Mark to walk through as he hurried to follow. Some crazy night bird was crying up ahead, sounding like a crow with a bad cold. And the light was different now, no longer dull and yellow but dwindling to gray. The trees cast cold blurry shadows on the snowy ground.

Things got thicker—there were brambles here. Mark walked through nettles that clawed at his pants, stepped high over piles of sticks and dead saplings that lay like discarded bones. It was tough going, keeping up with these two. A crazy thought sailed into his mind, pushing aside the present worries and making new ones of its own. They would come upon a new clearing in these dense woods and there would be a big steaming cauldron over a fire, grinning vultures would be perched on the overhanging branches, bones and skulls would be scattered across the ground. *Welcome home*, the Weird Sisters would say, indicating the pot with long and warty fingers. *Won't you step inside?*

Welcome home indeed. Mark shook his head to clear it, closing his eyes for a second and catching a branch in the face for his trouble. He fell back with powdered snow wafting around him like sparkling dust, ducked, and went on. Somehow the way seemed vaguely familiar, even for a failed Boy Scout like him. Wasn't it here that he and Glenn had paused for breath three years ago during that late-night jaunt to see the fallen-down old homestead? Wasn't it? No, it was impossible to tell. In deep woods everything looks the same. A thousand lost hunters could testify to that.

Mark's foot struck something that clanked and rattled and he stopped long enough to look down, thinking briefly that he had narrowly missed stepping into a bear trap or something. He saw that he had kicked a beer can out of its hiding place under the snow. He picked it up and held it close to his eyes.

Budweiser. Crushed in the middle and folded over, the way Mark liked to crush a beer can in his hands when he was done, faded now and yellowing. It was here, then, that he had finished his beer that night so long ago.

That meant the old place was just up ahead. That further meant that the Weirdo Twins up there were leading him directly to it. Old Benjamin Hastings' place, his long-ago refuge from the church and the law.

No. Ridiculous. Why would two women be hanging around *that* old ruin?

He walked on, thinking, perplexed. The night bird continued to shriek its nasal call, farther away now, crying plaintively in the dwindling light. His feet crunched over sticks and twigs as he pressed forward; the brambles and scrub trees seemed to rise up in a final barrier, and then gave way on a clearing.

The old cabin bulked ahead of him, nestled in a pale circle where snow drifted quietly down. It had been rebuilt. Smoke curled out of the chimney. Light shone in the windows. Off on the northern side a flat roof protruded from the outer wall, something which Mark mistook at first for a carport until he heard the soft nicker of horses inside and smelled the rich mulch of their manure.

Horses. How quaint. And wouldn't a horse or two be just the ticket for pulling a truck off its side?

Mark hurried to the front door, which was just falling shut, full of relief and excitement and gratitude to whatever gods existed for having the foresight to cause someone to rebuild this place and supply it with horses. He rapped on the door, hesitated, rapped again. He thought he had seen the two women go inside as he broke out on the clearing here. He knocked again, hard, with the side of his fist. No answer.

He opened it, squinting in the light. Old-fashioned glass-bulbed kerosene lamps burned cheerily inside. Fire popped and crackled in the fireplace. Straight-backed wooden chairs sat around a table, where several large books lay. Mark recognized one as a Bible. To the left of the table was a kitchen of sorts with pots and pans and utensils hanging from hooks on the wall. Knives, a big spoon, a meat cleaver with a wooden handle. It was all neat, all tidy and good.

Bring him here, a voice in his head seemed to whisper.

If only I could, he thought, and stepped inside. There was some kind of lingering odor in here, the hint of perfume, perhaps, and a deeper, less identifiable smell. Meat cooking, maybe. It was like entering the warmth and light of someone else's house just after suppertime. He let the door fall shut behind him and looked around briefly, his eyebrows drawing together with consternation. The women were gone. He had seen them come in but now they were gone.

No, no. He had to be mistaken.

"Hello?" Mark called softly, his eyes wide and searching.

The feeling of being an intruder was upon him now, making him want to scuttle back out the door and do some more knocking. But Glenn was still back there, still bleeding in the snow, and this was no time for niceties. "Yo," Mark called, taking another tentative step inside. "Anybody home?"

There was a large metal tripod on the hearth from which hung a big black pot. Mark sneaked over to it, licking his lips and thinking briefly of ham and beans. One quick spoonful, and then back to the business at hand.

The pot was empty.

He strolled over to the table, glancing at the books there. A Bible lying open, yes, and another religious-looking book with a title written in archaic flowery script lying closed beside it. *The Book of Mormon.* Beside that was another closed book, this one smaller. There was a large blunt pencil on top of it.

"Hmm," Mark muttered to himself, not really thinking about these books at all but about the way the two women had simply up and vanished. But come to think of it, he hadn't really seen them come inside at all, had just seen the door closing against its frame. The wind could have done that.

He went across the room with his boots thudding quietly on the floorboards. There were beds over here in the corner, nicely made up with heavy quilts. They were both big, big enough for two. Mark ran his fingers lightly across the pillows, making small clucking noises with his tongue, trying to seem nonchalant so that when the proprietors broke in on him he wouldn't look like the curious snoop he was.

The pillows were stuffed with straw. That was odd. He lifted one corner of a quilt and took a peek at the mattress beneath. It looked lumpy and incredibly uncomfortable. Yellow ends of straw poked up through the coarse fabric in spots. Who would spend the money to build this place and then cheap-out on the bedding like this? Who would spend the money to build this place here in the middle of nowhere, anyway? Yet John Phillips had done the same thing barely a quarter mile from here. Go explain the rich. The owner of this cabin was undoubtedly a kook like Phillips. So how would the kook feel about someone borrowing one of his horses without asking?

He heard them whinny outside and kick at something.

Mark picked up a lamp and went to the door, placing the mystery of the disappearing women into the same mental file as the mystery of the saw and the trees, things which he was already in the process of digesting and rationalizing. So two women had led him here and then went on about their business—big deal. The fact that they had led him to these horses was explanation enough for now. Mark had business of his own to attend to.

He stepped outside with the lamp held high, walked around to the stable with lamplight pooled in a circle around him, his shadow bobbing stark and black inside it. He saw that the horses were penned inside by a gate made of thin logs braced in an X pattern, and began to search for a latch. The horses nickered and made spooked, nervous movements inside their stall. Mark found the latch and lifted it. He was not familiar with horses at all but knew that they generally wore halters and would walk where you led them. That, in a nutshell, was the sum of his equestrian knowledge. With a rope and a horse he thought he could do Glenn some good, and that was what mattered.

Ah, a rope, he thought despairingly, and lifted the lamp higher. Stables usually had nails in the walls with all sorts of goodies hanging on them—saddles, bits, mysterious leather straps, spurs, and ropes—and this one should be no exception, newly built or not. Careful not to stand directly behind the horses—one swift kick to the nuts and you're a dead man, he knew—he swung the gate open and stepped inside, keeping close to the wall. Something darted past his legs in a swift oily motion and he recoiled, nearly dropping the lamp. The horses whinnied and squealed. An animal, some small thing like a dog, had run through the circle of light and into the stable.

A coyote.

The horses reared and bucked, braying and snorting. The one nearest Mark swung sideways and for a brief moment crushed him against the wall with the terrible weight of its haunch, driving the breath from his chest. The light from the lamp wobbled and stuttered, glinting off the horses' wild eyes. He saw them rear and try to turn. The coyote darted between their legs, biting at them, dodging their hooves. It was over before Mark had time to draw his breath again; the horses backed out and scattered into the darkness, the clop of their hooves muted on the snow. They galloped into the trees, crashed through the brambles and brush, and were gone.

"Jesus Christ!" Mark howled, filled with rage and pain. His chest felt as if it had been cracked in two. He stepped to the middle of the empty stall, swinging the light in a high circle,

his breath pumping up and down in his bruised lungs like painful fire, steaming out in clouds.

The coyote sat in the corner calmly regarding him. Its black tongue came out and curled slowly across its muzzle.

"Bastard," Mark hissed. He stepped forward, drew his right leg back, and aimed a kick at it. The coyote attempted to dodge but was slow; Mark's kick sent it skidding across the stable's dirt floor. It found its feet and darted out of the light. Mark heard it scramble through the underbrush and run away into the dark forest beyond. He went to the gate and hurled the lamp after it in a final gesture of hate. The lamp arced through the darkness and shattered in the snow with a bright eruption of fire that sizzled briefly and went out. Mark stood for a while slumped against the open gate, dejected, hurting, angry enough to scream. That damned coyote had been hounding him all night. On top of everything else, a goddamned senseless wild animal had to come along and screw up Glenn's last chance of survival.

The wind kicked up and the gate swayed, creaking on unseen hinges. Mark pushed away from it, stepped out, and slammed it back against its latch, damning the world and the gods that had brought him such miserable luck. He turned and was about to walk away when it came to him that he had been leaning on Glenn's salvation, had, in fact, just slammed it shut. The gate was made of logs. Thin ones, but maybe not too thin to make a respectable lever. And the ones that formed the X had to be at least ten feet long.

A satisfied little smile spread across his face. Screw the gods, and the bad luck, and the coyotes of the world. Even a lousy Boy Scout had to have his day.

He bent to the task of pulling the gate apart.

Ricky was not sleeping well.

Things were growing out of the sofa on which he slept, sharp things that he now knew to be straw. Or hay. Or something like that.

It was bothersome, anyway.

And the voice was there, a big booming baritone of a voice, thudding in his head like an endless bass drum, repeating the same thing, telling him the same things he had already heard before.

No rest, and no forgiveness.

And a higher voice, a forgiving voice, promising him something he could not yet understand: *Sometime after sundown.*

Ricky turned on the sofa, mumbled in his sleep. To the casual observer he would have been a young boy roughly four feet tall with dark hair falling across his closed eyes, wearing a blue snowsuit with mittens dangling from the wrists like extra hands (these mittens had a connecting string on them that ran across his arms and shoulders inside the snowsuit; this way he couldn't lose them) and red galoshes whose buckles were unbuckled and jingled softly whenever he turned in his sleep on the sofa, which he was doing now. The casual observer would have noticed this in an instant and gone about his business, because there was nothing remarkable about Ricky at all, nothing at all. A little boy taking a nap on a couch in a rustic-modern cabin where a fire burned flickeringly in the fireplace on the south wall and overhead beams cast bars of shadow across the ceiling.

To the casual observer.

There were no observers. Jill was staring at the fire, Linda was pacing the floor, lost in her own thoughts. Mark was slogging his way through deep woods dragging two long logs behind him, exhausted and unsure of his direction, pausing now and again as if to sniff the wind. Glenn was bleeding to death in the snow.

Ricky!

He turned on the sofa, unable to find a comfortable position. Things stuck him through his coat.

Should have seen that one.

Sometime . . .

He dreamed of being lost on an endless field of snow. The moon hung cold and dead in the sky, a grinning white face. He was taller now—the snow was barely up to his waist in spots. There was a great burning sore in his stomach and his feet were gone, the flesh sloughed off up to the knees to reveal the skeleton beneath. He walked on skeleton feet through an endless field of snow, a tall boy on aching stilts, searching, screaming . . .

Brigham

. . . hoping for the sun and food and life.

Demons cavorted around him. Pink things whispered by, reaching out to stroke his face with long tendril fingers. The moon danced in the sky, opening its great cratered mouth to speak as it danced.

No rest.

Ricky turned in his sleep. His galoshes jingled.

No rest.

Linda came to him and put her hands on his face. He felt feverish. He was about to fall off the couch so she reached under him to scoot him back. It was barely twelve o'clock noon but such a weird and spooky darkness had descended outside that she had lit a lamp and placed it on one of the end tables. It was over this lamp that she now bent, careful not to get so low as to singe her coat, scooting her hands under Ricky in order to give him a firm push back onto the center of the couch.

"Ouch," she said, and pulled her hands away. She looked at them. There was a series of parallel white scratches on the rawness of her cold-reddened knuckles. She lifted Ricky and looked beneath him.

Yellow straw was poking up through the sofa cushion, a stubbly field of it perhaps half an inch high. Some of it was crushed where Ricky was lying on it. Linda ran her hand over it, able now to even smell it—a dry, dusty odor that reminded her of the dark musty interior of a barn.

Ricky mumbled in his sleep. As she watched, a sprinkling of ice began to form over the straw, shafting twinkling bits of lamplight into her eyes. There were thin crackling sounds as it solidified to a sheet.

"Jill," Linda said, jerking her head in a come-here motion. "Look at this."

Jill turned away from the fire. "What?"

"This. Look."

Jill came over. She moved robotically, as if in a dream. In her eyes Linda could see a faraway kind of pain, a dazed sort of fatigue. She looked down at the couch and arched her eyebrows momentarily. "How 'bout that," she said offhandedly.

"Do you see it? The straw or hay or whatever it is?"

"Just couch stuffing," Jill replied, and wandered back to the fireplace.

"There's ice, too."

"It is kind of cold in here."

"Yes, but not *that* cold. Didn't you see?" Linda moved Ricky to the other end of the couch and settled him there. The straw slithered back down inside the sofa and the ice melted instantly. Linda blinked, looking at the droplets of water where ice had been before. They were beginning to soak into the fabric now.

"It disappeared," she said. She looked over at Jill with a mystified half-smile on her face. "It *disappeared*."

"Is that so?"

"Didn't you see it? The way that straw disappeared?" She pressed her hands on the cushion but could feel only firm foam rubber. "There's no straw in this couch at all," she said, frowning. "How can that be?"

"Oh, would you stop it!" Jill suddenly shouted.

"What did I—"

"My husband is lying out there dying and all you're concerned about is some stupid stuffing in a stupid couch! We should all be out there trying to lift the truck instead of standing around here wondering about the stupid *furniture*!" She went to the door and threw it open. Linda saw without much surprise that she was crying again.

"Jill, wait," she said. "Mark's doing all that can be done."

"No, he's not!" Jill shrieked. "Because if he was doing what he should Glenn would be in here with me and not still out there in that awful *storm*!" She ran outside, leaving the door drifting slowly back and forth on its hinges. Linda went to it and shut it. She couldn't blame Jill for the sudden outburst. If it were Mark instead of Glenn out there she would be going nuts herself.

The commotion had awakened Ricky. He got off the couch looking groggy and disheveled. "No rest?" he said, looking around dazedly.

Linda went to him and hugged him. "Not on that couch," she said.

Mark got back in time to see Jill come flying out of the cabin and run to the truck. He saw her stoop by Glenn, heard her wail. Then she backed up a few paces and hurled herself at the truck. There was a hollow sheet-metal thud as she boomeranged off the roof and fell backward. She got up and did it again, cursing and shrieking.

Mark broke into a lumbering trot, crossing the clearing with his logs dragging and thumping behind. He got to Jill as she collapsed in a huddle beside Glenn's prostrate form, sobbing. There was a respectable dent in the roof now.

"Jill, honey," he panted, dropping the logs and kneeling beside her, "don't crack up on me now. We all need to keep our heads."

She raised her head and looked at him with bright hysterical eyes. "He's dead," she wailed. "Dead!"

Mark looked at Glenn's pallid face. His skin was a flat pasty gray. A rime of snow lay on his forehead and cheeks, not melting. Mark picked up Glenn's wrist and felt for a pulse, his own heart thumping heavier in his chest. Could it have happened that quietly, with no fanfare or pronouncement from heaven? Can a man slip so stealthily into death? Can a man die from a crushed arm and shock and the loss of a few pints of blood?

Apparently so. There was no pulse. Mark peeled the blankets apart, unzipped Glenn's coat, and pressed his ear to his chest.

Nothing. And then, faintly—*lub-dup.* A single beat. Mark strained to hear, which was hard to do over the sounds Jill was making as she slipped noisily into hysteria. And then, again, *lub-dup.*

"He's not dead," Mark said, adding a mental *not yet.* He would be dead soon, by the sound of his heart. The beats were fully five seconds apart. Mark took Jill by the shoulders and pulled her close to him. He smelled the fragrance of her hair, some kind of perfume she had applied this morning when things were still fine and the world was bright and cheerful. Lilacs and honeysuckle, he would have guessed. He smoothed her hair with his hands as she sobbed into the hollow of his collarbone.

"Don't let him die," she whispered. Her breath was warm and moist on his neck. "Please."

"I'll try," Mark said. "I can only try."

She pulled away from him and got to her feet. Snow clung to her pants, white frosting. "Is there anything I can do?" she asked levelly.

"Not right now," Mark said. "I have to make a lever first." He indicated the logs. "With these."

"Okay." She nodded, took a deep breath, nodded again. Behind her the sky was lightening to yellow and gray, the snow streaming down in an endless shower. "Okay, Mark."

She walked back to the cabin. Mark zipped Glenn's coat back up, relieved, and was adjusting the blankets when Glenn's hand began a slow spider-walk up his sleeve again. Mark froze, watching it crawl up his arm toward his shoulder, seized with a ghost of certainty that it would walk all the way to his throat and strangle him. *Been hugging my wife,* Glenn would croak. *Been thinking dirty thoughts about her.* And they would both die out here, Glenn for no reason, Mark for a crime he had not meant to commit.

The hand stopped at his shoulder. Glenn's eyes burst open, wide and staring. A wave of strange horror rolled through Mark. The whites of Glenn's eyes were now yellow, but that had to be an optical trick of the yellow sky. The blue irises looked muddy brown. These stranger's eyes rolled in Glenn's head and came to a stop focused on Mark. "Get out," he whispered.

Mark leaned closer. "We can't leave you."

"She's trying to trick you, Mark. She wants him back."

"What?"

"The bitch. She'll do whatever she has to."

"Sure," Mark said. He could smell Glenn's breath, thick and pasty. His teeth even looked yellow in this light, Glenn's perfect white teeth that had inspired jokes about dentists. "Sure, Glenn."

Glenn's face contorted with pain. A spasm rippled down his body. "She's growing trees, Mark. Trying to take him back. Taking us all back. She'll do whatever she has to."

Mark tucked the blankets tighter up under his chin. "I found some logs, Glenn. I can try and get you out."

He shook his head from side to side. "She won't let me go, Mark. I've seen her face-to-face. I'm a dead man."

"Nonsense."

Glenn convulsed again. "Stranger things in this world than you know," he gasped. "Stranger things." He bared his teeth in a snarl of pain. "Get out of here, Mark. Get them all out of here."

He began to flop and jerk. Fresh blood spurted from his shattered elbow, spraying out across the snow and Mark's right leg in bright crimson streaks. Mark shuffled backward on his knees, his face drawn with helpless terror. He was watching the death agony of his best friend and was powerless to stop it. Glenn turned on his side and clawed at the roof of the Blazer. He worked his ruined arm back and forth as if trying to pull it free from the door. Mark heard the splintering grind of bone on bone and felt cold revulsion crawl up his throat.

Glenn was trying to tear his own arm off.

He rolled from side to side. His feet came out of the wrapping of blankets and dug trenches in the snow. He put his free hand on the Blazer's roof and pushed, forming a fresh dimple in the bright expanse of metal.

"Glenn, stop!" Mark shouted, and then his hands flew up to his mouth to choke off a scream. He did not want Jill or Linda to hear and come out, did not want anyone to see this agony, did not want to see it himself. A dull, sweeping horror fell over him. Glenn was going to do it. He was going to writhe and twist in the snow until his arm came off.

Mark moved toward him against what seemed like a weight of rushing water, drugged with terror, reaching out, needing to stop him and this unnatural, unbearable act. He crawled up on Glenn's heaving chest and swung his fist in a short arc. It caught Glenn under the chin and his teeth clicked shut. His frantic motions faltered for a moment, and Mark was no longer riding a bronco.

Then he started again. Blood drooled from the corner of his mouth in a bubbling trickle. Instead of ending his torture, Mark had only increased it. Hot tears sprang into his eyes as he swung again. His fist smashed into Glenn's cheekbone, flipping his head sideways with a snap. His legs stopped drumming the ground. Slowly, like a knotted flag unfurling, he stretched out to his full length and was still.

Mark climbed off of him, shaking. That had been awful, too awful to endure. The sleeve of Glenn's coat was a torn and bloody rag now, and where it dead-ended at the Blazer's closed door a white knob of bone peeked through like a large bloody pearl. The belt had come unwound and lay in the spreading pool of blood and its bright red splatters, useless. Mark tightened it around his bicep again, getting his fingers sticky with blood, until the flow trickled off. The brine smell of it was in the air, thin and pungent. He washed his hands with snow and dried them on his pants, then got to his feet.

Glenn turned his head. His eyes fluttered open, dull yellow.

"No rest, and no forgiveness," he croaked. His lips curled back from his teeth. "No rest for him, Mark. Never."

Mark bent over him. "What, Glenn? What?"

"No rest." A tremble passed through his body. "When we're gone, she'll still have him. I can see it all. The dead can see it all." The muscles of his face relaxed and his eyes slid shut.

"Glenn?" Mark knelt by him again and lightly touched his face. "Glenn?"

His eyes opened again. He swallowed. "Listen to what I have to say, Mark. Listen to a dying man's last words."

"Nonsense," Mark said, but knew it was a futile defiance.

"A terrible thing happened. So long ago, but it doesn't matter." His voice was a bare whisper now. "She's going to set things right. An eye for an eye. She's waited for him all these years."

"Who, Glenn?"

"The bitch. You can't do what he did, see. You can't. God, how clear it is to me now. I have to tell you . . ."

A low rumbling sound to his right made Mark snap his head around.

Sticks were worming up out of the ground in a line by the trees. Writhing and twisting, they pressed up through the snow cover like questing snakes, pushing piles of black earth up with them, extending upward. Black and pointed sticks, strange poles thrusting up into the sky, growing thicker.

Trees.

Mark watched in stunned disbelief as they grew before his eyes. Branches budded, extending out like bony searching fingers, sprouting a fur of green needles like a trick of time-lapse photography. A new line of trees was forming, a new circle of trees on the rim of the clearing, shrinking it.

They grew to ten feet, twenty feet. The wind sprang up and they swayed and creaked, huge and imposing and impossible, fully formed trees.

Mark got to his feet and took a staggering step backward.

More trees were growing in front of these new ones, bursting up even faster, spraying snow and dirt in their climb to the sky. Fresh black bark crackled and popped. The earth shook. There was a feeling of heaviness in the air, as if lightning had struck nearby and thunder were rolling through the atmosphere. Mark felt sudden pressure in his ears and almost cried out.

New treetops appeared in an arrowhead toward the Blazer, throwing snow aside. The arrowhead reached the Blazer and disappeared underneath. Glass broke with a sudden muted crunch. The Blazer shifted to the right.

Glenn screamed.

Two trees were bursting up through the Blazer's windows in a spray of glass and were thick enough now to hoist the truck off the ground. Glenn was lifted by his shattered arm, writhing and kicking. Branches grew out and snaked around his legs, cupping him in their basket of needles. Instinctively Mark lunged for him, clawed for a handhold on his feet, and managed to pull one of his boots off before he was lifted out of reach. Thrusting branches pushed Mark aside as one of the blankets that had enfolded Glenn wafted down. The rest were scattered on the rising limbs like cast-off rags.

The wind kicked up in earnest, howling and screeching. Mark saw the tips of trees shoot up, radiating inward toward the cabin like the spokes of a wheel, bursting up with a sound like dull cannon shots. The world became a green and white confusion. He turned and sprinted for the cabin just as the door burst open, and there was Jill and Linda with Ricky between them, looking out with their faces round and pale. He saw Linda's mouth stretch open in a noiseless shriek of wonder and terror, saw Jill look around like an awestruck child. Ricky lunged forward and took hold of Linda's right leg in a bear hug.

There was a huge jabbering crash of wood and stone as the trees smashed their way up through the cabin's foundation and floor. Through the open door Mark saw floorboards explode upward in jagged confusion. Furniture tilted and fell over. A tree grew up through the chimney, bursting it in an explosion of stone and cement dust. Trees punched through the roof, their expanding branches rippling through the shingles like roots before flipping them skyward to pinwheel down into the snow. Behind the cabin Mark saw the outhouse ride to the sky with its door flapping. A moment later it burst apart in a shower of ruined plywood.

Linda, Jill, and Ricky stumbled down the steps and into Mark's arms. The wind rippled their clothing into crazy shapes as they stood, huddled, watching with disbelieving terror as the world went insane. A tree shot up beside Mark's right elbow and his face was full of sudden branches as it hurled him aside. Ricky was snagged in it for a moment and lifted a few feet off the ground before Linda, with a shriek, hauled him back down.

"Glenn!" Jill screamed.

Mark looked back. The Blazer rocked and swayed, pierced now with even more trees, perhaps twenty-five feet off the ground. It was bent and mangled. Still Glenn hung by his arm, twisting and kicking at the enfolding cocoon of pine branches. As Mark watched, the door levered open and Glenn fell to the ground with a long, wailing scream. He landed on a tree that had thrust up out of the snow. The tree punched through his back in a geyser of blood, pushing him back up. A thin black branch wormed out of his open mouth as he rose, choking off his last scream. Sharp tendrils from it punched out his eyes, growing, thickening. There was a loud crack as his skull shattered. The tree shot skyward, bending in the wind, becoming green and luxuriant. Unrecognizable bloody pieces slid down the branches and pattered on the ground.

Jill's legs buckled and she fell against Mark. He picked her up, staggering from the force of the wind. "This way!" he shouted, and began to run across what was left of the clearing with Jill flopping in his arms. Linda took Ricky's hand and they followed, bent to the wind. Mark glanced back to make sure they were with him and saw the cabin's walls fall outward, collapsing like a giant's house of cards. Snow whoofed out in billowing clouds.

"Stay with me," he shouted. He knew where to go, so long as this unnatural disaster wasn't occurring all over this mountain, all over this world. He had a brief vision of a world of trees, of cities collapsing and skyscrapers falling, of people fleeing in panic like he was fleeing right now. It was a vision from a nightmare.

He carried Jill and ran as the trees took over everything behind him.

PART THREE

Sundown

CHAPTER THIRTEEN

Eddie Chambers was in pretty bad shape by now.

Viewed from the outside he was his normal self, good old Eddie was: skinny, dirty, little more than a skeleton cloaked in pallid flesh and army fatigues, with a shadow of reddish whiskers on his chin and cheeks and big purple circles around his closed eyes. There was the added touch of a sheet of dried vomit lying in a crust across his chest and a big wet stain of urine in a circle around his crotch; to a passerby it would have been the smell of Eddie that revolted more than anything: dried piss, dried puke, drying shit, old sweat, bad breath, B.O.—you name it, Eddie smelled like it. A garbage dump simmering under a midday sun would have had nothing on good old Eddie Chambers, brother to Jill Pruett, Eddie lying on a forgotten back road just west of Tremonton, Utah.

But inside, inside—Eddie was undergoing extensive changes. His heart was fluttering as weakly as the wings of a dying bird. His abused kidneys were about ready to call it quits for the day and stomp off in a huff of total renal failure. His eyes rolled in sockets as dry as old gourds, seeing things. His tongue was a hot swollen lump in a mouth as dry as the dust he lay in. His ears rang with the maddening high whine of tinnitus induced by overdose, hearing things. His cracked, sunburnt lips moved, and he spoke.

"Robin?"

His eyebrows drew together. A frown settled on his face.

Eddie was conversing with the dead.

He cried out in his stupor. A killdeer, trotting importantly beside the road, rose to the sky with a startled squawk and a sudden flapping of wings. Bugs, Mormon crickets and locusts, ceased their endless droning chatter for a moment, thought about

things for a while, then went back to talking. A light spring wind
made dust devils out of sand. Puffball clouds slid across the sky,
casting fat round shadows that chased across the endless bowl
of desert floor where Eddie lay so near death.

On the distant western horizon the rambling camel humps of
the Wasatch lay capped by black and ugly clouds.

He gnashed his teeth. His fingers went to his mouth and made
eating motions. Then he was still for a long while.

A blowing trail of dust became visible on the eastern horizon,
growing, approaching. Soon a blue dot was visible beneath it,
shimmering and wavy through the gentle ripples of midday heat.
The sound of a motor made itself known, rattling in the thin
warm air.

It was a blue pickup truck following the winding road. Eddie
could hear nothing, could see nothing except his vision. He lay
on the ground, a human roadblock, and presently the truck came
upon him and stopped with a squeal of brakes and a wash of
dust that obscured the sun momentarily.

A man opened the door and got out, leaving the engine idling.
On the passenger side a woman wearing a red bandana over her
hair sat watching. She had a toddler on her lap who was noisily
sucking a yellow pacifier. In the truck bed behind them sat two
Honda three-wheelers tied down with ropes.

"Jehoshaphat," the man said, walking over to Eddie and
stooping over him. He straightened, holding his nose. "Deader'n a skunk," he called out to his wife. He adjusted his cowboy hat higher on his head, perplexed.

Eddie groaned and shifted in the dirt.

"Whoops," the man said. "Cancel that."

The woman got out, leaving the baby in the truck with an
admonition not to touch the gearshift lever. She walked over to
Eddie with her shadow puddled at her feet. "Pee-yoo," she
said. She had an open, honest, sunburnt face and looked like
the type of woman to call a spade a spade if that's what the
situation called for, a no-nonsense daughter of solid pioneer
stock. Her name was Madge Pickens; her husband, Ralph. The
toddler in the truck playing with the gearshift lever was little
Tony.

"Guess we ought to help him out," Ralph said. "You take
his feet."

They picked him up. By shuffling along they were able to get
him beside the truck and hoist him up.

"Careful, now," Ralph said. He was getting puke on his hands but didn't mind all that much. This fellow looked deader than most corpses and obviously needed help in a bad way. It was like handling a light sack of bones. They lowered him down in the pickup's bed beside the three-wheelers and got back in the truck.

"So much for three-wheeling," Ralph said resignedly, swatting Tony's hand off the gearshift and grinding it into first. He popped the clutch and swung the truck in a tight circle, spewing dust. They headed back to the highway.

"Going to take him to the hospital?" Marge asked.

"All the way to downtown? I don't feel *that* much like a Samaritan. We'll just take him home and get some water in him. I figure that's probably what he needs most."

"What do you suppose happened to him?" Her eyes widened speculatively. "Do you suppose he's got the plague or rabies or something? I've heard of that happening. We could be opening ourselves to a world of hurt by even touching him." She scrubbed the palms of her hands on her Levi's. "That scares me."

"Nonsense. All that's wrong with that fella is an overdose of the bottle. He got lost out here and just plumb passed out."

"It's a long way from town for a drunk to walk."

Ralph nodded. "Drunks do amazing things."

They came to the highway and went left. The truck bounced up onto the pavement and Ralph, irate at having lost an afternoon of fun on the Hondas, burned a little rubber getting it up to speed. Little Tony squealed with delight.

Eddie, bouncing in the back, caught in a vision, didn't seem to care all that much.

Ricky was out of breath and feeling scared.

It was a terrible feeling, but a familiar one. They had crashed through the final barrier of briars and brambles ten minutes after leaving John Phillips' ruined cabin and Glenn's ruined Blazer and the trees that Ricky had watched, bug-eyed with wonder and terror, that grew like magic where no trees were supposed to be. Mark was staggering under Jill's weight, his breath rushing out in huge clouds of steam like a locomotive, his legs wobbling and scissoring, and Linda had Ricky's left hand in a crushing, tugging grip as she pulled him through the brambles at a dead run. It was terrible for him to see his mother and father so completely afraid, these big important grown-ups who up to now had known no fear. Not fear of the dark, fear of the night, fear of the monsters that lurked in closets and under beds. In Ricky's sight they had been, up to now, immune to the emotion he had grown so familiar with over the last few days. For him it was nightmares and the voices. For Mommy and Daddy now, it was the magic trees.

They came upon a cabin Ricky had never seen before, a big one made of thick stacked logs with brown stuff smoothed into the chinks, and it seemed dreadfully familiar to him in a way he couldn't understand. As Linda towed him up to the front door he began to cry, and she dutifully soothed him, thinking he had been stuck by the briars that had ripped across his snowsuit with a noise like zippers opening. Then Mark, a civilized man even in this uncivil situation, knocked on the cabin door with his foot, staggering a little as he did.

No answer. Linda hauled the door open and Mark maneuvered Jill inside. The wind howled at their backs and the snow sprayed down in a torrent. Ricky went in last, almost reluctantly, and stood inside, looking around with a strange new sensation of dread flooding over him like high water. This was not a good place. Yes, there was a cheery fire burning in the fireplace, and yes, it was infinitely warmer than it had been outside, but no, this was not a good place. Bad things would happen here. Had, perhaps, happened before.

He stood like a large doll in his blue snowsuit, staring at the floor and the melting snow around his galoshes now, too scared to look around anymore, too full of this eerie new feeling to move. Mark went across the room and laid Jill on one of the beds. She moaned and moved her hands in front of her face like weak fish flopping. Then she made an awful face and screamed.

It was loud, unbearably loud. Ricky felt tense and jittery, as if some small caged thing inside him was about to claw its way out, scurry up his spine, and attack his brain. This thing was a rat called PANIC, and he knew well enough what kind of rat that was. It was the rat that was attacking Jill right now, making her writhe and scream, and it was the kind of rat that jumped from person to person until everyone was screaming. He looked up at his mother and saw fear etched into her face in big dark lines. The rat was attacking her, too. His daddy looked small and shrunken, his dark hair full of snow and falling down across his eyes; there was a rat inside him as well.

They listened to Jill scream for a while, jittering on the edge of panic.

"We've got to get ahold of ourselves," Mark said, becoming tall again. He sat beside Jill on the bed and shook her by the shoulders. She lunged up suddenly and held him in a tight embrace, sobbing.

Linda went to Ricky and began to mechanically peel him out of his snowsuit. The rat was gone for now, but still this cabin was not a good place. It was almost like a smell, a thin undercurrent of something foul here. Ricky sniffed, not quite placing that smell. One time in the basement of their house on Westfire Road he had seen a smashed cockroach on the wall by the washing machine, one his mother had swatted with a slipper a few days before and never gotten around to scraping off the wall; with a child's curiosity he had gotten close and sniffed the dried green squashed innards of the cockroach, and that smell was something like this one. The low, lingering musk of rotten things.

"Whose cabin is this?" Linda asked as she pulled Ricky's galoshes off.

"I don't know," Mark said. He pulled Jill's arms away and pushed her back down on the bed. She whimpered and moaned. Ricky saw him bend down and give her a quick kiss on the cheek, then look up, startled, as if to see if anyone had seen him. His eyes met Ricky's and held them for a moment. Linda was busy setting the galoshes by the door. It seemed to Ricky that his daddy's face got very red all of a sudden. That was strange. And that kissing deal was strange. Daddy *never* kissed anyone but Mommy, sometimes bending her over backward and tickling her fanny while he did, making her laugh. But laughter was very far away now, and everything was different.

Mark went to the table, pulled out a chair and sat down. He put his hands between his knees and knotted them. "This is all very strange," he said. To Ricky he looked sick, like he was about to fall out of his chair. He pulled his hands apart and rubbed his face wearily, then put his hands back together. "Everything's gone crazy. Did you see what happened?"

"The trees," Linda said. There was awe and wonder in her voice. "They grew."

"Right. Right." He seemed lost and dazed. He looked at Ricky and attempted a smile that came out looking wobbly and miserable. "Are you hanging in there, Ricky?" he asked.

"Yes, Daddy."

"Good boy." His eyes took on that vacant look again. "Right out of the ground," he murmured. He raised his hands suddenly. "Zoom."

"Zoom," Linda agreed.

"Utterly impossible."

"Yes. But it happened." She shook her head and water flipped out of her hair. Some of it landed in the fireplace and sizzled there. "Just like that, it happened. Zoom."

"Right," Mark said. "It happened."

They stared at nothing, distraught. On the bed Jill covered her eyes and sobbed.

"Glenn's dead," Linda said. A terrible expression of pain settled on her face. "The trees, they . . . they . . ."

"Grew," Mark said.

Linda began to cry, too. Ricky looked up at her, and over to Jill. Both of them were sobbing and shaking. Linda began to walk in a small circle around the cabin, passing the fireplace, passing Ricky, who still stood by the door like a large doll. She twisted her hands in her hair while tears coursed down her cheeks. Mark sat glumly regarding his knuckles. Outside, the wind whooped and howled.

Benjamin.

Ricky jerked.

Benjamin!

"What?" he said.

Mark looked up. "What?"

"That voice," Ricky said.

"Voice? What voice?"

Ricky shuffled toward him, wanting to be held, wanting to be away from that door and the howling, talking wind outside. "Somebody said something," he said, putting his small hands on Mark's knees.

Mark ruffled his hair, but it was an automatic, meaningless gesture. His hand felt big and cold and hard on his head. Ricky snuggled up closer. "Just a voice."

Mark stretched an arm across the table and drummed his fingers on one of the books there. He hadn't heard, wasn't aware. Ricky pushed away from him and went to the fire. At least it was warmer there.

"The trees," Mark said, sitting bolt upright. He jumped up and went to one of the cabin's small frosty windows, peering outside. "Goddamn dark," he said. "But we're okay."

"Are we?" Linda said. "Are we really?"

Jill sat up in bed. Ricky looked over at her, feeling afraid all over again. Her hair was a wild wet tangle; beneath it her face was twisted into sharp shadows and lines. Her eyes flared weird and orange in the firelight. "You could have helped him," she shrieked, making tingles jump up and down Ricky's back. She reached out with a finger and pointed. "You could have pulled him out and saved him!"

Mark looked at her, mutely shaking his head.

"Yes! It was up to you!"

"I tried," Mark said. "Honestly I tried."

"Now he's dead," she shrieked. "Now they're all dead!" She turned suddenly on the bed from her back to her stomach and crushed her face into the pillow.

"I'm sorry," Mark said miserably. "I'm so sorry."

Her head snapped up and she glared at the pillow as if it had stung her. She picked it up and hurled it across the room. It landed on the floor in front of Ricky's feet with a solid *flump*.

There was straw sticking out of it.

No rest, and no forgiveness, the wind whispered outside.

Ricky began to tremble even though the fire was toasting his backside. He had never felt quite so cold, quite so utterly, utterly afraid.

"For everything that happens on this earth there is a rational explanation," Mark said. He was keeping vigil by the window now, feeling a bit like a pioneer farmer watching for Indians, only these Indians wore green and sprang up from the ground and defied rational explanation. But he was trying.

"I figure it like this," he said. "Some years ago the government used this mountaintop for testing some kind of chemical—a new fertilizer, maybe. They probably sprayed the area with something like Agent Orange, only this was Agent Green or something. Maybe it didn't work, so they gave up. Why they would want to have trees grow so fast is anybody's guess. I'd say it's to help the big logging companies, the paper mills, the state parks—you know, so all the trees we need could be cut down and then instantly replaced. It'd be a great thing. Only what they didn't count on is that this new Agent takes a few months or years to work. Maybe it lies dormant in the ground—who knows? At any rate, it suddenly started to work over the last day or two. That would explain why the road is gone, and what happened to us at Phillips' cabin. That would explain everything.''

He turned to see if anyone was listening. His mind was desperate to make sense out of the nonsensical and rationalize the irrational. The trees had been growing stealthily, just so slow that you wouldn't notice, creeping up in secret. Then all of a sudden, they went berserk. But why? And how, for Christ's sake?

"Anybody buy it?" he asked, looking around. Jill was sitting up on the bed, rubbing her face miserably. Linda was at the window on the other side of the door, watching.

"The same thing happened to the road?" she said. "Why didn't you tell me?"

"It was just too crazy."

"Everything's crazy now."

Mark nodded. "Let's assume I'm right on this. Let's assume the Agent did its work and that it's done. That means we're safe."

"What if we assume it's not, and we're not? What then?"

"Then we go out into that snowstorm and try to walk the thirty miles back down to the highway, that's what. We get lost and freeze to death. Is that what you want to hear?"

"How about this," she said softly. "We stay here while the snow piles up. We don't have any food, so we starve to death. Is that what *you* want to hear?"

Mark shook his head. "It won't happen. There are other people here on Spike with us. You saw a man. I met two women. In the last three years since we were up here cabins have been sprouting up like weeds. It's a regular state park up here now. We're not the only ones stuck in this storm, you can bet on that."

"Then why isn't there anybody stuck *here*, Mark? Someone built a big cozy fire and then got out in a hurry. They knew better than to stick around with the snow coming down like this. What if everybody else on this mountain is getting out, too? That leaves us alone with no way out." Her voice was rising, taking on an edge of bitter panic. "What will we eat, Mark? Snow? Trees? I checked all the cupboards here and they're empty. And I'm *hungry*, Mark. Even after seeing what happened to Glenn I'm hungrier than I've ever been in my life. We need something to *eat*."

Mark nodded, realizing with dismal certainty that she was right. He had seen Glenn torn to pieces but it hadn't ruined his appetite. Something like that should have made him swear off food for a week. He wetted his lips, pushing the fresh memory of Glenn's death from his mind, aware of a dull fleshy taste in his mouth. His stomach had a painful cramp in his belly. A side effect of overexposure to Agent Green? he wondered. The victim feels an overwhelming hunger and is driven mad by the desire for food? As trees burst up around him he pines for a hamburger, if you'll pardon the pun?

Maybe. A hamburger wouldn't be all that bad about now. And wasn't that just a terrible thing to be thinking about under these circumstances?

"I'll go find somebody," he said.

"How?"

"By looking. That's all I can do."

"You'll freeze to death."

"Not if I keep moving." He went to the door and put his hand on the wooden block that served as its knob. Was he really going to do it—go out there into that howling maelstrom and tromp around until he blundered onto another cabin? Or was he really sitting in the back of the Blazer, dozing and dreaming, about to wake up from the most macabre nightmare of his life? For a moment his mind teetered, not wanting to accept this reality, convinced it was, after all, just a dream.

"If you have to," Linda said, and came to him to slip her arms around his neck. She kissed him lightly on the lips.

I'm not going out there, Mark thought. *I'm not even really here.*

"Don't go, Daddy," Ricky said, and rushed up to cling to his legs.

"I've got to before the snow gets too deep," Mark said, and stooped to give him a hug. It was all unreal, this. Mark Butler was not going out and risk his life in a snowstorm for the simple reason that it was not an item on the master plan of his life. Other people did heroic and reckless things, usually winding up dead for their trouble. Mark Butler was the manager of a finance company and got his thrills from movies and TV and an occasional overdose of Budweiser beer. He was a sedentary man with a bit of a paunch growing around his middle and an ass that was beginning to spread from too much time parked in a chair. He was not about to risk his life now because none of this was happening.

He opened the door and the wind blew into his face like a

screaming ghost, lifting his hair and tattering it wildly, bringing
tears to his eyes. Gray-black clouds boiled overhead, dumping
snow, dumping snow. The trees that stood in a circle around the
cabin bent and swayed like clumsy dancers. It was cold and
bitter and real.

He stepped out and pulled the door shut behind him.

"It's just you and me now," he said to himself, hunching his
shoulders against the wind. The mountain suddenly seemed vast
and endless, the forest dark and foreboding and full of mysterious shadows. He took a few steps, stopped, and looked back.
Linda was at the window, watching. She raised a hand and
waved.

He turned and went on. The briars had been swept aside and
crushed down when they came through a half hour before and
he stepped through them easily, mentally beginning to form a
map of where he intended to go and how he intended to get
back. It would be easy enough to keep tracking in a general
western direction, as that was the way this side of the mountain
sloped. It would also be easy enough to walk in a semblance of
a straight line with occasional side trips to the right and left to
scout for cabins, if only there weren't so goddamn many *trees*
blocking the way, making a straight line impossible. It seemed
inevitable that he would walk a zigzagging path that would eventually form a large circle, for even though he was no outdoorsman he knew the age-old truth that you tend to walk in a circle
when you're lost. Something to do with one leg being stronger
than the other. And if that were the case, he would eventually
wind up back here at the cabin, probably three days from now,
dragging himself on his hands and knees, frozen and delirious.

Yuck.

He walked into the thickness of the woods, moving slowly,
already afraid and unsure. He glanced back and the cabin was
still there, a giant Lego construction on a small field of snow,
and there was Linda's shape still at the window. The wind was
dragging across the elongations of his tracks, obscuring them;
they would be invisible in ten minutes. And inside the deep
woods, with no tracks to follow back, he would be helplessly,
hopelessly lost.

An idea struck him and he stopped beside the thick trunk of
a pine, digging in his pocket. He withdrew his penknife, which
up to now had been used for nothing more severe than opening
the morning mail at the office, and stripped a section of bark

free. There was good white wood underneath, unmistakable as long as the light held out. He counted out ten more steps and marked another tree. Looking back, he could see—almost— where he had scored the first one, a ghostly beacon.

Better than nothing. Better than footprints that didn't last or bread crumbs that weren't available. He made his way deeper into the woods, marking trees, walking, marking trees. The light here under the canopy of branches was shadowy and dim, the wind capricious and gusty. The trees creaked and rustled, whitening under the new barrage of snow. He wondered how long he could keep this up, how long it would be before he just plain got too cold or the knife slipped from his numbing fingers and lost itself in the snow. He pulled his sleeve back from his watch as he walked and saw that it was approaching one-thirty now. He would do this until four and then head back. That would put him back at the cabin at six-thirty, just before nightfall and utter darkness.

Darkness.

Wasn't it dark already, though? Wasn't it darker now than it had any right to be, heavy cloud cover or not? Mark had the sudden pervasive feeling, as he stopped by a tree and cut away the bark, that time had somehow gone awry here, that day had exchanged itself for a dim, hazy twilight that might be approaching day, or approaching night. His internal clock seemed to have come unwired, making him check his watch again and hold it to his ear. And what had Glenn said in his delirium? Something about towing the sun backward. The bitch, he had said. She's towing the sun. That was a strange thing for Glenn to say.

Thinking about Glenn was too painful, too real, so he moved on, counting his steps, dodging some trees and marking some, glancing back at his footsteps to see what kind of path his feet had taken, ducking under low-hanging branches, moving forward, looking back, moving forward.

It was with no surprise that he came across one of the Blazer's doors lying at the bottom of a nest of trees like a big red plate in the snow. His botched internal homing system had directed him back to the Phillips cabin, the only path he knew in these woods. He stopped with dread and revulsion crawling up the back of his throat, cold and foul. Truck parts littered the ground here like a snow-dusted junkyard. A few feet away the ground was dotted with bright splashes of blood. One of the pines had red sap coursing down its scaly bark. And lying under a thin

pallet of snow was something that looked like an arm and hand
with its fingers curled toward the sky. And there were . . . other
pieces.

Mark veered hard to the right and lurched ahead, filled with
unease and revulsion. The forest was dense here, a jungle of
pines. He smashed boughs away with his fists, swinging his knife
like a tiny machete, needing to get away from this spot and the
things that littered the ground. Branches sprang into his face and
he knocked them crazily aside, wondering if the smell that filled
his nostrils was ordinary pine or the deadly scent of some miracle Agent. Perhaps, a far, gibbering corner of his mind reasoned with placid stupidity, the Agent will begin to work on me
and I will grow thirty feet tall. Perhaps I will sprout branches.
Perhaps I will grow roots.

Something crashed in the woods ahead of him and he stopped
with his breath pumping coldly in and out of his lungs. A dim
shadow bulked between the trees, moving toward him, some
low, snuffling thing that rustled the trees and caused snow to
powder down. Mark raised a hand and opened his mouth to
shout, forming a mental image of a man bent low to dodge the
branches, a man cursing under his breath and about to straighten.
That image died instantly and he was seized with a numb, crawling terror as a bear emerged from the dimness ahead and lumbered toward him, its massive head low to the ground, its eyes
small and beady. It was sniffing the snow with quick sweeps of
its nose.

Mark's mind went black for several seconds as he stood frozen, unable to do anything but stare at the bear that was barely
fifteen yards ahead now. Small thoughts flared through his mind
like bursts from a flashbulb, illuminating and fading, patterned
on the wall of fear that was growing around his brain like a
shell, followed by the cold placid voice of reason. The first flash
was a single word—*bloodsmell*. Then, rapidly, a series of flashes.
Grizzly. No grizzly bears left in the Wasatch. Killed off by hunters ages ago. *Hungry.* Smelling Glenn, Glenn in pieces. *Kill me.
Eat me.*

The flashbulb faded and Mark was left with the bright image
of himself being torn to pieces by this grizzly, the last remnant
of a dead race in Utah. He took a hesitant step to the right and
the bear stopped.

They regarded each other.

Nice bear, Mark thought dreamily. *Nice old bear. Goooood old bear.*

The grizzly reared slightly on its hind legs, searching the wind with its nose. Its forepaws paddled the air briefly.

Going to smell me . . .

The bear opened its jaws and roared. The forest seemed to shake. It raised itself to its full height, snapping branches behind it. Then it dropped down and ran toward Mark.

Jesus Jesus Jesus . . .

The bear closed the distance in three seconds.

Of course none of this was happening, Mark knew. There had not been a grizzly bear loose in the Wasatch since the turn of the century. You might find a black bear minding its own business now and then, but they were small bears, the kind to turn tail and run if they got a whiff of a man. This grizzly with the open mouth and teeth like small white tusks and black-pearl eyes was not here, could not be here, was not about to kill and eat the sedentary manager of a finance company. No way, no sir.

He turned and ran, too terrified to scream. He went face-first into a tree and began to shinny up with small questing branches gouging at his eyes. His hands found a large branch and he hoisted himself up, his feet kicking wildly at the air.

The bear reached up and swatted him out of the tree. Pain exploded in his side in big searing stitches. He tumbled to the ground and got a faceful of snow.

The bear reared up, towering over him. Its roar was a combination of thunder and pig squeal. Mark looked up at it, still magically displaced from this scene by the sheer impossibility of it, noticing the way the bear's big ponderous belly jiggled as it did a two-legged dance over him, noticing the way its coarse brown hairs all seemed to be standing out at attention. He rolled to the side as a paw roughly the size of New York State swooped down and tried to behead him. Snow and dirt burst up from the ground, showering him. Mark got to his hands and knees and scurried away, a groan of denial escaping his clenched teeth. He came to another tree and clawed his way up, his boots scraping the trunk and raining bits of bark down. The bear caught up to him and cuffed him down again, tearing the back of his coat to instant rags and knocking the breath from his lungs. He rolled to the ground with his face screwed up in pain.

Play dead!

He got to his feet again and discovered that his penknife was

still in his right fist. The bear, on all fours now, lunged at him
and he feinted to the left, a slick matador without a cape. His
side hurt and there was blood trailing down his back in sticky
runners. Still it was not real, not yet. Just another nightmare.
The bear spun in the snow, pedaling furiously, and rounded on
him again. It reared up and swatted. Mark stuck the knife in its
left paw as he fell backward to avoid the three-inch claws that
swiped by his face. The bear, sporting a chrome thorn in its paw
now, shrieked like a woman and tried to bite his face. Mark
noticed its breath now. Awesomely bad.

Okay, Androcles, he thought wildly, *what next?*

The bear pulled Mark's minuscule penknife out of its paw with
its mouth and flung its head sideways to spit it out. Blood flipped
through the air in big drops. Mark scuttered backward through
the snow, getting a cold load of it down the back of his pants
and almost losing his boots. The bear dropped down to all fours
again and clamped its jaws over his right shin. Bone crunched,
sending a shudder of agony all the way to his hip.

Mark screamed. The bear shook him like a puppy playing tug-
of-war, flipping him left and right. The world blurred out of
focus. Mark fought for a handhold on the ground, flipping up
black dirt and tearing his fingernails. His mind jumped back a
few hours to Glenn, Glenn hanging by his trapped arm, twirling
and screaming. Now it was Mark, and his leg was coming off
like Glenn's arm had come off.

He sat up and clawed at the bear's huge face. His fingers raked
across the furry slickness of its muzzle. Blood, Mark's blood,
bubbled there between its jaw in a crimson foam. He screamed
again and kicked at it with his left foot.

The bear let go. There were dark scuffs of dirt on its head and
muzzle now where Mark had landed a few good kicks. It reared
back and pawed at its face, bellowing.

Play dead!

Obeying the instinct this time, Mark rolled over with his arms
crossed beneath himself. But would it work? Or was the bear
too far gone now, too angry and hungry for blood? He sensed
the bear coming low again, dropping down to bite and claw. His
heart, already racing so fast it hurt, began to hammer in his
chest, filling his ears with the roar of rushing blood. How long
could he lie still while the bear chewed and clawed his backside?
Would there be anything left of him when it finally grew tired
of gnawing on a living corpse?

The bear bent down with a wet, guttural growl and fastened its teeth on his leg again. Mark cried out in pain and terror. It had taken him by the same leg and was shaking him again, flipping him around like a stuffed doll, pounding his head in the snow. The pain in his leg was enormous, the most enormous thing in the universe. Hot blood ran inside his boot. He felt his consciousness begin to gray out as if a great fuzzy blanket were being thrown over the world. The bear tossed him into the air and he landed on his elbows and knees and stayed that way, wobbling like a drunk trying to crawl home. His hair hung over his eyes.

The penknife lay in front of him. There was blood and snow smeared on the small chrome blade—bear blood. Mark picked it up, weeping and drooling, and staggered to his feet as the bear charged him again. He held the ridiculously tiny knife in front of himself like a lance, wobbling on his feet, knowing it was not enough, that it would be a mere pinprick even if he stuck it in the bear's chest directly at the heart—wherever that was. The bear reared up and waddled toward him, howling and slavering. Its eyes shone with mindless animal hate.

Mark heard another growl, one higher in pitch but just as menacing, coming from the woods off to his right. The bear halted and turned its head, sniffing. Mark shuffled backward a step, looking wildly about for a direction to run. His eyes caught a blur of something brown streaking through the woods, coming toward him.

Another bear? Oh, God, no!

Only it wasn't a bear, it was something brown and furry and bedraggled. The forest rang with a volley of growls and barks now.

A dog.

A dog?

A dog bounded out of the forest to Mark's right and hurled itself at the bear, its jaws open wide, its muzzle wrinkled back, teeth flashing. The bear fell back with a squeal of surprise.

Mark blinked. All of this had to be a hallucination because it was a famous television dog attacking the bear like a crazy wolf, a famous dog that looked for all the world like Fred Mac-Murray's dog Tramp on *My Three Sons*. Only this dog was wet and scruffy, a mat of knotted hair, as if it had traveled a long, long way up Spike Mountain, say, about thirty miles or so.

Beast.

The bear lunged at him but the Beast, tired and bedraggled or not, was too quick. Snarling and yapping, Beast went after the bear's hind legs, making it shuffle and dance. A huge paw swung

down in a blur but Beast dodged it and dived in again. The bear
seemed to have totally forgotten its plan to tear Mark to pieces and
was intent now on defending its own shins. Mark took another step
backward and his torn leg unhinged, nearly spilling him over.
Grimacing against the pain, he took off at a loping trot, aware that
his leg was not broken but that his foot didn't want to operate
properly. It squished wetly inside his boot and bright pain bolted
up his leg with each frantic step, but it didn't matter, nothing mattered at all except getting out while the getting was good.

He ran for five minutes before he dared to slow down. His
head was pounding and his breath whooped in and out of his
lungs. Long stripes of pain ran across his back where the bear's
claws had gotten him. The noise of the fight was a distant thing,
not so intense now. It was mostly Beast doing a lot of barking.

He bent over to look at his leg and the world went gray again.
His blue jeans were torn to tatters below the knee and it seemed
that his leg there had been plastered over with bleeding hamburger. The bear had done good work: red-white flecks of bone
dotted the wound like bloody salt. Mark had little doubt that in
another minute or so the bone would have been chewed through
and his leg would have been torn completely off. The pain was
a sharp steady throb. And it would get worse, he knew that much
about pain. In his life about the worst he had had to endure was
a deeply cut finger or a hammer-smashed thumb, and they hurt
like the dickens. This one made every pain he had ever experienced before seem like a chuckle in comparison. And it would
get worse, get so bad he would be screaming in agony. In a few
hours he would wish he were dead.

He straightened, aware that a fine mist of sweat had sprung
up on his forehead despite the cold. Beast was no longer barking;
the forest was silent but for the hissing wind. He saw that he
had been leaving a trail of blood in the snow; Mr. Bear could
follow that easily enough, if he wanted to. Wouldn't that be a
lovely prospect, having to face that bear again? Fear reached up
and gripped his heart, squeezing insistently. He would go mad
from fright if he saw that bear again. The damn thing wouldn't
have to touch him at all; he would simply keel over with his eyes
bulging and his brain shorting out like a bad fuse.

That would leave Linda and Jill and Ricky alone with no hope
of getting out. Mark wondered briefly if Glenn had bothered to
tell anyone besides John Phillips where they had gone. Mark
knew *he* hadn't, and neither had Linda. They'd simply told their

bosses they were taking a few days off. It would be days, maybe a week, before anyone got around to asking why they weren't back. It might be another week before concern grew to the point where people actually began looking for them. A lot could happen between now and then. A lot had already happened, and they'd only been up here a day and a half. What would the situation be in two weeks? Three weeks?

Something moved in the forest and Mark's heart seemed to freeze in his chest. He turned his head on a neck that creaked like an old hinge, sensing bear, seeming almost to smell it. But it was only Beast, snuffling along with his tail wagging. He saw Mark and bounded up, mad with joy.

"Beast," Mark said, bending slightly to ruffle his fur. Beast wriggled in ecstasy under his hand. "Beast old boy, how did you do it?"

Beast sniffed at his wounded leg. His tongue flashed out and licked at the exposed meat. Mark winced and pushed him away. "Careful, old buddy. I've got a little hurt there." He regarded Beast with almost fatherly affection. "How did you find us, boy? Did you see us drive past? Was that how? Man, you've got a hell of a sniffer."

"Woof," Beast allowed.

"Goddamn good dog. *Damn* good dog." Mark tickled his ears, smiling in spite of his pain. If Beast hadn't showed up he'd be dead. That simple. Perhaps there was a God in heaven who allowed small favors from time to time. What other explanation for this miracle?

"Let's go, boy," Mark said, and started back, following his own blood trail. His fear of the bear was as good as gone now with Beast by his side. Now there was the matter of finding the trees he had marked and following them back to the cabin. There he could get Linda to wash the bear spit out of his leg and bind it up with something, and then . . . and then . . .

And then what? Take a week or two to heal up and then try again? Send Linda or Jill down the mountain this time? What?

"Stay with me, Beast," he said.

"Woof," Beast answered.

They made their way back to the cabin together.

CHAPTER FOURTEEN

Ricky was sitting at the big square table where the books lay, his chin propped on his hands, wishing someone had thought to bring his Transformers coloring book and the big box of Crayolas with the sharpener in the back when they started out on this vacation yesterday morning. Having something to color would take his mind off things. Having something to color would help kill the butterflies that fluttered and flapped in the pit of his stomach. But there was nothing to do but sit and stare at Mommy standing by the window, or at Jill sitting on the bed with her face in her hands, or at the huge fireplace where a big stack of logs was burning so cheerily and casting orange dancing shadows on the rough walls of the big cabin. There was nothing to do but sit and listen to the shrieking wind outside and feel afraid and wonder why.

His fingers reached across the table and flipped idly at the pages of the big book, the Bible. It was bound in floppy black leather and had a purple tassel on a cord sticking out between the pages, somewhere near the middle. He played with the tassel, shook it a little, tried to make something interesting out of it. That grew tiresome in ten seconds. He thought about school, and what he was missing during this horrible vacation. Mrs. Penstock would expect a note of explanation from his parents when he got back, and he wondered what the note would say. Dear Mrs. Penstock: Please excuse little Ricky for his absence, he was taken on a vacation he didn't want to go on and wound up in a cabin he didn't want to be in. He was bored and scared.

He put his hand on the other book, one bound in stiff brown leather with gold lettering across the front. He opened it slightly and flipped through the pages. This one had a flat fabric marker in it with an angel blowing a long trumpet embossed on it. It hung out of the top of the book like a golden tongue. The book looked like it had been read a lot. The pages were crinkled and torn in places. In some spots passages had been underlined with thick pencil strokes. Ricky shut the book and sighed. This was no fun at all.

The third book presented possibilities, though. There was a fat pencil lying on top, which Ricky picked up. It was a funny pencil—no eraser on top, and made of plain unpainted wood. The lead was thick and blunt. Ricky stuck it over his ear and pulled the book toward him, opening it. The pages were blank, like the old diary Mommy kept in a shoe box in a closet at home.

Ricky flipped through the pages of this book. All blank. It smelled funny, all musty and old; nothing like Mommy's book, which was scented with a delicate perfumy fragrance. Here was something desperately in need of his artist's talent. He plucked the pencil off his ear, gnawed the tip for a moment, and flipped back to the first page. With sure, jagged strokes he sketched a crude Christmas tree that filled the entire page. He drew boxes underneath, which became presents. Circles became ornaments. A stick figure with no feet and large, two-fingered hands denoted a little boy in the throes of Christmas Day happiness. Ricky drew a star on top of the tree and sat back to regard his creation. Pretty good, all in all. Too bad no crayons were available to color it.

He began to place dots all over the tree to denote needles. Crisscrossing lines became popcorn strings. On one of the branches he drew an angel, copying it from the bookmark, long clarion trumpet and all. When that was done he sat back again, chewing the pencil, trying to decide what kind of picture to draw on the next page. This one looked neat and complete. When Daddy got back Ricky would show it to him and get the customary "That's great, Ricko" before Daddy turned to other business and forgot about it. Maybe if he got back and saw that Ricky had managed to fill every single page of this little blank book he would be more impressed than usual. It was something to do, anyway. But what to draw? Monsters were always fun, but the last thing he wanted to see right now was anything remotely scary—and the Christmas tree wasn't all that cool, considering what had happened.

He placed his hand loosely on the page with the tree, poised the pencil, and added a few dots. Perhaps he could draw a house on the next page, a house heaped with snow and with reindeer

on the roof. Or just Santa Claus with a big fat bag over his
shoulder, except that Santa Claus always came out looking like
a stick figure like all the others.

He added rays to the star to make it shine. Then more dots to
the tree. It was a regular dot-to-dot now. Idly, he connected a
few of the dots with lines. This ruined the picture—almost—
until he decided these lines were strings of tinsel. Now the tree
was becoming quite a work of art. The pencil seemed to have a
talent of its own, for now it was making lines and squiggles
while his hand tagged along. The pencil jittered in his fingers,
drawing lines and connectors and dots. Some of them went outside the tree altogether, making a ruin of the picture. Ricky
clenched his hand around the pencil hard enough to make his
fingers hurt, but it just kept on moving, making small block
letters now, writing things of its own accord. The butterflies in
his stomach wheeled and flapped, excited, turning his belly into
a crawling, tickling pit. The pencil wrote and Ricky's hand went
along for the ride, frozen to it by muscles that wouldn't unclench
anymore. His eyes grew wide in his face. Out of the jumble of
crude letters forming on the page, words that even a six-year-
old could read were beginning to take shape like the face of a
puzzle when the pieces are joined together. Ricky leaned over
the page and the skittering pencil, wondering what magic was
causing him to write when he should have been drawing tinsel,
filled with both wondering dread and curiosity, suddenly afraid
his mother might look away from the window and see him doing
this weird and wonderful thing, or that Jill might look over and
let out another one of her awful screams. He curled his left arm
around the book to hide it, and read between the lines of his
drawing.

TU SDAY MARC 10 1896 T DAY A COYOT
CHASE THE HORSES OFF O PRECI US JESUS
WE WILL SURV VE WIT YOUR HELP SAT RDAY
MA CH 14 189 TRIED T GET ELP WAS
BITTEN BY A BEAR TH NK Y U JESU LORD FOR
OUR DOG HO SAVED M BUT WHAT
SHAL WE EAT WE ARE S ARVING

The pencil was busily filling in the missing letters, making
the words complete. Ricky grabbed it with his other hand and
dragged it toward his chest, making a jagged lightning bolt down

he page. The top half of the pencil broke off with a snap and
e was left with a piece in each hand.

Linda turned at the sound. "What are you doing, Ricky?"

He looked up, guilty and confused, hiding his hands under
he table. "Just drawing."

She frowned. Her face looked drawn and haggard, the face of
omeone growing old very fast. "Don't mess with other people's
hings, Ricky," she said, and turned back to the window.

Ricky laid the two pencil halves on the table beside the book
nd closed it softly. That smell blew into his nostrils again, the
roma of old books left in some damp sunless place to rot. All
f these books smelled that way. Ricky wrinkled his nose and
ushed them away. They were no fun at all. They were, in fact,
cary. Especially the blank one.

He looked around for something to do, saw nothing more
xciting than his mother and Jill and the pots and pans and
tensils hanging on pegs to his right, and felt his eyes drawing
ack to that little black book with the blank pages. He had
nessed with someone else's things and wound up breaking their
encil. When they came back they might be plenty mad about
t. But somehow he knew they, whoever they were, wouldn't be
oming back. Hadn't his mother said they got out when the storm
it? Maybe there was no one left on this bleak and lonely moun-
ain but Mommy and Daddy and Jill now. And Glenn, up in the
rees, dead.

That thought blew a cold draft of fear down his spine. His
omprehension of death was limited but served him well enough.
Being dead meant you went away and never came back. Being
lead meant they put you in a long shiny box with two lids on it
nd people sat around crying for you. And then they buried you
nderground forever and kept on crying the way Jill kept on
rying for Robin. And for Glenn, now. Poor Jill. For her there
vas nobody left.

He stared at the book. It lay just beyond the reach of his hand.

"Oh, Glenn," Jill moaned, and Ricky looked over at her. She
vas sitting all clenched up with her head in her hands. Her hair
tuck out in spikes between her fingers. She was rocking back
nd forth, making the bed she was sitting on creak. Ricky caught
glimpse of her eyes, all puffy and red. Her face was pasty
vhite. Ricky liked Jill because she was a great cookie and cake
aker, and in the old days before Robin skateboarded to her
leath they used to come in after a hard afternoon of play and

pig out on chocolate chip cookies and thick slices of devil's food
cake. Jill kept a Kool-Aid pitcher with a smiley face on it in her
refrigerator at home and you can bet that pitcher was always full
of Kool-Aid, yes it was. Jill was pert and pretty and treated kids
like they ought to be treated—with food and smiles.

But now she was ugly. She looked like a witch out of somebody's bedtime book. Ricky looked away from her and the hag
she had become, and stared at the book that lay just beyond the
reach of his hand. Something about it, something familiar. That
book belonged to someone else, but somehow someone that he
knew, or had known.

The book gave a little jump, all by itself. Ricky blinked. The
book slid across the table with a quick rasping sound and bumped
against his knuckles. He jerked his hand away, stifling the yell
that leaped up into his mouth. The pencil halves were rolling
after the book, bumping and jostling each other. They jumped
up atop the book and the jagged broken ends slid around until
they had joined together. It was just one pencil now with a tiny
healed scar zigzagging down the middle.

Ricky picked the pencil up and the book opened itself. The
pages made small ruffling sounds as they flipped back and forth.
After a second the Christmas tree with the writing across it lay
exposed again, only the tree was dimmer now, as if someone
had tried to erase it. The boxes under the tree and the stick
figure boy were gone entirely. The musty smell of the book
mushroomed out in a cloud.

His hand was pulled down to the second page.

The pencil began to write again.

WEDNESDAY MARCH 18 1896 TRAPPED AND
STARVING TWELVE DAYS NOW WE TRUST IN THE
LORD JESUS FOR HE HATH PROMISED GLORY TO
THE FAITHFUL

Hunger leaped into Ricky's belly in a sudden driving spasm,
pushing the breath from his lungs and doubling him over. The
pencil flew from his hand and rolled across the table. The book
fell solidly shut just as Linda looked over again.

"Ricky?"

With an effort of will he straightened and put a semblance of
a smile on his face. There were secret things going on here,
things no one else should know about.

"I'm okay, Mommy," he said. "Just a little hungry."

She came to him and knelt by the chair, put her hands on the small roundness of his shoulders, and pulled him close. "We all are, honey," she said. "We all are."

"Is Daddy bringing groceries back?"

She pulled away and looked at him, smiling in a bemused but worried way. There were dark hollows under her cheekbones, Ricky noticed. And her eyes seemed to have sunk in their sockets a little too deep. She looked like somebody who needed some food pretty fast. But hadn't it only been a little while since everybody had eaten? Hadn't it? And didn't Mommy look a lot thinner than she had yesterday? Ricky searched his mind and came up with a mental picture of his father as he had looked when he left the cabin an hour or so ago, his bright blue coat zipped up all the way to his chin and his hair a wild snowy tangle. His face had been thinner, too, but that might have just been from the worry. But hadn't his coat hung a little looser on his shoulders than normal? Weren't his blue jeans just a little baggier, a little flappier around the thighs? And Jill—wasn't she just the slightest bit skinnier now, too?

He decided it was the wild run through the forest that had done it to them. Exercise makes you lose weight. That's why people jogged and went on diets. Thing was, Ricky had no idea it worked so fast. Why were there so many fat people in the world when a short jaunt through the woods and a day without food could make you noticeably thinner? If this kept up, why, they would all look like those Africans in the desert on TV, the ones his daddy called the Bone People because they were nothing but walking skeletons.

"Your daddy went to get help," Linda said, and stood up again.

"I hope he finds some fast," Ricky said, and shuddered. A couple more days like this and they would be Bone People. A week or so like this and they would be . . . Dead People. Yuck. But no, none of that would happen. Daddy would be back soon and everything would be all right. Everything in storybooks ended happily and everything in real life did, too. Even Glenn would be all right as soon as help got here. He just needed an ambulance.

"Hang in there," Linda said, and went back to the window.

"I'll be okay," Ricky said, folding his hands on the table.

Slowly, sneakily, the little black book slid across the tabl
toward him.

"Leave me alone," he whispered to it.

The pencil rolled over and nudged the little finger of his righ
hand. He turned his nose up and ignored it.

The wind outside snarled and howled.

Jill Pruett was losing her mind.

She had been born the daughter of Jack and Mary Chambers
a bright and pretty girl in a well-to-do family who happened t
live in a small town on the Oregon-Idaho border called Ontaric
Jack was one of the founders of a company called Lami-Tech
which started out as a one-horse operation manufacturing lami
nated wood products and grew, over the space of twenty-fiv
years, to one of the major corporations in little Ontario. Jill
life had consisted of church every Sunday and Wednesday, wher
she was indoctrinated good and well into the Mormon faith, an
of school, where she always did better than average work. Sh
was a cheerleader. She was a Thespian and an active participar
in Glee Club. She dated good-looking boys and always kept thei
hands at bay. She saved herself for marriage, got married, an
moved to Salt Lake City. There was nothing truly remarkable i
her upper-middle-class life at all save for her weirdo brothe
Eddie. Now, at thirty-two, she was the mother of a dead child
and a widow. And she was, at this moment, losing her grip o
sanity.

Something was pressing her stomach. She recognized it dull
as the need to urinate. That information was transmitte
throughout her brain, seeking a response. There was nothin
there to receive it but synapses shorted out by grief, and shock
and horror. The monstrous blow of finding her daughter dea
on the sidewalk in front of her home six days ago had bee
superseded by the even more monstrous blow of seeing her hus
band torn to pieces in a pine tree.

But of course none of that had really happened.

She was Jill Pruett, the mother of Robin, the wife of Glenn
Nothing would ever change that. Robin was not dead and neithe
was Glenn. It was all a horrible, even comical, mistake. Some
one had erred because there was a God in heaven and he did no
allow such atrocities to occur to his children. All her life Jill ha
been taught that a merciful God sits on a mighty throne in Heave
and dictates the course of individual lives. For God to have dic

tated this course for her was unthinkable. Ridiculous. Funny,
when you got right down to it.

She began to giggle. She was only dimly aware of her friend
Linda Butler over by the window staring at her with shocked
amazement, and of Linda's little boy Ricky over in a chair at
the table. She was only dimly aware of this because she was not
here in some forsaken mountain cabin with a dead husband stuck
up in a tree, she was in actuality at home waiting for Robin to
come home from school and Glenn to come home from his office. None of the things her senses offered up to her was real.
She stood up, giggling, realizing that if she didn't find her way
to the bathroom soon she would wet her pants.

She made her way to the door. Linda said something but it
didn't register. Linda put her hands on her arm but it didn't
register. Jill pulled away with a clumsy exaggerated twist and
fumbled for the doorknob. Linda was saying things in a pleading
voice that didn't make any sense at all. Jill simply needed to go
to the bathroom and this was the bathroom door.

"I have to use the bathroom," she stated flatly, with a little
irritation, and that seemed to satisfy her bothersome neighbor.
Why Linda would want to keep her from going into her own
bathroom was a mystery she would have to ponder later. She
pulled the door open and stepped out into the snowy twilight,
nearly stumbling down the sudden low step to the ground. The
wind tore at her clothes and hair but went unnoticed.

"There's probably an outhouse out back," Linda called behind her before shutting the door against the wind.

Jill shook her head in bewildered wonder. What in the world
was Linda talking about? Was the poor girl losing her mind?

She stumbled through the snow, looking for the toilet. Now,
something was definitely odd here. This was like being in a
dream, wandering around in a cold world of shapes and shadows, looking for something misplaced. The toilet was misplaced, as well as other things. Where was the sink, the bathrug,
the towel rack with the His and Hers towels hanging neatly folded
across the chrome bar? Was this one of those I-have-to-go-to-
the-bathroom dreams where you get up, walk to the bathroom,
do your business, and then wake up to find it was all in your
mind, thankful at least that you didn't wet the bed?

Jill walked in a large circle around the cabin, beginning to
weep a little now out of frustration. She needed to wake up out
of this howling, freezing dream. Dream snow stung her face and

eyes. Dream trees swayed overhead as dream wind rushed between the branches with a noise like distant dreamy freight trains. Everything was jumbled and crazy. She stumbled past the door again and Linda stepped out.

"Isn't there one back there?" she asked, her voice rising to compete with the hurricane noise of the wind. It was very nearly necessary to scream.

Jill could only weep in reply. Her hair blew wildly and wisps of it stuck to her wet cheeks.

"Come on, honey," Linda said, and took her arm. They walked around to the back of the cabin and there, a few yards away, stood a tall narrow box of an outhouse made of rough-hewn boards peppered with knotholes and cracks. Jill had passed it without seeing, or perhaps it had not been in the jumbly world of her dream until now. "In there," Linda said, pointing. "Do you understand?"

Jill nodded. The dream was fragmenting itself back into reality. It was cold and her hair was full of snow. Icy fingers of wind were pushing through her clothes. Robin was dead and so was Glenn. The world was all black and gray, endless night.

"Will you be all right now?" Linda asked.

Jill nodded, but it was a lie. She would never be all right again. Her family was dead and God was a cackling monster in a black and murderous heaven. Perhaps if she had gone to church more faithfully things would have been different, but there never seemed to be time anymore. Now it was too late. She had incurred his wrath. *I am a vengeful God,* he had said once to one of his prophets. How utterly true that seemed to be.

"Are you sure?"

"Sure," Jill croaked.

"Okay, then." Linda squeezed her arm briefly, turned, and went back around the cabin.

Jill opened the flimsy wooden door of the outhouse and looked inside. Snow had been driven through the cracks and holes in the walls and was settled in shallow piles across the board that served as the toilet seat. The opening in the board was a chopped-out black hole. All manner of creepy crawly things could be lurking underneath, bats or spiders or bees, but it didn't matter because Robin and Glenn were dead and no horror from the damp swampy depths of an outhouse could match that. Besides, it was winter and the filth would be frozen. It didn't even smell bad.

She stepped inside and hoisted her coat to unbuckle her belt. The door gusted shut on rusty hinges and she was left in darkness with the wind moaning and whistling through the cracks in the walls. Jill looked around, aware that her eyes felt hot and puffy and that this outhouse was like a dark refrigerator inside. And there was a smell in here now that the door was shut and the wind wasn't blowing through so strong, the stench of rot and decay drifting up from the hole. She worked her pants down and lowered herself gingerly onto the board, wincing. Weak light from the knotholes dappled her face and the pale whiteness of her thighs. Why oh why, she wondered, had Glenn loved the rough life of the outdoors so much? It was all bother and hassle. And in the end it had killed him.

Something moved in the cold depths beneath her. Ice broke with a brittle crunch as if something heavy had shifted. Jill jumped to her feet, thinking of animals that creep into dark places to hide. She pushed the door open with her pants still around her knees, her eyes wide and terrified, and took a waddling step outside. For the first time in six days she was no longer worried about Robin or Glenn or anything connected with the past at all. Something was moving in the dark cesspool under the outhouse.

"There are worse places, dearie," someone said in a small hissing voice that drifted out from the hole. Jill turned, unconsciously pulling her pants up. Something was rising out of the hole in the board, some round thing like a hairy white balloon. Jill recognized with dim, swooning terror that it was a woman's head. Bits of ice and filth were stuck in her hair.

"Worse places than this," she said. Now her head had risen three feet out of the hole on an incredibly long stalk of a neck. Fat winter beetles moved sluggishly on her face. "Worse places than this in this world," she said.

Jill moaned, shaking her head slowly back and forth in unspoken denial. The woman put small bony hands on the rim of the hole and pulled herself up. Her neck was three feet long and her head swayed atop it like some grisly voodoo trophy. The smell of rot and excrement rose up with her. Her long back dress was smeared with slime and clung to the bones of her legs as she clambered out. She was wearing a decaying black shawl. Her heavy grandma's shoes clunked on the board, leaving smeared tracks.

"Worse sins than murder," she hissed, and lunged at Jill, who fell backward with her arms thrust out. The woman fell atop her with cold fingers clawing at the warm flesh of her throat. The tube of her neck snapped down across Jill's face, blocking her sight and filling her nostrils with the putrid stench of winter's slow decay. Jill struggled beneath her, getting handfuls of cloth and flesh that tore free with sickening, greasy ease. She tried to scream but the woman's cold questing thumbs had found her windpipe and were pressing it insistently shut.

"It's not so bad being dead," the woman said in her buzzing, reedy voice. Her hands were icy clamps, her body soggy dead weight. Jill bucked and reared, growing light-headed, suffused with panic and mad terror. Her feet scattered snow and black earth. Colored pinpoints of light began to flash and sparkle across the dark field of her vision, growing brighter, moving faster. The need to breathe became consuming, overpowering. She arched her back, thinking wildly of Glenn, Glenn who would come to save her if only he weren't dead.

The colored lights began to fade. Warmth spread in slow waves from her throat to her scalp. A distant and remotely pleasurable noise began to whine in her ears. She thought of Robin, dead with her head turned backward. She thought of Glenn one final time, and then her hands unclenched and fell away from the thing that was lying on her. Her fingers dug themselves into the snow and were still. Her knees relaxed and dropped slowly to the ground.

"Forgiveness will be mine," the woman on top of her said. Her head rose up on its elongated neck. The pasty, bloated face grinned. The wind caught her dress and ballooned it upward, revealing rotted yellow petticoats.

"Now," the woman said.

The dress fell in on itself, empty. It settled on Jill, a black shroud. After a moment the wind picked it up and hoisted it skyward, where it floated away like a dark pinwheel to be deposited in the trees some distance away.

Jill stirred in the snow. She sat up and brushed herself off. Her face, which had been purple in death, assumed its normal color.

"At last," she breathed.

She got up and walked around the cabin and went inside. Linda met her at the door, her face drawn from too much worry, her eyes bright and questioning.

"So cold out there," Jill said.

"Poor thing," Linda said, and hugged her. Jill hugged back. Her eyes went over to Ricky at the table, and over Linda's shoulder she smiled wickedly at him. He smiled back uncertainly.

"I think I'd better use that rest room, too," Linda said, releasing her. "Will you watch for Mark?"

"Mark?" Jill frowned, then nodded. "Of course, dearie. You go on ahead."

Linda looked at her strangely, then shrugged to herself. She opened the door to a blast of wind and went out. The door slammed shut. Jill stood regarding Ricky, beaming at him. She crossed the room and bent over him.

"Welcome home," she whispered in his face.

He drew away, wrinkling his nose.

"Rest," she said. "Rest, and forgiveness. It's been a long time, hasn't it?"

"Jill?" Ricky said. "Jill, are you okay?"

She kissed him on the mouth. He jerked back so hard the chair he was sitting on scooted across the floor with a harsh squeak. Jill grinned, testing her lips with her tongue, her eyes wide and bright.

"My, you taste good," she said, and then her face fell together and she burst into tears.

Ricky decided she was nuts.

Mark made it back an hour later, practically on his hands and knees as he had feared, hobbling through the drifting snow with Beast by his side. His right leg was a steady throbbing agony and there were stripes of fire across his back. Footprints of blood lay in the snow behind him, big crimson dollops that had squished up out of his boot and run down his heel and the tatters of his pants leg in scarlet streamers. He estimated he had lost about two pints. He was limp and exhausted and freezing. But he was back, and that at least meant warmth and a place to lie down. He was fighting his way through the briars that encircled the clearing around the cabin when the door flew open and Linda rushed out.

"Mark!" she cried, slipping and sliding her way through the snow toward him.

He stopped, standing on his good foot with his arms waving for balance, never so glad to see someone in his life. She pushed through the brambles and slid up under his arm for support, her face ghost-white. "What happened?"

"Bear," he said, grateful to be leaning on someone warm and alive. "Grizzly."

"Up here?" She helped him forward, pushing briars away from his injured leg. "There aren't any bears up here."

"Should have seen that one. Mmm. Big one. Yeah." He was aware that he was becoming shocky the way Glenn had become shocky; everything was taking on a shiny plastic sheen of unreality. The cabin looming before him seemed inordinately small and distant, the field of snow around it unusually bright and sparkling. The sound of the wind rushing in his ears was a pleasant low drone, something he could listen to forever. Anything to drown out the piglike squeals and bellowing roars of that bear that seemed to echo again and again in his head. He squeezed his eyes shut and shook his head. No sense slipping into the warm and falsely pleasant world of shock. There was too much reality to be faced here.

They came to the cabin, Mark hopping on his good leg that was heavy and shaking with fatigue, Linda grunting as he lurched against her. Blood spilled down his foot, making red holes in the snow. Jill stood at the doorway watching and there was Ricky behind her, his dark eyes seeming to fill his face, which was small and drawn.

"Daddy," he said, "where'd you find Robin's doggie?"

"He found me, Rick." Mark took the step up with what seemed to be the last strength in his leg, and forced himself to make the last few steps to the nearest bed. Ricky picked up the pillow Jill had thrown on the floor and pushed it under Mark's head as he lay down on his side, then smoothed his hand over Mark's hair.

"What happened, Daddy?"

Mark draped an arm across his forehead, groaning with the pleasure of being off his feet. "A big bad bear got me," he said. The walk back had seemed like twenty miles, though it couldn't have been more than one. So much for the rescue mission.

And what about those trees, Mark old boy? Forgotten about them?

No, he hadn't forgotten. Impossible trees and an impossible bear. A monster snowstorm and endless twilight. Glenn dead and his own leg mangled beyond apparent repair. Mother nature gone berserk up here on Spike Mountain, the vacationer's paradise.

Watch out for the bitch, Mark. Glenn had said that. Is that what he meant, watch out for some old bitch-bear that'll try and tear your leg off? Did he know about the grizzlies on Spike? Or had he meant something else?

"You'll be fine," Jill said. She was standing at the foot of the bed, smiling down at him, while Beast sniffed up and down her leg. Mark decided she must be out of her senses with grief. She hadn't even noticed that the dog he was supposed to have shot was back from the dead. And she looked so placid and composed now, though her eyes were a bit puffy from crying. Once again he felt that crazy surge of love for her, stronger now than ever before. She was one hell of a brave woman.

And just what are you thinking about? Glenn's dead, you've just survived being eaten by a bear through some miracle, and still you lust after his wife. Just who's out of his senses here?

He dropped his arm, took Ricky's hand, and squeezed it. "Don't look so worried, Ricky Ricardo. I'll heal up. Then we'll get the hell out of here." His eyes caught Linda's and held them. There were so many things to see there—fear, worry, doubt, but above all, perhaps, the desperate glistening sheen of hunger. She even looked somehow gaunt and shrunken. Mark's own belly was a bottomless chasm shouting to be filled despite the hammering pain in his leg and the roaring gouges on his back.

"What should we do?" Linda asked, hovering over him. She lifted his torn pants leg and grimaced, then peeked over at his back. "Mark, you're torn to bits."

"Well stated, nurse," Mark retorted and offered her a weak smile. "Just put me back together as well as you can."

"And then what?" She scrubbed her face with her hands. "We can't just stay here with you like this. You need a hospital. We need food." Her voice was rising into the high whining tones of despair. "We'll never get down now. We'll just be stuck up here forever. If there's a bear out there none of us can walk out!"

"Steady now," Jill said, putting a hand on her shoulder. "We can't go losing our heads. Mark's bleeding and we have to get it stopped. We'll worry about that first and the rest later. Everything will be fine."

"Will it?" Linda's face screwed up and she began to cry. "Nothing has been fine so far. This whole trip has been a nightmare."

"Everything has a purpose, dearie," Jill said.

Mark glanced at her. Her face was set and peaceful. It oc-

curred to him that she had undergone a remarkable transforma-
tion in the last few hours. Maybe it wasn't the shock of grief,
then. Maybe the real Jill was surfacing, a strong and purposeful
Jill, a woman made of sterner stuff than he ever could have
imagined. It was a Jill he could love forever.

"We need boiling water," Jill said, and indicated the pot
hanging from the tripod by the fireplace. "We'll wash out the
wound and bandage it up. The claw wounds on his back aren't
deep and will heal without trouble. It's the leg we have to con-
centrate on."

"Right," Linda said, sounding dazed.

"So take that pot and fill it with snow. I'll tear a sheet into
bandages. Then we just have to settle in and wait."

"Wait? For what? Don't you see how impossible—"

"For him to heal," Jill snapped. "Time passes quickly on
Spike Mountain. Everything will be fine."

Linda opened her mouth as if to say more; Mark waved a
hand indicating she should do as she was told. If Jill was to be
in charge of this doomed little troupe now, then so be it. He was
more than glad to unshoulder this burden and pass it on. Frowning, Linda went to the fireplace and unhooked the pot from its
chain. It was big and soot-blackened; grunting, she carried it
outside.

"She'll do fine," Jill said, bending over Mark and adjusting
his pillow. He noticed bruises on her neck that were beginning
to purple, but passed it off as his fault; he had probably bashed
her neck against a small tree during the run through the woods
when he had carried her, unconscious, to this cabin. That had
been barely two hours ago but already it seemed far away and
nearly forgotten, as if it had occurred days and days ago and
was no longer remarkable enough to be remembered. But that
had to be one of the symptoms of shock, no doubt; the patient
believes that days are passing instead of hours. Or maybe it was
because of the endless twilight outside and the storm that seemed
to have been raging now for weeks and weeks instead of one
day. In any event, for Mark time was losing its perspective. He
felt drowsy and vaguely confused.

"You'll do fine, too," Jill said, and kissed him lightly on the
cheek.

He began to drift off, letting the pleasant unreality of shock
and warped time take his mind and carry it away and away to a
dreamless stupor.

• • •

The pot seemed to weigh fifty pounds.

It was a big round-bottomed affair with a heavy curled rim and a big hoop of a wire handle. Lugging it with both hands, Linda struggled through the snow to a deep drift at the western side of the cabin and dragged the pot through it. The wind tugged at her clothes and hair and blew powdery ice crystals like sand into her face. She wondered what had come over Jill all of a sudden, how she could go from being a weeping wreck one moment to the take-charge matron she had become the next. But it didn't matter, really. Her husband was dead and Mark seemed to be the next on the list. Linda had never seen such wounds in her life. And Mark was being remarkably brave about it. Somehow she had secretly suspected that Mark was not the kind of man who could endure much pain, but so much for that idea. Perhaps it was turning out that the weakest person among them was Linda Butler, who had been too weak and squeamish even to go to a little girl's funeral, her best friend's daughter's funeral.

She set the pot upright and used her hands to shovel snow inside. It was so cold it hurt but it had to be done. She shivered as she worked, not wanting to be outside alone anymore. She looked around, her eyes wide and wary, her breath steaming out of her nose in tattering wisps and her hair blowing into her face. There were worse things than trees up here. Now there were bears.

"Worse things than that," a high reedy voice said from inside the pot.

"What?" Linda replied automatically.

"Worse things," the voice said. A bony hand wormed up out of the pot, pushing snow aside. Snowy fingers snapped at the air and settled on the heavy rim. Another hand pushed up, weaving like a snake in a basket. It caught hold of the rim on the other side and the pot wobbled in the snow.

"Jesus," Linda whispered.

A woman's head poked up between the hands. Snow cascaded down her hair. "Worse things," she said with slow and terrible sagacity. Her yellow, bleary eyes rolled in their sockets. Her paper-white skin was cracked and peeling like old paint. She grinned at Linda and pulled herself up. "Worse things in this world."

Linda staggered back as the woman came fully out. She was wearing a long black dress that the wind pressed hard against her body. She was little more than a skeleton. She bent and picked up the pot by its wire handle.

"Forgive me," she said, and swung the pot as if it were weightless. It caught Linda behind the left ear with a hollow bong and flung her sideways into the deeper snow beside the cabin.

For Linda there were no last thoughts. Just brief pain and blackness.

And when she got up again, she was grinning.

CHAPTER FIFTEEN

Ralph and Madge Pickens lived in a rusting MobilDream trailer at lot 17 of the Ranchero Mobile Home Park in the southern outskirts of Tremonton. The trailer was nothing to brag about but it was a rental anyway and someday, when enough money had been saved from Ralph's job as assistant manager of the local Timberland lumberyard, they would be able to buy a real house and move out of this dump forever. But for now this was home to Ralph and Madge and little Tony, and it was here that they brought Eddie Chambers in order to fix him up.

Ralph pulled the truck into the gravel parking space beside the trailer and stopped. Dust blew by in a cloud, scattering across the neighboring yard where Rolando Garcia, the Pickens' neighbor for the last two years, sat in a ruined lawn chair slugging down Olympia beer while his five children played noisily around him. In the summer Rolando worked in the beet fields with the migrants and in the winter and spring he stayed home and drank beer while his wife worked in the Tremonton McDonald's slinging hamburgers. Now he stood up and ambled over. "I thought you was going three-wheeling today," he said in a vague but pleasant Mexican accent.

"My first Friday afternoon off in six months and I thought we were, too," Ralph said, getting out and slamming the door. "We found a bum out in the desert."

Rolando peeked over into the bed of the truck. He wrinkled his nose. "Woo-ee. Stinky fucker."

"Pretty bad shape," Ralph said.

Madge got out with Tony on her arm and they stood beside the truck looking down at their prize. Rolando's kids came over in a pack and clambered up, jabbering and laughing. "What you going to do with him?" Rolando asked.

227

"Clean him up and send him on his way, I guess. Couldn't hardly leave him out there to die."

"Hippie-looking bastard, isn't he? Let's cut his balls off."

"Oh, Rolando," Madge said. "You're so mean sometimes."

"Me?" He drained his beer, belched, and tossed the bottle over into his yard. "Hey, little compadre," he said, taking Tony's hand, "can you say bum? Can you say wino?"

"Ca-ca," Tony said proudly.

"Damn right, ca-ca. This guy's covered with it."

Ralph took his hat off and passed a forearm over his face. "Help me get the guy inside, will you? It's roasting out here."

"Not much better inside, man. Just toss him in the yard and I'll piss on him. That'll wake him up."

"I think a bath would do better. Come on."

"I ain't touching no fleabag bum. He might have AIDS."

"Oh," Madge blurted. "Ralph, I never thought of that."

Ralph put his hat back on. "Would you two stop acting like he's death itself? Give me a hand."

"The things I do to be a good neighbor," Rolando grunted, and leaned over into the truck. "I'll take the fucker's feet. Worst I can get is athlete's foot, I guess."

They carried him across the yard into the trailer. Madge held the door while they maneuvered him inside and down the narrow hallway to the bathroom. Flies buzzed in the somnolent heat, and already it was just hot enough inside to be unbearable. Going to be a bad summer, Ralph thought as they deposited Eddie in the rust-stained, chipped bathtub. Going to be one hell of a bad summer.

"Going to drown his ass, eh?" Rolando said.

"Just enough to wake him up." Ralph sat on the edge of the tub and turned the water on. Madge stood at the doorway holding Tony, who was watching everything with an infant's studious gaze.

"Baf," he pronounced solemnly.

"Yes, bath," Madge said. "We're giving him a bath."

Rolando grinned. "Now might be a good time to cut the bastard's hair off. I'll do his balls, you do his hair." He laughed uproariously at this.

"Thanks for the help," Ralph said.

"Anytime, anytime." He edged past Madge, still grinning. "Nail his nuts to the front door and you'd have a hell of a doorbell, don't you know. Every time somebody pushed on them this

dude would scream. Aaiieee!'' He clapped his hands to his crotch
and performed a little dance. ''Aaiieee! Aaiieee!''

''So long,'' Ralph said.

''Aaiieee,'' Rolando shrieked, going down the hall. ''Wahoo!
Yowee!'' The front door slapped shut and they could hear him
out in the yard, laughing and screaming.

''He's so cruel sometimes,'' Madge said.

''Just full of bullshit.'' Ralph eyed the tide of water that was
rising in the tub. Eddie's hair floated on it like dead seaweed.
The stench of vomit and excrement in the little bathroom was
thick and cheesy. ''Madge, get me a cup. I'll get some water in
him.''

She left and returned with a plastic mug. ''I'll boil it later,''
she said.

Ralph held it under the faucet. ''Lift his head for a minute.''

Madge put Tony down and hoisted Eddie's head upright by
the wet ropes of his hair. His jaw hinged open and they could
see his tongue, a brown and swollen lump. Ralph poured some
water in his mouth and it all drooled out. ''Never seen anybody
quite this far gone,'' Ralph said. He filled the cup again and
dumped the water over Eddie's head.

''We should have taken him to hospital,'' Madge said. ''He
might be dying.''

''He'll snap out of it. Tip his head back.''

He dumped a cupful in Eddie's face. This time Eddie spluttered and retched. Ralph got more water and poured it into his
mouth. Eddie's tongue moved weakly as he tried to swallow.

''Now we're getting somewhere.''

Eddie's hands came up and wrapped themselves around the
cup. He shifted in the tub, which was half full of water that had
gone black. Ralph reached over and turned the faucet down to
its normal steady drip. ''Let him go,'' he said.

Madge let go of his hair. His head fell back and disappeared
under the water. Bubbles rose up, gurgling. The cup fell from
his hands and floated off.

''It's now or never,'' Ralph said.

The bubbles stopped. Ralph and Madge looked at each other
and shrugged. ''I guess he's drowning,'' Ralph said, and chuckled.

''Oh, you.'' Madge reached into the water and pulled his head
out. Eddie's eyes came open and swiveled mindlessly in their

sockets. He wrenched his mouth open and screamed loud enough
to rattle the loose mirror in the vanity.

"A sign of life," Ralph said, rubbing his ears with his knuckles.

"Jill," Eddie croaked. His eyes fell shut and he went limp.

"Dunk him," Ralph said.

Madge dunked him. He squirmed under water, blowing bubbles. She pulled his head back out and he screamed again.

"Life's a bitch sometimes," Ralph said. "Hey, partner, snap
out of it." He reached out and slapped Eddie lightly on the
cheek. "Come on, flower child. Make our day."

Eddie sat up and rubbed his face, blinking. Madge let go of
his hair and reached for a towel, grimacing. "Water," Eddie
gasped.

"Water it is." Ralph got the cup and refilled it from the tap,
then guided it into Eddie's shaking hands. He drank it down and
let the cup fall into the water. "Oof," he said.

"You going to make it now, friend?" Ralph asked.

Eddie leaned toward him, belched, and threw up in his lap.

"Nice touch," Ralph growled. "Madge, hand me that towel."

She handed it over. Ralph dried himself off, glad that it was
only water and not more of the stuff that was floating in the tub.
When he was done he handed the towel back, which Madge
accepted with two fingers and dropped into the sink.

"Feeling better?" he asked.

Eddie nodded. His head wobbled like a plate on a stick. He
tried to stand, grappling at the loose tiles on the wall, but his
legs buckled and he splashed back down. "One step at a time,"
Ralph said. "First you wash off, then you can get out."

"No," Eddie said. "I have to—I have to—"

"You have to wash off, my man. Can't you smell yourself?
You been out in the desert for who knows how long, laying in
your own shit and piss."

"It was forever," Eddie said. "A million forevers." He
touched his shaking fingers to his face. "I hurt."

"Nasty sunburn. I'd say you been out there two, maybe three
days. Must have been one hell of a party."

"Oh," Eddie said. "Oh, God."

Ralph turned to Madge. "I'm going to shinny him out of his
clothes, babe. Care to step outside? Or do you want to see the
show?"

"That I can live without," she said. She left, shutting the door.

"Okay, strip down," Ralph said. "I'll drain this garbage out."

Eddie looked around with wide, puffy eyes. "I gotta get out of here."

"First you hose off."

"No, listen." Eddie stood up, clutching the walls for support. Water sluiced down his clothes. Ralph rose up with him and pushed him back down.

"Listen, hell. You listen. You can't slosh your way through my house with all this crud hanging off you. Now, get undressed."

"Something bad's happening," Eddie said. He ran his hands over his hair, squeezing out water. "On a mountain. Spear? Pike? What was it? She told me."

"Clothes off," Ralph commanded.

"Pike. Okay, yeah." He was breathing fast, wheezing like an asthmatic. "I saw it, see. I mean, I've been there. Robin showed me. I know what's happening."

"Now," Ralph said.

Eddie stood up, pushing Ralph's hands away. "I've got to go there. It's up to me."

Ralph stepped back to regard him. It was a pity, really, such a young guy all strung out on God knew what, or totally insane, or alcoholic, whatever. A young dude about his own age, totally ruined, useless to anybody. "So something bad is happening on Pikes Peak, right? And you have to get there, right? It's such a goddamn emergency you don't have time to wash the shit off your clothes. How the hell do you expect to get to Pikes Peak all burnt up and dried out? It's a long walk, my friend."

Eddie stepped out of the tub, pooling water on the floor. "Pikes Peak? Is that it?" He rubbed his hands together, looking worried and sick. "My sister's there. And—other people. Other things. Bad things."

"Get back in that bathtub," Ralph said. He was twice the size of this skinny weirdo and if it came down to it he would muscle him back into the water, pathetic misfit or not.

"Don't you understand?" Eddie cried. "I saw it all. I felt it all. It's been over a hundred years but time doesn't matter. *They're still alive if I hurry!*"

"Who is?" Ralph shouted. He didn't intend to get angry but

this whole day was turning out to be a pain in the ass. "Who' still alive if you hurry?"

"I don't know," Eddie said miserably. "Strangers. And—my sister. But it's too late for her, isn't it? Too late for Jill." He pu his hands to his face and began to cry. "I'm so sick of all th dying."

"Christ." Ralph hesitated, unsure of what to do. They hac not found a drunken bum out on the desert at all. They hac found a madman. And madmen could get violent and do violen things. Was it worth the risk, standing here arguing with a lu natic? "Okay," he said gently, "you can leave if you want to But Pikes Peak is in Colorado, man. How you going to get ther in the shape you're in?"

"It's not Pikes Peak!" Eddie shouted. He ground his fists int his eyes. "Dammit! I lived there! What was it—Spire? Spike?"

"There's a Spike Mountain a ways from here," Ralph said "It's a couple hours' drive, though."

"Salt Lake," Eddie said. "It has something to do with Sal Lake City."

"That's the place. East of Salt Lake City."

"That's where I have to go. Again."

"First you rinse off."

"Damn you and your 'rinse off'! People are dying up there!' Ralph gritted his teeth. "You've been out like a light for two or three days, man. Whatever's happening can wait."

"It's barely started," Eddie moaned. "God, I saw it all. Like it was, and like it is. All of it." He looked at Ralph with bleary eyes that seemed old and incredibly sad to Ralph. He felt it wa: like looking into the eyes of Father Time himself. But wasn' that the way lunatics looked, so wise and old and weary? But ir their fevered brains silly things went on. Gears spun out of mesh and cogs twirled uselessly. Lunatics were like broken clocks Lunatics were like this emaciated, dried-out shell of a man. I occurred to Ralph that he didn't even know his name. And no that it mattered.

"Do what you have to," he said resignedly. "You've already soaked the floor."

"Okay," Eddie said. In spite of the heat he was shivering "Thanks, man."

He stumbled out. Ralph hooked the towel out of the sink anc began to mop up after him. "Goddamn nut," he growled as he worked. "Goddamn nut."

• • •

The pain was growing unbearable for Mark.

He was lying on his stomach on the prickly mattress, drifting in and out of consciousness. It felt as if the bear was still gnawing his leg, biting and releasing, biting and releasing. With every beat of his heart his leg throbbed like a huge, angry tumor. Linda had washed his wounds with hot water, and Jill had torn a sheet into strips, binding his leg up tight with them. They had removed the remains of his coat and shirt to expose the deep gashes across his back, which were beginning to blacken and itch. The bed was soaked with water and blood.

"I hurt," he groaned. Three hours had passed since the incident with the bear. Outside, the storm still screamed in the unending darkness.

Linda came to him and knelt by his side. She pressed a hand to his forehead, smiling. "A bit of fever, but that's to be expected," she said. "Just lay still and heal."

He reached up and took her hand in his own. It was cold. He glanced over to the fireplace where Jill stood and saw that the fire was dying, just a pile of glowing ashes now with a few unburnt ends of logs sticking out. Linda saw him look at it and pressed his hand.

"If it goes out, it goes out," she said. "It doesn't matter."

He squeezed his eyes shut against the pain. In the brief darkness he saw the bear again, heard its angry roar. He snapped his eyes open, numb with horror. It just never ended, this pain and this nightmare. He still could not believe it had happened. "We'll freeze," he said.

"We'll make do. For as long as we have to, we'll make do."

"We'll starve before long. We're starving now." He considered the implausibility of that statement, judging it against the time that had passed. Perhaps eighteen hours ago they had eaten, Spam and bread and hot dogs and relish. But perhaps that was a week ago, perhaps two weeks. The overturned truck and the magic trees had occurred so long ago that the keen edge of remembrance was dull now and fading. A lifetime ago, he had been the manager of a finance company who took a well-deserved short vacation in the mountains. A lifetime ago, he had been Mark Butler struggling to make ends meet in a house he couldn't afford. None of that seemed real now, none of it. Here everything was solid and touchable and real. He was a man stripped of everything but his life.

"You have to have faith," Linda said gently.

Mark went up on his elbows to regard her. In her green eyes he saw strength and compassion, in the angle of her face he saw determination. Beneath her coat and blue jeans he saw a body wasting away to bones. Impossibly, she was shrinking. Jill looked gaunt, standing by the fire staring at him. Only Ricky, sitting at the table petting the dog, looked the way Mark felt they all should look, looked the way he knew he himself looked: scared. "You seem to have gotten religious on me, Linda Butler," he said. "Please spare me."

"Maybe a faith in our Lord is what we all need right now."

He slumped back down onto the pillow, smiling bitterly in spite of his pain. The miracle had occurred. His wife had found God. He resisted the urge to laugh in her face. "I congratulate you on your conversion," he said, "but unfortunately I can't share your new ideas. They say there are no atheists in foxholes. Can there be agnostics on Spike Mountain?"

"Sleep now," she said, and smoothed his hair.

"I will not sleep," he snapped. "We're in one hell of a situation here and you've decided to start handing out tracts. Dammit, Linda, we're *dying* up here."

"No one dies on Spike Mountain, Mark. Everyone does what they have to do to survive."

"And what the hell does that mean?"

"It means go to sleep."

"Yes," Jill echoed from across the room. "Go to sleep."

Mark crushed his face into the pillow. Straw stuck him like dull needles, grating across his whiskers. He wondered why he felt so angry, so outraged and betrayed. Was it because Linda had acknowledged the hopelessness of their situation and had accepted the only remaining hope for them? When all else failed, the meek turned to God. And now, with all else failed, Linda had done just that. He looked at her again, and at Jill. Both women had risen remarkably to the task of facing a freezing and uncertain future on a mountaintop where there was no chance of rescue or escape. Both looked peaceful and composed, neither blaming him for being the miserable failure he was. What was the source of their inner strength, and most galling of all, where could Mark find that strength for himself? Perhaps with God on his side he could figure out a way to save them.

But no, too much water had passed under that particular bridge. He had spent a lifetime denying religion, even scorning it, and he was too stubborn to cave in now. If they were to survive, it would be because Mark Butler thought of a way to save them, not God. Mark was willing to accept the blame if they died. He was just as willing to take the credit if they survived.

"Sleep now," Linda said again.

"I'm not tired," Mark said, but it wasn't true. This endless pain was wearing him out, holding him tantalizingly close to the comfort of true shock but never quite letting him sink fully into it. He had dozed for a while an hour or so ago, but it was a false sleep, one filled with pain and disturbing half-dreams like pale nightmares. In his dream he was hungry, mad with hunger. In his dream he had eaten some warm bloody thing and immediately vomited it up.

Jill came over and knelt beside Linda. She pressed her face close to Mark's. "Sleep," she whispered. "Sleep now, and let time pass. Time passes quickly on Spike Mountain, you see. Very quickly."

She kissed him lightly on the mouth. Linda looked on with an expression of bright happiness.

Mark drew away, shocked. But it seemed all right, very right. He reached out and took both their hands, squeezing them. He did, after all, love them both.

One big happy family.

Allison Parker was shitting in the snow with the storm howling and whooping around him. He was squatted in a square of yellow light thrown from one of the shack's windows, his ass hanging in the wind, his eyes wide and thoughtful as he surveyed the black and menacing scenery around him and wondered just what the hell was going on.

His property was shrinking.

In the spring of 1946 he had come up to Spike Mountain with a burning grudge against the man who had stolen his woman, fifteen hundred dollars in G.I. loan money, and an ax. With that ax he had single-handedly cut down three hundred and eleven trees, counting each one, counting each swing of the ax, picturing Jackson's face on each trunk as he worked. He had cleared an area thirty yards by thirty yards, dug around the stumps by hand, and burned them where they stood. It had taken eight months and a hell of a lot of sweat. Now that didn't seem to matter much. His claim stake was disappearing.

He squirted a turd onto the snow and fumbled with the roll of toilet paper in his hands, looking around. It was dark as night. The spires of the trees were visible against the sky as a deeper, more foreboding black. Low boiling clouds scudded overhead. The wind blasted powdered snow against his face and hands and ass, stinging hard enough to burn. It was cold, he guessed maybe ten degrees at best. Welcome to springtime in the wilds.

He wiped his ass, inspecting his toilet paper for signs of blood. One eye he kept nervously on the treeline, hoping to see how all these trees were appearing, but not really all that anxious to. He had seen enough mysterious things in the last twenty-four hours to last him a lifetime. And not too long ago he had heard strange boomings and crackings going on up near the doc's place, followed by screams. Human screams. And five minutes ago, just before he came out here in the storm to relieve his bowels, he had heard some strange sounds coming out of the forest around his shack. Rustlings and creakings. Thumpings and bumpings. The brittle snap of new bark cracking in the cold. Eerie things.

Allie was wiping his ass for the third time when he saw something that made his heart stop in his chest and his blood freeze in his veins. He shifted closer to the light, holding the wad of toilet paper inches from his face, aware that his ass was no rose but a damn sight better than Jackson's smelly feet. He uttered a strangled wheeze.

There was blood on the toilet paper. Blood running out his ass.

Cancer.

He got to his feet, feeling as if his insides had turned to glass and shattered in the cold. He tossed the roll of toilet paper into the wind, watching it blow away and unravel like a dismal party streamer. Mom and Dad had each gotten bowel cancer, and died in utter misery. He had known it would be his someday, a dark lurking enemy waiting to knock on the door and let itself in. He tied the rope that served as his belt around his waist and shuffled back around the shack, trees and property forgotten.

Jackson had finally gone and done it. Him and his flapjacks. Jackson.

He pushed the door open and stepped inside. Jackson had the stove open and was jamming a log inside, bent over with his back to Allie. Allie got his rifle off its pegs by the door and levered a round into the chamber.

Jackson heard it click, and froze. "That you, scumbag?" he said to the stove.

"Say goodbye, you murdering cocksucking beady-eyed bastard," Allie growled.

Jackson dived off to the right. The bullet hit the stove, leaving a bright metal streak in the rust and ricocheting off with a high whine. Allie fired again, blasting a hole through one of the windows. The rifle was tremendously loud in the confines of these four walls. Jackson ducked and dodged, scurrying around the room and overturning furniture. The shack filled with drifting blue gun smoke.

"Hold still, dicklicker," Allie said, tracking him with the sights.

"What did I do?" Jackson cried. He dodged behind the table, where plates and a skillet, one of the murder weapons, sat in preparation for tonight's supper. He flipped the table over and crouched behind it. Plates rolled on edge across the floor.

"Killed me, that's what you did. Killed me deader'n shit." Allie squeezed off three more rounds, decorating the tabletop with holes. Wood chips and sawdust blew out all over Jackson.

"What the fuck are you talking about?" he shrieked, poking his head up. "You're still on your feet."

"Goddamn son of a *bitch*!"

Jackson fetched up the skillet and shielded his face with it just in time. Allie popped another shot, catching his skillet dead center. It rang like a large tuning fork.

"Take yer medicine, dammit!"

Jackson hurled the singing skillet at him. It went end over and bonged musically onto the wall beside Allie. Allie stalked over and kicked the table aside. Jackson dived into the corner and huddled behind one of the hundred-pound sacks of pancake flour, another of the murder weapons. Allie pumped lead into it in a frenzy. Flour puffed out in spurts.

Jackson jumped up and heaved the sack at him. It bowled Allie over on his back, rupturing on his chest when he hit the floor. White flour, the colon's nemesis, exploded outward in a cloud. The light got hazy and it became hard to breathe.

"You ain't getting me without a fight," Jackson crowed triumphantly. He picked up the fallen rifle and aimed it down at

Allie's chest, blinking in the haze. His beard and hair had gone
white as snow.

Allie sat up. Flour cascaded off him. He was a spook with
dark circles for eyes. "You can't kill a man twice," he snapped,
coughing a bit. "You've done give me cancer already."

"Did not," Jackson said. "Did not."

"Did so. You and your fucking flapjacks. I'm a dead man."

"Then die, already," Jackson said, and pulled the trigger,
aiming just off to the side and hoping to do no more than rattle
Allie's eardrums a bit. The gun clicked. He levered it and tried
again. Click. "Damn!" he screeched.

Allie lunged up at him. They embraced, wobbled, fell back
down in the flour. They rolled in it. Loose floorboards rattled
and thumped. Flour dust boiled up in bright clouds. Fists
flew.

"Die!" Allie screamed, choking Jackson.

"Eat shit!" Jackson snarled, clawing at his eyes.

They rolled around. The bunk bed went over next with a crash,
hitting the lantern on a wire in the center of the room and sending it swaying. A chair was ground to sticks beneath them. The
table, which only had three good legs left to it, lost two more.
The lantern bobbed overhead, casting weird, swinging shadows.
The two had tussled a thousand times before but this was turning
out to be a lulu. Allie got ahold of Jackson's hair and pounded
his head on the floor, grinning.

"Take that," he panted.

"Take *this*," Jackson said, and kneed him in the crotch.

They broke apart, howling and cursing. The walls were white
with flour, the air thick with it. Both men staggered to their feet,
panting and coughing. They had become ghosts. Allie pulled his
bowie knife out of his boot and waved it around, blinking away
the dust in his eyes. "Now, cocksucker," he breathed. "Now
you pay."

Jackson scurried across the room and hefted a table leg. He
swooped it in a series of arcs. "Come and get me if you can,
dildo," he said.

Allie lunged. Jackson cracked the table leg down across his
head and he saw stars, moons, Saturn's rings. He roared with
pain and slashed out blindly with his knife. He felt it connect
with something solid and drove it home, nearly losing his balance.

"Yow!" Jackson wailed, falling back. When his head had

leared, Allie saw he had stuck his knife in Jackson's left bicep.
Blood dribbled out of a slit in his shirt sleeve, not much of it,
but enough to look brilliantly red against the backdrop of white
flour.

Jackson looked at his arm, his eyes widening behind his thick
spectacles. "Jesus," he said wonderingly. "Jesus God, you
stabbed me."

It occurred to Allie to say that he was sorry. Perhaps in his
forty-year feud with Jackson he had never really intended to hurt
him, at least not hurt him badly. They had broken furniture over
each other's heads before, had punched each other silly, had
cracked ribs and split each other's noses, but this was the first
time a weapon had been used with any effect. Yet crazy things
were going on now, perhaps should be going on now. The mountain Allie called home had turned dark and foreboding overnight, had become a strange place where women screamed in
the dark and dead coyotes got up and walked and blood appeared
on toilet paper to announce the sure onset of death. Allie felt his
rage building instead of ebbing, felt that he could no longer look
at Jackson and his thick reflecting spectacles without going mad.
An inner voice, a furious and impatient voice, seemed to be
urging him on. An eye for an eye. Death for death. It was the
law of the wilds.

"Damn right I stabbed you," Allie said, breathing hard,
heeding that inner voice. "An eye for an eye."

He jumped forward with uncanny speed and stabbed Jackson
in the stomach. The knife slid in all the way to the hilt. He
pulled it out. Jackson wheezed and fell back. The table leg
dropped from his hands and clattered on the floor. For a moment
the screaming wind outside died down as the world seemed to
hold its breath.

Jackson made faces. He clutched his stomach and staggered
around. Blood dribbled out of his mouth and down his chin in
a sudden crimson trickle. He stared at Allie as he walked, gaped
at him with terribly sad and wondering eyes. He tripped over the
fallen bed and crashed over on his face.

Allie stalked over to him. Blood was pooling on the white
floor under Jackson. Allie's rage built higher, became an unbearable fire in the pit of his stomach. He knelt beside Jackson
and raised the knife. Saliva drooled down his lips. He stabbed
him in the back. Once, twice, three times. The knife made thin
wet punching noises as it pierced Jackson's back. Four, five, six

times. Blood flew from the knife and splattered the walls. Jack
son twitched and flopped. Allie raised the knife, swung it down
The bobbing lantern made crazy shadows. He raised the knife
swung it down. Seven, eight, nine times. An eye for an eye.
tooth for a tooth. He swung the knife, swung the knife. Bloo
spread thickly across the floor, dripped down the walls. Th
wind screamed outside.

Allie swung the knife.

"Is he asleep?" Jill asked.

"Passed out," Linda answered. She smoothed Mark's hai
He lay facedown on the bed, not moving.

"He doesn't believe, does he? He doesn't believe even th
most simple truth of all. He will never believe."

"Indeed. A strange man from a strange time."

The cabin door gusted open. Snow danced in, seeming to tak
brief shape before drifting to the floor. Beast padded over, th
fur on his back bristling. He stopped and sniffed the air with
low growl rising in his throat.

The door blew shut with a bang.

Jill nodded and went to the fireplace. She put both hands i
the glowing ashes and withdrew the smoking remains of a lo
by its burning end. She carried it like a cumbersome baseba
bat across the room to the bed. Smoke curled in lazy silve
strings to the ceiling. The smell of burning flesh grew in th
air.

Ricky, sitting at the table, saw this happening and sucked i
his breath.

"Okay," Linda said dreamily, rising and stepping out of th
way.

Jill hefted the log up over her head, taking a small step back
ward to keep from overbalancing. Bits of ash sifted down on he
hair. With a grunt of effort, she smashed the log down acros
Mark's head. Smoke and ash burst up. Mark flopped once an
was still.

Ricky screamed.

"Again," Linda said.

Jill raised the log. The flesh of her palms sizzled and smoked
She brought it down, grunting. This time it broke across Mark
head into two pieces, one burnt, one unburnt. The unburnt piec
hit the floor and rolled away.

"Daddy!" Ricky cried.

Jill tossed the burning end aside and went over to the table. She reached past Ricky's head to the utensils hanging from pegs on the wall there, and unhooked the big meat cleaver. She turned it over in her blistering, black-sooted hands. The blade glittered weak orange in the dying light. She grinned, breathing hard in his face.

"You're next," she said.

CHAPTER SIXTEEN

Madge Pickens had secured a can of Cherry Coke from the refrigerator in the kitchen and stood now with Tony on her arm, drinking her Coke and occasionally tipping the can to his mouth for him to take a drink, watching Ralph clean up the mess the drunken hippie had made in his staggering charge from the bathroom to the front door. There were wet bootprints in a meandering track across the carpet, and puddles on the linoleum where he had detoured through the kitchen in his search for a way out. Madge had watched him do this without comment. There had been a crazy gleam in his drunken bum's eyes, the shine of madness to them as he hunted for the door and muttered to himself. Muttered to himself like Ralph was doing now as he mopped up.

"Goddamned weird-ass crazy-acting son of a buck."

"At least it was interesting," Madge put in.

He looked up at her. "A day shot to hell, that's what it is. And for what?"

"What did you expect? A thank-you card?"

He picked up the towel and waved it around. "I expected more than having to clean up the damn house afterward. I expected maybe some common courtesy." He slapped the towel back down to the floor and pushed it in quick circles. "You can bet your ass that's the last time I help anybody out. Goddamn nut." He duck-walked to the next puddle and wiped it up. The towel had gone dingy brown and was doing more smearing than wiping. "How do you like that guy," he muttered. "Just how do you like that guy."

"The day's not ruined, Ralph. We can still go three-wheeling." She shifted Tony to the side and looked at her watch. "It stays light till eight, and it's only four now. What do you say?"

"Forget it. The day's shot." He went to the front door, opened it, and threw the towel out into the yard. "When that sucker dries I'm going to burn it," he growled. "Goddamn nut."

Madge looked at him curiously. "Why are you letting it bother you so much? We got him back on his feet, and that's all we set out to do. So what if he left? It's no big deal."

"I don't know." He shook his head, exasperated. "He's trying to get to Spike Mountain, you know. That's a good three-hour drive from here if you know the right roads, and soaking wet and covered with shit like he is, nobody's ever going to pick him up. I think he's crazy enough to try and walk all the way, and you know as well as I do he'll never make it. I'll bet money he'll get about a mile from here and fall over dead by the road. Christ, we only gave him a lousy cup of water. He'll never make it. Never." He went into the kitchen and Madge heard him wash his hands. He came out a moment later, frowning deeply, absently wiping his hands on his shirt. "We should have at least got a meal in him. You ever see anybody so skinny?"

"Can't say as I have," Madge said.

"Poor bastard. We should have fed him. Maybe I should have conked him one over the head."

"Too late now."

"Yeah." He nodded. "Yeah, it is." He went to the door and looked out. "There he is, staggering down the road toward the highway. He hasn't made it a hundred yards yet and he looks like he's on his last legs already. Damn." He turned away, frowning. "He's never going to make it."

Rolando Garcia hopped up the front steps with a beer in his hand, and pressed his face close to the screen. "Your wino's getting away, man," he announced gravely.

"So he is," Ralph said.

"Want me to go kick his ass before he gets out of sight? Just for general principles?"

"No thanks. The dumb bastard'll be dead soon, anyway."

Rolando thought about it. "If I was out on the road I'd run his ass down just for the hell of it. He walked by me when he left and I felt like just killing him for being alive. You ever felt that way about somebody? Just want to kick ass for no reason?"

"I suppose I have, man."

"That bum won't make it ten feet out of town. When the rednecks get sight of him they'll tear him up. Dumbass, anyway. Dripping wet. Mucho loco, that guy. Fucking hippie." He swirled his beer reflectively. "Somebody's gonna stop and kill him just for the hell of it."

Ralph nodded. "It's a tough old world. The guy ought to know that by now."

They watched Eddie go. A red Pinto cruised slowly by him, the occupants, local teenagers Ralph had seen in town before, hanging out the windows shouting and laughing. One of them threw a paper Coke cup at Eddie after they had passed. Crushed ice sprayed against his back, twinkling like diamonds under the sun. He walked on without looking back. And here, Ralph thought, you have the story of that guy's life. The eternal victim.

The Pinto cut a quick U-turn on the street and moved up behind Eddie, practically on his heels, its horn blaring. He lurched ahead, ignoring it. The car stopped and four boys jumped out to tag after him. Their laughter floated back to the trailer like distant music. One of them pushed Eddie and he fell heavily to his knees.

"Ah, shit," Ralph breathed. Madge moved beside him to watch.

Eddie got up. One of the boys crept behind him on his hands and knees while another circled around front. There was a brief one-sided conversation, followed by a shout. Eddie was shoved backward and fell over the other boy, his arms pinwheeling. Ralph imagined he could hear his head and elbows crack on the asphalt.

"Well, damn," he said, and motioned Rolando aside. He opened the screen door with his face tightening in anger. "I'd better go save his ass before things get serious. I'll be back later."

"I'll fix him something to eat," Madge said as the door slapped shut.

He hurried to his truck. "Don't waste your time," he called back.

"You need a hand?" Rolando said, following him across the yard.

Ralph got in the truck and started it. "Just a bunch of punk kids, man." He put it into reverse and backed up. "I can handle them."

"Up to you, man." Rolando raised his beer bottle in salute. "Bring the scumbag back and we'll have a de-balling party."

Ralph put the Ford in first gear, nodding absently. He peered through the cloud of dust his tires had raised and could see that

e kids had formed a circle around Eddie, who was on his hands
nd knees trying to crawl past them. They were shoving him
ack inside the circle with their feet. Just roughhouse stuff, re-
lly, kids having a little Friday afternoon fun after school, noth-
g serious. At least not yet. Ralph eased the clutch out and
rove down the gravel road that served as the Ranchero Mobile
lome Park's main drag, went left at the asphalt, and pulled
p behind the Pinto. He got out, leaving the truck idling, and
lbowed his way into the circle.

"Leave him alone," he said.

They regarded him, youthful faces squinting in the harsh
unlight. Eddie pushed himself laboriously to his feet. Foul-
melling traces of steam drifted out of his clothes. Ralph won-
ered briefly what he was doing this for, why he would risk a
ght for the likes of this nameless bum. He searched his mind
r ready answers and found none. Just rooting for the underdog,
aybe. And there was never a dog so under as this.

"He's ours," one of the boys said. The others nodded agree-
ent. "We found him first."

"I told you to leave him alone," Ralph said quietly. He moved
ver to the boy who had spoken, and pressed close to him. "Do
have to say it again?"

The boy thought it over. Ralph guessed his age to be about
eventeen, old enough to have a man's body but young enough
be unsure of himself. His eyes darted to the others in the
roup as if seeking support. "Who's gonna make me?" he said,
ut there was no strength in the words.

"Just me, I guess," Ralph said.

The kid snorted. He scratched his nose. "Come on, guys."

They drifted away and got back in their car, leaving with a
ew mumbled remarks and a short squeal of tires on the pave-
ent.

Ralph breathed a sigh of relief. It was just too hot to be flirting
vith fistfights today. He turned to speak to Eddie and saw that
e had already walked off down the road a few yards, planting
ne foot in front of the other as if each step hurt his feet, his
houlders drooping, his hands dangling limply at his sides. The
um was just walking away as if nothing had happened, as if a
ind stranger had never bothered to intervene and save his skinny
ss from a crowd of rowdy kids. Ralph passed a weary hand
ver his face. Basket case. "You're welcome," he called after
im.

Eddie stopped. He executed a slow, stumbling tur
"Thanks," he said simply, turned again, and went on.

"You'll never make it," Ralph said.

Eddie shook his head as he walked. "Got to, man. Got to.

Ralph watched him go. Another mile at best, and he wou
collapse, or else a carload of older, more dedicated rowdi
would descend on him before then and work him over good. (
maybe a helpful soul like Rolando would simply veer off th
road to run him down and end his misery. The dude was de
tined for a world of hurt whichever way you looked at it. "I
drive you," Ralph said. It came out before he had a chance
fully realize what he was saying. The afternoon had been ruin(
by this bum, and now he was being offered the evening as wel
It would be ten o'clock before Ralph got back, and then only
he made good time. He resisted the urge to punch himself
good one across his own big mouth. It was out, and he wou
stick by it. Ralph Pickens was a man of his word.

Eddie stopped and turned. On his face Ralph could see reli
spread like a slow wave across his bony features. "Thank
man," he said, and hobbled to the truck.

Ralph looked back to his trailer. He waved and pointed sou
down the road. He made hand signals that indicated driving, ar
hoped Madge would understand. He went back to the truck, g
in, swiped at the sweat that was trickling into his eyes, a
decided that this was the craziest thing he had ever agreed to (
in his life. "I guess I ought to ask your name," he said as the
got under way.

Eddie looked at him with his sunken and fevered lunatic
eyes. "I have many names."

Ralph grunted. "I just need one."

"Edward," Eddie said. "That is my current name."

"Okay, Ed." Ralph dropped the shift lever into third ar
settled back for the long drive. "Tell me what this is all about.

Eddie laughed then, a low, unhappy chuckle. He hung h
head and swung it slowly back and forth, making the dangli
wet ruin of his hair sway in front of his face. "You're going
think I'm nuts," he said.

"I already do."

Eddie nodded. "Then what I tell you won't matter."

"Probably not. But I'd be interested to hear it, anyway."

"Okay." Eddie sat up straight and crossed his arms over h

est. The wind streamed through his hair, flapping it in a single
t knot. "What day is this?"

"Friday. Twentieth of April. Ten after four in the afternoon."

"Right, right. It was Wednesday morning when they got me.
at means I was dying for two days. Two whole days that
emed like ten thousand years. Hell, it *was* ten thousand years.
aybe a million. I was even a caveman, back in the beginning."

Woo-ee, Ralph thought, unconsciously imitating Rolando. *To-
lly fried.*

"I was dozens of people. I mean, I was really *them*. I knew
y name, I knew what I was doing, I knew where I was. But
ere were spaces, you know, spaces in between. That's when I
lked to Robin."

"Uh-huh," Ralph said. He came to the I-84 ramp and joined
affic headed east. "Go on."

"I tuned in on her. She called me Batman. I didn't really see
r, but I heard her. She showed me things. Took me places.
e took me back to Spike. When I woke up in that bathtub,
at's where I was. Reliving everything that had happened, see-
g it all real clear, and seeing what was happening now. Robin
owed me the bitch." He chuckled again. "That's what fuck-
ad kept saying, Glenn I mean. I shouldn't call him that any-
ore. He's dead, you know."

"Mmm."

"But she is a bitch, he was right about that. She wasn't al-
ays, though. She was—what do you call them?—a nymph, a
rt of nature. An ancient soul who attained the ninth level, and
came like God himself. She has powers, though they don't
ach far. Spike Mountain is the place, her only place. It belongs
her." He laughed out loud. "And to think I thought I was on
e eighth level, one step away from the ultimate. Man, I've
rely started, maybe hit the third or fourth. We all have a long
ay to go to become like her, and even she's not perfect. Look
what she's doing now, taking Spike back to what it was so
ng ago. She's killing, man, killing in a frenzy. She's gone
ts."

"Nuts," Ralph agreed.

"Do you see what that means? Even the perfect aren't perfect.
ey've got emotions, just like us. They can get mad, they can
t sad, they can screw up like we screw up. When you reach
e ninth level, you're back on level one of a new plane, man,
arting all over on a higher plane. And how many planes are

there, how many levels in all? God!'' He was bouncing in th
seat now, slapping his thighs with his hands. ''Robin got throug
She got through and talked to me!''

''Whoa, now,'' Ralph said gently. ''Don't flip out on me. Ju
let it all out slow, and I'll listen to every word.'' Was this, h
wondered, the proper way to handle a case like this? Or wou
Ed get so fired up he'd jump out of the truck? Ralph eased u
on the accelerator a bit, wishing he could reach over and loc
this Edward fellow's door without being obvious.

''She showed me one last life,'' Eddie said, growing sobe
''Not my last one, that was in the trenches. She showed me th
worst one of all, saved it for last. And I think I know why sh
did. Hell, I *know* I know why she did. Because she loves h
mommy. She did it for Mommy's sake, only Mommy's dead no
and so is Daddy. I was too late. The whole frigging family
dead.'' He covered his face with his hands and sobbed. ''And
treated them all like shit. I've treated everybody like shit. N
wonder people hate me.''

''There, there,'' Ralph soothed, squirming inside with di
comfort. ''I don't hate you, pal. Hang on to that thought.''

Eddie looked up. His eyes were red and wet. ''It's up to m
now. I'm the only one who can stop the bitch. She wants th
kid and she's killing people to get him. She's setting things u
rolling time backward, bringing the dead back to life. An ey
for an eye, that's what she's thinking. An eye for an eye. B
she's wrong, she's gone crazy. God, but she has power. Can yc
imagine it?''

''Hard to,'' Ralph said warily. ''Damned hard to.''

''I have power, too,'' Eddie said after a pause. ''I think I ha
power, too.''

Ralph felt his flesh crawl as the full awareness struck him th
he was sitting in this old blue Ford pickup driving down th
freeway with a pair of old Hondas in the back, chauffeuring
man who was utterly, totally, fabulously insane. He wondered
somewhere, deeply hidden in his baggy clothes, good old nut
Ed was carrying a knife. It would be just perfect.

''I can stop her,'' Eddie grunted. ''I think I can stop her.''

Ralph nodded and put on a smile. ''Sure you can, Ed. Su
you can.''

Eddie looked at him sourly. ''You're humoring me.''

''Just agreeing, Ed, just agreeing.''

''Ah, you think I'm nuts.''

Ralph shrugged. "I'll be honest with you, Ed, and I don't want you to take it the wrong way. Nothing you've said has made a lick of sense so far. You're rattling on about things that, well, sound crazy. I'd like to understand, you know, so I can . . . help you. And if I can't help you, we'll find somebody who can. There are places in Ogden where they treat, um, people with problems. They treat people who need help. Want me to take you there?"

"A nuthouse, you mean."

"An institution. Someplace like maybe you've been before."

Eddie hooked an arm out the window and let the wind play across his hand. "I'll bet I do sound insane," he said. "But after what I've been through, after what I've seen, anybody would. It's like the whole picture has become clear for me, all the old questions answered. I finally tuned in on the dead, and the dead told me everything." He took a deep breath and exhaled noisily. "Maybe I can put it so you'll understand, uh— what did you say your name was?"

"Ralph. Pickens." He took a hand off the wheel and extended it to Eddie. "Your friend, if you need one."

"Friend." Eddie shook his hand. "I haven't had many of those."

They smiled at each other. Ralph brought the truck up to sixty-five, putting the worry that Ed might jump out away from his thoughts. He felt he had created some sort of bond with him now, and that bond, no matter how new or shaky, would keep him from going off the deep end until they reached Ogden and the mental hospital there.

"Do you believe in God?" Eddie asked suddenly.

Ralph shrugged. "Guess so. I don't get to church that much, though."

"Okay, you believe. You believe that an invisible spirit exists in heaven. What if I told you invisible spirits exist on earth, too?"

"Ghosts, you mean."

"Sort of. What I mean are people who have lived so many lifetimes that they've become too advanced to be ordinary mortals. They become minor gods, you might say, and are given power over parts of the earth. Let's say you, Ralph Pickens, become perfect, so I, God, give you a piece of land to call your own. I make you a god over that land, give you total power over it and the people who live there. It'd be like a training area for you. You rule the area for a few thousand years, you do good, so I advance you up the ladder and give you a planet next. I make you a god over an entire planet. Sound plausible?''

''I suppose so,'' Ralph said. ''When it comes to religion, anybody's idea is just as good as the next guy's.''

''Okay, let's say there's a spirit that rules an area. Let's say something happens there a long time ago that is so horrible, so totally awful, that the spirit can't forget about it. The spirit broods about it, gets mad about it, eventually goes insane with anger about it. Let's say she decides to set things right.''

''She?''

''The bitch. A female goddess.''

''Like, uh, Diana? One of those?''

''Yeah, just like that. Let's say she's willing to break any rule, kill anybody, destroy anything, to get her revenge. Let's say she's doing this, and there's nothing to stop her. Except me.''

''You.''

''Me.''

Ralph chewed his lower lip thoughtfully. ''And this goddess, this bitch, is on Spike Mountain, right? That's where she lives.''

''Right now that's where she is,'' Eddie said. ''But maybe she can go anywhere, do anything. She probably caused Robin to die, and set everything in motion. She has awesome power.''

''But you can stop her.''

''I think I can. Robin thinks I can.''

''Who's Robin?''

''My niece. She's dead. She talked to me when I was laying out on the desert.''

''Oh.'' Ralph resisted the urge to roll his eyes and just laugh out loud. ''Sorry to hear it,'' he said instead.

''It was a pity. Her funeral was on Tuesday.''

''Then I am sorry to hear it. Is that what kind of pushed you over the edge? Finding out your niece died?''

Eddie shook his head. ''Nothing pushed me over the edge, man. I'm as sane as you are. Just wore out, that's all.''

''Right. Okay, so we've got this bitch goddess going nuts on Spike. What's she doing?''

''Taking it back. Making it to what it was about a hundred years ago, setting the stage for her revenge. A terrible thing happened up there so long ago, and she's going to make the people who did it pay. See, there were two women, and a man, and a boy. There was—cannibalism involved, but that's not the worst. She kept the spirits of the women, but she lost the man, and the boy was innocent. They got away. For a while, anyway. It's the man she's after.''

"And what's she going to do to him?''

Eddie put a hand over his mouth, shuddered, and spoke softly between his fingers. "Same thing he did. She's going to eat him.''

"Eat him?" Ralph made a face. "Jesus.''

"Even Jesus can't help him now," Eddie said. "Only me.''

"You? If this bitch has got all that power, what can you do against her?" Ralph blinked, surprised he had gotten so caught up in the conversation that he was asking questions as if this were all true and not some madman's delusion. The whole story was preposterous and insane. He took the truck up to seventy, which was hard on the old Ford, but he wanted to make the Ogden exit as soon as possible and begin scouting for the mental hospital there. Old Ed was a worse case than he ever would have believed possible.

"I think I can stop her," Eddie said, as if to himself. "I'm not sure how, but I think I can. Robin thinks I can, too. She said Batman can do anything.''

"Sure," Ralph muttered, and they drove on in silence for a long time then.

For Mark the long descent into cold bottomless darkness began with a crashing pain in his head. There was a burst of light inside his brain, a shattering explosion of light and pain, and then a slow tumble down a black and seemingly endless hole. After a while another burst of light came, this one less intense, less important. He fell then in utter silence, utter blackness, slipping down through a hole in reality, barely aware of his own existence, only dimly aware of lingering pain and an aching regret.

Dim things swirled past him. He reached out in free-fall, wrenched his mouth open to scream. His fingers caught at nothing and his scream was soundless, endless. He was drifting now, being buffeted like a small cloud across a chasm of black sky, dissipating into nothingness. His consciousness began to fragment like a poorly remembered dream, unraveling into threads of a life that no longer had meaning. Behind it all he began to hear the pulsing of his own heart, thudding noisily, faltering, growing erratic, growing slower.

He realized with a sudden burst of cognizance that he was dying. A hideous terror seized him, and with it the certainty that he must not fall farther, that to fall was to abandon reality and himself forever. His thoughts twitched wildly from memory to memory, seeking himself, seeking a past. He thought of his wife, and of his child. His own name came to him and he opened his mouth again and screamed it without sound.

His falling slowed. In the dark around him the drumming of his heart echoed and faded, echoed and faded. Looking down, he could make out faint light in the yawning blackness below, rushing up to meet him.

He landed softly on his face in cold wet snow, whole again. He pushed himself up on his hands.

He was in the middle of the old cabin, naked. The crumbling chimney stood before him like a gaunt skeleton, shrouded with mist and obscured by blowing snow. The low decaying walls jutted up around him in a large square. Wind moaned past the corners, whispered through the surrounding trees, shifting the drapery of mist that seemed to enclose him in a gloomy, twilit sphere. The world had become an eerie shadowland, dreamlike, unreal. He got to his feet, shivering from the cold, and took a shuffling, hesitant step forward. The wind pressed hard against his naked chest.

No rest . . .

He turned in a clumsy circle, hearing a voice carry with the wind.

No forgiveness . . .

The blowing snow danced and swirled in front of the chimney, drafting upward, sinking down. It began to rotate in a thin, nebulous tornado. Mark felt a bitter chill sweep over him. The snow was taking shape, becoming identifiable as a human form. He had the impression of diaphanous clothes, of long white hair streaming in the wind. He perceived the dark snowless holes of eyes that seemed huge and full of monstrous anger. A dark and numbing dread suffused him. It came to him with overpowering sureness that he had died.

The tornado drifted toward him, swirling, changing. Now it seemed to be a man crouched on his knees, a large man with a ragged beard and some pointed thing in his upraised fist.

No rest . . .

The snow swept down and became a small doglike animal, a

coyote on its haunches with its muzzle pointed to the sky. Baleful black eyes seemed to gleam in the whirling snow of its head.

No forgiveness . . .

Now it took the shape of the angry woman again, larger this time, standing ten feet tall with her clothes streaming out beside her, sharply defined in white against black, her face twisted with rage, her hair a pile of writhing snakes, her eyes gleaming black orbs the size of tennis balls that sparkled with stunning, murderous hate. She took a giant's step toward Mark, shaking the ground, shaking the universe. He staggered backward, fighting to keep his balance in the whirlwind. The cold became arctic deep and unbearable. His breath was pulled from his lungs in a sudden wheeze. The decayed remains of the cabin walls collapsed around him with a splintering crash. The chimney exploded into fragments that corkscrewed into the hurricane. He felt himself being lifted off the ground, dissolving again, his identity and his soul being blotted out by the shrieking wind and the overpowering presence of a giant ghostly woman made of snow and wind and hate.

An eye for an eye.

He began, as he rose through the blackness and conscious thought was inexorably torn from him, to forget who he was, and who he had been, and what the name Mark Butler had meant at all.

Ricky saw his father stir on the bed. Relief broke over him in a great wave and he struggled to get up out of his chair. Jill held him down with one hand on the top of his head. In the other hand she held the cleaver. Ten minutes had passed since Jill smashed the burning log over Mark's head and in those endless minutes Ricky had sat, mute and stunned, while Jill and Linda held him down, looking at him as if he had become a highly interesting bug. Beast padded restlessly back and forth from the door to the table, growling and whining.

"It will be time soon," Linda said.

Jill nodded. "Time at last."

The fire had died and the temperature inside was dropping. Two lamps, one on the table and the other on the fireplace mantel, cast dull flickering light through the room. Facedown on the bed, Mark groaned and moved. There was a dark smear of blood oozing from the back of his head. Thick rivulets had run down both sides of his jaw and stained the pillow. Ricky strained to see what he was doing, knowing that any minute his daddy would wake up and make Mommy and Jill stop acting so crazy, so mysterious. Jill had cracked him a couple of good ones over the head but Daddy was too tough and too smart to let that lay him low for long. He had survived a bear bite, so a few conks on the head weren't much. Pretty soon he would get up and see to it everything was straightened out around here.

"Such a pretty boy," Linda said. She reached down and stroked Ricky's cheek with the back of her fingers. "See what a fine little man he's turned into." She pinched his cheek between her thumb and forefinger, bending close, wagging his head, hurting him. "Aren't we just the luckiest little boy in the world? Aren't we?" She pinched his cheek harder, making him cry out. Her face grew sharp and slowly angry. "Over a hundred years we've waited for you, my darling, waited for you while we crawled in hell. But you were the lucky one, weren't you? You're the one who got away."

"Mommy," Ricky moaned, "you're hurting me."

She pulled her hand away, opened it, and slapped him hard across the face. He drew a sharp, surprised breath, his eyes wide, and then his face crumpled and he began to cry.

"Faker!" Linda snarled. She took him by the shoulders and shook him. "You left us, you bastard! You left us and got away!"

"Mommy, don't!"

"I'm not your mother, you stupid little man!" She stopped shaking him and pushed her face close to his. Her eyes were drawn down to dark slits, her teeth bared. Beneath his mother's skin Ricky could see the dark, twisted features of someone else, as if a secret inner person were hiding there behind the bones of her face, slowly surfacing. "You killed him," she breathed. "I didn't do it and neither did Jenny. We didn't do it, didn't do it at all. And you're the one who got away." She put her hands under his arms and suddenly hugged him, weeping. "Oh, God, dear God," she cried. "Oh, how I love you. It's been so long!"

Ricky sat woodenly, letting her hug him, filled with the desire to hug her back and make everything all right, yet sickened by her nearness. This crying, crazy-acting woman was not his mother. Somehow, this was not his mother anymore.

Jill took his hand and squeezed it. "And I love you," she said, going down on her knees. She put the cleaver on the floor and kissed his hand. "After all that's happened, I still love you." She began to cry, too. Linda covered his face with sloppy, drooling kisses. She found his mouth and he felt the tip of her tongue play across his lips. For a moment he felt a strange inner twinge, the hint of a memory still veiled, too cloudy to bring into clear focus. He jerked back and wiped his mouth with his free hand.

Mark made a noise on the bed. Both women looked over expectantly.

"Daddy's waking up," Ricky said, glad that this little horror show was almost over. He was ferociously hungry, and Daddy would fix that, somehow. Daddy would fix everything.

Jill stood up and looked at her burned hands. Ricky saw an expression of mild sorrow pass over her face. "There was no other way," she said as if to herself, looking over to the burned piece of log that lay on the floor by the bed. "He never would have done what has to be done." She put her face in her hands and sobbed. "Oh, all the killing, all the killing."

"But he loved us," Linda said to her, drawing away from Ricky. "Just like Ben did. The spirit of God was moving in him, slowly moving in him."

Jill shuddered visibly. "Not God. *Her.*"

Mark pushed himself up on his elbows, making the bed creak.

"Daddy!" Ricky cried, and escaped from his chair to rush over to him. What he saw in the dim lanternlight made him stop halfway to the bed, made his hair crawl on his scalp and his breath freeze in his lungs.

His daddy had turned as white as a drift of winter snow. Blue veins stood out in his face and neck in a crazy network. His mouth was a thin blue slash against translucently white skin, his hair a tangled black cap. Blood dripped leisurely from his jaw to the pillow in big crimson drops. He swiveled his head. His eyes, which seemed overly large for his face, rotated in a circle and came to a stop staring at Ricky.

He got out of bed, tottering and bowing, his arms outstretched as if for balance. Above his blue jeans his stomach and chest were chalk-white, the hairs on his arms starkly black. He took a lurching step forward on his bare white feet and collapsed heavily to his hands and knees in front of Ricky.

Beast barked and clawed at the door.

Mark raised his head and looked up at Ricky. His voice, when he spoke, was the high, whiningly petulant voice of someone else, the voice of a shrew.

"On the fifteenth day without food, much as it pained us, we

ate our brave dog,'' he said. He began to crawl shakily across
the floor. His blue lips were stretched in a crazy, off-kilter grin.
He crawled to where the cleaver lay, and picked it up. Slowly
he got to his feet, clutching the table for support. He turned and
lurched stiff-leggedly toward Ricky, who stood petrified, afraid
to move, afraid to make a sound.

"On the fifteenth day without food, much as it pained us, we
ate our brave dog,'' Mark recited in his old woman's voice,
advancing on Ricky. He raised the cleaver and swooped it down.
It made an unpleasant whooshing sound as it cut the air. "Much
as it pained us, we ate our brave dog.'' He raised the cleaver,
swooped it down. Ricky cringed backward, raising his arms in
front of his face.

"We ate our dog,'' Mark crowed, swinging the cleaver. He
went past Ricky and stood over Beast, who clawed at the door
in a frenzy.

"On the fifteenth day without food, much as it pained us, we
ate our brave dog!'' He hefted the cleaver in both hands and
poised it over his head, turning to look at Ricky with his large
stranger's eyes gleaming and insane. "That you did, that you
did. *But first you had to kill it.*''

He swooped the cleaver down.

"Daddy!" Ricky screamed, but it was no longer his daddy
standing there gripping the handle of a meat cleaver that had
buried itself halfway into Beast's back, it was no longer Mark
Butler jerking the cleaver free again and swinging it down to
hack a good and faithful family dog into two blood-spraying,
jittering pieces. The body of Mark Butler bent down and hauled
a handful of hot entrails from out of a severed half of the dog.
He raised his hand up, holding a bloody mass high for all to
see. Bright lines of blood tracked down the marble-white skin
of his forearm and dripped off his elbow.

"You ate your brave dog,'' he said with cold and serene
sweetness, "and then you got hungry again, didn't you? Then
you decided to kill the boy, didn't you? But you didn't quite have
the courage, did you? You had the courage to face a bear, but
in the end you didn't have enough courage to kill the boy. I could
have forgiven *that.*''

He dropped the handful of entrails to the floor and lurched to
the table. With one blood-smeared hand he picked up the small
black book. Jill and Linda fell back, cringing in terror.

"Write it," he said in his high, warbling voice. "Write it all down again."

He hurled the book at Ricky. It landed open on the floor and slid to his feet, riffling open to the pages he had magically written a few hours before. Slowly, without haste, it flipped over to a fresh page.

"Write it, and everything will be as it was," the thing within Mark said. "Write it, and then we'll eat."

CHAPTER SEVENTEEN

Ricky picked up the book with fingers that didn't seem to want to operate right anymore. He was stiff with terror, as if his bones had fused together in his fright and become a solid structure beneath the meat of his body, and the act of bending down seemed to take all his strength. When he straightened again with the book in his hands it was with a groan of effort, an old man's groan. Something twinged in his knees and his back popped.

He held the book to his chest and looked up at his father. New fear and wonder bristled through him like a low charge of electricity. His daddy's messed-up black hair was acquiring white roots, was becoming bizarre punk rocker's bleached-out hair. Locks of it had gone white all the way to the ends. Purple veins stood out in a crazy threadwork in his eyes. He raised the hand that held the cleaver and something slid across the table and hurled itself past Linda and Jill across the room to the bed. Ricky jumped sideways with a small yelp. It was the pencil, flying through the air as if by magic. And it *was* magic, Ricky thought as some strange, half-remembered part of him awakened. An old and terrible magic.

"Write," Mark growled.

Ricky reached back to the bed and picked up the pencil. His fingers shook and he dropped it.

Mark made a motion and it jumped back up into his hand. The pencil pushed itself down to the page and in weak scrawling letters he wrote:

> march 21 on the fifteenth day
> without food much as it pained us
> we ate our brave dog

The pencil stopped. A memory rose in his mind like a great bubble struggling upward through dark, murky water, a distant memory as pale as a yellowed and faded photograph. Something about a dog, and ferocious hunger, a weakness of body and a fever of the mind. It was too dim to be perceived clearly and faded away in an instant, leaving behind a cold dark space in his thoughts. Bitter revulsion filled that space, and a desperate sense that all these things should remain forgotten, must remain forgotten.

Mark lurched over to the two large pieces of the dog and hefted one by the leg. Blood splatted on the floor in stringy drops. He carried it dripping to the table and began to hack it into pieces. Ricky's flesh crawled at the solid chunking sound the cleaver made as it drove through to the tabletop. When Mark was done he handed a piece to Linda, and one to Jill. They looked green and sick, holding the pieces away from themselves as if they were diseased. Mark came across the room, hobbling on his bandaged leg, bringing one to Ricky. He stopped before him and held it to his face with one hand. With his other hand he brandished the cleaver.

"Too weak and broken to gather wood, you ate it raw. Freezing on your bed, you ate it raw."

It became bitterly cold in the cabin. The walls and floor creaked in sudden contraction. Steam drifted off the hairy chunk of meat Mark held out to Ricky, steam heavy with the coppery smell of blood. Ricky's aching stomach twisted inside him, making him gasp with pain.

"Eat," Mark commanded. "The boy was too weak so you fed him. Now I will be you, and you will be Brigham. The circle will be complete. Eat, Brigham. Do what your father tells you, Brigham. Eat your nice doggie, Brigham. Eat so you'll be nice and *plump* when the time comes to eat *you!*"

He shoved the meat into Ricky's face.

"No!" Ricky cried. He stumbled backward and landed on the bed, dropping the book and the pencil to the floor. Straw stuck his arms and back. The mattress was still wet and beginning to freeze. Mark bent over him, scrubbing his face with the bloody piece of Beast. "Eat! Eat so you may live, Brigham. Eat so that we may all eat you one day, Brigham. Eat so your father and his wives might butcher you soon like a hanging carcass, Brigham. Eat!"

Ricky pushed furiously at Mark's cold white hand and the

warmly slimy meat. "I am not Brigham," he shouted. Memories burst inside him as the name spilled out, but he pushed them away, too. *"I am not Brigham!"*

"You will be," Mark screeched, jamming the meat into his mouth. "Full circle, full circle! Then you were Benjamin and now you will be Brigham. Let the punishment fit the crime. An eye for an eye, Benjamin Hastings, and a tooth for a tooth. It is God's law, and my law, for I am God, and you WILL BE PUNISHED!"

Ricky gagged, clamping his teeth down hard on the meat. It was tough and bitter. He tore a bite away, turned his head, and spat it out. He looked up at the chalk-faced caricature of his father with his eyes hard and narrow. "You're not God," he said. "And you're not my daddy, either. My daddy's name is Mark Butler and he knows there is no God. So leave me alone."

Something flitted briefly through Mark's wide, bulging eyes then, a glimmer that seemed full of fear and remorse. For a moment his twisted face fell together and lost its glacial whiteness. "Ricky," he whispered, but then his lips curled into a leering snarl and he straightened with the color sinking from his features as if a drain had been opened. His mouth hinged open and he began to bellow. "I am God. I AM GOD!" He stomped his feet, rattling the cabin and causing the bandages on his leg to come undone and lazily unwind to the floor. He lumbered to the fireplace and back trailing bandages behind his foot, waving the cleaver and the piece of meat. Jill and Linda cringed away from him, whimpering. "I am God, Benjamin Hastings, and you will be Brigham. Soon you will be Brigham, and I will be you. At sundown I will be the father, and you will be the son." He lowered his arms and looked at him with insane, leering graveness. *"Ten days now since we killed our dog, and still the storm rages. The boy is growing weaker. He will be the first to die. Write it!"*

"No!"

The book flipped up off the floor with a papery rattle and slapped itself into Ricky's hands. He shook it off as if burned and it fell to the floor again.

"Always the stubborn old man," Mark said. He advanced on Ricky, wagging the cleaver. "You *will* write it, Benjamin Hastings. By sundown, you will write it. And sometime after sundown you will die." He glanced at the table, and a chair there began to vibrate and rattle. "You got away once, old man, but this time you will be mine.'' The chair propelled itself backward across the floor with a wooden screech, picking up speed. Ricky blinked instinctively. A moment later the chair smashed into him, bowling him over onto the bed. He lay still, feeling enormous pain and tasting warm salty blood where the back of the chair had cracked across his mouth. He felt a child's urge to cry at this outrage, but it was a muted urge, as if he were not really a child at all. He sat up and kicked the chair away. How small his feet were, he noticed as he did. Short little legs and short little feet. A ghost of memory flitted through his mind, a memory of seeing himself longer, with knobby knees and longer feet, but he pressed it back into the recesses of his mind. He wiped his mouth with the back of his hand, looking to his mother for solace, but saw only the strange woman wearing his mother's body watching him with a mixture of pity and secret glee. She took a bite of meat and chewed it reflectively.

''Write,'' Mark said.

Ricky bent down with a defeated groan and picked the book and pencil up off the floor. He sat back up on the bed and pressed the pencil to a blank page.

> ten days now since we killed
> our dog and still the storm rages
> the boy is growing weaker
> he will be the first to die

Now the urge to cry broke over him again, but not because of the chair or his bleeding mouth. A stupendous, crushing sorrow welled up inside him, the clear memory of a terrible, terrible thing, and below that a feeling of great and consuming hunger. He knew that he must not let this magic book and pencil write any more, because with each newly filled page came memories that belonged to someone else, hideous memories that hurt his brain and his heart.

His hand was jerked to another page and against his will he wrote.

> twenty-six days of storm
> the women too weak to move
> this small book will be our
> epitaph
> to those who find our remains

> i say
> we trusted in the lord our god
> and he ignored us
> is it evil to have two wives
> if so then the boy is a bastard
> and the cause of our misfortune

Ricky hung his head, overswept with raw, surging emotions and sickened by them. He pressed his eyes shut and in that darkness saw a ghost of a face, a thin and shrunken child's face.

"Write," Mark said.

Ricky shook his head. The ghost face floated across his vision, opening its mouth as if to scream. He opened his eyes and looked up at the monster that had been his father. Perhaps, he reasoned in a coldly adult way, the real monster is sitting on the bed with an unwritten diary in his hands. But that could not be, could not be. The monster is only a child. "I will not write any more," he said. His voice sounded flat and dead, too hoarse to be a child's voice. He felt stiff and incredibly weary.

Mark tossed aside the piece of meat he had been holding and put his blood-smeared hand on Ricky's shoulder. The cold from his palm seemed to sink down through Ricky's flannel shirt and settle in his bones, making them ache. He compressed his hand, and Ricky cringed. "You will write," he whispered fiercely. "On the twenty-seventh day of our misery we tried to eat our leather things, but found it impossible. God has cursed me for my wives, condemned me to death for a son born of a sinful union. There can be but one remedy."

Ricky jerked away. "No!"

"The boy must die—"

"No!"

"The boy must be erased like my sin—"

Ricky threw the book aside and covered his ears with his hands.

"The boy is my curse."

"NO!"

"Write it, Benjamin! Write it all down again, and then you will know your crime!"

Ricky stood up with his face contorted, ready to cry now. Emotions and memories crashed through his mind, alien memories and unbearable, devastating emotions. "I am Ricky Butler," he screamed. "I am only Ricky Butler!"

But he knew now with terrible sureness that it wasn't quite
~~ue.~~

Allison Parker sat on the flour-dusted floor of his shack with
~~is~~ rifle between his legs and the barrel of it in his mouth. He
~~as~~ leaning against the wall beneath the window where Jackson
~~ad~~ seen the woman last night, with his outstretched feet touch-
~~ng~~ the table Jackson had overturned during the fight, looking at
~~hat~~ remained of Jackson over on the middle of the floor, Jack-
~~on~~ in a large puddle of blood with the hilt of a knife sticking
~~ut~~ of his back. Jackson's blood was all over Allie's hands, thinly
~~ed~~ in the lanternlight. It had splattered his shirt and pants and
~~ade~~ red circles on his knees. The brackish smell of it hung in
~~e~~ air like gas.
   Allie whimpered. His eyes were big and white above his beard,
~~rking~~ back and forth, at times rolling up into his head. His
~~upils~~ had shrunk to pinpoints. The storm had died to a breeze
~~ad~~ in the relative silence he could hear Jackson's blood dripping
~~rough~~ the cracks in the floor to tap the frozen ground below.
~~ew~~ trees had crept up around the shack and rustled now against
~~e~~ walls as if whispering impatient secrets.
   His hand slid down to the trigger. He found it with his thumb.
~~fter~~ a moment he pushed it.
   Click!
   Tears seeped out of his eyes and rolled down his cheeks, eras-
~~ng~~ the flour in lines. He set the rifle aside and got laboriously
~~~ his feet. Stumbling and lurching, he searched the wrecked
~~om~~ for his box of bullets, found them at the former site of his
~~ed,~~ and got one out. He went back to the rifle, veering wide
~~ound~~ Jackson's remains, picked it up, and managed to push
~~e~~ bullet in the proper slot. He worked the lever and sat back
~~own~~ on the floor. He stuck the barrel between his lips and
~~ested~~ his teeth on the cold hard steel. The trees rustled, scrap-
~~ng~~ against the walls and against the windowpanes. They seemed
~~nxious.~~
   His hand slid down the barrel, down the pitted wood of the
~~orestock,~~ down past the sights. He watched his hand move with-
~~ut~~ the direction of his thoughts. His hand had a life of its own
~~ow,~~ and that life seemed determined to snuff itself and his life
~~ut~~ as well. His thumb stuck itself out and slid between the
~~igger~~ and trigger guard. It rested itself lightly on the trigger.
   His dazed thoughts began to coalesce. Just what in the fuck

was he doing? He was a murderer, and of course murderers ha
to be punished. Murderers had to die. But had he really mu
dered Jackson? Hadn't something, some weird power, shor
circuited his brain and done the killing for him?

His fingers wrapped themselves tight around the stock. H
watched his thumb begin a slow downward push. He tried
pull it back but it seemed disconnected from his brain, someon
else's big age-wrinkled thumb pushing down on the Wincheste
trigger. With a cry he pulled his head back and to the side ju
as the rifle fired with a noise like a thunderclap. His left eardru
went temporarily dead save for a high-pitched squeal. The wi
dow above him shattered and rained down on him in cold shard

"Jesus," he whispered. He disengaged himself from the rif
and screwed a finger back and forth in his ear. He got to his fe
amid a clatter of glass, tiptoed through the blood, and squatt
beside Jackson's body. Gently, he turned him over on his sid
"Christ, I'm sorry," he said.

Mark screamed. The cleaver fell from his hand and bange
on the floor. Ricky cringed back, not knowing what new horr
to expect. He saw his father's unfamiliar face twist up with rag
"No!" he shrieked, waving his fists. *"No no no!"* He bared h
teeth in a snarl. "Everything will be as it was! I command it!

His legs buckled and he crumpled to the floor.

Ricky held his breath. The women peeked down at Mark, st
holding their gruesome pieces of dogmeat. The wind howle
briefly outside, blowing the door open. It fell shut with a ban

Ricky breathed again. The monster had died as suddenly as
shot through the heart. He walked hesitantly toward Mark, wh
lay facedown with his legs folded beneath him and his arn
outstretched, like someone bowing to Allah. The cleaver la
beside his right hand, the broad blade pink with blood. "Hey,
Ricky said. He prodded Mark's hand with a foot. "Hey, God.

Nothing. He bent and warily picked up the cleaver. Anoth
barrage of memories rolled through him, keen and piercing. H
had used this cleaver before. Many times. More times than h
cared to remember. The solid weight of it made him feel sic
He went to the door, pulled it open, and threw the cleaver wi
all his strength. It went end over end and tumbled to the grour
in a puff of snow a respectable distance away. He heard one
the women cry out, it was hard to tell which one, and not th
it mattered anymore. They were both strangers, both intent

acting out the monster's terrible play until the finale, and Ricky's death. He was sure of that. It was all a repeat of some half-remembered tragedy of long ago.

He turned around and leaned onto the door, thinking about leaving, not sure what to do. The world was too vast outside, too dark and full of snow and trees and cold, but the world in here was not much better. He looked over at his mother and saw fear and indecision on her stranger's face. Jill looked lost, too, standing there with her own dog's blood on her chin like melting lipstick and a big hairy piece of him in her hands. Their little drama had been cut short. Ricky looked down at Mark and saw color rising in his skin. A moment later he groaned, and it was with his own voice, his own reassuring man's voice.

Ricky knelt beside him, smiling, near tears. The whiteness was gone. Daddy was waking up. Daddy was coming back.

Allie was still apologizing to Jackson when Jackson opened his eyes and sat up. He looked around for a second, raised his arms, and clamped his hands around Allie's throat.

"Holy fuck," Allie said before Jackson's thumbs cut his wind off.

Things cracked in his throat. His eyeballs bulged. He put his arms on Jackson's and the two performed a swaying little waltz, one kneeling, the other sitting. For a dead man Jackson had amazingly strong hands. His face had gone as white as a dead fish's belly behind his mask of flour, and his forehead and nose had blue twists of veins showing through. He was snarling without sound.

"Rrrrrkkk," Allie said. Things were getting swimmy. His right ear began to ring as bad as his gunshot-deadened left one. Jackson's face seemed as big and white as the moon, filling his entire vision. His glasses had fallen off during his murder and his eyeballs looked as big as two eggs rolled up side-to-side. Old blood bubbled and foamed between his lips. Allie felt a familiar anger begin to build inside him, not an unreasoning rage like before, but a very satisfying sense of betrayal. Jackson was dead. He ought to stay that way.

Allie let go of Jackson's arms. He raised his right hand and formed a V-for-victory sign with his first two fingers. He brought his arm horizontal, pulled back, and poked Jackson in his big egg-looking eyes as hard as he could poke. His fingers sunk in almost to the second knuckle.

It made Jackson let go. He scrubbed at his face like a chipmunk. There was wet stuff drooling out his ruined eyeholes,
some kind of clear fluid with bits of eyemeat in it. Allie breathed
again and felt like barfing. He wiped his fingers on his pants.
This time he had fucked old Jackson up but good. He felt gen-
uinely sorry for him, but then it dawned on him that Jackson
had been absolutely, positively dead, dead and practically gutted.

Like . . . the coyote.

He got to his feet, nearly slipping in Jackson's blood. The
forest had gone insane outside, the weather was any madman's
guess, there had been blood on his toilet paper, and now Jackson
had come back from the dead like the coyote and was sitting on
the floor pawing at his face with a knife sticking out of his back.
Allie backed away from Jackson and watched with surprise as
he stood up, jerking and twitching like a puppet on tangled
strings. Stepping absurdly high, Jackson followed him with his
arms stuck out straight and his hands snapping open and shut.
His head grazed the hanging lantern and he stumbled backward,
swatting at it with a jerking sweep of his arm. Allie put more
distance between them, angling for the door. He stepped on
something and glanced down quick enough to see that it was the
rifle that had almost shot him. He bent and picked it up.

"Another step and I'll have to pump you full of lead," he
warned, standing his ground. He levered the Winchester and
realized it was empty. He realized just as swiftly and with rea-
sonable sureness that he could perforate Jackson like a Swiss
cheese and still he would keep on coming, because this lurching
Frankenstein monster was not Jackson at all. Allie took the Winchester by the barrel and held it to his shoulder like a baseball
bat. When Jackson was close enough to hit he swung it, smashing him full in the face. The wooden stock broke with a sharp
crack, as did various bones in Jackson's face. It rocked him back
on his heels, but then he leaned forward and came on regardless.
His nose was a smeared lump now. A hook of bone protruded
out of it, pearly white.

"Damn," Allie said, dropping what remained of the Winchester. He went to the door, snatched up his coat and hat, and
lifted the latch. The door sprang open of its own accord, pushed
by snow-dusted evergreen boughs that cascaded down around
Allie's head. The smell of them was thick and sweet. He ducked
under them, squinting and cursing, and saw that the trees had

grown up too thick here to penetrate, as if frustrated in their inward progress by the shack's flimsy walls. But that couldn't be true, Allie thought. The damn things could hoist the shack to the sky if they wanted to. It was as if they had been waiting. Waiting, maybe, for that final push of the trigger. Now they stood too close together to squeeze past, a dense thicket blocking the doorway. He dropped his things and ran to the broken window, dodging past Jackson, who reached out clumsily as he passed and tried to snag him in a bear hug. In his mind's eye Allie saw himself take a flying leap at the window, shoot through like a bullet, and wind up on the safety of the other side. But the big spears of glass still stuck in the window, and the pine branches that had thrust through like questing arms made him pause to consider. He glanced at the window on the other side of the shack and saw nothing but pine waiting to burst through.

Caught, his thoughts told him calmly. Caught in a trap with a living corpse. The nice gentleman with the cancer in his colon must now perform the waltz of death eternally with the man he murdered. Welcome to hell, Mr. Parker.

He reached up and worked one of the spears of glass out of the ruined window. It was about ten inches long and two inches wide, about the same size as his bowie knife. He turned. "You touch me and I'll cut your fucking throat," he snarled at Jackson, wagging the glass at him.

Jackson stopped. He grinned a hideous grin. His teeth looked twisted and yellow behind the blue lines of his lips. His chest heaved as he drew in a long, whistling breath. "You've got *cancer*," he said, in a shrill, cackling voice. Air seeped through the cuts in his back as he spoke, sounding like miniature farts. "I gave you *cancer*, old man. I gave you *cancer* and you're going to *die* and be with me in *hell*."

Allie shook his head. "I spent forty years in hell with you already, dicklicker." He shifted the glass knife to the other hand and thrust it at Jackson's face. Jackson didn't flinch. Blind, then, blinder than a bat. Then why did he seem to be able to see so well? Allie circled to the left, walking through the puddle of blood. Jackson turned, following him without eyes. When Allie was in front of the overturned bunk bed Jackson raised a hand and the bed jumped up and hurled itself at Allie. Allie got knocked to his knees and scooted through the blood. The bed crashed against the wall. It was a pretty nifty trick, he had to admit. Old Jackson was just full of hidden talent.

He got to his feet and lashed out with the piece of glass. The
tip of it grazed Jackson's throat, laying it open. It did not bleed.
Allie tried again, this time succeeding in removing most of Jackson's right ear. Allie felt nausea rise in him like hot fluid. He
could cut Jackson to pieces and still he would keep on coming.

The overturned table began to rattle and thump on the floor
off to Allie's left. It rose, spinning and wobbling, and floated
through the room. Allie watched it, blinking. The table began
to corkscrew violently, sliding toward him like the giant blade
of a buzz saw. Its lone remaining leg became a blur. Allie estimated that if it pushed into him it would surely break some
bones in the process. And Allie with broken bones was Allie
immobilized, and Allie immobolized was Allie at Jackson's
mercy. And the eyeless dead thing that was Jackson was not
likely to have much mercy.

The table continued across the room with a low whirring
sound, getting close now, close enough for Allie to feel the
breeze from it. It made up his mind for him. If the world was
going crazy it would have to do it without Allison Parker around
to watch. He threw the glass down and sprinted across the shack,
pressing his hands together as if to pray. When he got within
jumping distance of the broken window he extended his arms
up over his head in a classic diving pose, and launched himself
through. As he flew he heard Jackson let out a high-pitched,
girlish scream of anger and heard the spinning table clatter to
the floor. Glass crunched against his hands, and his face was
full of pine needles. He scuffled his way out, clawing at the
close-standing trees and pulling himself through, wondering if
he had gotten cut but not really caring all that much. A severed
artery would be preferable to facing the ruined monstrosity that
used to be Jackson. He fell to his knees and elbows in snow and
scurried to his feet. The cold pierced his clothes but that didn't
matter, either. Nothing mattered but getting away. He pushed
through the unfamiliar new forest that had been his clearing,
angling downhill. Spike Mountain had pulled its last trick on
Allison Parker. It was time to get out. And the dumb son of a
bitch Jackson could go to hell alone.

As he went he heard branches snapping behind him. Jackson
was coming through the window. A little whimper escaped Allie's mouth. The dumb son of a bitch didn't have eyes. The dumb
son of a bitch was short an ear. The dumb son of a bitch had
more holes in his back than your average sieve, a throat that was

s good as cut, and a nose as flat as a flapjack. Yet he was still
oming.

Allie poured on the speed and ran down the mountain with
ackson hard on his heels.

Something strange happened at the Ogden exit. Ralph saw the
ig green and white sign that said "Ogden next right," and
lowed just a bit in unconscious preparation for the turnoff. He
vas already formulating his excuse for taking the exit, knowing
hat Ed, in his hurry, would be mightily upset about any delay.
he excuse was nothing brilliantly original but would have to
erve: Ralph was going to say he had to stop for gas. The Ford's
as gauge needle was hovering just below full, but that could be
xplained away by saying it was stuck there and couldn't be
lepended on. There were plenty of gas stations just off the exit
nd Ralph intended to pass them by, saying he had a credit card
or some obscure station like Citgo or some such, and that a
tation by that name just happened to be downtown. He then
ntended to stop for a bit of gas and ask directions to the mental
ospital. From there on he would play it by ear.

And he hated to do it, really. Ed was being real cool, now
hat his crazy story was out and he thought he was going to
pike Mountain. He was sitting on the passenger side quite
almly with his elbow hooked out the window, his hand lazily
urfing the wind. The wind and heat had dried his clothes pretty
vell and turned his hair into a frizzy tangle. There was color in
is cheeks and a kind of lopsided, determined little grin on his
ace. For a lunatic he was remarkably well behaved now. But
hat would surely change once they pulled up at the mental hos-
ital. Ed might just go berserk then, at which point the white
oats would come and drag him away, and Ralph would be done
vith him. It was, Ralph had decided, not going to be a pretty
cene, but one that had to be played out. Taking Ed to the san-
tarium was the best and only way to do this. The man needed
rofessional help, anybody could see that. The man was suffer-
ng from delusions. So why, Ralph wondered as he made ready
o take the Ogden exit, do I feel so damned guilty?

He rested his fingers on the turn signal, ready to pull it up.
Ie would later recall glancing in the rearview mirror and seeing
he chrome grille of a big Navistar semi behind him glitter cru-
lly in the sunlight. He would recall blinking at the series of
tuttering flashes, momentarily blinded, and weaving a bit on

the road. He would remember hearing Ed let out a peculiar little
sigh, and seeing out of the corner of his eye Ed slump slightly
forward in the seat. There was a feeling of gravity doubling, a
pause in the roar of wind passing through the open windows.
He had the impression of being pushed sideways. And that was
all he would remember of that instant just before the Ogden
turnoff on I-84, when time clicked out of sync and he began to
doubt Ed's sanity less and his own more.

The exit never appeared. They rolled on across the bright cement ribbon of highway with the sun glinting off the pickup's
blue hood and the wind blasting through the windows, and presently another big green sign loomed, this one proclaiming that
the Kamas exit was one mile up the road.

"What the heck?" Ralph said. His voice was hoarse and dry
as if he had just awakened from a deep summer nap. He swallowed, feeling thirsty and somehow woozy.

"Jesus," Eddie said. He rubbed his temples with his fingers.
"What was that?"

Ralph craned his head around, frowning hugely. Past the
handlebars of the Hondas he could see that the big Navistar truck
with the chrome grille was gone, replaced by a rusting orange
Chrysler trailing blue exhaust. He turned back with his heart
skipping a beat or two faster. The Kamas sign flashed past, big
and green and undeniable. It was noticeably cooler outside, and
big dark clouds spread in a low sheet across the eastern sky,
threatening to block the sun in a moment. To his left a dark line
of mountains bulked high toward the sky.

Whoa, now, Ralph thought, nervously checking the instru-
ment panel. He half expected to see the gas gauge settling down
past empty, proof that he had been hypnotized by the road and
the rushing wind. Time had a way of slipping past you on the
highway, but never before like this. He looked at his watch and
saw that it was five o'clock. Time hadn't slipped past at all. And
it didn't *feel* any later, either. He wondered if the highway crew
hadn't made a mistake and put the road sign in the wrong place;
Kamas lay at the southern base of Spike Mountain, more than
two hours from here, wherever here was. Just what the hell had
happened?

"We're getting close," Eddie said softly. He had his eyes
closed and his fingers pressed to his temples, like a mystic receiving messages. "I can feel it."

"Gas," Ralph said automatically. He was feeling more than

little scared, and didn't like it. His sense of place had been stolen, and he was disoriented. Something had been taken from him, something indefinable. On the middle of the open and familiar road, he was lost. "We need gas in Ogden. I have a Citgo credit card."

"There are other spirits," Eddie said. He turned his head and grinned. "There are other spirits, too!"

"Bullshit," Ralph said. The highway curved east, broadening to an exit, and the sun disappeared behind the clouds. Light drizzle began to spatter on the windshield. The air carried the clean scent of rain and distant pine. Ralph swung right onto the exit, forgetting to signal, forgetting all manner of driving courtesies. The steering wheel seemed to turn of its own accord, as if lightly pushed by overactive power steering, and he tried to fight it, succeeding in making the truck fishtail a bit on the wet pavement. The Hondas clunked and moved in the back.

"Go left at the stop sign," Eddie said, pointing ahead.

"I know the way, goddammit," Ralph snapped. He passed a hand over his eyes. Maybe too many late nights sitting under the stars in one of Rolando's broken lawn chairs guzzling down Olympia had finally taken their toll. He was suffering some kind of mental lapse. Had they really started out from Tremonton about an hour ago? Or had it been longer? His watch could be broken, might have a weak battery or something. He tapped it with his finger.

"We're not alone," Eddie said. "No one is ever really alone. Fantastic."

Ralph brought the truck to a stop at the sign and got out. He took a quick walk around the truck with the falling drizzle stinging cold against his face. Steam drifted lazily off the tires. The motor sounded fine. Everything was intact. He rubbed his eyes again. What had he really expected? Speed burns in the paint? Tires gone bald from the supersonic rate they had traveled? What?

He got back in and looked at Eddie squarely. "Tell me I'm nuts."

"They have power we can't imagine," Eddie said.

"We're almost there." Ralph smiled miserably. "Almost here."

"A battle between good and evil. I guess it never ends, no matter what plane you're on. There must ultimately be a winner."

"I feel so tired. Like I've been out of it for a while. Like I've been knocked out or something."

"We're soldiers in a bigger battle. A battle of the gods."

"Wait till I tell Madge about this." Ralph put the truck in gear and went left. "She'll have *me* locked up."

"The enemy is death. Death, and hatred. Robin died to show me the way."

"They'll throw away the key, so maybe I better keep my mouth shut."

"It's all up to me now."

They drove east along the winding two-lane highway, talking to each other without hearing. The rugged expanse of Spike Mountain stood before them, a looming shroud against the darkened backdrop of sky.

CHAPTER EIGHTEEN

"Wake up, Daddy!"

Mark drifted upward toward consciousness as if spinning through a dense white fog. His drifting thoughts fused together, pulled by the sound of his son's voice. The pain that had become distant and forgotten in the time he had been lost to himself came surging back, crushing agony in the back of his head, stripes of fire on his back, a deep, shuddering misery in his leg. He cried out, then came to with the sound of his own scream rattling in his ears.

Small warm hands tugged on the cold muscles of his shoulders. His face lay pressed to the floor, his nose mashed against it. He heard Ricky's voice again, coming from somewhere over his head. "Come on, Daddy, *come on*!"

He turned his head, opening his eyes, and saw dark, unfocused things. Wooden boards with wet, spattered drops of dark liquid. The legs of furniture some distance away. A cold dead fireplace. A burned length of log lying on the floor. Feet. Everything looked absurdly distant and dreamy. Ricky's voice was far away now, close again now, fading in and out of range. His own heart thumped in rhythm to his pain.

"Ugh," he said. His tongue felt cold and dry against the roof of his mouth. He swallowed and his head responded with a brutal thump.

"Daddy, hurry!"

Hurry. Yes, that was the key word. Something dreadful was happening and there was a need to hurry. But what was it? He had a hazy memory of his son lying sideward on a bed shouting at him. In that moment he had almost awakened, had drifted out of the fog and whispered Ricky's name. But that had been ages ago, or a second ago. Everything was jumbled. He pushed him-

self up on his hands and fell back again. His body ached like
something stretched on a torture rack.

Ricky let out a squawk and his hands were pulled away from
Mark's shoulders. Mark was aware of feet moving and thumping
near his face. He heard a fleshy sound and realized it was the
slap of a hand on skin. Ricky cried out. Another slap, then a
solid, heavier blow. Another. Ricky screamed.

"Nnngg," Mark said. It was his current version of *no*. Someone was beating his son. Someone was hitting Ricky Ricardo.
He went up on his hands again, wobbling like a fallen boxer. He
was shivering, freezing. It was incredibly cold in the cabin.
The world canted sideways and he rocked over onto his side,
hitting his head on the floor. Pain exploded in his skull. It had
not been like this in the dream world he had just arisen from.
There all was fog, except for that brief moment when things had
instantly gelled and he had seen Ricky on the bed. There had
been something like a poorly peeled chicken beside him on the
bed, a hairy rack of beef with the bone sticking out. Ricky had
been shouting at him. That was so long ago. Ricky was shouting
now, shouting for help. There was a lot of tussling going on.

"*Daddy!*" he screamed.

More slaps. Mark went up on his knees. His head bobbed on
his neck as if mounted on springs. He squinted against the wavering glare of lamplight and saw a tilted image of his wife and
his best friend's wife beating and kicking Ricky in a frenzy.
Ricky had gone into a squat in the middle of the floor and covered his head with his arms. He was crying and squealing. Jill
was kicking him with her exquisitely patterned cowboy boots.
Linda was swinging wildly with her open hands. She was no
longer quite recognizable as the woman who had been Ricky's
mother for six years. Another face had pushed through, changing the angles and lines into a strange caricature of someone
much older. For Mark it was like looking at a poorly taken
photograph found in a dead relative's attic, a photograph of
someone barely known and barely remembered. The Linda of
yesterday was not this old, not this skinny. And Jill was no
longer quite Jill, either. She was a starved-looking young woman
with blood smeared on her mouth and a crazy vengeful gleam
in her eyes.

"Linda, stop it!" Mark shouted, wincing at the pain it
brought.

They looked over at him, startled. There was a long moment

of guarded silence. Then Jill's face twisted into a horrible, vulpine grimace and she shouted. "You're dead! You have to be dead!"

"Daddy!" Ricky scurried over to him and threw his arms around his neck. There was blood tricking down his chin and one eye was puffing shut. He was white with fear. "She's not Mommy anymore, Daddy. And Jill's not Jill."

"Huh?" Mark pressed his fists to his eyes to stop the crazy rotation of the world. What had been happening while he floated in that misty nothingness like a cloud? He disengaged himself from Ricky's arms and tried to stand, desperate to make sense out of things.

"And you were somebody else, too. You screamed at me. You did magic."

"What?" Using Ricky as a crutch, Mark pulled himself to his feet. His injured leg roared pain at him and he had to stand on one foot. The room twirled and rocked like a carnival ride. He touched the back of his head and found a huge bloody goose egg just above the base of his skull. When had that happened? And Beast, for Christ's sake, look at Beast. Half of him, the half with his head, lay by the door in a wash of blood. The rest of him was pieces on the blood-soaked table.

Jill stepped toward him. He squinted at her. It was Jill, of course it was Jill. She just looked so different in this weak light. And the way the world was spinning it was hard to tell what was what, anyway. Linda hung back, seeming to take small sideward steps toward the big fireplace. "Jill?" Mark said. "Jill, what's been happening?"

"I killed you," Jill said, and now her voice was different in a slight and barely noticeable way, as if she were trying to imitate someone and just now getting the hang of it. "She told me to and I did it. She promised me an escape from hell. She promised me rest."

She drew closer, bringing her hands up, reaching out for Mark. He saw with a burst of shock that the skin of her palms and fingers was charred and blistered. Her red shirt and blue jeans seemed suddenly far too baggy for her body, as if just beneath the flannel and denim little more than a skeleton moved. Above her collar her neck was a thin stalk. •

"Murder can be forgiven," she said in her new voice, and cupped her black fingers around his throat.

Mark gasped and jerked back. His legs gave way beneath him

and he fell heavily to the floor, hitting his head. Pain knifed through his skull and reality dimmed again. Jill swatted Ricky aside like a doll and stood over Mark, seeming absurdly tall to him, her head seeming to scrape the beams of the cabin's darkly shadowed ceiling. Her hair had dried in ugly strings that stood out from her head like wires. She grinned down at him and sat on his stomach. Her fingers spidered over his chest and walked on his throat. She found his Adam's apple and pressed it with her thumbs. "It's not so bad, dearie," she whispered. "Not so bad at all."

Gristle crunched in his throat. His lips stretched wide in an involuntary grimace. She had powerful hands, too powerful. He thrashed and bucked, batting at her arms. His hands moved up and clawed her face. Ricky scrambled to his feet and hurled himself at her. Still she hung on with him kicking and clawing at her back, leaning forward to press her full weight on her hands. "Stop it!" Ricky shouted, his child's soprano cracking into a strange bass register on the last syllable. He tore at her hair. "Stop it, Jill," he shouted again, this time fully in a deep, resonant man's voice.

Jill straightened abruptly. Her fingers loosened slightly. She craned around to look at him.

"Jennifer," he said. His face took on an odd mystified expression, and a shadow had passed over his features. *"Jennifer!"*

"Ben," she whispered, and shifted on her perch on Mark's stomach to turn and face him. "Oh, Ben."

Mark balled his right hand into a fist. He thought of Glenn, of Robin, of Jill the happy housewife in a neat suburban world. None of that existed anymore. The old world was dead, had died the moment the truck overturned and the horror started. He swung out with all his strength and hit her between the eyes.

She slid sideways off of him and thumped to the floor, then went immediately up on her elbows. Mark sat up and saw Linda shuffling toward him with the wire handle of the big black pot in her hands and the belly of it swinging between her legs. She pulled it up over her shoulder, leaned forward, and ran at him.

"No!" Ricky cried. His voice was a cracked basso-soprano. In the shadow-streaked lamplight his face looked old and haggard. "Dorothy!" he screamed. "Dorothy!"

She swung the pot down. Mark lunged aside and heard it crash onto the floor behind him. He pushed himself up on his feet,

noring the pain in his leg, turned, and took her by the shoul-
ers. She was bent over, struggling to lift the pot again. He
lled her upright and shook her. Out of the corner of his eye
e saw Jill stand up. "Linda, for Christ's sake," he shouted.
What are you doing?"

She snarled at him. Her breath carried a smell like old meat.
his close he could see that very little remained of his wife.
eneath her familiar dark brown hair was the twisted and unfa-
iliar face of a stranger. "You have to be dead," she screamed,
ruggling under his hands. She clawed at his chest and face.
Dead!"

He pushed her away. "What happened to you?" he shouted.
What happened to Jill?"

"Dead," she sneered. "Dead like *you!*" She hoisted the pot
) in one lithe motion and swung it at his head. He ducked
ick. The handle tore from her fingers and the pot flew across
e cabin to land in the fireplace with a muted thud and a burst
' ash. Then she came at him again, scratching and hitting.

"Aw, Linda," he moaned, fighting off her hands. He made a
st and drew it back, full of misery and terror. He drove his fist
to her cheek, snapping her head around. It was hard enough
knock her out, had to be hard enough. She stumbled back,
en straightened and grinned at him. Her teeth looked incred-
ly yellow, like the teeth of a corpse. Her skin was sagging,
axen. She hooked her fingers into claws and came at him.

"Look out!" Ricky screamed.

Mark turned at the sound and saw Jill coming up behind him.
ne had the burned piece of log in her hands. He felt Linda's
nds close around his throat, saw Jill swing the log back. He
ied to duck but Linda held him upright with unusual strength.
e saw the log pause in its arc, saw smoke waft from its crooked
). He could smell it, the smell of childhood campfires, the
nell of cozy grown-up fireplaces. It swung toward him. He
eard a dull whooshing sound and instinctively closed his eyes,
ondering why this was happening, wondering stupidly what he
d ever done to womankind to deserve this frenzy of hate.

He heard a loud, brisk *thok* just above his right ear. He was
vare of smoke and soot thickly in his nostrils, and of the world
lting sideways, and then he was falling as he had fallen before
rough a swirling world of white.

• • •

"Again," Dorothy Hastings, dead wife of Benjamin Hasting
said.

Jennifer Hastings, his other dead wife, swung the log. Ma
Butler lay on the floor. The log cracked down across his sku
Blood filled with bits of ash flowed through his hair.

"Again."

She swung the log. It crunched dully on his skull. Ric
screamed, a warbling, high-again, low-again scream. The bo
of Mark Butler jerked and spasmed.

"Again. We have to be sure this time."

The log swooped down.

"Again."

"It's gone," Ralph said. He put the truck in neutral and hu
his head out the window. Cold rain mixed with snow hit
face. "There's a gravel road right along this stretch. It goes
the way up the mountain, almost. But Jesus Christ, it's *gone.*"

"Evil forces," Eddie said. "Trying to trick us."

"Don't give me that shit. There's a fucking *road* here. I'
camped up here before, drank beer up here when I was in hi
school before. It's been a while, but I know there's a gravel ro
right here."

"Civilization doesn't exist on Spike anymore. There are
roads. She's taken it back, made it to what it was before."

"Bullshit. It's just too dark to tell." He idled the truck fo
ward, squinting. Trees loomed high on both sides of the blackt
road, dark and foreboding, rustling in the rain. This lone
stretch between Kamas and Hanna was deserted but for Ralph
blue pickup and the two figures peering out from inside.
turned the headlights on, staring through their sudden wet gla
on the pavement. No sign of a road. He swiped at his chin.
had to be here someplace.

"A spirit sent you to me," Eddie said suddenly.

Ralph grumbled something.

"No, really. There are spirits at work here. They'll show
the way."

"There is no way," Ralph said. "The road's gone."

Eddie touched his temples. "The way is behind us."

"What are you, a psychic or something?" He looked at Edc
and snorted. "A pretty lousy one, I'd say. I checked every in
of the road behind us. It's just not there. Maybe the Parks D

rtment planted it over. Don't ask me why. It's been years since
ve been up this way."

"The answer is behind us," Eddie said. He jerked his head.
Your motorcycles in the back."

"Ah." Ralph nodded knowingly. "The spirits want us to
eeze our asses off, maybe get lost, huh? The spirits have never
:en on a three-wheeler in this weather, have they? The spirits
ve never run across a fallen tree in the dark and broke a leg,
ve they?''"

"I never said the spirits made it easy on mortals. But they do
ake things possible. Why else would we have the motorcycles,
aless we were supposed to use them? Why would they send
ou to find me if it wasn't for a specific purpose?"

"Nuts," Ralph growled. He stopped the truck and turned to
ce Eddie. "I hate to say this, old pal, but you're nuts to the
one. Nuts if you think I intend to get my ass out in that freezing
in. Nuts if you think I'm going to let *you* do it. We're heading
ıck."

Eddie opened his door. "Not me, man. I'll walk if I have
."

Ralph sighed. He had helped Ed about as far as he was going
help him. If the man wanted to lose his life stumbling around
ı some freezing mountain, then maybe he ought to have the
portunity to do just that. The Good Samaritan in Ralph had
orn itself pretty thin. And that business about traveling from
emonton to Kamas in under an hour—that would take some
ınking about, but he suspected it had been hypnotism after all.
y the dark look of things here at the base of Spike, it had to
: nine or ten o'clock. Maybe Ed was some kind of amateur
'pnotist, and had set Ralph's watch back during the trance. It
as a goofball explanation, but the only one that came to mind.
l was a weird one. Not dangerous, that seemed unlikely. Just
eird. Weird enough to kill himself following spirits.

"Stay inside," Ralph said.

Eddie slid out, stood, and turned to lean back in. "I'll walk,
ıt I'd rather ride," he said. He held out a bony hand. "Give
e the keys to one of them."

"No way. I paid six hundred bucks each for those, and that
as used. Get back in."

Eddie's eyebrows drew together reproachfully over his bleary
own eyes. "The spirits command it, Ralph. You can feel it the
me way I can."

"All I feel is pissed, which is what I'm getting. Get back in.

Eddie drew himself out and slammed the door. He walked i front of the truck and passed through the twin beams of th headlights, a long-haired scarecrow in flapping green army fa tigues. A moment later the dark forest swallowed him up.

Ralph deliberated for a moment, tapping his fingers on th steering wheel. He leaned out the window and shouted. "Yo don't even know where you're going!"

Eddie's voice drifted back to him, calm and resolved, a spoo voice out of the dark. "Yes, I do."

"It's thirty miles to the top, man. Thirty miles."

"Not if I go straight up."

"It's cold outside."

Eddie's reply came from farther away now. "I'll survive."

Ralph pulled his head back in with his mouth twisted up in disgusted grimace. "Suit yourself," he snapped, and jamme the shift lever angrily into first.

The motor died. Something banged in the back and the truc gave a little backward lurch. Ralph snapped his head around a saw past the Hondas that the tailgate had fallen open. The re lights were a dull red glow on each side of it.

"What the shit?" he said. Gooseflesh broke out on his arm It seemed eerily quiet inside the truck now with the motor dea Rain ticked lightly on the roof. He bent to turn the key and th headlights went out.

"Hmm," he said aloud, knowing that there was a ration explanation for everything under the sun, but beginning on again to doubt it. He turned the key and nothing happene Presto, he thought. World's deadest battery. And the damn thi is almost new.

His door clicked, and began slowly and stealthily to op itself.

Ralph's eyes widened. His hair began to stand up under h cowboy hat. He slid gingerly across the seat to Eddie's sid levered the door, and got out. He backed up a few steps wi his heart thumping in his throat, staring at his truck that no seemed spooky and haunted. His eyebrows arched up till th touched the sweatband of his hat.

The tires were swelling. There was a distant hissing sour coming from them, the sound of air moving under pressure. T truck rose an inch or two higher on its axles.

"Ed," Ralph called out with a voice that was remarkably dr

The tires became swollen black doughnuts. The hubcaps were silvery dimples in the centers. Rain sheeted down in a fine icy mist, dotting the rubber where it stuck out past the fenders.

"Oh, Ed," Ralph called, backing away.

The front tire nearest Ralph went first, blowing with an explosive hiss. The Ford settled heavily on the rim and the hubcap popped off to roll lazily across the road into the weeds behind Ralph's heels. The other tires squeaked and grunted like man-handled balloons. Another one exploded.

"Ed!"

A distant, eager reply. "Yo!"

"Get the fuck back here!"

Eddie came running. The remaining two tires exploded as he passed, and the truck clanked down onto its rims. It looked decidedly dead. "You get the bikes off, and we'll do it," Ralph said to him, breathing hard. Dead or not, he did not want anything to do with his old Ford for a while. He fished the Honda keys out of his pocket and handed them over.

"The spirits know one of their own has gone bad," Eddie said, sounding happy and dazed. He accepted the keys and ran to the truck. "The spirits are with us," he shouted. "Can you believe it?"

Ralph nodded miserably. He was ready to believe anything now.

Allie's age was beginning to tell on him. He had outdistanced Jackson for the first few minutes, managing to run headlong into a few trees in the dark and knock himself down, but now, ten minutes into the chase and with his face full of scratches and his clothes white with snow, he was spent. He stopped and put his hands on his knees, bent forward to catch his breath, desperate for oxygen. Dammit, he thought. You can't turn seventy and come down with cancer and still expect to win footraces. You just can't. And still Jackson was coming, also seventy years old, crashing drunkenly through the forest a hundred yards or so behind him, doggedly trailing him in the dark without eyes. The dumb son of a bitch was inhuman.

Allie waited until Jackson's crashing footfalls were close, then straightened and struck wearily out again. The brooding forest enfolded him like a tomb, and branches slapped his face and crunched past his ears. It seemed alien and mysterious here now, no longer like home at all. The sour smell of pine was thick and

pungent as his breath steamed in and out of his nostrils. He wa
going more by feel than by sight, aware of the slope of th
ground under its six inches of snow, able to see only a few fe
in front of himself. At least the wind wasn't blowing so ba
anymore. He guessed that he would continue on until his leg
gave out or a dead branch poked him in the eye, whichever cam
first and stopped him the longest. Then Jackson would have
him, and the age-old fight would come to an end.

He ran into a barrier of interlocked branches that yielded in
ward like a springy wall, grew firm, then heaved him backwar
His feet skidded in the snow and spilled him on his butt to th
ground. His remaining teeth clicked together, nipping the side
of his tongue, and he tasted blood.

Fucking Jackson.

He got to his feet, pushing himself upright with his hand
growling. Snow clung to his fingers like freezing mittens. H
shook them off and backtracked, hearing Jackson coming inex
orably closer. He found an opening and plunged through wi
pine needles combing through his hair and gouging his face.
small sapling passed between his legs, ripsawing along h
crotch, hurting. He thumped into a tree and stumbled bac
blinded by powdered snow and branches. "Yaahhh, *shit*!" H
screeched, turning in a circle, snapping dead black branche
with his elbows. This was not the forest he had lived in sinc
the age of thirty. This was an overgrown jungle, a wooded nigh
mare. He had made yearly trips down the mountain using roughl
this same path, but now it was different, gone. Jackson cam
closer, perhaps fifty yards away now, moving fast, as if the fore
were no stranger to him at all. Allie backed up again, lookin
for a way out. This was a wall of pines here, thick and tangled
It was a choice of go left or go right.

He went right. The trees seemed to squeeze in on him again
bunched together trunk-to-trunk with tangles of mountain bria
growing between. He arrived at an impasse and went right again
This brought him closer to Jackson instead of farther away. Curs
ing, he turned around, squinting in the dark for a sign of saf
passage. He fought his way forward perhaps ten yards befor
realizing he had run out of ways to go. Somehow he had gotte
himself boxed in, and the box was only open on the side tha
led to Jackson. And Jackson was at this moment bearing dow
on him like a bloodhound.

The crashing noises were pretty close now. Allie bared hi

eeth unconsciously in a snarl. So this was the way it would be, ꞏuh? Face-to-face with that creepy no-eyed fucker once again. ꞏt was a prospect he didn't like one bit. He reached up and ꞏrabbed a dead-looking branch, pulled it free with a snap, and ꞏleaned the twigs off it. About four feet long and as thick as his ꞏvrist, it would make a handy bat, or spear, or ass-reamer if it ꞏame down to that. He turned and stood his ground, ready to ꞏnake war. The trees ahead of him jostled, their branches parting ꞏs Jackson pushed through. Allie hefted his weapon and pre-ꞏared to kill the silly dead fucker once again.

Only it wasn't the silly dead fucker that came through the trees ꞏnd stood before him. It wasn't the silly dead fucker at all.

Allie felt his remaining strength drain from his body as if ꞏomeone had popped corks in his heels. His bowels tightened ꞏp and then went strangely loose. The branch fell from his hands ꞏnd thumped softly in the snow.

It was a bear.

"Shit," Allie breathed. Warmth splashed down his thighs as ꞏis bladder let go. In all his years in the wilds he had rarely ꞏncountered a bear, and never one like this. Never a grizzly that ꞏtood twelve feet high on its hind legs and had a mouth like an ꞏpen cave full of pearly stalactites. Man-eaters like this had died ꞏut a hundred years ago.

"Oooohhh, fuck," Allie moaned.

The bear came at him, strangely quiet, strangely intent. Allie ꞏhought, but couldn't be sure, that he saw Jackson standing off ꞏo the side like a ghost, grinning. Allie closed his eyes as the ꞏear shuffled up to him and took hold of him in a cold, loveless ꞏmbrace. He was too surprised to fight back, too weak to do ꞏnything but stand there and breathe a few final curses as its ꞏead slung downward and its jaws closed wetly over his face.

Bones crunched. Brains and blood squirted out on the snow.

The women weren't looking. Ricky edged toward the door, ꞏvatching them, stiff with terror, barely able to move his legs. ꞏhey were inspecting Mark for signs of life. Their backs were ꞏurned. Jill was bent over prodding his arm.

He got to the door and eased it open. The hinges creaked ꞏoftly. His foot struck one of the red galoshes his mother had ꞏet by the door so many ages ago, and the buckles jangled. No ꞏne noticed. He opened the door wide and peered outside. It ꞏvas dark out, but not too dark to see, as if it were just about sundown on a day of bad storms. He looked back at his father, facedown in a pool of blood. Grief squeezed his heart. They had surely killed him this time. Now there was no one left. And no place to go, really, but anywhere was better than this.

He slipped outside and pulled the door quietly shut, straining to hear. There came no outcry, no sudden thump of feet. Busy with Mark, they had not noticed. He let himself breathe again. So far so good. He turned and tiptoed out through the deep snow that had drifted up against the cabin. It was up to his thighs, powdery and easy to push aside. It sifted down into his shoes immediately, bitterly cold around his ankles. It would be a long walk, and a freezing one. He had a vague idea which way to go, a faint memory of having gone this way before. But in the dark, with no coat and no boots, six years old and alone, he knew he would never make it. Yet there was no other choice.

He came to the tangle of briars that ringed the clearing and signaled the start of the woods, and picked his way through. He was shivering now, shivering miserably. He began to cry. The forest was dark and alien. The trees stood like foreboding black towers. There were bears here, too. One of them had gotten to Daddy, and look what happened to him. What would one do with a little boy?

He hesitated, looking back at the cabin where weak yellow light burned in the windows. Much as he was afraid of the forest, he could not go back there. Death waited for him back there, perhaps something worse than death. Once again cloudy memories chased through his mind as he stared at the cabin. An awful thing had happened there. It would happen again if he stayed.

He was about to turn around when the door was jerked open. Mark stood there, framed in a rectangle of light. It was impossible to see his face, but he looked oddly bent, like an old hag with bone disease. His head swiveled back and forth above the dark bulk of his shoulders.

"Benjamin!" he screamed. His voice was high and crazy. *"Benjamiiinnn!"*

Ricky turned, whimpering, and ran into the forest.

Old Ed was nuttier than a fruitcake. Ralph was sure of it now. He had rolled the three-wheelers off the truck in a frenzy, listened impatiently to Ralph's instructions on how to operate the things, fired his up, and gone roaring off into the woods with a mad cackle and a burst of blue exhaust before Ralph could even

get his started. Now Ralph, no amateur at three-wheeling, was
having trouble catching up with him, and they were ten minutes
into the ride. Ed was driving like a dirt-track rider, his headlight
cutting a wildly swinging beam through the darkness, his rear
tires spewing out fountains of snow and clotted mulch. The
Honda blatted like a power mower gone berserk. When he leaned
into the turns to avoid trees, Ralph was sure he was going to
spill over. Somehow he managed to hang on, all bony arms and
legs and flapping clothes and streaming hair.

"Slow down!" Ralph screamed at him, squinting against the
pelting snow and rain. Trees seemed to loom out of nowhere.
He had lost his hat to a low-hanging branch. He was soaked to
the skin and freezing. He did not like any of this at all, but by
God this business about spirits seemed to have some weight to
it. Ralph calculated that the spirits owed him about four hundred
dollars for new tires. Crazy.

"You're going to kill yourself," Ralph shouted, then had to
dodge left to avoid a tangle of branches that appeared, stark and
skeletal, in the bright slash of his headlight. The forest seemed
denser up this high, denser than Ralph remembered it. And Jesus
in heaven, the wind streaming against him was cold. He tracked
on Eddie's taillight, which was a good distance up ahead. Where
the hell had the dude learned to ride like this? Were the spirits
helping him out? Driving for him? Possibly, just possibly. Anything was possible with old Ed around.

Grumbling, shivering, he manhandled the Honda around a
thick scaly tree and came back on line with Eddie's tracks in the
snow. He did seem to know where he was headed, this strange
guy did. He was arrowing straight up the mountain, not wasting
any time. If the winding road had still been there it would have
taken them an hour to follow it. Like this, they would be at the
top long before that. Ralph wound the Honda out as tight as its
big 250cc motor would wind, crouched low to the handlebars.
Hanging branches whipped his face and dumped fine snow down
the back of his neck. A real picnic, this. Something to tell the
grandchildren about some future day, if he lived long enough to
tell it. He opened his mouth to shout at Eddie again to slow
down and was whacked in the face with a bushy branch. He
spluttered, his teeth crunching on sour-tasting pine needles. This
was like being hit again and again in the face with a broom while
trying to break the world's land speed record.

The way grew steeper. They were getting to the tough part,

the part where Spike got mean and rocky. Eddie's headlight cut
the dark up ahead like a brilliant sword, outlining nothing but
trees and more trees. The rain was gone, pure blowing snow
now. Ralph hunkered down lower, determined to catch up to Ed
and scream in his ear. You simply do not take an unfamiliar trail
at top speed. You go slow and pick your way. One low branch,
one hidden pothole, and your bike leaves you behind on your
ass.

Eddie's headlight swooped suddenly up, a rising white finger
probing the sky. The motor freewheeled in an angry howl. Ralph
saw the Honda flip end for end with Eddie still on it, heard it
crash down. The motor clunked a few times and quit. He drove
up beside it and stopped.

It was on its side. Snow sizzled beneath the hot motor. Eddie
was still perched on it as if determined to ride it sideward through
the snow.

"That ought to teach you," Ralph said, and leaned down to
offer him a hand.

Eddie raised his head out of the snow and screamed. Ralph
shrank back, wondering what the hell was wrong, thinking that
Ed's leg was under the muffler and being burned. Then he saw
that Eddie's left foot, the one under the Honda, was twisted back
between the motor and the frame, turned almost backward, the
toe of his boot pointing at the tire. It was an odd angle, an
impossible angle. No wonder he was screaming. Ralph got off
and dropped to his knees for a closer look.

Something was broken here, whether Eddie's ankle or his
whole leg he couldn't tell. Eddie thrashed and groaned. Gingerly, Ralph disengaged his foot from the frame and tried to turn
it back the proper direction. Eddie screamed again. "You've
busted something," Ralph told him. "Real bad, too."

Eddie raised himself on one elbow and looked up at him. He
shook his head. "Doesn't matter. Let's get going."

Ralph stood up without comment and set the Honda back on
its wheels. He was past the point of being surprised by the things
Eddie did. If Eddie told him he would now proceed to tap-dance
the rest of the way up the mountain, Ralph would pretty much
expect him to do it. If he told him the spirits would lead the
band while he did, suitable music would probably drift down
from the heavens.

Eddie got up, grimacing and snorting, and got back on. He
thumbed the starter button, and after a few dull farts the motor

caught. "We're on our own now," he said, looking grimly at Ralph. "This is her territory, the bitch's territory. What happens now is up to us."

"You can't ride," Ralph said. "How are you going to shift gears?"

Eddie reached down and jerked the foot lever with his hand. "Piece of cake," he said, straightened, and pushed the throttle. The Honda crawled up the hill, spitting snow. "Come on," he shouted.

"Sure thing," Ralph shouted back, almost angrily. "Why let a broken leg slow you down?"

He got back on his three-wheeler and roared after him.

CHAPTER NINETEEN

Ricky plunged madly through the forest, skidding in the snow and tripping over roots, falling, getting up again, falling again. His flannel shirt and blue jeans were dusted with snow like fine sugar, his hair and face full of stinging ice crystals. Branches seemed to reach down and grab at him, slowing him down, blinding him. His heart thundered in his chest as if ready to burst. Mark lumbered after him, shouting in his high, screeching voice.

"Benjamiinnn! Benjamiinnn!"

Ricky sobbed as he ran. His terror was enormous, a huge deadly thing that made it hard to think, hard to see, hard to do anything but run and cry and wish for an end to this. He tripped again and went sprawling. Snow slid down the front of his shirt and pushed up his sleeves, painfully cold on his belly and forearms. When he scrambled to his feet he found that one of his shoes had come off. He ran, weeping for it and for his father who had died and come back to life as a monster.

"Benjamin! You can't run from me!"

But he did run. Stooped over, batting at low branches, his wet sock trailing behind his foot, he ran even though he knew it was hopeless. Mark crashed through the woods behind him, calling in his macabre voice. On his big grown-up legs he was closing the distance. It really was hopeless, Ricky knew, unless the monster was as stupid as it was mean. He slipped behind a thick tree and stopped, breathing hard, listening for him, thinking that he would pass by. He cupped his freezing hands over his mouth and breathed through his fingers, frightfully tense and aware. Mark came closer and Ricky shrank against the tree, forcing himself to hold his breath.

He came past the tree and slowed. Ricky almost cried out.

288

This shambling, bleeding monstrosity was not his father. He was bent and shrunken, icy pale, almost blue. His chest and pants were smeared with blood. Blotches of it had dripped on the tops of his bare feet. Scarlet rivers of it had flowed in zigzags from his battered scalp down across his face. His eyes were huge and bulging.

He stopped. He turned. His blue lips spread wide in a terrible smile.

"Time to come home, Benjamin."

Ricky pushed away from the tree to run. Something laid ahold of him then, a power like a hundred invisible hands, something that tugged him backward, pulling him toward Mark. He shouted and struggled. His feet, one with a shoe and one without, kicked at the snow. Mark's cold hand closed over his left wrist and jerked him back toward the way they had come.

"No!" Ricky screamed.

"Oh, yes. Yes yes yes, Benjamin. Time to face up to what you did. Time to pay." He chuckled mysteriously and began to walk, dragging Ricky along. "Everything is as it was, and it's time to pay at last. Sundown, oh sundown, yes yes yes."

He forced Ricky back up the slope. His hand on his wrist was a crushing vise. Ricky clawed at it, opening the skin in lines with his fingernails. Bluish-red blood dripped thinly out.

Ricky heard something then. It was a distant blatting noise, like a chain saw being revved far down the mountain slope. He strained to hear. Not one chain saw, but two. Someone was down there in the dark. Mark heard it, too. He stopped dragging Ricky and craned his head around. His wide eyes blinked owlishly. Then he turned and moved forward again, faster. Ricky twisted and bumped along behind him, being dragged on his knees now. They came to the ring of briars and hurried through. One of the women swung the cabin door open and Mark hauled Ricky inside. He threw him down on the bloody floor and stood over him. The book snapped up off the floor and landed on his chest. "On the thirtieth day," Mark shouted triumphantly, "I made my decision. The—"

He stopped. He seemed perplexed. His face twisted in a ghastly expression of dumb surprise. He stepped back and looked around with his huge, blue-veined eyes wide and full of suspicion.

"I threw it away," Ricky said, and sat up. The book slid off his chest to the floor. "I threw it where you'll never find it, you crazy old monster."

"Evil man!" Mark cried. "You horrible, evil man!" He hurried to the door, kicking Beast's carcass aside. The noise of the chain saws was loud now, loud enough to be heard inside. Mark pulled the door open, stood in the doorway, and raised his right hand. Past him Ricky could see the spot where the cleaver had landed. The snow began to boil in a circle there. The handle of the cleaver thrust up. He hadn't tricked the monster at all.

He got to his feet, full of weary desperation. The monster's back was to him. He charged forward and ran into him with all his strength. One of the women uttered a warning cry, too late. The monster catapulted out into the snow with a short cry of surprise. Ricky fell behind him on his hands and knees, got up, and began to run again. The sound of motors was close, just a ways down the hill. That was where salvation lay. He saw the cleaver rise from the snow and tumble lazily through the air, the monster's magic. He imagined the monster was back on his feet by now, was receiving the cleaver by now.

He almost made it to the briars when invisible hands grasped him and stopped him dead. He turned his head and saw the monster coming at him with the cleaver in his hand.

The noise of the chain saws hesitated. A second later they stopped. The forest grew quiet but for the gentle hiss of the wind. The monster came up behind Ricky and put a cold rough hand around the back of his neck. He leaned close, grinning.

"Now you pay," he said.

The forest was thick. Even Ed, the World's Most Determined Man, had to admit that. They had come upon a wall of tangled trees and brush, tried to push through, and gotten nowhere. Eddie had managed to kill his engine, and now Ralph pulled up behind him and turned his off. It was time for some common-sense talk.

"Looks like the end of the trail," he said. He was shivering so bad his teeth clicked. "Besides, there's nothing up here. No reason to keep going at all."

Eddie shook his head. "More reason than ever, Ralph. Look up there."

Ralph looked. In the dual beams of their headlights he could see only dark forest with snow drifting down. No people in trouble, no dead people, no insane goddess tearing things up. Just trees. "Big deal," he said.

"Down on the ground."

He looked again. A few yards ahead there was something lying between the trees. Under its dusting of snow it looked like a car door. And there were other things, other parts. He saw the glitter of chrome, and a portion of a license plate. Farther off, where the light got fuzzy, a dashboard was cocked up against a tree, its gauges reflecting balefully. Odd place for a junkyard, he had to admit.

"That was Glenn's truck. What's left of Glenn is up in one of the trees. We're pretty close now." He started his motor again. "Let's go."

"There's no way through, man. This is the end of the line."

"I'll find a way," Eddie said.

Ricky heard the motors start again. His heart leaped. The monster heard them, too. He hauled Ricky around and raised the cleaver. "*On the thirtieth day, I made my decision. The boy must die, and we must live.* Say it, Benjamin. Remember it!"

Ricky shook his head, full of sudden misery. He did remember it, but still in a foggy way, as if it were something from a dream. But if he spoke those words he might remember, and that memory would be too terrible to bear.

"*Say it!*"

"No!"

The monster tilted his head back. His throat seemed to swell. "Jennifer," he said in a deep old man's baritone. His head rocked back and forth. "We must obey God, Jennifer. He has commanded me to slay the boy, just as Abraham was commanded by God to slay Isaac. Stop your weeping, woman, and help me off this freezing bed. The boy must die so that we might live."

"Stop it!" Ricky shouted. He covered his ears. That voice was as familiar now as his own. It was the voice of a monster of a different sort, the voice of an old man driven insane by hunger and religion. Tears sprang into his eyes. That voice had been his own in the dim and forgotten past.

"But you couldn't kill him," the monster said. His voice was high and screeching again. "You kept him alive so that you might *eat*!"

Ricky shook his head in a blur. The motors were coming, the

sound of them filling the air. He saw the two women come out, Dorothy and Jennifer, his wives reborn. Everything tilted out of focus. He loved them both, yes, he loved them, but it was sin, he was living in sin. A man may not have two wives. The storm was proof of that. This endless hunger was proof of that. It was God's revenge.

"*On the thirty-first day, sometime after sundown, we cut off the boy's arms, and ate them.* Say it!"

"No!"

"*We bandaged him up as best we could, but still he screams!*"

"NO!"

"*Tomorrow we shall eat his legs!*"

"NO! NO!"

"*When he is eaten up, our sin will be gone!* SAY IT!"

Ricky doubled over, racked with great, heaving sobs. He had done the unforgivable. He had eaten his own son while that son still lived. He remembered it now, remembered it all. The chunking sound of the cleaver. The way his wives cringed and sobbed. The sweet warm taste of human flesh. The cabin filled with Brigham's horrifying screams. Dorothy dying in bed. Jennifer, pretty young Jennifer, hanging herself from the rafters. His wrenching remorse, the flight down the mountain with the demons of insanity on his heels. The accusing face on the moon. The endless, endless snow.

"I'm sorry!" Ricky screamed. He went down on his knees. The motors were close, right behind him, but it no longer mattered. Justice was being served here. "I am so *sorry!*"

"Not good enough, Benjamin. An eye for an eye, and a tooth for a tooth. Sundown has come. Now we will eat *you.*"

He raised the cleaver higher. With his other hand he held Ricky's arm horizontal, steadied it there. Ricky could not fight him anymore. An eye for an eye. It was justice. God's justice. He looked up at the broad silver blade, welcoming it. He had sinned and must pay.

The blade started down. It stopped, wavered. Ricky looked questioningly in the monster's eyes. In them he saw a remnant of his father. "Oh, Ricky," Mark whispered miserably, and then the remnant was gone. The monster lifted the cleaver again.

The motors stopped. Ricky heard thudding footsteps in the snow. He struggled to free his arm. The monster held him tight.

• • •

Eddie Chambers ran on his broken leg, aware of tremendous pain but ignoring it. He saw a white-faced creature that he had seen before in a dream, in a trance, in a nightmare. Robin had showed her to him. He saw the bitch as she lifted the cleaver.

"You can't!" he shrieked, and then his leg hinged sideways and he crashed over in the snow. He tried to get up but the pain was too fierce, his body too tired and abused. He saw Ralph run past him, kicking snow high in the air. He heard him growl. The bitch swung the cleaver down. Ralph launched himself at the little boy crouched on the ground and knocked him out of the way. The bitch screamed. Eddie crawled toward her as fast as he could crawl.

"I forgive him," he shouted at her, scurrying forward on his elbows. "Do you hear me? *I forgive them all!*"

She looked at him. Her bulging eyes narrowed. She bared her teeth in a snarl. She tilted her head back and howled like a wounded animal.

She charged at him with the cleaver.

Eddie rolled to the side as she rushed up and swung the cleaver down. It swooped past his ear and buried itself in the ground. She jerked it free and hoisted it up again. Eddie looked up at her and smiled. "And I forgive *you*," he said. "I forgive you for letting it happen."

She began to shake. The cleaver jittered out of her hands and dropped to the ground. She raised her fists to the sky and screamed.

She collapsed in the snow.

Eddie crawled up to the little boy. The kid looked miserable and frozen. Eddie pushed himself up on his knees and took the boy's hands. "I forgive you," he said.

The kid sniffed. He looked at Eddie warily. Slow realization spread across his face. "You do?" he said. He began to cry. Eddie hugged him, crying a little himself.

"Don't you know me?" he shouted to the women. "Aunt Dorothy? Mommy? I was Brigham. *I was Brigham!*"

The younger one, Jennifer, took a tottering step toward him. He reached for her and she fell over, thumping facedown in the snow. The other one, Dorothy, cried out. Then she collapsed, too. Eddie nodded. He had expected nothing else. They had been dead for a hundred years. The bitch gave them life only so she could act out her play of revenge. Now they were gone, back to the dead zone, waiting to be reborn. The bitch had tormented

them in a hell of her own making, and now had no hold over
them. They were forgiven. Jill had died for this. One of them
dead on the snow was her, his own sister.

Ralph got to his feet, dusting snow off his clothes, breathing
hard. He looked around with wide, incredulous eyes. "Man,"
he murmured. "What the hell was going on here?"

"Terrible things," Eddie said. "But I think they're over now."

As if in reply the wind kicked up, pushing through the forest
with a low moan, building up. The trees bent in unison.

"It's gonna blow," Ralph said.

Eddie nodded. "She's pissed, all right."

Ralph nodded toward the cabin. "Let's wait it out inside."

"Huh-uh. Worst mistake a man can make. We've got to run."

"Christ, man, you're in no shape. And what about these people? Do you just want to leave them?"

"They're dead," Eddie said.

"What?"

He knelt beside the body of Jennifer and turned her over.
Snow clung to her face, but Eddie saw now that it was Jill's face
she wore. In death she had become herself again.

Ralph picked up her wrist and felt for a pulse. She was already
stiff. "I'll be damned," he whispered.

"Same with the rest," Eddie said.

"No!" Ricky cried. "My daddy's alive." He went to him and
dropped to his knees by his side. Tears spilled down his cheeks.
Eddie saw that the kid had lost a shoe and a sock. His foot was
cruelly red. How long had he been out in the weather like that?

"Wake up, Daddy," Ricky said, bending over him. "Please
wake up."

Nothing. Blowing snowflakes tumbled across the icy paleness
of his face and settled in the hollows of his eyes. The blood on
his face had dried to cracked streaks that were turning brown,
almost black. His lips were slightly parted, the tip of his tongue
showing between them. Ricky had never seen someone who
looked so utterly, terribly dead, not even Robin in her coffin.

He took his father's hand, his pale white hand with the
scratches Ricky had put there when the monster had been inside
him, and squeezed it in his own. "Daddy," he sobbed. "Come
back, Daddy."

Nothing. And then . . . Mark's eyes moved beneath his closed
eyelids. It was almost imperceptible, but Ricky saw it. They
moved the same way Robin's had moved, back when Ricky had

uched her as she lay in her coffin. They moved just a little bit
ecause she had been trying to warn him the only way she could,
ut his daddy was not warning him now. His daddy was saying
at he was still inside.

Ralph came over and felt his heart. He took his pulse. He looked
Eddie and nodded. The wind howled and moaned, and now
ddie saw out of the corner of his eyes that the cabin was disap-
earing, shimmering like heat waves over a desert. He shivered.
y the time he turned his head fully and looked at it, it was gone.
othing but a rotted shell with the stump of a broken chimney
aching dismally to the darkened sky like a crooked skeleton's
nger. Snow began to pour out of the sky in earnest.

"Can you handle him?" he said to Ralph. "I'll take the boy."

"It'll be a tough ride," Ralph said. He bent and picked Mark
p, then carried him to his three-wheeler and draped him over
e gas tank. His hands and feet still dragged the ground and
is cheek was resting against the motor. Ralph winced and
oved him back until he was over the big knobby rear tires. It
oked uncomfortable as hell, but it would do. They would have
go slow, though. He went back and was helping Eddie up
hen movement on the other side of the remains of the cabin
aught his eye. He stopped, staring hard at it, thinking that
aybe another dying soul was wandering around on this brutal
ountaintop. Then his eyes bulged in his face as he realized
hat he was seeing.

Eddie and the boy turned and saw it, too.

It was the biggest one Ralph had ever seen in his life. The
iggest, hairiest, meanest one he had ever seen. It was waddling
ward them like something out of a circus act, only there wasn't
y circus here and this was no act. It was the king of the bears
o on his hind legs, and he was coming fast.

Things speeded up. No one said a word. Eddie found that his
roken leg was not so bothersome after all, and sprinted to his
ree-wheeler with the boy in tow. They got on, Eddie in front,
e boy in back, and the Honda chugged, wheezed, and started.
ddie reached down and worked the gearshift. Eddie took off.

Ralph got aboard his. He thumbed the starter and listened to
e motor chug hollowly. The same thing had happened down
n the road when they first got under way, which was why he
ad been so far behind Eddie. This particular Honda had a ten-
ency to need a bit of cranking before it finally decided to run.

The bear roared. Ralph's skin crawled, lifting all his body

hair. He didn't dare look back. If he looked back he would tu[n]
to stone, or salt, a pillar of salt like Lot's wife. He would sh[..]
his pants and wet himself. He reached down and worked th[e]
choke. No good. The Honda was cantankerous, especially whe[n]
it was hot. Why, sometimes you just had to get off the thing an[d]
wait fifteen minutes or so for it to cool down. Sometimes yo[u]
got so mad at it you swore you'd drive it straight to the junkya[rd]
if it ever started again.

"Oh, jeez, *please*," Ralph said.

Now the battery was sounding weak. The motor just wasn[t]
turning as fast as it should. The bear advanced with thunderin[g]
footsteps. The wind seemed to chuckle. Ralph thought of Madg[e]
and Tony, and the futility of life when you wound up dead at th[e]
age of twenty-six. He worked the choke in a frenzy.

Something scraped across his back. Something grabbed h[is]
shirt. He screamed and whipped around.

It was the guy on the back, the one with no shirt or shoes. H[e]
was waking up. The bear was five feet behind him.

The motor caught, died, caught again. The motor ran.

Ralph crunched the gear lever down and peeled out, awa[re]
that his skin had been crawling so hard it felt loose and wrinkle[d]
now as it relaxed. He reached back and held on to the guy's bu[tt]
to keep him from bouncing off. The guy's bare feet scrape[d]
troughs in the snow.

Eddie had driven in a circle around the clearing. Now he pulle[d]
up beside Ralph and shouted. "We can't go back the same wa[y.]
It's too thick." He cocked his head down at Mark. "He'll g[et]
knocked off."

Ralph shouted back. "It's probably thick everywhere." H[e]
had a vision of them driving in an eternal circle with the be[ar]
giving mad chase. Until the gas ran out. "What'll we do?"

"Play it by ear," Eddie said. "Follow me."

He veered right and drove into the woods.

Ralph followed. So did the bear.

They lost it a short while later. But by then they were los[t]
too. Snow swirled thickly down. In spots it had drifted up [as]
high as the handlebars. Ralph guessed the guy on the back ha[d]
terminal frostbite by now. He knew he had it himself. His cloth[es]
were frozen to his body. His face ached from the wind. H[is]
hands were clenched to the handgrips as if welded there. He wa[s]
too cold even to shiver. At least the forest was more spaciou[s]

here, the trees standing far apart from each other. It looked like a different mountain, and for all Ralph knew, it might be. Eddie didn't know where he was going, that was obvious. At times he stopped and looked around. The spirits seemed to have deserted him. But still they drove on, because that was the only thing left to do. When the gas ran out, which it must do shortly, they would be stuck, and they would die. Ralph was too cold even to care about that. He was beginning to get drowsy. Bad sign.

A while later Eddie ran out of gas. They ditched the Hondas and began to walk. Eddie hobbled along with the boy, who had told them his name was Ricky Butler, and Ralph carried the guy, Mark Butler, who drifted in and out of consciousness. They took frequent rest breaks. It was pitch-dark. The wind shrieked and whooped. It took them an hour to go one mile, even though it was downhill all the way. After a while everything began to blur into one long agony. Eddie no longer had the strength to walk, so he dragged himself on his hands and knees. The boy walked with his one bare foot, not complaining. Ralph's heart ached for him, but there was nothing he could do. They went on as best they could.

A few minutes later they came upon a road. A yellow Caterpillar snowplow was chugging its way up it, its headlights boring twin paths in the dark. The driver stopped and eyed them.

He swung his door open and leaned out.

"It's warmer in here," he said.

To his own everlasting surprise, Ralph burst into tears.

EPILOGUE

It was fourteen months before Eddie found his way back to Salt Lake City. By then he was moving nicely up the ranks at Lami-Tech, his father's company, and no one doubted that the new Eddie Chambers would inherit the business someday. He owned a small house on the outskirts of Ontario, and a brand-new Mercury Topaz. It was in this Mercury that he drove one weekend, clean-shaven and combed, back to Salt Lake. There was a little bit of business he had to attend to. On the way he stopped in Tremonton, but found a new family living in the run-down trailer house Ralph and Madge had rented. They, too, had moved up. Rolando was still in his lawn chair. He didn't know where they had gone. He called Eddie "sir."

Eddie located Mark Butler in the SLC phone book. He no longer lived on Westfire Road. The house had gone up for sale a few weeks after he and Ricky were released from the hospital. There had been an inquest, a lot of police activity, five bodies brought down off the mountain by helicopter. Funerals. It had made the papers briefly. Eddie had told the truth and was passed off as a lunatic. Mark knew only that he'd seen trees grow like magic and been mauled by a bear; that was as far as his memory went. Ricky was sullen and morose and was pretty much disregarded. That left Ralph. He backed up Eddie's story of spirits. He spoke of tires. He was told politely to go peddle his papers. The books were closed. Verdict: five dead in Utah's worst bear attack since the turn of the century.

He found Mark and Ricky living in an apartment complex on the outskirts of the city. He drove there on Sunday morning, a fine Sunday morning, hot but not too hot, pleasantly dry. The sun burned down out of a flawless sky. They were sitting on the front steps. Mark had the Sunday paper in his hands. There were several fingers missing, and Eddie knew that inside his shoes he had only seven toes. That was the extent of it. Ricky was reading the funnies. He had grown an inch and filled out a bit. A count of the toes on his right foot would have revealed a curious number: three and a half. That, too, was the extent of it. He looked up and saw Eddie and his face went pale. He nudged his father. They stood up.

"It's just me," Eddie said.

"Hi, Eddie," Mark said. These two had done a lot of talking in the hospital. Eddie had told him everything. About Robin, about Benjamin, about Brigham, about reincarnation. Everything. And he believed. "How have you been?"

"Good. How about you, Ricky? Been okay?"

"Fine," Ricky said. It sounded like a lie. The boy looked sad, as if the memories locked within him were still fresh and hurting.

"I've been talking to Robin again," Eddie said matter-of-factly. "She's been coming to me in dreams. She wants me to tell you something."

"She does?"

"Sure does. She wants me to tell you that your mommy's fine. She misses you, but she'll see you again. It'll be a few years, and she'll be somebody else, but you'll know her. Just like you knew me."

"Really?"

"Really. It won't be long. She told me that."

Ricky smiled. Eddie hesitated, then bent down and hugged him. Ricky hugged him back.

"I *do* forgive you," Eddie whispered fiercely. "But you have to forgive yourself, too. Understand?"

Ricky drew away. A tear tracked down one cheek, but he nodded and managed to smile.

After a while they went inside to get out of the sun, and drank Coke, and talked of other things.

The new spellbinder by
New York Times
Bestselling Author

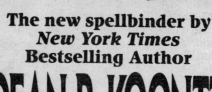

DEAN R. KOONTZ

The grand master of menace

LIGHTNING

THE SECOND TIME IT STRIKES, THE TERROR STARTS.